Retribution

Rebecca Deel

Copyright © 2017 Rebecca Deel

All rights reserved.

ISBN: 1979818398
ISBN-13: 978-1979818391

DEDICATION

To my amazing husband.

ACKNOWLEDGMENTS

Cover design by Melody Simmons.

CHAPTER ONE

Katie Henderson coughed, wrinkling her nose at the acrid scent. Nearby, a dog gave a strident bark, frantic to gain someone's attention.

She frowned and settled deeper into her pillow. Why didn't someone check on a dog in obvious distress?

Another cough. She tried to draw in a breath and broke into a sustained coughing fit. Her lungs and throat burned. Was she sick? Had she fallen asleep too close to the campfire? Something niggled at the back of her mind, but Katie couldn't drag herself out of bed to take a pain reliever or check her temperature. Too tired. In the morning, she promised herself.

Sighing, she felt herself drifting off again until a muffled shout dragged her closer to the surface of wakefulness.

Hard hands shook her. "Katie, get up! The house is on fire!"

Fire? No, please, not again. She moaned, coughed. Katie forced her eyelids open, blinked against the sting as she peered through a thick haze of smoke.

"Good girl. Let's get you out of here."

She recognized her cousin Lance's voice. His engine company must have responded to the alarm. "Charlie," she croaked. "Save Charlie."

"Katie loved her three-year-old Search and Rescue partner, a black Labrador Retriever. Losing that sweet boy would break her heart.

"We got him. He's safe." Lance lifted her into his arms. "We have to leave. This baby is burning fast and furious." He hurried to the hall and raced for the front door. He pulled up short when he reached the living room. "The fire spread. Our escape route is blocked."

Her cousin twisted toward the back door, but the undulating orange glow told the tale. A fire blocked that exit from the house as well. Bitterness swelled inside Katie. What were the chances an accidental fire had blocked both the front and back doors? Nil. Someone was trying to kill her. Again. And from the look of things, this time he might succeed.

Flames roared, and inside the house, the heat rose. They had to escape now or she and Lance would burn alive.

Lance ran to her bedroom, the room farthest from the fire. Not much protection. Flames were spreading fast. Someone must have spread an accelerant. Her cousin cleared the threshold, slammed the door closed, then crossed to the window and unlocked it. One of his firefighter buddies reached into the room and helped Lance carry her outside. Her cousin cradled her in his arms as he raced away from the house. Before they reached the emergency vehicles, the windows in the living room exploded outward.

Her cousin angled himself to better protect Katie. More coughing to expel the smoke she'd inhaled. Man, how long had the flames been burning before Lance and his co-workers arrived on the scene? EMTs from the waiting ambulance strapped an oxygen mask over her face as soon as Lance laid her on the gurney.

"You're going to be okay, Peaches." He gave her a quick hug, then backed out of the ambulance. "I'll come to the hospital as soon as we're finished here." Lance closed the door and signaled that he was clear.

Within minutes, the ambulance parked at the ER entrance and Katie was whisked into the hospital. Medical personnel directed the EMTs to one of the exam rooms where a doctor evaluated her. After being poked, prodded, and questioned extensively, Katie was grumpy and still coughing, though the spasms were spaced further apart.

Two hours after her arrival, her cousin hurried into her treatment room, his hair still wet from a recent shower.

"You okay, Katie?"

"I'll live," she said, her voice raspy. "I'm well done, though."

"You have burns?" His expression reflected his horror.

"No worse than a sunburn. I'm okay, Lance." She grasped his hand. "You saved my life. I'll never forget that. How is Charlie?"

"He's safe at the firehouse. The guys are having a blast with him. They'll watch over him, Peaches."

"Spring me. I'll take him to the vet, have him checked out."

"Johannsen's brother-in-law is a veterinarian. He stopped by the station and checked Charlie. He's fine. No burns, minimal smoke inhalation. You're worse off than Charlie, Peaches. Once you're discharged, we'll go pick him up."

"And then what?" Her gaze locked with his. "What are we going to do?"

"Run," he said, his voice grim.

Her heart sank. "When does it stop?"

"I know a guy who owns a private security firm. He owes me a favor. I'm collecting."

She dreaded having to uproot their lives again. "Do we have another choice?" Something better than reinventing themselves for the fifth time.

"We can give up and let him burn us to death next time."

She flinched. "No thanks. Sorry. Didn't mean to whine. When do we leave?"

"As soon as you're released," he murmured. "We'll collect Charlie and go. Nashville is four hours from Atlanta."

"What about our belongings?" The house would be too hot to salvage anything for a while yet.

"There's nothing left." Anger flushed Lance's face. "He did a good job. The house and everything in it was a total loss. If our engine had been five minutes later, we wouldn't have saved you or Charlie."

"Lance, Katie, come into my office. Bring Charlie." The tall man with the blond buzz cut stepped aside for them to enter his office.

Katie slipped past Brent Maddox into a large office with several televisions on the walls, each one displaying continuous news or feeds of military operations. She frowned. Why would Maddox have access to government soldiers? Maybe the uniformed people were his.

Maddox waved them to the chairs in front of his desk, then sat in his own. "Tell me what's going on, Lance."

Her cousin gave Maddox the short version. Katie wanted to laugh. Lance had left out a lot of details. Fifteen years this had been going on. By the time they finished answering the Fortress CEO's questions, exhaustion weighed her down like a suit of armor.

"What do you need from me?" Maddox asked.

"New identities in a new place," Lance said. "We just want to live in peace."

"I can do that. There's only one way to stop the fires, Lance. Expose the arsonist."

"Then find him and rip off his mask," her cousin snapped. "You can drop kick him off the nearest cliff for all I care. I just want Katie safe."

Maddox studied them a moment. "I hope you mean that."

Oh, man. Katie didn't like the sound of that. "We want to be left alone. When you find him, turn him over to the police. If you and your people are as good as my cousin claims, it should be child's play." Right. That's why she and Lance had never been able to uncover this guy's identity.

He was silent another minute. "Katie, have you and your cousin been separated when you changed locations and identities?"

Alarm shifted her heart rate into the stratosphere. "We've been together since I was ten years old."

"That's about to change."

"What? No!" Lance surged to his feet. "You can't send Katie off by herself. This monster wants to kill her. Who will protect her?"

"I have a safe place in mind for her and Charlie." He turned to Katie. "Interested in training Search and Rescue workers?"

Talk about a dream come true. That's what she'd wanted to do since she and Charlie became partners. She should consider adding another dog to her family after Maddox caught this creep. Katie's hand dropped to the top of Charlie's head. The silky fur of his ears soothed her ragged emotions. "I would love that."

"Good. I'll arrange it. Fortress has a bodyguard school. Personal Security International is expanding their training program to include Search and Rescue. I think you and Charlie would be perfect. We already have an experienced

S & R man on board and PSI begins training the first class in two months."

Two months? What would she do in the meantime? Sit around the house and wait for the arsonist to catch up with her? No thanks. Too much time on her hands left her too much time to think. Not good when her circular thoughts centered around the person who had sabotaged her life for years.

"I don't like this." Lance scowled at Maddox. "She shouldn't be alone. If this madman comes after her again, who will protect her?"

"I have people in place. Good people. They'll watch over Katie."

"What about Lance?" Katie asked.

"I can take care of myself," he insisted.

Unlike her? She sighed. Might as well face reality. More often than not, Lance had saved her. Didn't mean she liked to acknowledge her failure. So much for being independent and self-sufficient. "Mr. Maddox, will my cousin have protection?"

"It's Brent and yes, he will have bodyguards. The arsonist has almost killed both of you more than once. Neither of you will be without backup until the arsonist is behind bars or dead."

"We've tried for years to figure out his identity."

Maddox smiled. "You didn't have Fortress. We'll uncover this clown's identity and give you back your life."

"I hope you're right. In the meantime, what will I do for two months until the S & R program is ready?"

"Do either of you have weapons or self-defense training?"

They glanced at each other, dread curling in Katie's stomach. She hated guns. No, she corrected herself. She didn't know how to use one and so she was afraid. Time to change that.

"No training," Lance admitted.

"Past time you got some." His gaze locked with Katie's. "The training might save your life."

CHAPTER TWO

Katie turned off the engine of her SUV and stared through the windshield at the uninspired brick building in front of her. Not Katie now, she reminded herself. Heidi Thompson.

Minimal landscaping, she noted. Then again, no one could plant in February if they even bothered to worry about the greenery. Personal Security International probably wasn't concerned about the outward appearance. No, their important work went on inside the building and on the grounds. She doubted they cared about flowers or shrubs.

Scanning PSI's grounds, Heidi stopped when she saw a town. Intrigued, she opened the door and stepped down. A whine from the backseat drew her attention to the black Labrador Retriever watching her, his tail slapping against the upholstery. "Want to stretch your legs, Charlie?"

A yip answered her query. She grinned. "We have a few minutes before the interview." Heidi grabbed Charlie's leash and attached it to his harness. "Let's go, buddy. I hope this is going to be our new workplace." Maddox had said the job was hers, but she was afraid to believe his words.

Heidi locked the vehicle and crossed the grassy expanse. A fake town. Training, she realized. Hostage situations, urban warfare. Impressive.

She breathed deep of the cold, pine-scented air, hopefully the scent of a new beginning. Heidi thrust her troubling thoughts aside. Time enough to wrestle her demons in the dead of night.

Charlie growled. Heidi glanced at her canine partner, then turned her attention to the man striding toward them. She used a hand signal and the growls stopped although Charlie remained alert, his gaze fixed on a potential threat to his mistress. Watching the man, Heidi decided Charlie was right. He was a threat to her equilibrium and peace of mind. He reminded her of the reasons she avoided dating seriously. This man would be lethal to a woman's heart. Not hers, though.

The closer the male came to her, the larger he appeared. By the time he reached Heidi, she realized he was tall, powerful. Broad shoulders, arms roped with muscle, trim waist, muscled thighs, the stride of a man in peak physical condition. Sandy brown hair topped his head, a color Heidi would have given almost anything to have instead of her fiery red mop. She envied his tanned skin. She burned no matter how much sunscreen she slathered on.

Her gut clenched into a tight knot as she got a good look at his face. How could Maddox do this to her? To the good man standing in front of her? Quinn Gallagher had been more slender in his teens, but nothing could change those memorable brown eyes.

She prayed he didn't recognize the girl who had idolized him all those years ago. Her family had caused his nothing but grief and heartache. Not her doing, but the result had still left Quinn furious and devastated. He must have hated her. The rest of the town did.

"May I help you?"

The deep, rich voice sent a surge of goosebumps up her spine. Wow, really nice. Quinn's voice had deepened in the intervening years to something she would be happy to listen to for hours. Not likely to happen when he learned who she really was.

If his voice hadn't short-circuited her brain cells, she might have come up with ways for the source of her adolescent crush to help her. First on the list would be unloading the trailer filled with her belongings that she'd towed into Otter Creek, then left in the driveway of the house she had rented outside of town, sight unseen. Not a lot of options for housing and the owner of the house agreed to let Heidi set up Charlie's training equipment in the backyard. "I'm Heidi Thompson." She rested her hand on Charlie's head. "This is Charlie. We're here for an interview." And hopefully a job, provided this man didn't fire her before she worked one day.

If not, she'd start her own dog training school. Surely there were enough dogs in and around Otter Creek that needed obedience training. Hopefully, Quinn wouldn't object to her staying in town as long as she wasn't in his face often, reminding him of his painful past.

"Search and Rescue?"

"That's right."

"ID."

She froze. That fast? Please, no. She needed a job and a safe place to hide, and this was where Maddox had sent her. Security was their business, she reminded herself, while she presented her identification, and waited. Cold sweat formed at the small of her back.

After careful examination, Quinn gave back her ID and extended a hand. "Quinn Gallagher. Nice to meet you, Heidi Thompson."

Thank God. She breathed a sigh of relief. Quinn didn't recognize her. Maybe, just maybe, she'd have a chance to prove herself before he learned the truth. She smiled.

"Heidi." She glanced at Charlie. "Charlie, this is Quinn. Greet."

The Lab immediately sat and raised a paw.

With a chuckle, Quinn gently shook Charlie's paw. "Pleased to make your acquaintance, Charlie. You're a good boy." He straightened and turned to Heidi. "You'll interview with Deke Creed first, then with me and my teammates."

Butterflies dive bombed her stomach. Why two interviews? Maddox hadn't mentioned that possibility. In fact, he had approved her hiring provided Mr. Creed accepted her and Charlie. Heidi wasn't a great liar, a good thing under other circumstances. Now, her life depended on carrying off this role. She had to own this role, become Heidi Thompson, to convince anyone else, especially someone like Quinn who knew Katie Henderson. "Brent said you and your unit train bodyguards for Fortress."

"That's true." He sent her a level look. "We're responsible for any training at PSI. That includes S & R. While we may not provide intense training for your people, we will do hands-on work with them. We want them prepared for anything."

She understood why PSI and Fortress wanted that. In a search for a lost hiker, you might cover miles and the handlers went wherever the dogs' noses led. She'd run afoul of a pot grower on one search until the grizzled man learned she and Charlie were hunting for a toddler who wandered away from her parents' campsite. Heidi and Charlie found the blond angel a half mile beyond the pot grower's property. The girl had a few scratches and bruises, but was otherwise unharmed. She was lucky. Heidi and Charlie had caught up with her five hundred yards from a cliff. "A wise policy, Quinn. Does the training extend to the instructors?"

A grin. "Yes, ma'am."

Wonderful. More chances for Quinn to catch her in a lie. Heidi sighed. She foresaw sore muscles in her future. She trained with Charlie all the time, but she had a feeling her workouts weren't as intense as the ones Quinn and his teammates planned. If she landed this job. Her meager savings and what was left from her inheritance would last her a little longer. She rubbed Charlie's head. She needed a job to keep her buddy in kibble. If Quinn made it impossible to stay in Otter Creek, Maddox would have to relocate her. Again. Thinking of moving again made her hands clench.

She glanced at her watch. "I don't want to be late for the interview."

"I'll walk with you. I need to wrap up a few things before your interview." His blue eyes darkened, grim determination settling on his handsome face.

"Problem?" she asked as they walked to the back entrance of the brick building. Hopefully Heidi wasn't the problem. At least not yet. How long before Quinn learned the truth?

"Not for long." Quinn swiped a card, then entered a long security code at the keypad before the lock disengaged. "After you." He glanced at Heidi. "Have we met before?"

Her pulse pounded madly. "Why?"

Quinn frowned. "You remind me of someone I knew a long time ago."

Not what she wanted to hear. "I hope it's all right for me to bring Charlie inside."

A warm smile chased the grimness from Quinn's expression. Wow. Nice, really nice. "We'll get used to the sight. Besides, we don't have fancy furnishing or carpet. Deke also mentioned wanting to meet Charlie."

Heidi yanked her mind back on task. For the moment, her identity was secure. "What kind of dog does Deke own?"

"Australian cattle dog."

Delight bubbled inside her, banishing some of the nervousness. "Oh, man. Those dogs are super smart and a bundle of energy."

"That's Ace, all right. Some days I wish I could tap into that energy." He led Heidi and Charlie to an office at the end of the hall. He rapped on the door and received a growled response that Heidi couldn't make out.

Quinn opened the door and stepped aside for Heidi. "Heidi Thompson, this is Deke Creed. Deke, Heidi and Charlie." With that, Quinn left the office, closing the door behind himself with a soft click.

"Glad to meet you in person, Heidi." The tall, dark-haired man rose and circled the desk. Noting Charlie's alert, watchful stance, Deke extended a fist for the dog to sniff.

"Charlie, this is Deke. Greet."

He sat and raised a paw which Deke shook with a smile.

"Good boy, Charlie," he said before turning to Heidi and extending a hand. "Welcome to Otter Creek. Have a seat."

"Thanks." Heidi chose one of the two chairs in front of Deke's desk. To her surprise, instead of returning to the other side of his desk, Deke sat beside her.

"How did you get your start in S & R?"

Nothing like asking the toughest question first. "How much do you know about my background?"

"Only what's on the application Maddox forwarded. Dog trainer for eight years, S & R for five."

Meager details for a life impacted by a string of horrific events. Charlie pressed against her leg, bringing her back into the present. Heidi rubbed his head in silent thanks. "When I was ten years old, my younger sister and I were abducted from our beds in the middle of the night.

The police eventually tracked the kidnappers down, but not in time to save Moira." A true story, as far as it went.

"I'm sorry," Deke murmured. "How did that experience lead you to S & R?"

"The kidnappers kept us in a house less than a mile from our home. Our yard backed up to woods, and because they knocked us out, the two men carried us to the location using a trail through the forest. The police assumed the kidnappers used a car for a fast getaway. They didn't have a tracking dog or call in an S & R team. If they had, Moira would be alive today. I use that experience to help find others who are lost."

"How long did it take the police to find you?"

"Two days." Two interminable days when she'd been sure she would never go home again. Her baby sister hadn't. Heidi blinked back sudden tears. Enough. She couldn't help Moira by mourning her loss. Nothing would bring her back.

"The men are in prison?"

She swallowed hard. "One of them died in prison. When I escaped from the second kidnapper, he ran. The police never discovered who he was."

Heidi might not know who he was, but the creep sure knew her. The ghost in the night was never far away. She prayed this time she'd run far enough to finally be safe.

CHAPTER THREE

Quinn strode to the conference room where the rest of his teammates waited. As soon as he opened the door, all conversation stopped and his unit leader waved him to an empty seat.

"Well?" Josh Cahill asked.

"Confirmed."

Nate Armstrong, Durango's EOD man, shook his head. "Stupid."

"Carstairs took a shortcut that's going to cost him," added Rio Kincaid, his team's medic. "No wonder he refused a blood test."

A snort from Alex Morgan, their sniper. "Can't hide performance enhancing drugs."

"What's the point of taking that crap?" Quinn dropped into the chair, furious with the trainee who'd been doping to be the best in the training class and convinced five other classmates to join him in his stupidity. "The side effects of long term use are catastrophic. Who wants to roll the dice with your life?"

"You'd be surprised what people will do to get ahead."

A fact Quinn was all too familiar with, thanks to the Henderson clan. His world had changed forever because of them, not something he would ever forget.

Josh poured coffee into a mug and passed it to Quinn. "Maddox is waiting for a report."

He forced himself back on task. Months had passed since he'd thought of that fateful night so many years ago. Why now? Shoving the painful memories to the back of his mind, he said, "Make the call." He sipped the bracing brew while the call connected. Maddox would recommend immediate dismissal from training. These men couldn't be trusted in the field. What would prevent them from taking other, more harmful drugs while on an operation or accepting a bribe to feed their doping habit? Nothing.

"Talk to me," was Maddox's greeting.

"Josh Cahill, sir. You're on speaker with my unit."

"And?"

"Confirmed."

A growl from the Fortress CEO. "Take care of it. I'll process the release papers as soon as they're signed and faxed. Send the originals for their files."

"Copy that."

"Did Heidi and Charlie arrive?"

"They're with Deke," Quinn said.

"You talked to her?"

He stilled at his boss's question. Maddox hadn't asked if the team had met her, but him in particular. Why? "I talked with her briefly."

"Your impression?"

"Sharp, alert, confident in handling her dog. I didn't have much time with her, but they seem like a good team." What was it about her that bothered him?

"She's the perfect fit for an S & R trainer."

One eyebrow soared upward. A ringing endorsement. "We'll find out soon enough. She's scheduled to meet with us in a few minutes."

"Take care of this other matter before you talk to Heidi. I want those men off PSI grounds before the end of the day."

"Yes, sir," Josh said. After Maddox disconnected, Josh glanced at Quinn. "Call them in."

Quinn grabbed his cell phone and selected the number of the ringleader from his contact list. When the trainee answered, he said, "Conference room right now. Bring your buddies." He ended the call mid-rant from the trainee. This confrontation wouldn't be pleasant. Maybe they'd clear this crew out before Heidi and Charlie arrived. Then again, she needed to know how PSI ran. Deke and Heidi, if they hired her, would be required to enforce the same rules on their trainees.

"How are the wedding plans?" he asked Rio. His teammate planned to marry Darcy St. Claire at the end of the week.

"On schedule. Serena Blackhawk agreed to bake the cake."

Quinn blinked. "She's a thousand months pregnant. Is that wise?"

Josh, Serena's brother, chuckled. "Serena's backup is Nate. She told me the cake is already completed and in the freezer. All she needs to do is decorate it."

"I talked with Serena," Nate said. Their EOD man was also a trained chef, which made all the other Fortress teams envy Durango. "I know what she has in mind. We've got it covered."

"What about Trent?" Darcy's brother was also a Fortress operative and often out of the country, although lately he'd been taking longer breaks between missions. Might have something to do with that pretty nurse he'd been dating.

"In Nashville at the moment. Maddox promised to keep him off the duty roster until after the wedding."

A sharp rap sounded. Alex opened the conference room door to the six men. All but one looked belligerent. The remaining trainee's eyes were downcast, his expression showing remorse.

Quinn didn't know this guy well enough to judge whether the emotion was sincere. Didn't matter, though. There weren't second chances in PSI's training regimen. If he cheated by taking drugs, Fortress couldn't trust him to be honest about anything else, let alone watch another operative's back.

As soon as Alex closed the door, Josh stood. "Personal Security International has a zero-tolerance policy regarding trainee use of drugs not prescribed by a physician. Our policy mirrors the one used at Fortress. By using performance-enhancing drugs, you endangered your own health and the safety of your teammates."

"Who cares if we use something to make us a little faster or stronger?" the ringleader spat out. "Results count, not how we get them."

Guess Carstairs had enough steroids in his system to trigger aggression. Results counted, all right, and Quinn was looking at the result of drug abuse. Made him wonder how much Carstairs had been taking and the length of time he'd been doping. His best guess? Carstairs had started using immediately after his arrival in Otter Creek. Mediocre when he first arrived, Carstairs soon passed his fellow classmates.

Durango's leader said nothing. Quinn watched as one by one, the gazes of the guilty dropped. Yeah, he'd been on the receiving end of that cold stare more than once during his years in the Rangers and Delta. Major Cahill had intimidation down to a science and he wouldn't tolerate disrespect in any form.

"I wouldn't let you watch my six if you were the last operative standing, Carstairs," Josh said. "A man who continuously takes steroids will behave erratically. I have a wife I want to spend many years with. I'm not trusting my safety and future to you or your buddies."

"That's it, then?" A glare from Carstairs. "No appeal?"

"No appeal. Maddox agrees with our assessment. You're finished here." Josh opened the manila folder in front of him. "Your separation papers are ready. Sign them. You have fifteen minutes to vacate the premises."

The man's face reddened and his fists clenched. "You think you're better than the rest of us. You're nothing but a washed up soldier. You're responsible for this, not me. I won't forget your role in this, Cahill. One of these days, when you're least expecting it, I'll pay you back. You'll wish you'd never crossed me."

"What are you doing, man?" the guy next to Carstairs hissed. "Don't be a fool."

"Listen to your friend," Alex said, voice soft.

All six men froze.

No one did intimidation like one of the deadliest snipers on the planet. Quinn stood. "Want my advice?" he asked casually. "Don't forget Cahill is a cop as well as Delta. Another threat like that will land you in jail. If you make a move on him or his wife, you'll die."

Six pairs of eyes shifted to Josh, who hadn't moved a muscle, his focus still locked on Carstairs. The former trainee's face paled. Yeah, he should be afraid, Quinn thought. The clown hadn't believed Durango was Delta. Josh would wipe the floor with him in under a minute. His unit leader wouldn't tolerate a threat to his wife. Neither would the rest of Durango. Del was one of them. All of them would defend her and the rest of their women with their lives.

"Sign your release papers and get out," Josh said.

Quinn snatched up the papers, and distributed them along with a pen for each. They signed without further words. Carstairs was the first to finish. On his way out the door, he tried to shove Alex aside, failed.

In two moves, the sniper had Carstairs face down on the ground, arm wrenched high up his back. The trainee thrashed, howling, trying to throw Alex off. Quinn shook his head. Dumb move. Didn't appear Cartstairs had two brain cells to rub together.

At that moment, the conference room door opened to admit Deke, Heidi, and Charlie. Deke's eyebrows rose. "Need some help?" he asked as Heidi led Charlie away from the action.

Alex shook his head and jerked Carstairs to his feet. "Let's go."

With a resentful glare at each member of Durango, Carstairs stomped through the doorway with Alex trailing behind him to make sure he vacated the PSI campus.

The rest of the former trainees handed over their release papers. Each man left except for the one Quinn had noticed earlier. "What is it, Jackson?" he asked.

"Would it be possible to reapply at Fortress in the future?"

Quinn glanced at Josh, received a slight nod in response to his silent query. "Wait six months. We'll want a blood test proving you haven't used any non-prescription drugs."

"Yes, sir."

"Work on your conditioning, Jackson," Josh said. "You won't need drugs to do what we ask you to do. I'll send a conditioning program to your email. Eat healthy. No booze or smoking. If you want to work for Fortress, all it takes is discipline and hard work."

A determined expression settled on his face. "Thank you, sir. Thanks to all of you. I'll see you in six months."

Once he was gone, Nate said, "That one has a chance."

"I hope he makes it," Rio said.

"So we're down six, huh?" Deke asked.

"Steroids."

Deke turned to Heidi. "Heidi, these are my bosses. Josh Cahill, Nate Armstrong, Rio Kincaid, Alex Morgan who just escorted the troublemaker out the door, and Quinn who you've already met. Guys, Heidi Thompson and Charlie."

"Have a seat, Heidi," Josh said. "Welcome to PSI."

She blinked. "That's it?"

Amusement twinkled in his eyes. "You expected something more?"

"I expected a few questions, at least."

"Maddox wants you here. Deke sent me a text with his endorsement." Durango's leader shrugged. "That's good enough for me."

"How soon will you move to town?" Rio asked.

"My belongings are in a truck, waiting for me to unload everything into the house I'm renting."

"Need help?" Nate asked as Alex slipped back into the room.

"I would appreciate any help. Friends helped me load the truck, but I didn't know how I would unload the couch by myself."

Alex pulled out his phone. "What's your address?" After she gave him the information, he said, "I'll meet you there in an hour. I need to take my dog outside first. My wife is in class until six this evening."

"The backyard is fenced if you want to bring your dog. Charlie would love to play outside."

He smiled. "I might do that."

"I'll check with Darcy, see if she needs anything from me before I show up." Rio stood, extended a hand to Heidi. "Glad to have you and Charlie on board. I'll see you in a few minutes." With a wave at the others, he left the conference room.

"I'll call Del," Josh said. "Let her know I'll be late."

"When are you on duty, Major?" Nate asked.

"Have to go in at ten o'clock tonight for roll call."

Heidi frowned. "Roll call?"

"I'm also with the Otter Creek police department."

Nate stood. "I'll stop by Burger Heaven on the way to Heidi's and pick up dinner for everyone."

"Better include enough for our wives," Alex said. "I imagine Ivy will help after her class is finished."

"Same with Del. She'll be along after the bookstore closes." Josh turned to Nate. "What about Stella?"

He shook his head. "She's on shift until ten tonight."

"I'm out," Deke said. "I'm sorry, Heidi, but my daughters have a school function tonight."

She held up her hand. "Please, say no more. You can't miss something that important. Besides, sounds like I have plenty of help."

"Quinn, what about you?" Josh asked.

"I'll follow Heidi and Charlie to their place, unload what I can before the rest of you arrive."

As Durango left the room, each one took a moment to greet Charlie before leaving.

Heidi glanced at Quinn. "When do I start work?"

"Tomorrow too soon?"

A quick smile. "That's perfect. Charlie's welcome?"

"Of course. You can't demonstrate how a well-trained S & R dog behaves without him. Deke already set up a training area for the dogs and owners. You and Charlie can try it out tomorrow, see if we're missing anything. Your first class of trainees arrives next week. If you're ready, we'll head to your place."

"I hope you all have medical insurance," she muttered.

Amusement swirled through Quinn. "Why?"

"The couch is a monster-sized sectional."

"No problem." He escorted Heidi and Charlie from the building to the parking lot.

Heidi headed for a black SUV parked next to his. "Oh, goodness," she murmured.

"What is it?"

"Is that your SUV?"

"Yeah, it is. Something wrong?" He scanned his vehicle, stopped on the jagged scratch running the length of his ride. Fury welled up. Someone had keyed his SUV.

CHAPTER FOUR

Ethan Blackhawk, police chief of Otter Creek, leaned back in his chair, the annoying squeak as familiar to him now as seeing his face in a mirror. Hard to believe almost three years had passed since the day he first walked into this office, an outsider tasked with replacing the retired chief who served for thirty years.

Those first days were tough. In this small, close-knit town, no one trusted him. A smile curved his lips. No one, that is, except for a gutsy blond witness who had captured his interest and eventually his heart. Coming to Otter Creek, Tennessee, had changed his life. New job, a wife, and now in a matter of days, a baby.

Ethan's heart squeezed at the thought of the precious life growing inside the love of his life. With his background and career, he never thought any woman would risk loving him. But Serena Cahill Blackhawk had taught him the true meaning of courage, and his life would never be the same. All he could do was show her each day how much he loved her and their baby.

His assistant, Trudy, buzzed him. "Lt. Parrish is on line 1, sir."

"Thanks." He snatched up the hand set. "Lieutenant, it's been a while. How is your wife?"

A pause, then the deep bass voice said, "As beautiful as ever. And Serena?"

"She swears she'll be pregnant forever."

Parrish chuckled. "Not long now, I suppose."

"No, sir. Doc Anderson says the baby can come any time now. We can't wait to hold our child."

"Congratulations, Ethan. I'm happy for both of you."

"Thank you, sir." Something in his voice told Ethan his former commander was worried. Anything that made tough-as-nails Wade Parrish worry wouldn't be good. And though he and Parrish were friends of a sort, the grizzled cop wouldn't call just to shoot the breeze. Wasn't his style. No, something bad was going on. "What's wrong?"

A wry laugh drifted through the handset. "You always were the most perceptive officer under my command."

"Give it to me straight, Lieutenant."

"Someone needs to be with Serena at all times. Someone you trust implicitly and who is at least as dangerous as you."

Ethan stilled, his heart rate picking up speed. "Why?"

"Your old pal Hans Muehller escaped from Herlong."

Ice flowed in his veins even as his mind raced. Serena was with his aunt today, cooking meals for Ruth to store in her freezer and heat later. Home Runs, his wife's personal chef business, was booming these days, a fact which was good for their bank account but a source of worry for Ethan in light of her advanced pregnancy. He'd finally convinced Serena to carry a light-weight stool with her when she had these marathon cooking sessions. Although he hoped voicing his concern had persuaded her to take the extra precaution, he suspected it was her swollen ankles that led to her capitulation. Serena was stubborn, but she loved their baby as fiercely as she loved her husband. He was so blessed to have her in his life.

His hand tightened around the handset. No one, not Hans Muehller nor anyone else, would take her or his child. He'd kill anyone who tried. "Should have sent him to a maximum security prison."

"Agreed. Too bad the federal prosecutor didn't see it our way."

"Do the marshals know Muehller's loose?" Serena's friend, Pam, had testified against the man and had entered the witness security program. Though Ethan was concerned for his wife's safety, he didn't want the former citizen of Otter Creek caught off guard if the international assassin happened to track her down. His gut told him Serena was in far more danger than Pam. The courageous mother of his child had testified in the same trial and was responsible for his life sentence.

"The handler knows and is relocating the witness and giving her a new identity."

Ethan breathed a little easier. At least Pam should be safe from Muehller's reach. "Any indication where he's headed?"

"My guess is straight to Otter Creek. In reality, no one's seen him since he escaped. However, a murder in Nevada this morning matched his M.O."

"How did Muehller escape?"

"Female guard fancied herself in love with him, got him assigned to kitchen duty. Muehller killed a food delivery driver, stole his uniform, and drove out the gate without anyone stopping him."

"What about the guard?"

"Knocked her out and left her to face the consequences. She swears she didn't know he would kill anyone."

Ethan grunted. "What did she think he'd gone to prison for? Stealing Girl Scout cookies?"

A soft groan from his lieutenant. "Please. My wife has me on a diet that doesn't include cookies. Listen, I'll keep my ear to the ground, pass along any updates." He paused. "Unless you have your own sources to draw information from."

He thought about his new detective, Stella Armstrong, and her former US Marshal partner, Deke Creed, now working for Personal Security International. In addition, Fortress Security owed him a few favors. He'd call in every marker he had to protect his wife and child. "I have a few resources to tap. I'd still appreciate hearing anything you pick up."

"You got it. I'll be in touch soon." The call ended.

Ethan's lips twitched. Parrish never bothered with good phone etiquette. Between friends and former colleagues, the courtesy wasn't needed. He glanced at the clock, decided it might be wise to check on his wife.

After a stop by the diner to purchase three of the day's special, Ethan drove to his aunt's place. A quick knock at the back door and he let himself into the kitchen where he knew the dearest women in his life would be located.

Sure enough, he pushed open the door to see Serena and Ruth sitting at the kitchen table, a mug of tea in front of each woman.

"Ethan!" Serena's blue eyes lit from within as a broad smile curved her lush mouth. Yeah, he was still convinced Serena Blackhawk was the most beautiful woman on the planet. That sentiment would never change. "What are you doing here, love?"

"Looking for the two most gorgeous women in Otter Creek." He held up the large bag in his other hand. "I come bearing gifts."

Ruth's gaze took in the familiar logo emblazoned on the bag. "Anything from Delaney's Diner is mouth-watering. You're welcome to come any time without bearing gifts, Ethan."

"Good to know." He leaned down to kiss her soft cheek. "How is the new book coming?"

"Slow as molasses. I can't come up with an inventive way to kill the protagonist's uncle."

Ethan set the bag in the center of the table and distributed the to-go containers filled with meatloaf, green beans, and mashed potatoes. "Go to a movie with one of your friends. Might help you to think about something else for a while."

"Great idea. There's an action film at the theater that Alice and I have been wanting to see. Might be just what I need to jumpstart my imagination. Alice loves to brainstorm plots with me and she always has interesting suggestions."

He shared an amused glance with Serena. After spending so many hours with his aunt, his wife knew how Ruth's mind worked. The best-selling author had a penchant for trouble, though. A couple months back, she sprained her wrist while riding a hover board. She had been lucky the damage wasn't more severe. Doc Anderson had made Ruth to stay off hover boards in the future.

Ethan circled the table, leaned down and kissed Serena. "How are you, baby?"

His wife rubbed the mound of her belly. "Still pregnant."

He smiled, laid his hand on the side of her stomach. Seconds later, a solid thump nudged his hand and made him chuckle.

"Baby Blackhawk is running out of room in there," Serena murmured.

Kneeling, Ethan leaned in and pressed a soft kiss to her belly. He loved Serena and this baby so much he could barely breathe. Losing them would destroy him. He glanced up to find his wife watching him.

"What's wrong, love?"

Did she have to be so perceptive? He normally admired that about her, but not now and not in this situation. The last thing Ethan wanted was to worry Serena.

They'd never lied to each other. He wouldn't start now. He simply told her the truth. "Lt. Parrish called. Muehller escaped."

Color drained from Serena's face as her hands cradled her belly, unconsciously protecting their child. Man, he adored this woman more every day. Instead of being afraid for herself, her first instinct was to protect the small life she carried.

"What will we do?" she whispered.

"Wait, watch, prepare. If he comes to Otter Creek, I'll take care of him." *Permanently.*

CHAPTER FIVE

Heidi turned into her driveway and stopped a good distance from the loaded truck. She breathed a sigh of relief. Everything appeared untouched. Otter Creek wasn't a big city, she reminded herself. No need to worry about a crime wave. He wouldn't find her here. She was safe. For now.

Quinn Gallagher parked his damaged vehicle behind hers. Guess vandals lived in small towns, too. The fact the damage occurred on PSI grounds disturbed Heidi. Quinn definitely wasn't happy. Was the angry trainee responsible for the damage? The leaders of PSI had resources at their disposal. Whoever committed the crime messed with the wrong people.

Thinking about the confrontation between Carstairs and Josh Cahill sent chills over her skin. Heidi didn't know their military background, but Quinn and his unit had intimidation down to an art form.

Heidi released Charlie from the back. He stayed at her side. "Good boy," she murmured, rubbing his head. "Welcome home, Charlie." She unlocked the front door and waited for Quinn who spoke into his phone as he approached.

"Yeah, I know I should have waited at PSI. Tough, Rod. There's nothing to see in the parking lot. No broken glass. No convenient clues left waiting for you to process." He rattled off Heidi's address. "I'm helping our new S & R instructor move into her house. When you get a break, bring your kit. We'll feed you a hamburger." Quinn shoved his phone into his pocket. "Sorry. One of the police detectives griped because I left the scene of the crime."

"Go back to PSI. Your friends will be here soon."

"Rod knows where to find me."

"I don't want you in trouble because of me."

He sent her a look that quelled further arguments. Fine. Quinn was man enough to dig himself out of trouble with the law. He'd encountered more than his fair share of scrutiny as a teenager. Regret swamped Heidi. Her family had caused Quinn's such heartache. He must hate them.

Heidi opened the door. "Charlie, inside." Her Lab trotted into the house. The few boxes she'd unloaded by herself before the interview were in the living room against the far wall. She ripped the packing tape off a box marked *Charlie*.

"Give me the keys. I'll start unloading," Quinn said.

Once he left, Heidi took Charlie to the backyard with some of his toys and let the dog explore his new surroundings. After providing water for Charlie and checking the gate, Heidi returned to the driveway. Quinn was heading to the house with his arms full of boxes.

"Here." She hurried to him. "I can take one of those."

Quinn grinned. "Plenty more in the truck. These are mine. By the way, appreciate you labeling the boxes. The move will go much faster. Where's the master bedroom?"

"Down the hall, last door on the right."

"Charlie?"

"Backyard. He spent a long time in my SUV today."

Another SUV parked in her driveway. Alex climbed from his vehicle and opened the back door. A gorgeous blond Lab hopped out. Oh, man. Just look at that dog. So beautiful.

Heidi headed for the newcomers. "Thanks so much for helping," she said to Alex before turning her attention to the dog. "Hi, buddy." She held out her fisted hand for the Lab to sniff.

"This is Spenser."

"You are such a handsome boy, Spenser." She glanced at Alex. "Charlie's in the backyard." She led Alex and his dog around the side of the house and opened the gate. Charlie trotted over and the sniff-and-wag party began. Before long, the two Labs were involved in a game of tug-of-war with a rope.

Quinn came to stand beside Heidi and watched the dogs tussle. "Looks like Spenser has a new friend to play with."

Alex smiled. "So it seems. How long have you two been here?"

"Ten minutes." A scowl from Quinn. "Rod hassled me for leaving PSI without waiting for him."

His friend stiffened. "Something happen?"

"Someone keyed my SUV."

Alex frowned. "I followed Carstairs all the way to the parking lot. He didn't touch your ride, Quinn. Have you checked the security cams?"

"Not yet. Got to give Rod something to do."

Alex shook his head. "You like to live dangerously."

An unrepentant grin from the other man. "Been too quiet around here."

Heidi hoped Otter Creek stayed quiet. She'd had enough excitement.

"I love quiet evenings at home with my wife, buddy. Don't mess that up." Alex followed Quinn to the damaged SUV with Heidi trailing behind. He whistled at the damage. "Nasty. Gouge goes to the armor plating. Needs to be fixed soon, Quinn."

"I already called Bear and arranged to drop this off tomorrow morning and pick up a loaner."

"You have a session tomorrow morning?"

"CQC at eight."

"What's that?" Heidi asked. Sounded like some kind of military acronym.

"Close quarters combat." He turned to Alex. "Can you cover the class?"

"No problem. My first session is at ten."

"I owe you one."

Alex waved that aside and hopped in the back of the truck. He grabbed two boxes. "Guest room?" he asked Heidi.

And so began Heidi's duties as director of operations. The rest of Quinn's teammates and their wives or bride-to-be arrived and jumped in to help. Once the truck was empty and the front door closed, she brought in Charlie and Spenser. After making the greeting rounds, both dogs flopped down in front of the fireplace and fell asleep. The sight brought a smile to her face.

"Dinner time," Josh's wife, Del, said. "I'm starving."

"Me, too." Ivy dropped into the nearest kitchen chair. "Please tell me you brought soft drinks, too, Nate."

"In the refrigerator." While he carried drinks to the table, Darcy brought bags filled with foil-wrapped hamburgers and containers of fries to the table. On his last trip to the fridge, Nate grabbed a salad topped with grilled chicken and handed it to Darcy. He also pressed a bottle of water into her hand.

Darcy smiled. "You remembered."

"Always." He tapped her nose gently. "We want you healthy, Darcy. Someone has to keep Rio in line."

Heidi studied Rio's future wife. She looked tired, but healthy. Maybe when she knew Darcy better, she'd ask about the health comments.

In the middle of the meal, a sharp rap sounded on the front door. Heidi's heart leaped. Who was that? The only people she knew in Otter Creek were in her house. Breathe. Just breathe. The arsonist couldn't have found her. Maddox promised to protect her.

"Want me to answer the door?" Quinn asked, his gaze quizzical. "It's probably Rod Kelter, the police detective."

Great. Way to go, Heidi. Where was her spine? "Please." And thought herself a coward for letting one of her new bosses answer her door. Did she think the arsonist would knock politely? Besides, she had a house full of people, not the least of which were five very well trained men with distinguished careers in the military. Del, Ivy, and Darcy had been careful with the information they shared, but Heidi was good at reading between the lines, a necessary skill to survive. Her new bosses wouldn't let someone hurt her.

Her gaze tracked to Charlie, her constant companion. Though Charlie wasn't a protection dog, more than once her sweet Lab had stood between her and danger.

Not only were the Fortress operatives here, Heidi wasn't a helpless ten-year-old girl. She may not have worked in Special Forces like she suspected her bosses had, but she had a brain and wasn't afraid to use it against the man who terrorized her.

Quinn crossed the room, checked the peephole. He flung open the door and a tall, red-haired man strode into the house.

"What smells so good?" he said closing the door behind himself.

"Food from Hamburger Heaven."

The detective moaned in appreciation. "Thank goodness. Meg's on deadline, so dinner at our place will be whenever she finishes the newspaper copy. I'll be lucky to see her before midnight."

"I brought extras if you want to take food for Meg," Nate said.

"Oh, man. She'll be ecstatic. Serena's been stocking our refrigerator and freezer in anticipation of Baby Blackhawk's arrival."

"Guess that means Meg's tired of healthy food," Josh said. He grabbed a hamburger and soft drink and handed them to Rod. "Here. Enjoy. Once Serena's back on her feet, she'll resume her campaign to reform Meg's eating habits." He glanced at Heidi. "I have three sisters, Heidi. Serena, Meg, and Madison. Serena is a personal chef. She's made it her mission in life to retrain our taste buds."

"Hurts our bodies to eat like two-year-olds," Nate commented, his tone mild. He winked at Darcy, who smiled.

Alex rose. "Take my seat, Rod. I'm finished. I need to assemble the beds."

One more problem off Heidi's plate. She hadn't looked forward to assembling them after a long day of driving and moving. The headboards were heavy and difficult to secure to the frames by herself.

"I'll give you a hand," Josh said. He leaned over, dropped a kiss on his wife's lips, and followed his teammate.

Heidi sighed. That was the kind of relationship she wanted with the right man one day. After she unmasked the arsonist. She couldn't expect a boyfriend or husband to endanger himself by associating with her. Any man in her life might be a target.

The detective dropped into the chair beside Heidi and placed his meal on the table. He turned, blue eyes assessing her as he held out his hand. "Rod Kelter."

"Heidi Thompson."

"So you're working with Deke in the S & R program." Rod unwrapped his hamburger and took a bite.

"You know Deke?" She held up a hand. "Never mind. It's a small town and you're law enforcement. Of course you know him."

Rod chuckled. "I also work with Nate's wife, Stella. She and Deke used to be partners in the Marshals. Deke hopes to start an S & R unit in the area."

"Otter Creek is surrounded by mountains and not far from the Smokies. Easy for people to lose their way in the forest. The more S & R teams available and ready, the better chance of finding the lost ones before it's too late."

"How long have you been part of S & R?"

She smiled, amused at his cop's curiosity even in a social situation. "Five years."

"Ever tracked a fugitive before?"

The image of her sweet younger sister popped into the forefront of her mind. If she'd been equipped to lead a search for Moira, maybe her sister would still be alive. Heidi shook her head. "Lost hikers and toddlers. Anything else you want to know, Detective Kelter?"

His cheeks pinked. "Sorry. Occupational hazard."

Heidi grinned. "It's fine. I'm familiar with a number of law enforcement officers, friends with a few. They're nosy, too."

"Heidi, want help arranging your kitchen?" Del asked.

She jumped up. "Absolutely. I start work tomorrow."

"What about your playground equipment?" Quinn asked, a twinkle in his eyes.

Rod paused, hamburger halfway to his mouth. "Playground equipment?"

Her cheeks burned. "It's for Charlie."

"Show me where you want everything."

Rod crumpled the empty wrapper as he swallowed his last hamburger bite. "I want to look at your ride, Quinn."

"Need the keys?"

The detective shook his head. "I'll let you know what I find." With a last sip of his drink, Rod gathered his trash and threw it in the garbage can, then retraced his steps outside.

Heidi turned to Del. "I'll be back in a minute."

"We'll unpack boxes and stack dishes on the counter until you return."

In the backyard, Heidi showed Quinn where she wanted the barrels, teeter-totter, slide, ladders, boards, and balance beam before returning to organize her kitchen. The ladies had lined the shelves and drawers by the time she walked through the doorway. "Wow! You didn't waste any time."

"Don't have much to spare," Ivy said. "Josh goes on duty in a couple hours, I have papers to grade, and Darcy gets up early to open her deli."

She turned to Darcy. "You own a deli?"

"You passed it on your way through town." Darcy cut another piece of liner and handed it to Ivy. "That's A Wrap."

"I'll have to stop by."

"I'd love to show you around." She smiled. "Your first visit will be on me. A welcome-to-town gift."

Over the course of the next thirty minutes, her new friends and co-workers arranged furniture, and unpacked and organized the kitchen and bathrooms. Another quick knock and the detective returned.

"Where's Quinn?" he asked.

"Still out back," Del said. "I'm beginning to wonder if Rio and Quinn are trying Charlie's training equipment." That comment brought a round of laughter.

With a chuckle, Rod left again.

"Wonder if he found anything useful?" Ivy murmured.

"If he did, we'll have to wheedle the information from Nick or Stella." Del balled the last of the newspaper protecting Heidi's glasses and stuffed it into a trash bag with the rest. "Rod is closemouthed about his work."

"And Nick isn't?" Ivy asked, voice revealing her skepticism.

"He doesn't keep secrets from Madison. She's my information source most of the time."

"You're married to a cop," Darcy pointed out. "Why don't you ask Josh?"

"He's not a detective. Josh won't always have the information."

"The vandalism occurred on PSI property," Heidi said. "Shouldn't he have the inside scoop?"

"Good point," Del said. "I'll ask him if Rod won't talk."

Rod, Rio, and Quinn returned to the kitchen.

"Well?" Ivy asked Rod. "Did you find anything to identify who damaged Quinn's SUV?"

"Maybe. Pulled a lot of prints." He glanced at Quinn. "I'll run them, see if anything pops."

"As long as you don't slap those silver bracelets on me."

The detective smirked. "Got something you're trying to hide, Gallagher?"

"Not this week."

Heidi smiled. Good to know Quinn's sense of humor hadn't changed over the years and that her bosses seemed to have a sense of humor, too. She wasn't sure about Deke. He'd have to fit in with the PSI guys and you couldn't do that with no sense of humor. She'd find out soon enough. She could hardly wait to start her new life. If she kept Quinn in the dark as to her real identity until he got to know her better, maybe she could stay in this place she'd love to call home.

"I'll let you know what I learn," Rod told Quinn. He turned to Heidi. "I know you have your hands full moving in today, but you should secure your gas cans before you call it a night."

"Gas cans?" Puzzled, she frowned.

"Yeah, the two old-fashioned metal gas cans on your front porch."

Heidi felt the blood drain from her face. "Show me."

"Heidi."

She turned to Quinn who was watching her intently.

"Are you okay?"

She shook her head. Maddox promised she'd be safe, that the arsonist wouldn't find her here. Despite his precautions and stringent rules, the nightmare was beginning again.

CHAPTER SIX

Quinn's gaze sharpened, his focus riveted on Heidi's extreme response to Rod's comment about the gas cans. Unless he'd misread her completely, Heidi was on the verge of passing out.

Rio moved closer to Heidi. "Sit a minute, sugar." He moved a chair away from the table and motioned for her to sit.

When she just stared at the seat, Quinn took her by the upper arms and nudged her onto the chair. Nate handed him a bottled soft drink which Quinn opened and pressed into Heidi's hand.

"Take a few sips," he murmured.

She blinked, her expression blank.

Even more concerned, Quinn knelt on one knee in front of her. She acted as though she were in shock. From a simple gas container? "Heidi. Drink, babe." Babe? Where had that come from? He saw the looks of surprise from his teammates at the term of endearment. He ignored them. What they thought didn't matter. Only Heidi mattered and she was in obvious distress.

She sipped the fizzy drink for a couple minutes. "Thanks." Her cheeks flamed when she noticed the people around the room watching her with varying degrees of concern. "Sorry for the freak out. It's old history. I'm okay now."

Quinn didn't think so. Her hands were still shaking. All this from gas cans? Did the secret she hid have anything to do with his conviction that he knew this woman from somewhere?

Heidi focused on Rod. "Show me the gas cans, please."

Quinn rose and helped Heidi stand. She wavered, pressed her lips into a grim line, released Quinn's hand, and moved toward the front porch. Stubborn woman. Wouldn't have hurt to wait another minute for the shock to pass. He followed close behind, prepared to catch her if Heidi's wobbly legs gave way.

By unspoken agreement, the other members of Durango followed them to the porch. Two metal gas cans stood against the outside wall. Quinn was close enough to hear Heidi's quiet gasp.

He frowned. The gas cans hadn't been there when he and his friends moved Heidi's furniture and boxes into the house. He would have noticed them. He admitted to himself the beautiful woman distracted him a little. Okay, a lot. But not so much he would have missed something odd on her porch.

He exchanged a glance with Alex, noted the same wariness in his gaze that Quinn felt. He shifted his focus to the surrounding area. Nothing but trees and darkness, a few scattered streetlights. Many shadows. Located at the end of an older street on the outskirts of Otter Creek, Heidi's house was on a large lot butting up against the forest.

Good for Charlie, bad for Quinn's peace of mind. Too many places for someone to watch Heidi and not be seen until it was too late. The knot in his gut told Quinn trouble was coming. He prayed he and his teammates would be in the right place at the right time to offer assistance.

"Are these yours?" Rod asked.

"No." Heidi's voice was tight. "I don't have gas cans."

"How do you fill the gas tank on your lawn mower?"

"I hire someone to take care of the lawn for me." A ghost of a smile curved her lips. "I hate to mow grass."

"Did you purchase the house?"

She shook her head. "I'm renting. Why?"

"Any chance the owners left the gas cans for your use?" Rod asked.

Relief flooded her face. "Maybe that's the explanation. Why didn't the owner tell me he left them?"

Nate waved toward the driveway packed with cars and SUVs. "Perhaps he didn't want to interrupt."

"Makes sense."

Heidi wanted to believe that explanation, but Quinn noticed the unease as her gaze drifted back to the red containers. His protective instincts rose to the forefront. Something was going on with Heidi Thompson and he intended to find out what it was. His gut knotted at the prospect of going behind her back. He'd have to convince her to tell him the truth. Otherwise, he'd be forced to use Fortress resources to learn what he needed to know. Quinn would do what was necessary to protect her, because Heidi was in trouble.

"Is there anything else you need before we leave, Heidi?" Ivy asked. "I hate to leave you surrounded by boxes."

"I appreciate the help, but I've taken enough of your time. What's left now will wait until tomorrow. I'll unpack one box at a time as I have a few minutes free."

One by one, the others left with only Josh, Rod, and Quinn remaining behind. "I need your signature on the vandalism report," Rod said to Quinn. His gaze shifted to Heidi for a moment.

"I'll sign it in a minute. Josh, you have time to talk?"

"Sure."

Quinn glanced at Heidi. "Okay if I stick around and help for a while longer?"

"Of course. It's not necessary, though."

If the relief in her eyes was any indication, the lady wasn't quite ready to be by herself in the old house. "I'd like to help, if you'll let me."

"Thanks, Quinn." She glanced at Josh. "I'll see you tomorrow?"

A short nod from Durango's leader. "Afternoon, most likely. I have the graveyard shift. Your house is in my patrol area. I'll swing by a few times tonight, make sure no more surprises are left on your porch."

She smiled, then went inside the house.

"What's up?" Josh asked softly.

He waved at the gas cans. "You ever hear of an owner giving free gas to a renter to mow the grass?"

His friend frowned. "Can't say that I have."

"I'll take the gas cans, check them for prints," Rod said. "Want me to run her while I'm at it?"

Running her through the law enforcement databases seemed intrusive. Besides, Maddox must have conducted a thorough background search on her or, more accurately, had Zane Murphy investigate her. The Fortress tech guru would have caught any problems. Nothing slipped by Z.

Quinn didn't want to learn Heidi's background from Rod, Maddox, or Murphy. He'd prefer she told him the details herself. Didn't know why that was important to him, but it was. "Just check the gas cans. If the owner of the house asks about them, Heidi can tell him you have the cans at the station."

A nod from the detective. "I'll let you know what I find." He pulled on a pair of latex gloves and carried the cans to his SUV.

Quinn dropped his voice to a murmur. "Did you see Heidi's reaction to the containers? I don't like this."

"Extreme," his friend agreed. "Should I touch base with Z?"

Another head shake from Quinn. "I want her to tell me what's going on." He wanted her to trust him with her safety. For some reason, one he couldn't identify at the moment, he wanted to be the one she relied on for security and comfort.

"I'll leave it alone." A pointed look from his unit leader. "For now."

He got the unspoken command. Either Quinn learned the information they needed, or Josh would. If something in Heidi's past put PSI or their personnel in danger, they needed to know before being blindsided. Quinn understood. If he had a woman to protect, he'd be as protective as his teammates were of their mates.

His gaze shifted to the house, thinking of the drop-dead gorgeous woman inside. "I'll take care of it." And her. No one would harm Heidi on his watch.

"Good enough." Josh clapped him on the shoulder. "I need to go. I want to spend some time with Del before my shift."

"Go. I've got this."

"Call if you need me."

"If you notice anything out of the ordinary during the night, I want to know about it." He heard the sharp edge in his tone, wondered at it, but didn't retract his statement.

"Something you need to tell me, Gallagher?"

A feeling he couldn't put into words yet? He shook his head.

"When you figure it out, I want to be the first to know." With that, his unit leader climb into his SUV and drove away.

Quinn flinched at the tide of guilt flooding him. The members of Durango were his best friends. Without a doubt he could count on each one to cover his back. This situation with Heidi, however, was unique. He couldn't put into words what was happening. She was important to him, which was beyond stupid since he'd known her for a handful of hours.

Shoving the puzzle to the back of his mind for the moment, Quinn crossed the yard to Rod's SUV. He signed the report and handed the form to the detective.

"Nick's on duty at ten. I'll bring him and Stella up to speed on your SUV and the gas cans before I go off shift."

"Thanks, buddy."

"You know how to reach me if you need me, Gallagher. Later."

Quinn waited until the taillights of the detective's vehicle were out of sight, then one more time visually scoured the area. Still nothing. He couldn't shake the feeling something or someone was waiting, watching. He straightened, jaw flexing. Let him come. He'd be ready.

CHAPTER SEVEN

Heidi locked the door behind Quinn, then rested her back against the steel surface. She drew her first free breath in hours. So far, she hadn't tripped herself up and Quinn hadn't asked more questions about her background. The questions were coming, though. She saw them brewing in his gaze. The Quinn she remembered was sharp. That intellect was working on the connection. Sometime in the near future, the day of reckoning would arrive. If she was lucky, she'd have time to cement a good working relationship and maybe a friendship before he realized who he was dealing with.

Charlie sat in front of her, whined. A smile curved her lips. "I'm okay, buddy. Tired. Worried I'll slip with Quinn. Thrilled with the new job to feed us." Spooked.

She had reason to be afraid. Maybe the gas cans were a gift from her landlord. Heidi didn't think so. The landlord didn't appear to care about anything except the rent money and security deposit. From the way Quinn reacted to gas cans on her porch, the operative wasn't buying the gift explanation either. Fantastic. Quinn Gallagher probably had great instincts, ones that told him she was in trouble.

Understatement. She was in more trouble than her childhood crush knew.

Heidi glanced at her watch. A little early to call. Levi wouldn't mind. She missed him already. It was better this way. Safer for both of them if they were separated. So why did the separation feel like the wrong choice?

She grabbed the prepaid cell and tapped the only programmed number. One ring. Two. Three rings. With each unanswered ring, Heidi's anxiety ratcheted up another notch.

On the fourth ring, her call was answered. "Are you okay?" was her greeting.

A relieved grin curved her mouth. "Hello to you to, cousin." Man, it was so good to hear his voice. She missed not being able to pick up the phone whenever she wanted to call him. They'd been best friends since she'd gone to live with his family all those years ago. He should have spurned her like any normal high school sophomore. Instead, he'd taken up the mantle of protector and friend.

A pause, then, "You're an hour early, Peaches. What gives?"

She rolled her eyes at the childhood nickname. "Just missed you."

"Heidi."

She thought about the gas cans, debated not telling him. He needed to know. Levi should be prepared. "It may be nothing."

"Tell me what's happening." Alarm reverberated in his voice.

Heidi related the incident with the gas cans and the vandalism to Quinn's SUV. The two happenings weren't related, but it was safer for him to know everything.

"I'll come to Otter Creek as soon as I make arrangements."

"No!" This was why she hadn't wanted to tell him the truth. Levi couldn't break cover. He wasn't safe either.

"The police are on top of it. The leaders of PSI were here. They know what happened. You have to stay in place. Promise me." Heidi couldn't lose anyone else. She didn't think she'd recover if she lost her cousin and last remaining relative.

"I hate this," he muttered. "I shouldn't be hiding like a coward."

"You're not a coward, Levi. This freak tried to kill me more than once. When he failed, he came after you and almost killed you."

"Maybe I should come out in the open and let him do his worst. Then you might be safe."

For a moment, she was too stunned to say anything. Then anger surged to the forefront. "That plan is full of so many holes it resembles lace. Don't be an idiot. We've stuck together all this time. You've been my rock. You saved my life. I will never forget what risks you took for me. How will it help me if you're dead, Levi? I wouldn't have anybody."

Quinn's image popped into her mind with his thick, sandy-blond hair, and chocolate brown eyes. Right. She'd known him a matter of hours as Heidi Thompson. Though she knew him years ago in their hometown, Heidi couldn't count on him for support once he realized who she was. He was not hers. To think otherwise would lead to heartbreak. "We know the arsonist won't give up the chase because you're gone. I'm his primary target. This creep will still come after me even if you're dead. No, Levi, I'm afraid the blame lies with me and my wretched last name."

"It's not your fault, Heidi. Your father set all this in motion and his partner in crime is out for revenge. Unfortunately, we're both the victims of his continued cycle of violence."

She blinked away the tears stinging her eyes. Levi's words were kind, but untrue. If she had never lived with his family, at least his parents and siblings would be alive.

"If only we knew who we were dealing with."

A familiar refrain between the two of them. They could set a trap if they knew the identity of their stalker. As it stood, anybody could be the enemy. Maddox had told her and Levi they could trust the operatives he placed with them. Because Heidi had been the primary target, the Fortress CEO had sent her to PSI, run by his best unit. She hadn't known Quinn was part of PSI or she would have asked him to send her somewhere else.

She'd been honest with Maddox about her background and identity. Heidi frowned. He must know her connection to Quinn's family. Why did he send her to a man whose life had been impacted by her father's crimes? He must trust Quinn to do what was honorable despite their shared history.

Though Maddox hadn't explained what these men did, Heidi figured out Quinn and his friends had been black ops in the military. Alex's wife, Ivy, mentioned the men being in the Army together from basic. So that made them Rangers? Delta? Whatever they were, the Fortress CEO thought very highly of them. That made these men scary good. Good enough to take on this arsonist who'd proved himself determined and lethal over and over?

She sighed. Guess they'd find out because it seemed he had found her again. Heidi swallowed hard. She was so tired of running and looking over her shoulder. She wanted a normal life, whatever that was. "Maddox said the unit in charge of my new company is the best he's ever worked with."

"Yeah?" Skepticism rang in Levi's voice. "We've heard that before, Peaches."

"I'm sorry, Levi."

"Don't," he said.

For the first time since this nightmare began, she heard something in his voice that she didn't like. Heidi frowned. Fatigue? No, she realized, horror growing in her gut.

Resignation. That's what she heard. No. Just no. "Don't you dare give up. Not after everything we've been through. We can't give him that."

"How else am I supposed to feel, Peaches? This guy has taken everything. Our families, our identities. He stole our lives and he's still coming. When will it be enough?"

She didn't voice the truth they both knew. The nightmare wouldn't stop until either they were dead or the killer was. "Don't give up. I need you." Truthfully, Heidi didn't know if she could continue without him.

Charlie whined and nudged her hand. Sweet boy. He always knew when she was upset.

"Charlie okay?"

"He's fine, comforting me. Levi, please, don't give up. We'll find the answer and get our lives back. What about your friends?" she asked, careful not to reveal too much just in case. "Are you comfortable with them and their skills?"

A pause had her sitting up straighter, muscles tensing. "Levi?"

"They are very good. Relax, okay? I'm fine."

At least now she heard something different in her cousin's voice, this time something good. Heidi wondered if one of his bodyguards was a woman. Maybe when it was safe, she'd ask Maddox. Whatever the reason for the hesitation in Levi's voice this time, she was grateful.

"One of my new employers is Quinn Gallagher."

"Did he recognize you?"

"Not yet."

"But?"

"I'm on borrowed time. He'll figure it out soon."

"Tell Maddox to move you," he demanded. "Now, Peaches. If there's any chance he won't do his job…."

"He's not like that."

"You don't know what he's like anymore. You can't base trust on a child's fantasies."

"I know," she said, voice soft.
"Promise me you'll be careful."
"You know I will."
"I should go. We can't be on here too long."
"You be careful, too." Heidi would have said more, but her throat closed off. Man, she hated to let him go--for selfish reasons. Once she ended the call with Levi, she had to deal with her house on the outskirts of town which now seemed too far away from civilization. After having so many people helping her unpack, the place seemed huge and empty.

Right. She could try selling herself that fantasy, but it wouldn't work. The problem wasn't the house. The problem was the watcher in the darkness, the one she felt but couldn't see.

"Same goes, Peaches. Watch your back. Call me if anything else happens."

"I will. Promise." And then he was gone.

Charlie nudged her hand with his head.

Heidi pushed aside the desolation she felt at closing the connection to her cousin and shoved the instrument deep in her pocket. She never went anywhere without that phone, a lifeline to her former life, a life she would give almost anything to return to. Almost. Going back to her former life was impossible. She wasn't the same. Even if she returned to one of her former lives, Heidi wouldn't be happy. The only thing left was forging a new life, hopefully for the last time.

Dropping to her knees, she wrapped her arms around the Lab's neck and rested her cheek against the top of his head. "We did the right thing separating, Charlie." She infused her voice with confidence for the dog who watched her with worry in his gaze. Who was she kidding? She was trying to convince herself as much as her beloved dog of the wisdom of her and Levi's decision. Too many close calls convinced them it was necessary for their survival.

Heidi pressed a kiss to Charlie's head and stood. "We have curtains to hang before we sleep tonight, buddy. Let's get busy."

Close to midnight, Heidi breathed a sigh of relief. Finally, all the windows were covered and she didn't feel as if someone watched her every move. After one last check of the windows and doors, she completed her bedtime routine and crawled under the covers.

She awoke to Charlie's low-voiced growl. Heidi's eyelids flew up, heart racing. The Lab never growled. Had the kidnapper come for her after all? "What is it, buddy?" she whispered.

Charlie's response was a whine, though he didn't take his attention off the window across the room.

Something or someone was out there. Heidi eased her hand into the nightstand and grabbed her Glock. She wouldn't be caught unawares again. Maybe, if she was very lucky, Heidi could stop all this madness with the kidnapper once and for all. She'd love to end this tonight and tell Levi they were finally free.

Her lips curled. Then again, with her luck, Charlie might be alerting to a skunk or coyote. But he wouldn't growl. No, the Lab was sensing something else. She signaled her companion to be silent. The growls and whines stopped.

Heidi shoved her feet into her tennis shoes and shrugged on a heavy sweater in case she had to run. She started to turn on the light, hesitated. No. If she turned on the light, he'd know she was awake and aware, and she would ruin her night vision. The point was to catch this guy in the act if she could. Anything to stop him and protect Levi. Her cousin had suffered enough.

She walked across the room, skirting packed boxes. Instead of throwing aside the curtain as she wished, Heidi stepped to the side of the window and, moving the curtain as little as possible, peered into the darkness.

Pitch black except for the weak light from the moon. She couldn't see anything in the forest outside her window. Frustrated, Heidi moved away from the window and toward the door leading to the hallway. Maybe she'd see more from the living room window.

She padded down the hall, gun held by her thigh. Charlie stayed glued to her other side. With her free hand, she rubbed his head. She and Charlie cleared the threshold into the room when someone hammered on the front door.

"Heidi, open up." More pounding. "Heidi! It's Josh Cahill."

What was he doing here this time of the morning? She hurried to the door, checked the peephole to verify her new employer stood on the doorstep, and unlocked the door. "What's wrong?"

"Fire. You have to get out."

CHAPTER EIGHT

Quinn felt around on the nightstand for his ringing cell phone. He squinted at the screen, sat up abruptly. Josh. Heidi or another mission from Fortress? "What's up?"

"Fire at Heidi's house." His unit leader's voice was grim.

Quinn placed the call on speaker and grabbed his jeans from a nearby chair. "She okay?"

"Shaken up. Look, Quinn, something weird is going on."

He frowned as he tied his combat boots. "What do you mean?"

"Just get here. Heidi needs someone in her corner."

"That champion can't be you?"

Someone yelled Josh's name. "Got to go." Josh ended the call without answering his question.

Not good. Quinn tugged on a black long-sleeved t-shirt, strapped on his Sig and a backup piece along with his phone. A minute later, he drove toward Heidi's place. A fire. Couldn't be a coincidence, not after finding the gas cans on her porch. Trouble had followed Heidi Thompson to Otter Creek. Again he wondered what Maddox knew. Knowing their boss, the Fortress CEO was cognizant of more than he shared with Durango. If Quinn didn't get answers from Heidi, he would learn what he needed from Maddox or Zane. Heidi's eyes reminded him of someone from his past. But who?

Minutes later, he turned onto Heidi's street and found the place crawling with first responders. He whistled. Good thing she lived in a remote part of town. Otherwise, the chaos would have woken the neighborhood.

Quinn parked away from the emergency personnel and walked toward the action. Officer Hernandez tried to stop him until Josh said, "I called him. He's a friend of Ms. Thompson."

Huh. Quinn said nothing until he and Josh were several steps from the officer. "You aren't claiming a friendship with her? What's that about?"

"I need to be neutral." His unit leader inclined his head toward a nearby cruiser. Heidi sat in the front seat, face pressed against Charlie's neck. Quinn's heart squeezed at the sight. No one offered comfort to a distraught woman. Anger burned in his gut. Otter Creek's finest weren't doing anything except casting suspicious glances at Heidi. So much for southern charm. In her case, it was southern suspicion. He was disgusted with his adopted hometown's response to a crisis and not happy with Josh's neutrality. He understood his friend had a job to do. That job shouldn't be more important than supporting a colleague in need of support.

He saw Nick Santana talking to the fire chief. From the expressions on their faces, Quinn figured the fire was not an accident. Knowing Josh had to return to patrol, he said, "Thanks for calling me."

A snort from his friend. "Didn't think I had a choice after you demanded I call if there was trouble." His expression sobered. "Keep an eye on her, buddy."

"Count on it."

He closed the distance between himself and Heidi. He crouched in the open doorway and laid his hand on the back of her head. "Heidi," he murmured.

She slowly turned toward him.

Oh, man. Tears and pain shadowed her green gaze, something he couldn't stand from any woman. He didn't say anything, just enfolded her in his embrace. For a few seconds, Heidi remained stiff. When he simply held her, stroking her hair, she relaxed enough to lean against him and pressed her face against his neck.

Heidi drew in a ragged breath.

"Shh. We'll find out what's going on," he whispered, desperate to stop her silent tears. Those tears killed him. "You have my word."

She shook her head. "Stay out of it. I don't want you or your friends hurt."

So there was a problem and she was trying to protect them. From what or who? "Baby, we're hard to kill." He winced. Baby? Really? His teammates would wonder about him. Quinn had never called the females in his life pet names aside from his mother and sisters. Heidi was an acquaintance, although she was the total package for him. He'd always had a soft spot for green-eyed redheads with a sense of humor. Heidi's wicked sense of humor had kept him in stitches last night.

"Quinn, why are you here?"

He turned his head toward Nick. The grim-faced detective glanced at the woman in Quinn's arms before returning his attention to Quinn.

Yep, definitely suspicious of Heidi. Made Quinn wonder what the detective and fire chief discussed. Nothing good for Heidi, he was sure. A wave of protectiveness rose in him. "Supporting a friend. What happened here, Nick?"

"That's what I want to know. I need to ask your friend questions."

Quinn felt Heidi flinch. He tightened his arms around her. "Can we take this inside?" He hadn't seen any damage to the house when he parked, but that didn't mean there wasn't any out of sight of the road.

"The fire was contained in the garage." Nick stepped back for them to exit the vehicle.

Quinn pressed a kiss to the crown of Heidi's head. "Come on. Let's get out of the cold. Hope you unpacked the coffee."

She raised her head, mouth curving. "Last task before going to sleep. Can't function without the magic elixir."

"Amen to that." He helped Heidi from the vehicle and Charlie hopped down, pressing close to her side. Quinn scanned the Lab. "Charlie okay?"

She nodded. "He needs a bath before work. My buddy smells like he's been smoking." Heidi paused, her gaze searching Quinn's. "If I still have a job."

"Of course you do. Didn't you know? We thrive on trouble."

"Not this kind of trouble," she muttered. "No one thrives on this crap."

Her cryptic comments spiked his curiosity. Not here, he reminded himself. If someone had targeted Heidi, she was still vulnerable amid the chaos, maybe more so. Who would notice if someone slipped a knife into her body and walked away? She'd bleed out before anyone noticed.

Quinn walked on one side of her while Charlie kept pace on the other. The hair on the nape of Quinn's neck stood as first responders kept track of their progress to the porch.

A light shone over the kitchen sink. Quinn glanced around, noticed the curtains. He should have thought to hang them himself and wondered how long she'd been awake to accomplish so much after he left.

Heidi turned on the overhead light and started the coffeemaker. "The coffee will take a few minutes. I have cookies if you're hungry."

Nick's eyebrows rose. "What kind of cookies?"

"Almost any kind you can name." Her cheeks flushed. "Cookies are my weakness."

Quinn grinned. Good to know. He added that little tidbit to the all-things-Heidi file he'd begun forming in his head. "Chocolate chip cookies would be perfect with a steaming mug of coffee."

Heidi looked at Nick. "Detective?"

"Same here. Thank you, Ms. Thompson."

"Heidi." She turned toward the pantry.

When she opened the door, Quinn's eyes widened. He whistled. Must be fifteen types of cookies on her shelf with little else occupying the large pantry. "You couldn't have gone to the store after I left last night. Otter Creek rolls up the sidewalk at ten."

The color in her cheeks deepened. "I packed the cookies in a box labeled kitchen supplies." She snatched up a container of chocolate chip cookies along with a box of dog biscuits for Charlie and deposited the cookies on the table. She pulled two biscuits for the Lab and, after putting him through a series of commands, gave him the treat.

Quinn frowned. "Why didn't you just give him the biscuits?"

"Charlie's a working dog. He earns his treats and meals."

Nick dropped into the nearest kitchen chair, fatigue written on his face. "Long night?" Quinn asked his friend.

"You have no idea. Two burglaries to process, and an AWOL camel to track and return to Mr. Lawrence."

"Bonnie unlocked the gate again?"

"She's better with locks than most of the burglars I arrest."

"There's a camel in Otter Creek?" Heidi asked.

"Old farmer named Lawrence bought two for his granddaughter. Named them Bonnie and Clyde. Clyde's a homebody. Bonnie, on the other hand, hates to be penned up. She's the town troublemaker."

"How do you catch a camel?"

"I don't know how other people catch them, but Bonnie loves potato chips. She'll follow you anywhere if you have her favorite treat. We all carry a potato chip supply in our cruisers."

The coffeemaker signaled the end of the brew cycle. "Where are your coffee mugs?" Quinn asked Heidi.

"Cabinet to the right of the sink."

"I'll bring the coffee. Want anything added to yours?"

She shook her head as she dropped onto a chair across from Nick. Heidi opened the cookie container and pushed it closer to Nick.

"Thanks," he murmured and selected two cookies.

Quinn placed a mug each in front of Nick and Heidi before returning to pour his own steaming liquid. At the table, he sat next to Heidi and chose his own cookies. He wolfed one down in a couple of bites. He saw the wisdom of cookies this time of morning. They were tastier than the MREs he'd downed in the field over the years. On ops, you ate whenever you could. A five-course breakfast hadn't been on the menu.

"I'll have to take Madison muffins or donuts when I go off shift. I can't eat cookies for breakfast without providing my wife with something as good." Nick waited until Heidi finished her coffee before pushing his empty mug aside and grabbing a small notebook and pen. "Tell me what happened tonight, Heidi."

Her hands clenched around her mug. "Starting from when?"

"I understand you arrived in town yesterday. Start there."

Heidi recounted the time line for her interview and drive to her rental home. "Quinn followed me. My other bosses and their wives helped me unload the truck. Sometime after we unloaded the truck, Detective Kelter arrived. We fed him, then he checked Quinn's damaged SUV."

"Tell me about the gas cans." Nick's quiet voice sounded non-threatening, but Quinn suspected he was circling for the kill. The detective knew something about the fire and was slowly cinching the rope around Heidi's neck. Guess Quinn's initial assessment of the conversation between Nick and the fire chief was right. The fire which destroyed the garage must have been set, and the detective thought Heidi was responsible.

"Detective Kelter mentioned them, said I should put my gas cans away." When Heidi's dog laid his head on her thigh, she dropped her hand to rub his ears.

Nick's hand slipped under his jacket.

Crap. Quinn hated the suspicion he saw in his friend's eyes. "Nick," he murmured. When the police detective glanced his way, Quinn gave a slight head shake to tell him Heidi didn't have a gun pointed at his midsection under the table.

"I don't have gas cans," she continued, unaware of the byplay between Quinn and Nick. "I hate cutting grass so I hire a lawn mowing service to take care of the yard for me. I don't need gas cans."

He motioned for her to continue.

"The others left soon after Detective Kelter."

"I stayed for another two hours," Quinn added, holding Nick's gaze with his own. "We unpacked the living room." He smiled. "Heidi has quite a collection of books so it took a while."

Heidi shrugged. "So I like my books in a particular order. Sue me."

"And after Quinn left?"

Retribution

"I hung curtains in each room. Couldn't stand the thought of someone peering into the house."

"Your nearest neighbor is a quarter mile away."

"Doesn't matter," Quinn insisted. "Anyone would want curtains up for privacy, including you, Nick."

His lips curved. "Got me there. What did you do after you hung curtains, Heidi?"

"Prepped the coffeemaker and climbed into bed. Charlie woke me at three o'clock."

"Charlie?" Nick frowned.

"My dog. He was growling. I thought someone was outside."

"Did you call the police to investigate?"

She shook her head. "I didn't want to call before I knew someone was outside. We're in a new place. I wasn't sure what Charlie was hearing."

Quinn kept his expression blank although he knew Heidi was holding something back. From the way Nick sat unmoving, he suspected the same thing.

"Did you look outside?"

Heidi grimaced. "I did, not that it helped much. It's dark out here. I'll have to talk to the landlord about a security light."

Fat chance of him doing anything about it. Quinn had asked Zane to research Heidi's landlord. The quick response from the Fortress tech expert revealed a man who wouldn't spend more than necessary on his rental properties. Any improvements came out of his renters' pockets. Maybe Quinn could work out security upgrades with Maddox.

"What happened after Charlie woke you?" Nick asked.

"I grabbed my Glock and put on my shoes and sweater. I walked into the living room, hoping to see more from this end of the house."

The detective's pen hovered over the pad. "You have a Glock? Where is the weapon, Heidi?"

"I have a table with a drawer in the entryway. I left the gun there when Josh made me leave the house. I knew the police would respond to the fire and I didn't want anyone to look at me the way you are. I'm not a threat to you."

"You have a permit?"

"I do. You want to see it?"

"In a minute. You took the time to put on your shoes and sweater? Why is that, Heidi?"

"In case I had to run."

"Go on."

"As Charlie and I arrived in the living room, Josh Cahill pounded on the door to tell me there was a fire and I had to leave the house."

"What happened to the gas cans Rod found on your porch?"

Heidi blinked. "I suppose Detective Kelter took them. He was talking to Josh and Quinn when I went inside last night."

"He took them," Quinn confirmed. "I watched him put the cans in his SUV. What's going on, Nick? Why all the questions about the gas cans?"

Nick stared at Heidi. "I want permission to search your house, Heidi. I'd rather have your cooperation than have to get a search warrant, but I'll go after the warrant if I need to."

Quinn's gut twisted. "Why, Nick?"

"The fire in the garage wasn't an accident. Someone set the fire using gasoline as an accelerant." Nick's gaze focused on Heidi. "I think you know a lot more than you're telling me. Don't lie to me, Heidi. Did you set the fire?"

CHAPTER NINE

Heidi's stomach pitched, making her wish she'd passed on the cookies and coffee. She pushed back from the table, took her mug to the sink to give herself time to craft an answer Nick Santana's question. How much could she safely tell him?

She must be honest with the Otter Creek detective. Heidi couldn't divulge her cousin's location. Maddox had been careful not to say where Levi was living.

She didn't want Quinn to hear her explanation. The day of reckoning had arrived sooner than she anticipated. Heidi couldn't answer Nick's questions without spilling everything. Quinn would hate her. Heidi regretted the lost opportunity to work with her childhood crush. She'd looked forward to knowing the man he'd grown into. Now Heidi would never know the truth about him.

Heidi returned to the table and faced the detective who watched her every move. "I didn't set the fire. Search the house. Some of my belongings are still in boxes. If you open them, you won't find candles, matches, or lighters. I don't like open flames, not even a grill, indoor or outdoor. One of my requirements in renting was electric heat and air, water heater, and stove. No gas of any kind."

Nick tilted his head. "Let's hear the story behind that, Heidi. Afterward, I will search the house, including every box in your possession. If I find anything that raises my suspicions, I will take you to the station for more questions."

Not surprising. Didn't like it. Again, nothing different than what she'd faced before except she'd had Levi in her corner. Now, she had no one. Not even Quinn once he learned the truth. Would he believe her when he heard her story? Probably not. No one else had. "When I was ten, my eight-year-old sister and I were kidnapped."

Beside her, Quinn stiffened.

Heidi had planned to tell him who she was when no one else was around. She hated hurting Quinn. Then again, it wasn't her doing. The blame belonged to her father. Would Quinn recognize the distinction?

Nick frowned, straightened in his seat. "The cops catch the perps?"

"One of them died in prison." Exactly where he deserved to be for a long, miserable life. He'd cost her everything. Her home, what was left of her family, her life. Another prisoner had ended his life three years into his prison sentence. "The other one escaped and was never caught."

"Did they want money?"

If only the answer was that easy. The initial kidnapping was about money, but Heidi didn't know why she survived and Moira hadn't. Her father never said. Now it was too late to ask. "A ransom demand was paid."

The scheme had caused Quinn's family so much pain. She focused her gaze on Nick though she felt Quinn's hot gaze locked on her. "Detective Santana, my father was one of the kidnappers. He was captured and died in prison."

Quinn shoved away from the table and crossed the kitchen to stand with his hands braced on the counter, his back to Heidi and Nick. Anger practically radiated from his body.

Hurt twined through Heidi even though she knew it wasn't rational. Quinn Gallagher had every right to put distance between them. Her father's selfishness had changed Quinn's life and not in a good way.

"You or your family members never asked your father why he participated in kidnapping his own children?" Nick sounded skeptical. "I find that hard to believe, Heidi."

Yeah, he wouldn't be the first law enforcement officer with that reaction when hearing her story for the first time. If she hadn't lived the nightmare, Heidi wouldn't believe it either. "I couldn't ask him or my mother."

"Explain."

"My family was traumatized." So was she, but in the grand view of things, Heidi's trauma was minor. "The second kidnapper murdered my little sister." She tried to blink away the tears gathering in her eyes, but a slow trickle of moisture escaped despite her best efforts.

"I'm sorry," Nick murmured. "Did your mother offer any explanation or speculation as to the reason behind the kidnapping aside from money?"

One of her hands clenched in Charlie's fur. With her free hand, Heidi swiped the tears from her face. "No. By the time I could ask questions, she was gone, too."

"You have no other family?"

She refused to answer. Essentially, Nick was correct. She had no family members left except for one. Levi. She had to protect him.

Nick tried again. "How long ago did you lose your mother, Heidi?"

"Twenty years."

Nick scrawled a few notes on his notepad. "I know it's bad form to ask a woman her age, but I need to know how old are you now."

Man, this was going to be bad. "Thirty."

"Your mother died not long after you were kidnapped?"

"I lost my baby sister, then my mother, and an older sister a week later."

"How did they die?"

Heidi swallowed hard. She already knew what kind of reaction her answer would generate. She stole a quick glance at Quinn. "House fire." Quinn's hands fisted on the counter.

Nick's head snapped up, his laser gaze focused on her. "You were too young to live on your own. Where did you go? Foster care system?"

"I moved in with an aunt and uncle who lived in a neighboring town."

"Their names?"

"I can't tell you their names, Nick." Quinn's head whipped her direction, his eyes full of suspicion.

"Why not? It's not a secret."

"No, but it's safer for everyone involved if I don't divulge their names."

The detective studied her a moment. "Are you in witness protection, Heidi?"

"Sort of."

He said nothing, but his eyebrows rose.

Yeah, didn't figure that vague explanation would fly. What could she do? Heidi had to protect Levi. She also didn't want to land behind bars. Who would take care of Charlie? Being arrested would lead to exposure in the press. Talk about waving a flag at the other kidnapper if he hadn't already found her. Besides that, Levi would leave his protection to verify her story, putting him in the heart of danger again. Not something she wanted to contemplate. "The Marshals are not providing protection."

Nick's gaze immediately shifted to Quinn. "Fortress?"

He turned around though Quinn focused on the detective. "You know we can't confirm or deny without permission from higher up the food chain."

Heidi flinched. Quinn's tone was clipped, cold.

"I'll take that as a positive response to my question." He looked back at Heidi. "I assume your name is not Heidi Thompson."

She shook her head. "I like this name better than the others I've had."

"What's going on here, Heidi?" Quinn asked, finally looking at her. "Now is the time to come clean. We want to help you."

"You don't know what's happening here?" Nick asked, his voice rising. "You've got to be kidding me. I thought you were protecting her."

Quinn held up his hand, his gaze locked with Heidi's. "Talk to me."

"My aunt, uncle, and one cousin were murdered just like my mother and older sister."

"Another house fire," he said, voice flat.

"I know it seems suspicious."

Nick snorted. "You think? We don't believe in coincidence in our business, Heidi."

"That's because it's not a coincidence, is it?" Quinn said. "The fires are connected to your past. That's why you freaked when you saw the gas cans on your porch last night."

"They are the same kind used in the other fires." She glanced at the detective. "I don't know what Detective Kelter found on the gas cans, but I can guess. Nothing. No prints, no smudges, no fibers. Am I right?"

Nick's eyes glittered. "Yes, ma'am."

No question any more. The kidnapper had found her again. But how? How had he broken the security Maddox established for her? She dropped her face into her hands. Levi. She had to warn her cousin. If her security had been breached, his had most likely been compromised as well. Heidi raised her head. "I need to make a phone call right now. It's a matter of life or death."

Quinn crossed the kitchen in three strides and captured her chin in the palm of his hand and turned her to face him. "Who are you protecting?" he demanded. "Tell me. My teammates and I can help you if you let us."

He couldn't be serious. It sounded like he meant to put their murky past aside and protect her no matter what. She wanted to believe but was afraid to trust. Quinn had no reason to help her and every reason not to. "My cousin. He's under protection as well. If the kidnapper found me again, my cousin's security might have been compromised." She turned to the detective. "Please. I have to warn him."

"I'll take care of it." Quinn pulled out his phone.

"How? You don't know who I'm talking about." Or did he? Had Maddox shared more than she realized with the leaders of PSI? That couldn't be the case. Quinn hadn't faked the anger and hurt when she revealed enough of her background to confirm her identity. "I have a way to contact him, one approved by Maddox."

"I have a friend who will notify his security detail in less than a minute." He tapped his screen and placed the call. "Hey, Z. Need a favor. Heidi's security has been compromised. She's worried about her cousin. You need to warn his security team. Thanks, man." He ended the call, glanced at Heidi. "Done."

She blinked. "Just like that?"

"Just like that."

Heidi sat back with a sigh. "Thank you." At least Levi had a chance to defend himself if he and his team were attacked. Even if Quinn and his friends sent her back to Maddox for another identity change and relocation, at least Levi would have enough warning to protect himself.

Quinn's phone signaled an incoming message. He glanced at the screen. "Your cousin's security detail has been notified. They'll take appropriate measures to ensure his safety." He captured her chin again, his touch gentle. "Just as we'll do for you. You have some decisions to make."

Nick closed his notebook and slid it and his pen into the pocket of his jacket. "While you and Gallagher discuss a few things, I'm starting the house search."

Heidi waited until the Otter Creek detective left the room before beginning her last discussion with Quinn. "I'm sorry," she murmured. "I didn't know you were working with PSI or I would have asked Maddox to send me somewhere else. I never meant to hurt you, Quinn."

"Did you recognize me?"

She nodded, her lips curving. "It was obvious you didn't know who I was."

"You're no longer ten." He glanced around to be sure Nick was out of earshot before he leaned close and whispered, "What happened to you, Katie Henderson? You used to be a sweet, painfully honest kid. Now it seems you're an accomplished liar. Taking after your sorry excuse for a father?"

Stung, she glared at the man staring daggers at her. "That's not fair. I was following Maddox's instructions."

"Maddox has some explaining to do. He should have told me before letting my past blindside me."

Heidi sighed. "I'll ask him to reassign me."

"Did you lie to him, too?"

"No! My cousin and I told him the truth about everything."

"So he knows about our connection."

"I assume he does. I never talked about you by name."

"Didn't have to, sweetheart. The boss researches every prospective client before taking them on. Trust me, he knew who you were before he sent you to me."

"Then why didn't he send me to someone else? I never wanted to cause you more pain. I swear I didn't know you worked for Fortress or PSI."

Quinn closed his eyes for a moment, as if the sight of her hurt him. When his eyelids lifted, Quinn's gaze locked with hers. A moment later, his shoulders relaxed. "I believe you. Here's the bottom line, Heidi. You need me."

Her breath caught. "There are other bodyguards capable of protecting me." She didn't want anyone else, but that was a different matter.

"No. Durango is the best unit Maddox has. He knows we'll get the job done no matter what obstacles are thrown in our path."

Despite the tense circumstances, her mouth curved. "Not modest, are you?"

"Simply stating facts." He moved closer until his breath whispered across her lips with his next words. "Decision time, baby."

"What decisions?"

"How many different names have you had since I knew you as Katie?"

"Five."

"Do you want a sixth?"

Want one? No. She had changed identities so many times she almost didn't know who she was any more. "I like this name. I think I'll like this life. I want the chance to find out." She desperately wanted the chance to know Quinn as an adult. So maybe she wasn't a kid with a childhood crush. Perhaps she was an adult woman with a crush on an attractive man.

"Do you want to run again or do you want to stand and fight?"

Heidi wanted a life. Levi deserved that and so much more. He was a good man, one who had given up everything he had left to protect her. "My cousin and I tried that several times. Each time we almost died."

"You didn't have us before." He paused, then amended his statement. "You didn't have me before. If you want to start over somewhere else, my team and I will tap a few resources Fortress knows nothing about. You'll have new identities, new jobs, new housing in the same location. A fresh start all the way around if that's your choice."

The thought of reinventing herself one more time made her stomach hurt. "If I decide against that option?"

"Do you want to stay, Heidi?"

She was distracted for a moment by the way he said her name. Quinn didn't hesitate to call her by the latest name. "You find it easy to call me something besides Katie?"

"Katie was the adorable pixie from my hometown." He lifted one hand to cup the side of her face. "Heidi is the woman standing in front of me. Answer my question, baby. Do you want to stay or run?"

She wanted to stay. To be on the ground floor of building this S & R training program was a dream come true for her. Heidi could be part of something good, maybe prevent another tragedy like the one that had taken her little sister.

"To stay would be dangerous for everyone involved with me or my cousin. You have to know that. Your friends and their families need to understand that as well. I don't want to be responsible for another innocent person being hurt." Her gaze searched Quinn's. "What do you think I should do?"

"Do you want my personal preference or professional opinion?"

"Professional opinion." Chicken. She really wanted his personal preference. Did he want her to stay or would he prefer Heidi out of his sight and life for good?

"Stay. Fight. Otherwise you will always be watching over your shoulder, constantly on guard, monitoring every word from your mouth. You'll slip up. Word will leak. The kidnapper will find you again. If you take a stand now, we can end this for good, and you and your cousin will be free to live the life you want."

Did she dare? She wanted to say yes so badly she could almost taste it. Ramping up her courage, she whispered, "What's your personal opinion?"

Quinn's hand slipped around to the back of Heidi's neck. His thumb brushed over her skin. Just that light touch sent heat curling through her body. "Stay," he whispered. "Trust me."

"I thought you hated me. Why would you agree to protect me?"

Quinn's mouth brushed against hers, the touch so light she almost believed she imagined the kiss. "I don't hate you. I hate what your father did and the repercussions from his choices. He hurt a lot of people, not just my family. The company closing down cost many people their livelihoods."

Afraid to consider the light kiss as anything more than a friendly peck on the mouth or a gesture of comfort, she focused instead on his words. "Do you mean that? You don't blame me?"

His hand tightened at the back of her neck. That was the only warning she had before he pressed his mouth to hers for a deeper, hotter kiss. For a few seconds, Heidi froze, then her arms crept up to circle his neck. She lost herself in the heat and texture of his mouth. Heidi wished for time to stand still, to live in this moment, fear and uncertainty gone. Only Quinn holding her in his strong arms.

Quinn's phone signaled another incoming message. After a few seconds, Quinn broke the kiss, backed up a step, and pulled out his phone. Scanning the message, he frowned.

"Something wrong?" Heidi asked, struggling to focus after that mind-melting kiss. Who knew childhood crushes could kiss like that? Like a splash of cold water, her gaze dropped to Quinn's phone. Was Levi safe?

"Unexpected meeting at PSI in two hours. Guess I won't drop off my SUV for repairs today."

"Is that a meeting I should attend?" If so, she needed to get moving. Charlie wasn't fond of baths and Heidi would have to unearth his grooming supplies, then wrestle her eighty-five pound dog into the tub. The Lab was not going to be happy when he realized what was in store.

"Not sure. Let me ask." He tapped out a message. The reply came back less than a minute later. "You and Deke are both requested to be there as well." Quinn sounded puzzled.

"That's unusual?"

"In this case, it is. We're meeting with Ethan Blackhawk, Otter Creek's police chief." He slid his phone into his pocket. "So, what do you say, Heidi? Will you walk away or fight for what you want?"

She raised her chin. She was finished with the run-and-hide routine. "Fight." The decision felt positive, like she was taking a step forward. Heidi prayed she wasn't making a mistake that would cost her life or the life of Quinn or his friends.

CHAPTER TEN

Quinn strode into the conference room at PSI with a large cup of black coffee in his hand. He saluted his unit leader with his cup. "Looking a little tired there, Major." Something he could relate to considering his own short night. Josh, however, had one up on Quinn since he'd been up all night on duty.

"I'll catch some sleep after this meeting." He lifted his own over-sized to-go cup and sipped.

"Any idea what Ethan wants?"

"Nope. I'm as much in the dark as you are."

Not what he'd expected Josh to say. Once the meeting with Ethan ended, he needed to tell his teammates about Heidi. Quinn wouldn't let himself think of her as little Katie Henderson. For one, she wasn't little anymore. Katie had grown into a beautiful woman. Second, if he thought of her as Katie, the kiss that burned him to cinders a couple hours ago would feel inappropriate. Third, he couldn't think of the name Katie Henderson without associating her with her father. Thinking of Caleb Henderson always filled him with rage and he didn't want that feeling connected to Heidi.

She didn't understand how he could distance her from her father in his mind. The wariness in her eyes had made that obvious. Once he realized she was telling him the truth about not knowing he was with PSI, he knew where to lay the blame. Maddox. Quinn frowned. That was a conversation he'd have without Heidi or his teammates nearby.

The conference room door opened again and the rest of Quinn's teammates filed in, each with a coffee cup in his hand. Yep, they were dependent on the magic elixir as Heidi had named it. Each member of Durango had developed the coffee habit while in the Army. Those early mornings and late nights required vats of the stuff.

"Don't ask," Josh said to his team before anyone uttered a word. "I don't know what Ethan wants. We'll find out when he tells us what's on his mind."

"That's a surprise," Rio said, dropping into the nearest seat. "He usually tells you when he needs something from us."

"He said he needed a favor and would explain when we met." Amusement lit Josh's eyes. "My brother-in-law isn't one for repeating himself."

"Must be a big favor," Alex said as he took the seat next to Josh. "Our chief of police is one of the most capable men I know. I wouldn't want to go up against him. Not sure I'd come out on top."

And that said something about Ethan, Quinn thought. Alex Morgan was one of the deadliest men on the planet. An elite world-class sniper, Alex hit what he aimed at. Rumors abounded in the Special Forces community about Ethan Blackhawk. The six-foot-four Native American was in a class of his own as a tracker, and he was relentless. The most dangerous men Quinn knew gave Ethan a wide berth.

"Heard about the fire at Heidi's place," Nate said to Quinn. "She all right?"

"She's fine. So is Charlie. The blaze was confined to the garage."

"Electrical?" Alex asked.

"Deliberate. Arson, according to Nick."

Rio whistled. "Tough way to start a new life. Doesn't put Otter Creek in the best light."

Josh frowned. "Can't remember hearing of an arsonist in town."

Nate snorted. "In a place this size, a neighbor or friend would spot you doing the deed and call the cops."

His friends had no idea how tough this was for Heidi. Quinn admired her courage. She must be scared witless by the prospect of facing down the person targeting her and her cousin.

He scanned the faces of his teammates. He had to tell them what was going on. He would be depending on them to protect Heidi from this psycho when he couldn't be with her, which meant convincing them of her honesty. His teammates always had his back and they wouldn't like her not revealing her identity to Quinn when she recognized him.

Her silence smacked of deception, but he didn't believe that was the case. They'd talked while they bathed a very reluctant Charlie. Heidi planned to tell Quinn who she was today. The arsonist had forced her hand a few hours early.

Deke and his dog, Ace, came into the room. "Morning, guys." He placed three red and white boxes on the table, then flipped open the lids.

The yeasty scent of fresh donuts made Quinn's mouth water. He and his teammates reached into the boxes and grabbed a few donuts apiece. When Quinn reached for another couple, conversation in the room ceased.

He glanced around. "What?"

"Extra hungry today, Quinn?" Deke asked, eyes twinkling.

"These are for Heidi. She won't have time to stop for breakfast."

"And you know this how?"

"I just left her place a few minutes ago." He'd wanted to follow her to work, but she refused, insisting he go on to PSI while she showered. Once this meeting with Ethan was over, he'd talk to Heidi and the others about her security arrangements. Like it or not, she didn't have the option of being on her own when her stalker was in the area, too. He wasn't buying the possibility Heidi had a second arsonist in her life.

The only sound in the room was the breathing of his teammates. He frowned. "Problem?"

"You just left her place?" Alex asked, an amused twinkle in his eyes.

"It's not like it sounds," Quinn insisted, his cheeks burning. His aggravating teammates chuckled.

Ethan strode into the room as if he owned it, followed by Nick and Rod. Quinn straightened at Ethan's blank expression. Normally, the police chief was animated unless he was on police business. His expression indicated something more grim than normal police business on his mind.

"Outstanding," Rod said as soon as he saw the open boxes of donuts. "Meg will be envious."

Nick grinned. "A wise man wouldn't tell her."

"Wise for you, maybe. Madison is a gentle sweetheart. My wife has the nose of a bloodhound. I guarantee she'll find out. If it's junk food, she loves it."

"Be smart," Ethan said. "Take her a couple."

"You guys mind?" he asked the men around the table.

"I'll wrap them for you when you're ready to leave," Nate said.

Quinn glanced at his team leader while the others talked and downed donuts and coffee. Josh said nothing, but he was worried. Something big was up or Ethan would never have brought in Nick and Rod.

Nick turned to Quinn. "Where's Heidi?"

"On her way. She needed a shower after we gave Charlie a bath."

A quick smile from the detective. "For such a well-trained dog, he really doesn't like baths."

"I thought Labs liked water." Alex frowned. "Spenser loves baths."

"According to Heidi, her dog loves swimming. He's not impressed with a bath. That boy let us know he objected." In fact, Quinn had almost been as wet as Charlie by the time the bath was complete.

Nick chuckled. "My ears are still ringing from his howling. Charlie has a pair of lungs on him."

Heidi rushed into the conference room, Charlie by her side. "Sorry I'm late."

"We haven't started yet." Josh motioned to the coffee pot on a table at the back of the room. "Grab a cup. Quinn saved a couple donuts for you."

Her gaze skated to his. "Thanks." She motioned for Charlie to sit and stay beside Quinn before pouring herself a mug of coffee. When she sat in the chair next to Quinn, Josh said, "Heidi, you've already met Nick and Rod. This is Ethan Blackhawk, our police chief and my other brother-in-law. Ethan, Heidi Thompson is the newest member of PSI's S & R training staff."

"Welcome to Otter Creek, Heidi. Glad to have you as part of our community," Ethan said. "We've needed a search and rescue team in our area for a long time." He turned to Josh. "Anyone else attending this meeting?"

"No. What's going on, Ethan?"

"I received a call from my former lieutenant in Las Vegas." His large hands clenched into fists. "Hans Muehller escaped from prison."

"Oh, man." Rod scrubbed his face with his hands. "I thought we'd seen the last of him."

Deke's eyes narrowed. "Why does that name sound familiar?"

"International assassin who murdered a Marine veteran here in town and tried to kill my wife," Ethan said.

"What do you need, Ethan?" Josh asked, his voice cold. "Name it and it's yours."

"Protection for Serena when I can't be with her."

"You think Muehller is coming here."

"He never leaves a job unfinished. Serena was his last target." His eyes glittered. "Muehller failed."

"You're just as much a target as she is. He'll come after you as well. You are the reason his mission failed."

Ethan's face hardened. "I can take care of myself. I'm concerned about my wife and baby."

"You want Durango to provide security?" Alex asked. "Or PSI trainees?"

"Durango or Fortress," Josh said. "No trainees. Muehller is as lethal as any of the terrorists we've gone up against. He's also a master of disguise."

"You're positive this guy is coming to Otter Creek?" Heidi asked Ethan.

"There's been a string of murders with his signature," the chief said. "He beat them, then killed them with a bullet in the forehead."

"His motive for the murders?" Nick asked.

"Transportation, money, clothes, food. Since he was incarcerated in California and he must avoid detection, it will take him a few days, but Muehller is headed this direction."

"We'll be ready for him," Nate said.

"Wouldn't he have a large supply of alternate IDs and money stashed in different places?" This from Rio. "We do and I'd say you do as well, Ethan."

A small smile curved his lips. "You're correct, Rio. The assassin will go under when he reaches the location of his first stash site."

"That's when we need to worry," Deke muttered. "We won't know he's here until he strikes."

"He won't catch us off guard," Josh said.

"Why did you ask me and Heidi to meet with you, Ethan? We're not part of Fortress or a Special Forces unit."

"Muehller will tip his hand. He's too arrogant to do otherwise. Your first S & R job might be to track an escaped murderer."

Everything in Quinn rose up against Ethan's statement. No way. He didn't want Heidi on this creep's radar, especially not with her facing her own problems. "You're an expert tracker, Ethan. You could do this yourself." He ignored Josh's scowl in his direction. Heidi had no business tangling with this guy.

"True, but I can't be everywhere. I have a job to do, a town to protect. I can't afford for him to slip through the net. When the time comes to find him, speed will be the deciding factor. Charlie or Ace will tip the scales in our favor."

"Muehller is that dangerous?" Heidi asked, voice soft.

"Yes, ma'am." No surprise that Ethan sounded positive. When Josh had returned to duty after he'd been home on medical leave, he'd told the members of Durango his sister was lucky to be alive, that Ethan had tipped the balance in Serena's favor. And captured her heart in the process.

"Deke and I will need clothes Muehller has recently worn for a scent for the dogs," Heidi continued. "The clothes need to be collected with rubber gloves and placed in a zipped plastic bag. The fewer people who handle the clothes, the better. We don't want the scent muddied."

"I'll take care of it. You'll have the clothes tomorrow."

Rio pushed away from the table and freshened his coffee. "What about your aunt, Ethan?"

"She'll need protection as well, but Ruth won't be Muehller's primary target. She was an annoyance more than anything to him. Serena is the grand prize as far as he's concerned." His jaw clenched. "I would do anything for my wife and baby. If he captures her, he'll have both of us where he wants us."

"He won't touch her," Quinn said. Whatever it took, he and his friends would keep Serena and the baby safe, and protect Heidi.

"I'm counting on all of you," Ethan said. "Serena is my life."

Josh crossed to the coffee pot. "Who is with her now?"

"Henderson and Sanchez. Serena is cooking for the Watsons."

Rio put down his mug. "I'll go, Josh. I don't have a class today. Let me know the details after you hammer them out. Ethan, tell Henderson and Sanchez I'm headed their way. I would prefer not to treat my own bullet wounds from overzealous cops protecting the top cop's wife and child."

A quick nod. "Thanks, Rio."

The medic grinned. "Hey, protecting my favorite personal chef is no hardship. She's generous with the samples." And then he left.

Alex shook his head. "I think the rest of us just lost out on some very fine food. I'm on board for the afternoon shift."

Josh turned to Ethan. "I assume you want in on the planning of this security detail."

"Every bit of it."

"You have information on Muehller or should we tap Fortress resources?"

Ethan handed a manila folder to every person seated around the conference table. "Each folder contains pictures of Muehller and any information we have on him to date."

Quinn scanned the grim contents. "He'd give the worst terrorists we've encountered a run for their money."

A look of disgust crossed Nate's face. "Muehller loves his job."

"Then let's get to work." Josh set his cup down and moved to the white board. Grabbing a marker, he said, "Time to put this clown out of a job."

CHAPTER ELEVEN

Quinn shook hands with Ethan as he left, as did the others in the conference room. After the door closed behind Otter Creek's finest, Josh wiped the white board clean. Guess it was time to lay their cards on the table. Quinn took a deep breath and said, "We have another problem to deal with."

Alex set his coffee cup down. "Another one? An international assassin isn't enough for you?"

"What's going on, Quinn?" Josh asked as he dropped the eraser and marker on a desk nearby. "You've been antsy and unfocused since you arrived."

He rubbed the back of his neck, cheeks burning. Yeah, he had been although he thought he'd hidden his distraction well enough. Apparently not. He glanced at Heidi. She was a beautiful distraction.

"Should Heidi and I leave?" Deke rubbed Ace's head. "I wanted to watch Heidi and Charlie run through the obstacle course anyway."

Quinn shook his head. "This concerns Heidi."

Deke's eyebrows shot up.

"The arson?" Nate asked.

"That plus a lot more."

Josh's gaze searched his teammate's face, then Heidi's. He returned to his seat. "Let's hear it."

Heidi glanced at Quinn. "Where do I start?"

"The beginning. For your safety and theirs, don't hold anything back. You can trust them with the truth."

Heidi's gaze touched each of the men around the table before she began. "Part of my story, Deke already knows."

"Part?" The former marshal's eyes narrowed. "How much did you leave out?"

She grimaced. "About half of it. It's true I have a history with S & R. When I was ten, I was kidnapped with my younger sister, Moira. We were taken and held less than a mile from our home. The police found us two days later, but not soon enough for Moira. One of the kidnappers murdered her. That person escaped from law enforcement and has never been found."

"And the other?" Josh asked.

"He was captured and died in prison after three years. That kidnapper was my father."

Stunned silence greeted her statement.

"Go on, baby," Quinn murmured. Under cover of the table, he covered her hand with his. "It will be all right. You'll see." Quinn would do whatever it took to keep her safe and reunite Heidi with her cousin, to be free to live her life without a threat.

She squeezed his hand and continued her tale. "A week later, my home burned to the ground, killing my mother and other sister."

"How did you escape?" This from Nate.

"I was at a friend's house for an overnight stay. I was so traumatized by the kidnapping and Moira's death, I hadn't spoken a word after the initial police interview. My mother thought getting away from the media circus and doing something normal might help. Instead, everything was worse. The police said the fire had been set."

"Like the fire last night."

"It's like someone looked up the details in the arson investigator's file and recreated them."

"Did you end up in the foster care system?" Josh asked.

She shook her head. "I lived with an aunt and uncle in a town nearby. They, too, died in a house fire five years later. I lost everyone but one cousin. He and I were away at band camp at the time."

"Some might call that convenient."

"I was fifteen years old. You think I stole a car, drove an hour back to the only home and relatives I had left, doused our home in gasoline, and lit a match? I loved them. My aunt and uncle were the reason I started to talk again. I would never hurt them."

"Why didn't they wake up and get out of the house? Didn't they have smoke alarms?"

"They weren't working. The batteries weren't in the smoke detectors." She frowned. "My cousin and I never understood that. My aunt was obsessive about changing the batteries. She also tested them. Aunt Debbie would never have taken a chance by leaving the batteries out. Her family home burned in a fire when she was a child. She was paranoid about smoke alarms and escape routes in case of a fire. The circumstances didn't make sense to me or my cousin. We told the police. No one paid attention to us. Stuff happens, they said. They figured my aunt forgot to replace the batteries. That never would have happened. Period. Someone killed them."

"You were still underage at that point and you said you had no relatives. What happened to you? Who took you in?"

"My cousin was a freshman in college at the time and had turned eighteen. He petitioned the court for custody. He saved me from the system."

"At eighteen? Impressive and commendable. Most freshmen would have been more concerned with enjoying college than looking after a younger cousin." Alex asked. "What was he doing at band camp?"

"Chaperoning. He'd been part of our school band until he graduated that May. He volunteered to keep an eye on the boys in the dorm along with the band director."

"What happened when school started?" Nate asked.

"My cousin found an apartment near his college campus and I moved in with him. I finished high school while he attended college."

"Get back to your story," Josh said. "Two arsons in your past. One early this morning. Looks suspicious on the surface, Heidi."

She sighed. "It gets worse. Those aren't the only fires in my past. Every few years, a fire broke out wherever my cousin and I were living."

Durango's leader scowled.

"I know it looks bad, but I swear I had nothing to do with the fires."

"What about your cousin? Could he have blamed you for the deaths of his family members and decided to get even?"

"He's an arson investigator. He's seen the devastation fires leave behind up close and personal. There is no way he would do something like that. Besides, when we figured out the fires were connected and on the anniversary of Moira's death, we made sure we weren't anywhere near our home and were in plain view of other people."

"Why didn't you set a trap for the arsonist?" Alex sounded skeptical.

"We did. Each time he escaped. Somehow. I can't tell you how many times we had to start over because we lost everything."

"Maddox sent you to us for more than a job, didn't he?" Josh leaned back in his chair with a sigh. "I should have known something was up. He expected us to hire you on the spot and that isn't like him. Maddox left all the hiring decisions to us until you."

"I'm qualified for the position," Heidi insisted. "But there is another reason why he sent me to you."

"Maddox sent Heidi to me," Quinn said.

"Why to you specifically? And why wasn't I informed of this?" his team leader asked.

"Heidi and I are from the same town. I knew her when she was a kid."

"Why didn't you tell us?"

"He didn't know," Heidi said before Quinn could defend himself. "Quinn didn't recognize me. I've changed quite a bit since I was ten. Maddox sent me to Quinn and the rest of you because Fortress is protecting me and my cousin."

"Wait," Alex said. "Is this the same situation that led to the death of your father, Quinn?"

He breathed past the pain at the thought of his father's death. Even after all these years, he felt betrayed. They could have recovered financially and people in the company didn't blame his father. But to Mark Gallagher, it hadn't mattered. He'd lost his business and his reputation and couldn't face the fallout. He'd left his family to deal with it. "Yes, it is. Heidi had nothing to do with that, Alex."

"Your name isn't Heidi Thompson, is it?" Deke asked her.

She shook her head, glancing again at Quinn.

He gave her a short nod. Now wasn't the time to hold back. If Durango wouldn't help, he'd protect Heidi on his own. The one thing he would not do was endanger his teammates with a gap in their knowledge. "You can trust them to keep your identity a secret no matter what they decide regarding your employment and the protection detail."

"My name is Katie Henderson."

"And your cousin's name?" Nate asked.

"Lance. He goes by Levi now."

"Why didn't you tell us you were sent here for protection?" Josh asked.

"I followed Maddox's instructions. I planned to tell Quinn today because he was beginning to piece together my identity from his memory. I don't understand how the arsonist found me again. Maddox had his people check everything I own for bugs and tracking devices. How does he keep finding me?"

"We'll figure it out and stop him." Quinn laced his fingers through hers. "No one will hurt you on our watch." He turned his attention to his teammates. "Will they?" Although he heard the challenge in his voice, Quinn didn't back down. He hoped they would step up and do the right thing whether they fully trusted Heidi or not.

Alex studied Heidi for a moment. "You believe her, Quinn?"

"Yes, I do. Look, her father's choices hurt a lot of people, my family included. Whatever Caleb Henderson did is on him and his partner in crime. Heidi was a victim, not a co-conspirator."

His teammates exchanged glances.

"How do you want to handle this, Quinn?" Josh asked.

The ball of ice in his stomach melted. Given the circumstances, he wouldn't have blamed them for questioning Heidi further. That they didn't was a testament to their faith in his judgment. "She can't stay by herself in that house. It's too far out of town and the arsonist knows where she lives. No offense, Josh, but you being in the vicinity when her garage caught fire was luck. If the arsonist had waited another ten minutes, the outcome would have been different." Possibly fatal for Heidi because Quinn suspected the smoke alarms weren't working in that house, something he planned to check when he followed her home.

Her hand squeezed his. "What are you suggesting as an alternative?"

"You need someone staying with you. A bodyguard."

She stilled. "You?"

"Why not?"

"Has to be more than just you, buddy," Josh said. "You have to sleep sometime."

"Yeah, and the rest of you are newlyweds. That lets you out, doesn't it?" His teammates would do it, no question. Quinn didn't want to ask them for the favor. He wanted his friends' marriages to succeed where many didn't, especially in their line of work. Men and women in the military or para-military organizations were gone frequently. They missed birthdays, holidays, anniversaries, special events, things that made up a life. Hard to build and maintain a family like that. He wanted Durango's families to flourish as his own hadn't.

"Not necessarily," Nate said. "We'll coordinate our schedules to split the night shift with you."

"We'll make it work," Alex said.

"You won't insist Maddox find someone else to protect me?" Heidi asked.

Josh studied her face a moment. "Do you want to leave Otter Creek?"

"No. Since you're friends with Quinn, I thought you would insist I leave to protect him."

Expressions of amusement rippled across all their faces, including Deke's. "Heidi," Nate said. "Quinn can take care of himself. He doesn't need us to protect him from you or anyone else."

Deke watched her a moment. "You're ready to fight back, aren't you?"

"I am sick of having everything taken from me, including my identity. I want to live my life without fear. I don't know why this guy wants to kill me and Levi."

"You think the arsonist is a man?"

"I don't know. Levi and I never saw a person set the blazes."

"Look at it this way," Nate said. "The arsonist is here. You don't have to go looking for him. If you want to capture this person, now is the time to do it with Fortress to back you up."

Her gaze locked with Quinn's. A nod of encouragement was all it took for her to say, "Then let's do this. How many boxes of cookies and bags of coffee will I need in my pantry?"

CHAPTER TWELVE

Heidi pressed a kiss to the top of Charlie's head. "Well, buddy, what about some play time?" A loud bark and enthusiastic tail wag was her response. With a laugh, she grabbed her lined jacket and headed to PSI's training field, the Lab on her heels. Three intense hours of discussion about Serena Blackhawk's situation and Heidi's own had left her sluggish and Charlie antsy with the need to burn off energy. Deke was supposed to bring Ace so the two dogs could get to know each other. A smile curved her lips. It would also give the S & R program director time to see how she and Charlie worked together.

Her thoughts drifted back to Serena. Heidi was in awe of the police chief's wife. The pregnant chef must be one of the strongest women around to face down an international assassin with his stunning record of criminal success and live to tell about it. The information in the file on Hans Muehller was horrifying. This assassin had been responsible for the deaths of so many people. Some innocent, some not. Muehller was skilled at his work.

Her lips twisted. As if she didn't have enough problems to populate her dreams. Now she had those terrible pictures and stark, ugly facts imprinted on her brain. At least Muehller's escape allowed her to focus on something besides herself and her own problems. Compared to having a highly skilled assassin after you, she'd take the arsonist on any day. Hopefully, she would meet Serena soon. She understood from Josh that Serena had a Westie named Jewel. Maybe Charlie and Jewel could have a puppy play date.

With the prospect of facing off with the assassin, now more than ever Heidi was grateful for Charlie and her Glock. Maddox had insisted on her and Levi having weapons and self-defense training. She wasn't nearly as prepared as Quinn and his teammates were, but she could hold her own against most run-of-the-mill thugs and villains. Her cousin, however, had taken to the training at Fortress like he'd been born to it. Maybe her arson-investigator cousin should consider a career change and hire on with Fortress.

Soft laughter escaped. If he had a female bodyguard who caught his attention, he'd be able to pursue her in earnest. Boy, what she wouldn't give to see Levi's protectors. Maybe Maddox would divulge the names. Better yet, maybe Quinn could tell her. Then she wouldn't worry about the Fortress CEO changing her cousin's bodyguards. Levi wouldn't thank her for interfering in his life. She grinned. Even if he needed it, the excuse she'd used over the years to set up Levi's dates. With their life in the shadows, he'd neglected his social life until she stepped in. He'd had fun, even if Levi had never admitted it. The look on his face had been enough. Doing something normal for a few hours kept both of them from sliding into a funk.

Heidi signaled Charlie into the dog tunnel. When he emerged on the other side, she praised him, slipped him a treat, and sent him to the ladder for the slide. When he reached the top, he yipped, then slid to the ground and raced for the dog teeter-totter.

    A soft whistle sounded behind her. Heidi whirled on her heel, hand reaching for the weapon concealed at her back. Seeing Quinn, she relaxed. "Weren't you taking your SUV to the body shop?"

    "I thought you might like to meet Bear, our car guru."

    Her eyebrows soared. "Bear?" What kind of name was that?

    He shrugged one shoulder. "We all had names given to us in the military. Some good." His lips curved. "Some not repeatable in the company of women. That's the name Bear was given in the Army. I can't remember the last time anyone called him by his birth name with the exception of his family. Bear is the guy who beefs up our rides with armor plating and bullet-resistant glass as well as fixing any mechanical issues we have. For obvious reasons, we can't trust just anyone with our vehicles."

    She could imagine. They must have a hard time trusting anyone outside their own circle of friends and co-workers. Did that sentiment include her now? Or would she have to earn his trust? Sure, he'd aligned himself with her in front of his friends. Trusting her at his back was something different. With a fierceness that surprised her, she wanted that kind of relationship with him, one of unquestioning belief and support no matter the circumstances. Did the kiss indicate he wanted the same?

    Maybe. He might be attracted to her. Didn't mean he would act on it and pursue a relationship. Why would he, after all? She came with boat loads of baggage and she was connected to one of the most painful experiences of his life. As honorable as Quinn was, he might not be able to leave behind their shared painful history. "Would he look at my SUV if I needed repairs?"

    "Absolutely. He works miracles with anything mechanical. Bear's worked on a weapon or two for us."

Handy guy to have in your corner. "I'd love to meet him, but I'm meeting Deke to work with the dogs."

"Deke's already here," the man in question said, Ace trotting by his side. The former marshal stopped beside her to watch Charlie run through a type of jungle gym obstacle at Heidi's verbal command. "Nice. You can tell Charlie loves doing this."

"It's all about his play drive. He thinks this is a game. He views tracking the same way."

"For Ace, it's about work. Conquering the obstacles is his job and what he lives for."

Ace whined, glancing up at Deke. With a chuckle, Deke signaled him to join the game. Soon, both dogs were clambering over or through equipment. "Who did you want to introduce Heidi to?"

"Bear. I have to drop off my SUV for repairs." He glanced at his watch, grimaced. "I'm already an hour late."

Deke shook his head. "Oh, boy. Bear won't be happy."

"Nope. He'll probably charge me extra for the aggravation. This would be the third time in as many months I've been late getting a vehicle to him for repair."

"He'll be angry?" Heidi wondered what kind of mood Bear would be in if an unwanted visitor appeared along with Quinn.

"Not with you. He's a big teddy bear with the ladies. Kind of growly and gruff. He was like that with Andrea and the girls. They adore him. You'll enjoy meeting him," Deke said to Heidi. "Leave Charlie with me. I'll work with him and Ace until you return."

"Are you sure? I can meet Bear another time."

A snort from Quinn. "Not unless he wants to accommodate you. The man might be a mechanical genius, but he's a surly one when you cross or inconvenience him."

Deke chuckled. "He wasn't that way with my girls, just me when I ran late dropping off our minivan for him to reinforce. He'll enjoy meeting you, Heidi. I'll enjoy working with Charlie. In fact, my daughters should be here later. They'll get a kick out of playing with your dog." He smiled. "Go on with Quinn. We'll talk about the training program when you return."

"Come on," Quinn said. "I promise not to keep you too long."

She followed him to the parking lot. "Do you think we can uncover the arsonist, Quinn?"

"If anyone can unmask this person, it's my team." His hand clasped hers for a moment. "You and Levi have been on your own for a long time, babe. You aren't anymore. Trust us."

"I'm afraid to hope."

He sent her a pointed glance. "Don't be. We're good at our jobs. We aren't ordinary soldiers, Heidi."

"I kind of figured that based on the information the women shared with me last night. They're very protective of their men."

"It's for everybody's safety."

Interesting comment. Guess the woman who captured Quinn Gallagher's heart would be required to keep secrets about his work as well. That thought sent an arrow straight into her heart. The idea of another woman in Quinn's life hurt far more than it should. After all, what hold did she have on her childhood crush? Nothing much except a few sweet memories, a lot of bad ones, and a kiss that still made her knees want to buckle hours later. She reminded herself again that Quinn probably hadn't thought much about the kiss they shared. After all, why should he? A kiss was probably a frequent occurrence in his life. Not so in hers. No time for relationships while on the run.

At the passenger side door of his SUV, Heidi paused. "Can you tell me what kind of soldier you are, Quinn? It's okay if you can't, but I'd like to know." The information would help her understand him better.

He raised their clasped hands and kissed the back of hers, his gaze steady, watchful. "Durango is a Delta unit."

Delta? Stunned speechless, she stared into his dark eyes. Oh, goodness. No wonder the women were so determined to protect their husbands. A whispered word in the wrong ear would be deadly for them all. She couldn't imagine how many enemies Quinn and his friends had accumulated while in military service and in their jobs with Fortress. Heidi suspected more than one terrorist would love to get their hands on the Durango team or their mates and exact some revenge. "How long did you serve in that career?"

"Almost too long." With that cryptic comment, he dropped a light kiss on her mouth, then unlocked the door and settled her inside. He came around and climbed behind the wheel. Key in the ignition, he tried to crank the engine. Nothing but a clicking noise.

Heidi frowned. What was wrong with his SUV?

"Heidi, run!"

CHAPTER THIRTEEN

Quinn shoved Heidi out the door, bailed from the SUV himself, and ran. Before sprinting more than twenty feet, his vehicle exploded. The energy wave tossed his body into the air. Quinn hit the ground and rolled to a stop against the tire of another vehicle. The stench of burning metal and fuel made him cough.

Groaning, Quinn scrambled to his hands and knees, but the ground met him in a hurry, adding to his growing list of aches and pains. He had to move. Heidi was his priority. She had to be unharmed. The alternative didn't bear thinking about.

"Quinn!" Hard hands ran over his arms and legs. "Can you hear me?"

Another groan escaped. Man, everything hurt, including his head. And whichever teammate was with him sounded as though he was speaking under water. The blast had messed with his hearing. Should return to normal soon. He hoped. "Heidi," he rasped out. His throat burned. "She okay?"

"Josh is with her. An ambulance will be here soon. Don't move, Quinn."

Those same hands tried to hold him still when Quinn shifted to his hands and knees again. "Need to get to Heidi."

"She's not going anywhere."

Those words galvanized him into action. No! She couldn't be gone, not when he'd just found her again. He shoved off the restraining hands and lurched to his feet, stumbling as though on a drinking binge though he and his teammates never drank. They had to be prepared at any time for deployment on missions. They couldn't afford impaired judgment.

Nate grabbed him right before he face planted. "Hey, you lunkhead! You might have internal injuries."

"Have to get to her." Yeah, he was stubborn. "Is she okay?" Please, she had to be all right. "Nate?"

"I don't know, buddy. She's unconscious."

Grim determination filled him. Quinn turned toward the burning remains of his ride. Fire roared and black smoke billowed from the wreckage. Even from this distance, the heat seared. "Where is she?"

"Far side, near the building. She doesn't weight much, Quinn. The shock wave tossed her against the wall."

Dread swelled inside him. Heidi might have serious injuries. He wouldn't even allow himself to think of the worst case scenario. Before he staggered more than two steps, Nate draped Quinn's arm across his shoulders.

Once they moved past the inferno, he saw his team leader kneeling on the ground, talking on his cell phone. All he could see of Heidi were her legs. Not moving. Nate steered him further away from the blaze, then helped him the remaining thirty feet and eased him to the ground.

His heart clenched. Blood marred Heidi's pale skin, a macabre mask on her beautiful face. Quinn grasped her hand, afraid to move her though he longed to pull her into his arms, assure himself she was still alive. Her chest rose and fell with each breath and yet he feared any moment the motion would stop and he'd lose her for good. That couldn't happen. He wouldn't let it.

Somewhere in his throbbing head, Quinn realized he wasn't being rational. Couldn't make himself back down. Heidi mattered to him. He'd figure out how much she mattered and why later. Right now he concentrated on her breathing.

Josh shoved his phone in his pocket. "EMTs are two minutes out. Where are you injured, Quinn?"

"I'm fine, just worried about Heidi."

His friend's lips curved. "You'll still go to the hospital to be checked."

"Call Bear. Tell him I need a new ride." He shifted his gaze to his friend. "I want Bear to reinforce Heidi's SUV. I'm not sure what this was about, but she needs extra protection."

"I'll take care of it." He looked at Heidi. "Was the bomb meant for her or you?"

"Don't know. Could be either one. We need the surveillance tapes."

"We'll upload the security footage to your laptop." Josh frowned, glanced over his shoulder at the burning SUV. "Did you leave your computer in your ride?"

Quinn grunted. He'd been in a hurry after racing home to shower off the scent of smoke and wet dog.

"No problem. I'll bring you the laptop from your office. Focus on yourself and Heidi."

The growl of a siren stopped abruptly as the ambulance arrived. Quinn looked up to see two of his teammates keeping watch, weapons visible, standing between him and Heidi and threats in the area. He doubted anything further would happen. The bomber would be a fool to remain on the PSI campus. Trainees poured from the building and fanned out to search the grounds under the direction of PSI trainers who worked with Durango.

Good. If this clown was still here, somebody would lasso this guy and turn him over to the cops. Quinn scowled. Chances were, though, the bomber was in the wind. His gaze focused on Heidi. "Wake up, sweetheart," he murmured, stroking the inside of her wrist with his thumb. "I need to see those beautiful green eyes."

His team leader's head whipped his direction, eyes narrowed.

"Problem, Major?"

"How involved are you?"

"Not your business."

"Anything impairing your judgment is my business."

Quinn stiffened. "My judgment is as sound as yours was when you rescued Del and Ivy from Granger."

"No one touches what is mine." Ice coated the words of his friend. Anyone who came after Del would regret it.

Quinn's exact sentiments about Heidi. His gaze traced the delicate lines of her face. As a child, she'd wormed under his barriers. As a woman, Heidi was storming his heart. Should he let her? He wasn't perfect boyfriend material, if she would consider him in that role. A wise woman would kick him to the curb. One of Durango's enemies might try to exact revenge, anyone in his life a target. Heidi had spent her life on the run. He didn't want to add his problems to hers.

She should keep him as a friend, nothing more, but his gut cramped at the thought. Quinn didn't want to be a friend to Heidi Thompson. He didn't know what they were yet, but he wanted the chance to find out. Quinn wanted more than he should, more than was safe.

Josh moved aside as the EMTs rushed over, though he didn't move far in his role as temporary bodyguard. Minutes later, Quinn climbed into the back of the ambulance and sat as close to Heidi as he could without hindering the EMT.

He watched for any signs Heidi was regaining consciousness. Nothing. With every passing moment, he feared she'd never wake. The EMT relayed Heidi's vital signs to the hospital. To Quinn it was a bunch of jargon. He wished Rio had been at PSI. The medic would have been able to interpret the coded conversation. All Quinn could do was watch, pray, and will Heidi to wake and show him those remarkable green eyes which had haunted his dreams for years. If things worked out between them, he would tell her.

The ride to the emergency room was short. When the EMT threw open the doors, some tightness left Quinn's muscles when he saw Rio jogging toward him.

"You all right, Quinn?" Rio's eyes assessed him as he stepped down from the ambulance. "You need stitches, buddy."

"I'm fine." He gestured toward Heidi. "She's still unconscious. Rio, the blast threw her against the wall." His voice broke.

The medic squeezed Quinn's shoulder. "Josh told me. He and Nate are en route. Alex is with Serena. You want me to stay with Heidi?"

"I can take care of myself. She can't." Much as he longed to provide moral support and protection, the medical personnel wouldn't allow him in the examination room with her. He wasn't family. He wasn't her boyfriend. Yet. All he had to do was convince her to take a chance on him.

He almost snorted out loud. Sure. Like she'd want to throw her lot in with an operative whose job was slightly less dangerous than his military career had been.

"Stay alert," his friend insisted. "We don't know the motive behind this."

Rio didn't have to spell it out for him. No drugs to render him unconscious or impair his reaction time. The bombing was connected to her arsonist or one of Durango's missions. Would an arsonist change his MO from a fire to a bomb? He frowned, remembering his burning SUV. A bomb would take out the target and give the arsonist the thrill he sought watching the flames. "Don't let her out of your sight."

Rio hurried to the stretcher bearing Heidi. "I've got it, Mac. Help Quinn."

Their team medic might convince the medical staff to bend the rules. Not only was Rio well known and well liked in the medical community, he also trained the EMTs as an instructor at PSI.

Quinn followed them at a slower pace, Mac by his side. Though the other man didn't touch him, he looked ready to catch Quinn if he started to go down. Not going to happen. He wanted the focus on Heidi, not him.

As soon as they cleared the ER doors, someone called out, "Room 2, Mac."

"This way, Quinn."

He glanced up and the floor pitched. He prepared himself for the inevitable pain at the end of his journey to the linoleum.

"Whoa, buddy." Mac steadied him, then draped Quinn's arm across his shoulders. "Second door on the right. Your lady friend is in Room 1. Rio will update you on her condition."

Inside the room, Mac eased him down on a chair. "Doc will be here soon. You need to stay here, Quinn. I know you want to check on your woman. Don't. You can't help her if you collapse from internal injuries."

"I'm fine," he insisted again. Why wouldn't anyone listen?

"Tell it to the doctor, okay?" Mac's radio squawked. He sighed. "Gotta run. An accident on Highway 18."

Retribution

"Thanks, Mac."

"Yep. See you around." With that, the EMT dashed from the room.

Quinn thought about slipping into the next room, resisted when he swayed the moment he stood. Sinking onto his chair again with a disgusted sigh, he settled back to wait.

Just when he thought the doctor had forgotten his existence, a tall, athletic woman breezed through the doorway, her brown eyes twinkling. "Well, we meet again, Quinn Gallagher."

He blinked, at a loss for a moment. Ah. Susan Bailey, the doctor he'd met at a fundraiser for the fire department and EMTs in Dunlap County. While Otter Creek's fire department personnel were paid employees, the rest of the county wasn't so lucky. "Hey, Doc."

"I hear you tangled with a bomb."

Quinn grimaced. "Afraid so."

Susan's gaze swept over him. "Looks like superficial wounds, though the cut on your forehead needs stitching. Let me take a closer look at you. Take off your shirt and climb on the examining table, buddy. I want to make sure you don't have cuts or burns you aren't telling me about."

His lips twitched as he moved to the table. "You think I'd do that?"

"You are as macho as my cop husband. I'm positive you wouldn't tell me everything."

Smart lady. "Does Ken know he's a lucky man?"

"I remind him daily." Susan motioned with her hand for Quinn to take off his shirt.

He ditched the leather jacket that had protected him from burns on his arms and back, then peeled off his black t-shirt. Quinn would have to order a new jacket. This one now sported slashes and burn marks.

The doctor looked at his back and whistled. "You'll be colorful in a few hours." Her cold hands pressed against his back and ribs.

He hissed when she hit a particularly sore spot.

"We should do x-rays."

"If I had broken ribs, I wouldn't be able to breath."

"Had those before?"

"Oh, yeah. Not fun." Especially since he'd been on a mission and couldn't be airlifted out. Rio had taped his ribs and kept Quinn mobile.

Susan finished the exam, stitched his forehead, and declared him fit except for a slight concussion. His hearing and balance had already improved. "The woman who was brought in with me is a friend. How is she?"

Susan's eyebrows raised. "A friend, huh? Quinn Gallagher, is there something you aren't telling me?"

His cheeks burned. "Such as?"

"Maybe she's more than a friend."

Was he that transparent? "Planning to tattle on me, Susan?"

She laughed. "Not me. She would be lucky if she caught your interest. Too bad for the single women in town, though. You're going to break their hearts."

He shifted, uncomfortable with the direction of their conversation. In his view, Quinn wasn't a great catch. He was frequently out of town with his team so he couldn't be counted on for dates. Most women hated the uncertainty and turned him into a serial dater. What woman would tolerate his career long term? "Right. About Heidi?"

"I'm checking on her now." She nodded at his shirt and jacket. "Get dressed and wait in the hall."

As soon as Susan left, Quinn dragged on his t-shirt and grabbed his battered jacket. He leaned against the wall across from Heidi's room.

A couple minutes later, the door opened and Susan motioned for Quinn to step inside.

He drew his first free breath since seeing Heidi on the ground when she held out her hand to him. Thank God.

Quinn grabbed a chair and crossed to her side. Not wise to let Susan or Rio know his head pounded and the room spun. "Hey," he murmured, threading his fingers through hers as he sank onto the hard chair. He was vaguely aware of Susan and Rio leaving. He focused on the woman clinging to his hand as though he were her lifeline.

"Hey," she whispered. Her gaze scanned his face. She winced when she saw the stitches. "How bad?"

"Eleven stitches." He shrugged. "What does Susan say about you?"

"I'll live."

He waited, his gaze steady on hers.

"Concussion, maybe a cracked rib or two." She lifted trembling fingers to his face. "You could have been killed today. This is my fault. I never should have stayed when I realized you were here. I have to leave before something else happens to you."

CHAPTER FOURTEEN

Quinn's hand tightened on Heidi's. "We don't know the arsonist is to blame. The bomb might be connected to one of our missions. We try to keep our identity under wraps. Doesn't always work."

Heidi appreciated his attempt to take the blame. "You have people trying to kill you?" Skepticism rang in her voice.

His lips curved upward. "More than you realize. Durango makes enemies when deployed." He brushed his lips over hers in a soft parody of the intense kisses they'd shared. "Don't run, baby," he whispered against her lips. "Stay with me."

"It's too dangerous." He'd suffered enough because of her family. She wouldn't be the cause of more hurt.

"I told you, sweetheart. I'm hard to kill." He drew back enough to look her in the eyes. "Heidi, it's time to stop running. Don't let fear take away what you really want."

If he knew what she wanted most, Quinn Gallagher would put as much distance between them as possible. The one thing she wanted most was her childhood hero. Never happen, though. Sooner or later, he'd decide she wasn't worth the effort.

The voice in her head screamed at her to leave Otter Creek. Her heart, on the other hand, pleaded for her to fight back. What if the bomb was connected to Quinn's past? Fury that someone might hurt him surged ahead of the fear for her own safety and the conviction that Quinn would shatter her heart in a million pieces.

Hours earlier, she'd decided to stay and fight. Would the latest incident scare her off? Heidi raised her chin. No matter what happened, she wouldn't slink away in fear. She and Charlie were living in this quaint town. Sure, her heart was on the line with Quinn and maybe he'd decide against a relationship with her. But broken hearts mended.

The time to take a stand was now. She and Charlie were surrounded by good people with the best training the military and law enforcement offered. Heidi Thompson hid from no one. The arsonist wanted to come at her again? Good. She and her new friends would end his reign of terror. Then she could live in peace and fulfill the call of her soul, to be an S & R instructor. If she stayed, no matter what happened between her and Quinn, she could make a difference in this community.

Heidi cupped Quinn's face between her palms and kissed him. When she eased away, his eyes glittered. "I'm staying."

"No doubts?"

"None." Never again. Her decision was made, whatever the consequences.

Satisfaction gleamed from his gaze.

She prayed he didn't regret the support. "Is Charlie all right?"

"Deke took Charlie to his house. We'll pick him up after we're discharged."

Thank goodness Charlie hadn't been with her. Heidi wouldn't have been able to get him out of the vehicle in time. "When can we leave?" She detested hospitals, having spent more time in them than she cared to remember.

"Don't like the hospitality?" he teased.

"I want to wash away the smoke and dirt, and change into clothes that don't smell like I've rolled around in a fire pit." If she could stand up long enough. The concussion was messing with her equilibrium. A headache and nausea weren't helping.

A light tap sounded on the door. A muffled voice said, "It's Rio."

"Come." Quinn turned to face the door, his hand hovering over the weapon until his teammate cleared the doorway, with Josh close behind carrying a laptop.

When Heidi saw the grim expression on her new boss's face, her hand tightened around Quinn's. More bad news. Fantastic. Her resolve hardened. Didn't matter. They'd face whatever came.

Josh set the computer on a nearby counter and turned to Heidi. "How do you feel?"

"Like I went two rounds with a brick wall and lost."

He grinned. "What does Susan say?"

So he knew her doctor by name, too. Must be a small town thing. She considered Josh's other job. Maybe it was a cop thing. "Concussion, cracked ribs, a few stitches, and she's convinced I'm the luckiest person on the planet today." A sentiment Heidi might agree with, except she knew her survival had nothing to do with luck and everything to do with Quinn Gallagher.

"You are lucky." Quinn said, his voice soft.

Heidi's gaze found Quinn's. "It wasn't luck. It was you."

A ghost of a smile flickered on his mouth as he leaned down and kissed her, his touch light as a brush of a butterfly's wing. Heidi's heart lurched into furious rhythm. He'd kissed her in front of his teammates, as though claiming her.

When he eased away, Quinn's fingers trailed across her cheek before he turned to his team leader. "What did you find out, Major?"

Josh raised the laptop's lid and tapped a couple keys. A shot of the PSI parking lot filled the screen. "Watch." He touched another key and the minute counter at the bottom of the screen showed the security footage in fast forward.

Vehicles moved in and out of the parking lot. Josh pulled into a slot and climbed from his truck. Heidi frowned. She saw Quinn arrive in his SUV and walk to the building with a to-go cup in his hand, followed by his teammates, then Deke and Ace. Last, running late, was Heidi and Charlie. Yeah, her furry buddy hated baths with a passion.

The counter continued to race through the minutes until she and Quinn approached his SUV together. Another kiss. Heidi's cheeks burned. She didn't know the outside of the building had security cams. Should have known these men wouldn't leave anything to chance. What would Josh and Rio think about a relationship developing between her and their teammate? Heidi didn't know what to think about the change in her relationship with Quinn. She was afraid to trust such a dramatic shift. But she wanted to.

"That is not what I wanted to see." Quinn's eyes narrowed. "Did you double check the footage?"

"Had Zane do it. No tampering. What you see is what you get. Nothing."

As Heidi watched the scene unfold, the on-screen Quinn shoved her from the vehicle, bailed out himself and ran. The SUV exploded in a ball of flames.

She shuddered. So close. She'd come so close to losing Quinn. A heavy arm circled her shoulders. Quinn drew her against him, offering silent comfort and support.

"Did you have Z pull the footage from my home security cams?" he asked.

Josh nodded. "Nothing."

"The bomb must have been placed while I was at Heidi's this morning."

"Agreed."

"Which means he's watching either me or Heidi." Quinn scowled. "Doesn't help us narrow the target. At least if we knew which of us was being targeted, we'd have a starting point."

"Bold move," Rio said. "Not much opportunity with the fire department and Nick milling around the place. He could have been caught easily."

"He's either smart enough not to get caught or arrogant enough to believe himself invincible and got lucky. Nate have anything to add?" Quinn asked.

"He'll be here soon to tell us what he found when he examined the scene." Josh closed the laptop. "He was talking to Rod when I left PSI."

"I'm surprised Rod let him cross the crime scene tape."

"Rod's smart. Nate is a bomb expert. My brother-in-law won't let him sit on the sidelines when tapping his experience might lead to an arrest. OCPD doesn't have an explosives expert. If we had a bomb threat, Ethan would ask Nate to help."

"We have to install security in and around Heidi's house or move her to a safer place."

Were they kidding? Why worry about security at her rental when someone had tried to kill Quinn? "You're missing the point. Someone planted a bomb in your vehicle when you were outside my house, Quinn. It must be the arsonist. He's shifted his attention to you." A fact that made Heidi sick to her stomach. This was what she feared would happen. How did this man keep finding her?

Quinn was shaking his head before she finished. "The bomb could have been meant for me. They might have followed me from home to your place."

"And you didn't notice? Come on, Otter Creek isn't that busy. You would have seen headlights trailing you to my place."

"Not necessarily. The two times I made the drive I was distracted. Something else to consider, Heidi. If the arsonist planted the bomb, I've been on his radar for years but not worth his attention before now."

"Looks like that's changed, thanks to me."

"No guarantee the bomb was planted this morning," Josh said. "The bomber could have rigged the SUV last night. He had plenty of opportunity when the rest of us left to go home."

She frowned. "But why wait to set it off?"

"Timing wasn't right. The bomber wanted to make a statement."

He had achieved his goal. But what had he accomplished? He'd warn Durango one of their own was in danger which would make them more alert than normal. From what she'd observed, the warning would make her new bosses more dangerous. The bomber had made a serious mistake.

Another knock on the door and Nate announced himself from the hallway and strode into the room. He eyed his injured teammate, then nodded, seeming satisfied. He shifted his attention to Heidi. "How are you, Heidi?"

"A few stitches, concussion, cracked ribs. I'll live."

His lips twitched. "Your first war wounds?"

"Hopefully my last. I'm not a fan."

He chuckled. "Ditto."

Something told Heidi that Quinn and his teammates had many more war wounds than she did. Couldn't be otherwise considering their line of work.

"What did you discover from the crime scene?" Josh asked.

"The bomb was a simple device. Anybody with an Internet connection could rig this up. Ammonium nitrate with a blasting cap for detonation. The explosion was triggered by a cell phone."

"So the timing of the explosion was exactly as the bomber wanted." Quinn frowned even as he eased Heidi against his side again. "He was trying to kill one of us. The other was collateral damage."

"The question is, who was the target?" Heidi leaned her aching head against Quinn's arm. "Is there any way to find out?"

"Maybe," Josh said. "Zane can set up bots to scour the Net for any mention of Quinn or the rest of us."

"Doesn't he already do that?" Seemed logical to her that they should demand that kind of monitoring all the time.

"The bots are set for Fortress or Durango, not our individual names unless there's been a specific threat." He turned to Nate. "I assume the bomb materials are easy to find?"

A snort. "Yep. We might be able to trace the blasting cap if enough of it is left. Doubt it, though. Construction companies have them and there are a lot of those companies in and around Dunlap County."

"What are the chances the blasting cap came from Elliott Construction?" Rio asked. "They're the biggest construction group in the county. Several job sites for the bomber to steal a blasting cap."

"Possible." Josh picked up the laptop. "I'll call Brian on my way home." He glanced at his watch, sighed. "I have to go back on duty in six hours. Nate, you supervising the cleanup at PSI once Rod finishes at the scene?"

"Got it covered, Major. I'll call Zane about the bots. We need to know if our wives are at risk. Go sleep and spend some time with Del."

"I'll check in before I go on duty. Quinn, you and Heidi take the day off tomorrow." He held up his hand when they both started to protest. "That's an order,

Sergeant. Heidi, if you show up at PSI, you and Charlie will be gently shoved out the door. Rest. Recoup. Have Quinn show you the big metropolis of downtown Otter Creek." With that, he left.

Worry knotted Heidi's stomach. She'd been on the job for one day and already told to take a day off. What did that mean for her long-term employment? She wondered if Quinn would take the day as ordered.

"Perfect." Quinn smiled down at her. "I'll take you to Delaney's Deli. That's the town gathering place. You'll be able to meet several Otter Creek residents while we eat."

She studied his face. "You're not going to work."

He shook his head. "Josh outranks me."

"You're not in the military now."

"Doesn't matter. He's the leader of our unit. Besides, we'll be sore tomorrow. Taking the day off will give us a chance to work out the kinks."

"Take our word for it," Nate said. "You don't want to cross Josh Cahill. You will regret it. Lousy assignments. Terrible hours. Painful workouts." He shuddered. "I only made that mistake once. Learned a painful lesson."

Rio squeezed Heidi's hand. "If you're sore and stiff, Heidi, you won't be able to run if necessary. Do some light stretching tomorrow. Take the opportunity to explore the town."

"Might be good to find a map of Otter Creek and the surrounding area," Nate added. "Del can help you with that. She keeps maps stocked in her bookstore for tourists."

Relieved to do something pertaining to her job without ignoring Josh's orders, Heidi nodded. "I need to be familiar with the area when I'm called out for an S & R assignment." Maybe she and Quinn could drive around the area tomorrow.

Another knock on the door. Alex wouldn't abandon Serena, and Heidi had a feeling Ethan Blackhawk kept late hours with his job. He probably was on call all the time.

With Hans Muehller bearing down on them, there was no telling when the police chief would go home for the night.

Quinn must have been concerned about the unannounced visitor because he released Heidi and stepped in front of her, gun in his hand though he held the weapon by his side. He motioned for Rio to open the door.

A familiar figure pushed past the medic and stalked into the room.

CHAPTER FIFTEEN

Quinn's hand tightened around the grip of his gun as a large, dark-haired man shoved past Rio and raced toward Heidi. A split second before he raised the weapon, a spark of recognition hit him. Heidi's cousin. "Levi."

That brought the big man up short, his gaze whipping to Quinn's face. "Quinn, what are you doing here?"

"I'm with Fortress and PSI. Maddox sent Heidi to me for protection."

He waved that comment aside. "I know about your employment. Why are you at the hospital with Heidi?"

There were a lot of ways to answer that, most of them sure to cause a negative reaction from Levi. Quinn finally settled for the absolute truth. "I wouldn't be anywhere else."

With a frown, Levi shifted his attention to his cousin. "I heard about the bomb. How bad are you hurt, Peaches?"

A spurt of amusement shot through Quinn. Peaches? His gaze skated over Heidi's red hair and cream complexion, currently flushing a pretty peach color as temper simmered in her eyes. Yep, Peaches was an appropriate moniker for the woman staring down her cousin.

"Levi, what are you doing here?"

"You're kidding, right? Someone tried to blow you up and you think I'd stay in hiding?" His voice rose.

"Watch your tone, Levi. Where's your security detail?" Quinn snapped. At the very least, one of his bodyguards should have checked the room before he barreled in here. They shouldn't have allowed him to race ahead.

"The elevator was too full. I wanted to check on Heidi."

"No excuse for carelessness."

"What do you mean?"

Nate folded his arms across his chest. "You're lucky we didn't kill you when you shoved your way in the room."

Levi scowled. "No one will keep me from Heidi's side. Not you, not Quinn, no one."

"You have a security detail for a reason. The next decision you make to dodge them might be your last. I don't think you want to cause Heidi more pain."

The door opened again, this time to admit a tall brunette. She relaxed marginally when she saw Quinn, Rio, and Nate in the room. "Levi, you ditch me again and I'll report to Maddox that you aren't cooperating. You'll have a new team of bodyguards assigned."

Startled, he swung around to face her. "I can take care of myself for a couple minutes."

"Maddox must not agree since he assigned two operatives to your security detail," Quinn said. He glanced at Nate, indicated for his teammate to talk to Angel out in the hall. He didn't want Heidi hearing the operatives' dressing down. If Angel and her partner couldn't keep Levi protected at all times, then he needed a new detail. If Heidi's cousin continued to ignore the rules Maddox laid down, the Fortress CEO would cut him loose and let him fend for himself. The rules were to protect the operatives as well as their principal.

Angel noted the interchange between him and Nate, and she paled.

"Angel?" Levi murmured, stepping closer to her side. "What's wrong?"

"Hallway, Martinez," Nate said to Angel.

She swallowed hard and turned toward the door without addressing Levi.

"Angel? Hey, what's going on?" Levi frowned at Quinn. "He can't order her around."

Quinn waited until the door closed before rounding on Heidi's cousin. "Nate will talk with your protection detail."

"That's not his job. They don't answer to you."

Levi," Heidi said. "Knock that chip off your shoulder."

"My bodyguards answer to Maddox," Levi insisted. "Your team doesn't have the right to criticize Angel and Dane."

Quinn stepped closer, looming over the other man. "Fortress is run like the military. Angel and Dane are considered privates."

"And you aren't? They've been with the company longer than you."

His eyes narrowed. How did Levi know the length of time Durango worked with Fortress? Guess Angel and Dane had informed their principal, something he would address with the two operatives. They probably wanted to reassure Levi about Heidi's safety. Loose lips would endanger Durango and their loved ones. "Length of service with Fortress doesn't matter."

"Then what does?"

"Skills and training. Angel and Dane were law enforcement. My teammates and I are military."

A snort. "So being a gun-toting soldier gives you more rank than a cop?"

Anger burned in his gut. "In terms of experience and expertise, yes. You're missing the point, Levi. We outrank them. Angel and Dane made a rookie mistake that could cost them their jobs."

"What? No! I just wanted to check on Katie." He grimaced. "Heidi."

"You not only put yourself in danger with this stunt, you also endangered your bodyguards. You forced them to go into a situation blind which might have cost their lives."

Levi glanced at the closed door, a troubled look on his face. "I need to apologize. I wasn't thinking."

"You can't afford to act without thinking. Why are you in Otter Creek?"

"Heidi was almost killed by a bomb. Of course I'll be here. It's my job to protect her."

Quinn glared. "That job is mine, a job which you've made a thousand times harder."

"How?"

"Did the arsonist make a move against you at the safe house?"

A head shake.

"Then you should have stayed away. If the arsonist planted the bomb, he did it to draw you out. You handed him the response he was after and that multiplies the danger to you and Heidi. This guy now has you both in the same zip code. How much easier will it be for him to kill you both?"

Levi squeezed his eyes shut a moment. "I'm sorry. I wasn't thinking beyond the need to reach Heidi."

"Panic will kill you and your cousin," Rio said. "That's why you must listen to the operatives protecting you. They'll save your life if you're smart enough to follow their orders. If you won't do that, you're a dead man and there's a good chance your actions will cause injuries or worse to Heidi."

"I will listen to Angel and Dane from now on. You have my word."

"No more screw ups," Quinn said. "If we have to call your bodyguards down again, we'll send them packing. If they're lucky, they'll keep their jobs." Although Maddox would send Angel and Dane through PSI for re-training.

"I get it, okay? I won't mess up again."

The door opened and Nate walked back into the room with a silent Angel following close behind.

"Dane?" Quinn asked.

"On the door. No one will slip past him. I'm needed at PSI."

"Go. Rio, can you stay until Susan turns us loose?"

He pulled out his cell phone. "Need to let Darcy know I'll be late for dinner."

Quinn's lips edged upward. "You already sound married."

His friend grinned. "Six more days and I will be. I can't wait to marry her."

"Tell Darcy I'm sorry we spoiled her plans," Heidi said.

"Don't worry, sugar. I'll have her to myself for two weeks. I plan to make amends for every missed or late meal and event, and treat her like the princess she is."

Envy hit Quinn in the gut. He wanted the kind of relationship Rio and Darcy shared. His gaze shifted to Heidi and found her attention on him. Did she want the same thing with him? Man, he hoped so. Yeah, it was crazy. He'd only reconnected with Heidi two days ago, but he felt as though they had never parted.

Maybe the connection remained from the time their families spent together when they were growing up. Since their fathers were business partners, the Hendersons and Gallaghers often shared meals and celebrated holidays, even attended the same schools and knew the same people. He'd watched her grow, considering her a kid sister until

Caleb Henderson kidnapped Heidi and Moira. After the death of his father, Quinn focused on his own family, giving little thought to Katie as he helped his mother and sisters cope. Now, Katie Henderson was no longer a child. She'd grown into the drop-dead gorgeous Heidi Thompson and the feelings Quinn had for her were anything but brotherly.

Once Nate left, Levi turned to Quinn. "Guess Maddox's version of witness protection didn't work. The arsonist has found Heidi again. How will you and your buddies protect her?"

Quinn studied him a moment. "How did you hear about Fortress? We don't advertise."

Levi looked startled. "How does he find business?"

"People find us. Answer my question, Levi."

"I was a firefighter before I transitioned to arson investigator. My engine responded to a house fire. We rescued a mother and daughter trapped on the second floor. The daughter is Maddox's niece."

Quinn remembered Maddox talking about the incident. According to him, one of the firefighters had been burned saving the girl. Must have been Levi. Maybe the burns were the reason Levi had changed jobs. "Bet your career raised suspicions when you and Heidi were victims of fires."

"You have no idea. It was bad enough as a firefighter. As an arson investigator, I knew enough to set the fires, sit back and watch the show. The cops were wrong, but that didn't stop them from trying to pin the fires on me anyway."

Another knock on the door. Rio stepped into the hall, then returned with the doctor.

"Would you like to go home, Ms. Thompson?"

Heidi smiled. "How fast can I sign the papers?"

Susan laughed. "You'll be walking out the door in a few minutes. I'll have the nurse give you a sheet with instructions when you're discharged. Rio, I assume you'll watch them overnight. If you can't, I will keep them for observation."

"I'll take care of it." He slid them a pointed look. "I guarantee they'll stay quiet."

"Excellent. Heidi, Quinn, stay out of trouble for a few days."

"Susan, I hate hospitals," Quinn said.

"Something tells me you experience more than the normal bumps and bruises when on the job." She held up her hand. "I don't want to know. I can't speak about what I haven't seen. As a physician, I'm telling you to lay low for a day or two. Heidi, it's nice to meet you. Wish your welcome to Otter Creek hadn't been so dramatic."

"Thanks."

"Rio, call me if there are any problems." The doctor smiled. "I'll be on duty until six tomorrow morning." When Durango's medic saluted Susan, she grinned and left with a wave.

Thirty minutes later, Quinn escorted Heidi to Rio's SUV, idling at the ER entrance. Dane and Angel followed with Levi in their vehicle. With so many Fortress operatives in one place, Quinn decided returning to Heidi's house for the night was safe enough. Though he had better security at his place, Heidi needed Charlie's supplies and her house would accommodate all of them. He and Rio would spell the other operatives through the night. No choice, despite Susan's instructions for him to rest. Heidi and Levi must be protected and the arsonist had proved he knew Heidi's location. Now the cousins were under the same roof.

On the ride to Heidi's home, Quinn called Maddox.

"Talk to me, Quinn," was the Fortress CEO's greeting.

"You're on speaker with Rio and Heidi, too." With that warning, he dived into the most pressing issue. "Levi's here."

"Explain."

He reported the events of the past several hours and Levi's subsequent arrival in Otter Creek with his security detail.

"Why didn't I hear about the location change from Levi's security detail?"

"My guess is the principal didn't give them an option and wouldn't wait." With an apologetic glance at Heidi, he said, "Levi's determined to protect Heidi, no matter the cost to himself or others around him."

"Heidi? Opinion?"

She sighed. "Quinn's right. My cousin has been protecting me since I was ten. Even though we have bodyguards, he doesn't think anyone can do as good a job as he can."

"I'll talk to Josh, see what he wants to do."

"Give him a few hours before you touch base," Quinn said. "He's on duty tonight and is sleeping."

"Copy that. Want me to reassign Levi's bodyguards?"

"How good are they?"

"Good enough I planned to add them to a new unit. After their performance on this assignment, I might rethink that decision."

So, this was on-the-job training for the pair. Nice. "Nate had a talk with them. Run it by Josh, but my recommendation is to leave them in place for now. If there's another incident, we'll send them to Nashville or dump them into training at PSI."

"I like the PSI angle. Might do that anyway once this assignment is finished. I'll talk to Josh about designing a specialized training regimen for future units."

An excellent idea. Fortress constantly needed more units as the danger around the globe escalated. Made sense to have PSI design a program since the infrastructure was in place.

"Heidi, I need you to tell me the truth," Maddox said. "Did you break the rules?"

CHAPTER SIXTEEN

Heidi groaned. Man, Rio was right about the sore muscles. She rolled over, glanced at the window. Frowned. It was still dark. What time was it? After she and the others returned to her house the night before, they had eaten the day's special from Delaney's brought to them by Ivy Morgan. Following a reunion with Charlie, Heidi went to bed.

Squinting at the clock on her bedside table, Heidi sighed. Three o'clock? Knowing she wouldn't sleep now, she headed to the bathroom. After a quick shower, she dressed in comfortable clothes and running shoes, and patted her thigh for Charlie to follow her. She'd been so glad to see her furry buddy when Deke dropped him off. He'd laughed when telling her about Charlie being such a good natured, patient "victim" as his daughters played house and dress-up with him and Ace. "Outside, Charlie," she murmured.

When she passed the living room, the brush of fabric caught her attention. Heidi's heart leaped into her throat until she remembered her conversation with Quinn before she'd gone to bed. He warned her at least one Fortress operative would be on watch through the night. She hoped the guard was one of the others.

"Everything okay, Heidi?" Quinn moved into the dimly lit hall, concern on his face. "I can wake Rio if you need him."

He was concerned about her? What about Quinn? He must be exhausted. "I'm wide awake," she whispered. "I need to take Charlie out."

"I'll take him. There's fresh coffee in the kitchen."

She smiled. "I'll take you up on both." Early morning visits to the grass in winter with Charlie were her least favorite times with her beloved companion. Heidi poured herself a cup of coffee and had taken several sips by the time Quinn returned. Charlie dashed to his food and water bowl which Heidi had filled while he was outside. "Don't you ever sleep?" she asked Quinn.

He glanced over his shoulder as he relocked the door. "I slept."

"How long?"

"Three hours."

She stared. "How can you function on six hours of sleep in two days?"

He poured coffee for himself. "Military training. No cookies this time?" he asked, his lips curving.

Figuring he'd said all he planned to regarding his sleeping patterns, Heidi said, "I might be persuaded to eat one." Who was she to turn down a cookie? Any cookie. She glanced at the open pantry door at the brightly covered containers of pure goodness. Yep, definitely punchy from yesterday's excitement if she waxed eloquent over a cookie. "Maybe two cookies," she muttered.

With a soft chuckle, Quinn grabbed two kinds of cookies and slid them across the counter. "Guess the choices don't matter."

"I haven't found many that aren't good with coffee."

"Don't tell Rio about your eating habits, babe. He'll nudge you to better food choices."

"Too late." Rio walked in, yawning. He grabbed a cup of coffee for himself and sat at the breakfast bar with Heidi and Quinn. "Pass me two of those oatmeal things."

"Can't wait to tell Darcy about your late night eating habits," Quinn said as he passed his friend the container. "All your lectures about changing our eating habits must have blown past your ears."

"I made the change for my wife-to-be and I feel better physically. Galls me to admit Nate's been right about our juvenile food choices all these years." He narrowed his eyes at Quinn. "If you tattle on me, I'll let Alex stitch you up the next time you're injured."

"Ouch. Not nice, buddy."

"Alex isn't skilled as a medic?" Heidi bit into her cream-filled chocolate cookie. So good. Chocolate was good for you. She thought she remembered hearing that. Whether food critics agreed or not, chocolate cookies made her feel good.

"He's best with a rifle in his hand, not a needle." Quinn shuddered. "I'd rather stitch myself up than let Alex work on me."

She wrinkled her nose. "Have you stitched yourself?"

"We all have. You do what's necessary when in the field."

"How do you feel, Heidi?" Rio asked.

"Sore, but not bad considering I lost an argument with a brick wall."

"Headache? Nausea?"

She shook her head.

"Excellent. Stay with the plan for today and take it easy. Tomorrow, you can return to normal activity as long as you don't do anything too strenuous."

"No running marathons or scaling mountains. Check."

Rio looked surprised. "You done both?"

"Helps me prepare for searches." Heidi finished her coffee and cookie before turning to Quinn. "What are we doing today?"

"Breakfast at Delaney's at six." He winked. "A real breakfast. Then we visit Del at the bookstore to get a map. We'll drive around the county today." He pushed aside his empty coffee mug and turned to face her. "Up to answering questions this morning, baby?"

Goosebumps surged over her body, though she wasn't sure if his endearment or Quinn's ominous overtone caused them. Most likely both. "What do you want to know?"

"You told Maddox you followed his security rules. Have you remembered doing anything that might have compromised your safety and given away your location?"

Heidi thought about that question late into the night, racking her brain for any slip that might have led to another breach in her security. "I haven't talked to anyone from my past except my cousin. I only used the encrypted phone Maddox gave me to talk to Levi and only for very short periods of time."

"Did you run across anyone you met in one of your past identities?" Rio asked. "Maybe someone who called out one of your old names or someone from your childhood."

"Not that I remember."

"You would remember a scare like that. When you're on the run, you're paranoid. What about social media?" Quinn asked. "Did you have your picture on social media posts?"

She frowned. "I don't have social media pages, but someone might have posted a picture of me without me knowing. Are you thinking the arsonist is tracking me through other people's social media posts?"

"Something to consider."

"I can't see the boss missing something that basic." Rio selected two more cookies. "Zane would have conducted a facial recognition search, then scrubbed any images he found."

Heidi stared. "Can he do that?"

"There are no pictures of Fortress employees on the Internet. Our safety and the safety of our families depends on our secure identities."

"Maddox had your possessions searched for bugs and trackers before you came here?" Quinn persisted.

She gave a soft huff of laughter. "What possessions? Levi and I lost everything except one change of clothes in another fire the night before we met with your boss. We didn't have anything to search."

"What about after you met with him?"

"He shipped us off for defense training, then split us up. I came here. I don't know where he sent my cousin." Couldn't have been too far from Otter Creek since Levi showed up so fast after the bomb destroyed Quinn's SUV.

"Your vehicles?"

"Maddox went over them himself a couple times and said they were free of tracking devices."

"You brought nothing from your former life." Quinn was silent a moment. "What about Charlie?"

At the sound of his name, the Lab sat up on his chill mat.

Heidi stared at her canine companion. "Charlie's been with me for three years. I would never leave him behind. He's as much my family as Levi."

Quinn and Rio exchanged a look. "Did anyone scan Charlie for a tracking device?" Rio asked.

"I'm not sure. But how would the arsonist place a tracker on my dog? He's never out of my sight."

"Because he's a trained working dog, you must take him to the vet."

"Of course. I don't leave him, though. I go into the examining room with him. He's not fond of vet visits."

"Can't say that I blame him. I don't like doctor visits either. What about when he's at the groomers? Do you stay with him when he's groomed?" Quinn rose and retrieved the coffee pot, refilling each of their mugs.

"I usually don't." She rubbed Charlie's ears, feeling guilty all over again for leaving him even for those few hours. "It's hard to hear him kick up a fuss. He's vocal about his dislike of baths. You hear his howls all over the store."

Quinn flashed her an amused look. "I think my ears are still ringing from the bath we gave him." He turned to Rio, raised an eyebrow. "You want to check him?"

"Sure." He knelt beside the Lab and ran competent hands over him. The medic took his time, an expression of concentration on his face. Finally, he removed his hands from the dog. "I don't feel anything implanted under his skin."

"Heidi, have you changed Charlie's collar recently?"

Her gaze dropped to the red paisley strip of material around Charlie's neck, dread coiling in her stomach. "It's the same," she whispered.

Rio unlatched and examined the collar. He froze. "Where's your flashlight, Quinn?"

"In my Go bag." He left the room and returned a minute later with a small black flashlight in his hand. After passing it to his teammate, he held up a small hand-held slim box.

She frowned. "What's that?" The hard, black plastic was no bigger than a deck of cards.

"Finds tracking devices." He pressed a button on the side. A yellow light appeared, then a pattern of flashing red lights. Quinn frowned.

"Did it find anything?"

"Oh, yeah." Quinn dropped to one knee and took the collar from Rio, examined it. Satisfaction gleamed in his eyes. "Right here, baby." He pressed Heidi's fingers to the spot he'd been examining.

Her eyes widened as she felt the small, hard lump. In the light of the powerful flashlight, she spotted a small slit in the fabric of Charlie's collar.

Stomach in a knot, she looked at Quinn. "We've been trying so hard to stay out of the arsonist's clutches. I led him straight to us. He could have killed Levi and it would have been my fault."

Her childhood crush shook his head. "You didn't know what to look for, Heidi. The fault is ours. Fortress should have caught the tracker and removed it."

"I'll buy Charlie a new collar." She rubbed the Lab's head. "The idea of this guy knowing where I am all the time is creepy."

Another horrible thought surfaced. "Quinn, we have to warn Deke. He needs to protect his family."

"I'll warn him, but no one will catch Deke off guard, babe. The marshal is very protective of his wife and daughters." Quinn grabbed his phone and typed a message. "Done. Look, I know you want to get rid of the collar."

She didn't like the sound of that. "But?"

"Leave it. If the tracker signal disappears, the arsonist will know we're on to him. Instead, use it to draw him into the open."

CHAPTER SEVENTEEN

Ethan eased the curtain aside to peer into the darkness. Nothing moved. Not even a leaf stirred. Didn't matter. The skin on the back of his neck was crawling, something he'd learned over the years never to ignore. Trouble was coming, might already be in his picturesque town.

Would the protective measures he'd put in place be enough? They had to be. The alternative was unthinkable. Much as he wanted to send Serena to a safe house out of Muehller's reach, he couldn't. At this point in her pregnancy, his wife couldn't travel. Their baby was due any time and Ethan wanted to be at the birth, supporting the woman who'd captured his heart. His hands ached to hold that tiny miracle he'd all but given up hope of having until he met Serena. He never would have dared dream the tiny blond-haired, blue-eyed waif of his childhood would one day fall in love with him and enable him to be a father.

"Ethan?"

He turned at the soft voiced inquiry, dismayed. "It's early, sweetheart. Why are you awake?"

Serena moved into his open arms at an angle. She took one of his hands and pressed it to the side of her stomach.

After a few seconds, he felt a strong thump against his hand.

Ethan chuckled. "Ah. Baby Blackhawk is playing this morning."

"I think we're having a future soccer player."

"Or a place kicker for the Dallas Cowboys."

Serena grinned. "You still hoping for a boy, love?"

He bent down and kissed her, long and deep. Man, even after two years of marriage, her kisses still revved his heart rate, something his Ranger buddies would find amusing. He'd been known as steady and cool under fire. That was before Serena entered his life. He eased back, running the back of his fingers over her cheek. "I already love our baby. To be honest, I don't care if we have a boy or girl."

She studied his face a moment. "What's wrong, Ethan?"

Should have known his wife would pick up on his worry. "You know me pretty well, don't you?"

"Tell me."

"No proof, just a gut feeling."

"I trust your gut over hard facts any day. Is it Muehller?"

He gave a short nod. "Are you cooking today?"

"I'm preparing meals for my sisters so they won't be tempted to raid the junk food aisle at the grocery store. I'll be at Madison's this morning and Meg's this afternoon."

"Be extra careful today. One of Durango's members will be here soon."

"I wish that wasn't necessary, but I understand why we're taking the precaution."

"You'll cooperate?"

A gentle hand rubbed his back. "I would never risk myself or our child, love." She smiled. "Besides, I'm not fast on my feet these days. I can't escape Muehller if I have to run. I'm happy to have a babysitter."

"Thank you." His wife had a stubborn streak. If she'd set her mind against having a bodyguard, he would have had a hard time convincing her otherwise. He'd have managed, but the process wouldn't have been pleasant and he valued his excellent relationship with Serena. He didn't want to damage that.

The doorbell rang. Ethan checked, then unlocked the door. "Morning, Nate."

"Ethan." Durango's EOD man walked inside the living room and shook Ethan's hand. He turned to Serena and pressed a kiss to her forehead. "How are you, sugar?"

"Growing bigger by the minute. Thanks for asking."

He chuckled. "Still sassy, I see. Where are we going today?"

"Grocery store, then Madison's house this morning, Megan's this afternoon."

"Want help with the cooking?"

"That would be fantastic, but aren't you supposed to be covering the meals at PSI?"

"Josh arranged for Delaney's to deliver breakfast and lunch to the trainees and staff. Stella's in court this morning and sleeping this afternoon, so I volunteered to stay with you until Ethan is free."

More tension left Ethan's muscles. Not only was Nate a crack shot, he was also a professionally trained chef. With his help, Serena would finish her cooking responsibilities faster. "Need some chamomile and mint tea, baby?"

"Actually, I do." She slid Ethan a knowing look. "I'll be in the kitchen, gathering my recipes and making grocery lists."

Nate waited until Serena was out of the room before he said, "What's up?"

"Muehller's close."

"There's been a sighting?"

Ethan shook his head. "Gut."

The other man blew out a breath, his expression grim. "You need a security plan in place at the hospital when Serena goes into labor, especially if we haven't caught up with this clown before then."

His heart almost leaped out of his chest at the thought of his helpless child in the clutches of a ruthless assassin. Then his brain kicked into gear. Ethan shook his head. "Muehller doesn't hurt children." A memory surfaced of the 911 call the assassin had made to report one of his kills because a two-year-old was left in the apartment alone with his deceased mother.

"After the trouble you caused him, I wouldn't put it past him to use your child as leverage."

Ethan considered the wisdom of his friend's words. "Suggestions?"

"Ask Maddox to assign Remy and Lily Doucet as bodyguards for your baby. We'll call Remy when Serena goes into labor. They're only four hours away and can be here sooner if Fortress has a plane free."

He frowned. "Weren't the Doucets here a few weeks ago?"

"They came in with Zane and his girlfriend, Claire."

"Would you trust them with your child?"

"Absolutely," Nate said without hesitation. "We've been on several ops together. I would trust them at my back any time. No one would get through them to your baby. Not even Muehller."

The endorsement and confidence Nate expressed gave Ethan enough insight to know he could trust the Doucets with his family's safety. Having them on hand would free all the members of Durango should he need them to round up Muehller. "I'll talk to Maddox." His lips curved. "Your boss owes me. Might be time to collect on that debt."

Nate gave him a nod of approval. "Good. In the meantime, any instructions concerning Serena?"

"Keep her off her feet as much as possible."

"I'll do my best."

"Something happens, I want to know immediately."

"You got it." He clapped Ethan's shoulder. "I'll take care of her, Ethan."

"Thanks." Ethan went to the kitchen and found Serena sitting at the table, her recipe cards spread out, making a list of groceries to purchase for her day of cooking. "I need to go, baby."

Serena smiled as he approached.

Man, that smile still made his heart skip a beat even after two years together. He suspected he'd feel the same when they reached fifty years of marriage. Ethan knelt beside her and kissed her, lingering over the sweet kisses of the woman of his dreams. "I love you, Serena." Then he leaned down and pressed a kiss to her belly. "Be good, little one."

His answer was a swift thump against his cheek. With a chuckle, he rose to full height. "I'll check in throughout the day. If you need me, call my cell. I'll answer no matter what's happening."

"We'll be fine. Nate will take good care of us." Serena clasped his hand. "I love you, Ethan. Be safe today."

"Always, baby." With that, he made himself leave even though he longed to stay home for the first time since he'd taken the job as Otter Creek's police chief. He had a job to do, though. Part of that job included finding Hans Muehller before he hurt anyone in Otter Creek.

After making sure Nate had his cell number, Ethan climbed into his SUV. As soon as he left the driveway, he called Brent Maddox. He gave a passing thought to the early hour. Maddox would understand. The Fortress CEO wouldn't have hesitated to call in a favor from Ethan if their situations were reversed.

"Yeah, Maddox." No surprise the man sounded wide awake and alert.

"It's Blackhawk. Sorry to call so early."

"No problem. What's wrong?"

Ethan explained the situation with Muehller and Serena's advanced pregnancy.

"What do you need?"

"Remy and Lily Doucet."

"Done. How soon?"

"The baby is due any time."

"Expect them in Otter Creek by noon. They'll report to your office as soon as they arrive."

Relief rolled through Ethan. He trusted Nate to watch over his wife, but he valued his skills with his unit more, especially if Ethan needed to call on Durango. "Thanks, Brent. I owe you one."

"Not by my count. If you need anything else, let me know."

Ethan ended the call as he parked in the lot behind the police station. Once in his office, he sent Nate a text about the arrival of the Doucets. After clearing the pile of papers that had multiplied like rabbits in his absence overnight, Ethan picked up his phone and dialed a number he hadn't used in a long time. Time to call in a favor for information.

CHAPTER EIGHTEEN

"You're not using my cousin as bait!"
Quinn stared at the livid man in the kitchen doorway.
"I didn't ask your opinion or permission."
"No way," Levi insisted. "Heidi isn't expendable."
White hot anger swept over Quinn. Did Levi think so little of him? They'd been friends in high school. Not best buddies as they lived in different towns, but they'd spent enough time together at football games and at the local burger joint that he should know Quinn wouldn't treat Heidi as disposable.
"Quinn," Rio murmured. "Dial it down. Levi loves her."
Quinn cared about Heidi, too. A lot. Couldn't define their relationship. It was…changing. Not sure how yet. Quinn would find out if she gave him a real chance and her cousin let their relationship develop without interfering. One look at Levi convinced Quinn that Heidi's cousin believed the worst of him. Without taking his gaze from Levi, Quinn said, "Heidi, it's your decision. I'll support whatever you choose. However, this is the best option for what you want."

"Don't do it, Heidi," her cousin snapped. "We'll leave, set up somewhere else. Maybe this time, the arsonist won't find us."

"Like the other five times he shouldn't have found us?" Heidi sounded disgusted. "We can't hide forever."

"We'll go to the other side of the country and disappear again. We can start over, choose different jobs."

"I'm finished running. We have Quinn and his unit plus your bodyguards. This is the place to take a stand."

"Come on, Peaches." Another glare directed at Quinn. "This guy's using you to capture the man who contributed to the death of his father. He doesn't care about you." Bitterness rang in Levi's voice. "No one cared but my family. You're nobody to him."

Between one heartbeat and the next, Quinn slammed Levi against the wall, arm across his throat. As if from a distance, he heard Rio snap out, "Sergeant, stand down."

A soft hand touched his arm and the red haze clouding his vision began to fade. Quinn pressed harder against Levi's throat. When the other man's eyes widened, fear glittering in his gaze, Quinn said softly, "First, I would never let anyone hurt Heidi. If I couldn't protect her, that option would be off the table. Second, Heidi expressed her desire to stand and fight. She needs to feel as if she's in control of her life. I'm offering her a chance to fight."

"I just want her safe," Levi croaked.

"On that, we agree. I want her safe, too. Third, packing her off to another location with yet another identity isn't the way to do this. You two will slip up, he'll find you and will strike again. This latest incident is not the end. He's stepping up his game and Heidi is the prize." He leaned in close. "Fourth, you know better than to believe I would risk her. This is not about my ego, Levi."

"I haven't seen you in years. You're supposed to be some hotshot in the military. How do I know you're not just blowing smoke to stroke your own ego or score points with Heidi?"

"Tell him," Rio said. "We need to move past this. We have more important things to do than try to convince Levi over and over that you're not a wannabe."

"My teammates and I are a Delta unit."

"Delta? Is that like a special group or something?" Levi sneered.

Heidi growled.

"We're some of the best trained soldiers on the planet," Quinn answered, his tone wry, wondering if his friend had been living under a rock for the past fifteen years. "The military poured a lot of money into training us. We know what we're doing."

"Whatever. Why can't we escape this arsonist?" Levi asked. "I thought Fortress was supposed to be the best security firm."

"We are. Even the best miss things."

Levi stilled. "Did your firm miss something?"

"We did. A tracker in Charlie's collar." Quinn eased away from Heidi's cousin. "That's on us. The choice of what to do about it belongs to Heidi. She's made her choice. It's our job to make sure she's safe while we set a trap."

Levi was silent a moment. "I want to help."

Satisfaction bloomed in his gut. "I wouldn't expect otherwise from the man who helped raise her." Quinn understood. Levi wouldn't find it easy to step back and let virtual strangers step in and take over her protection. Levi was part of the decision Heidi was making. Though the woman he was coming to admire more and more didn't say the words, she wanted to fight for Levi's freedom and her own. She recognized that her cousin had given up everything to protect her. The price of their love and loyalty had been steep. Now it was Quinn's turn to make sure that sacrifice paid off with help from his teammates.

With Quinn's words, Levi's body sagged against the wall. "Tell me what I can do."

"Come to breakfast with us."

"How does that help?"

"Let's draw out the arsonist. Best way to do that is act as though we don't know he's out there, watching and hunting."

"And then?"

"We go back to the beginning." The prospect of making Heidi remember the kidnapping and subsequent fallout made Quinn want to barf. It would mean revisiting the death of her entire family, then Levi's. And the destruction of Quinn's family. He'd avoided thinking about that time in his life. Why bother to revisit the pain of the past? Nothing would change. His father would still be gone.

Now he had no choice. "The answer to the fires lies with the kidnapping. Nothing else makes sense. Maybe if we combine our knowledge, we can figure out who's behind this." He glanced at Heidi, noted the slow drain of color from her face. "I'm sorry, baby," he murmured, cupping her cheek with his palm. He wished there was another way. He couldn't think of one. "I wouldn't do this if I didn't think it necessary."

She nodded, then looked at her cousin. "We don't have a choice. We deserve a life, Levi. Our past can't hurt us any more than it already has."

"I wouldn't bet on that," Levi muttered. "We've been kicked in the teeth so often over the years, I'm beginning to expect the worst."

"I'd rather know and face the truth than live life scared of my own shadow, expecting a disaster around every corner. We've paid enough, Levi. We deserve to live free of fear."

Heidi's cousin looked as if he wanted to argue the point, but subsided with a nod. Time to come up with a plan.

By the time Levi and his bodyguards were ready, Delaney's was open for business. Since Quinn's SUV was toast, literally, he and Heidi rode with Rio. The others followed in the second SUV.

Business was booming in the restaurant as the staff waited on the early morning crowd. Quinn usually didn't have time to stop here on mornings he had an early training class which, unfortunately, was frequent. He never could figure out why Josh always scheduled his classes before the worms stirred. The rest of his teammates should share in the joy of an early class. Being in Delaney's on a weekday morning was a rare treat for him, one he intended to enjoy.

His hand rested against Heidi's lower back as he guided her into the restaurant. The company for this meal would also be a treat. He glanced at the others in the group. Well, most of the company would be fun. Levi was still unhappy about Heidi's decision and made no bones about expressing his displeasure.

As soon as he opened the door to the restaurant, heads all around the room turned their direction. Heidi slowed so he gently nudged her forward. Yep, he'd forgotten to warn her about small town life. Everyone in Otter Creek would be interested in them. There was a good side to the town's nosiness. They also noticed when strangers were in their midst. The downside was everybody knew your business almost as well as you did.

Otter Creek residents didn't understand why Durango didn't talk about their missions out of the country. They didn't realize the less they knew, the better for their safety.

Quinn decided to be proactive when conversation in the place dropped to nothing. "Morning, everybody." He waited for the greetings of patrons and Delaney staff members to peter out before continuing with his introduction. "This is Heidi Thompson, our newest employee at PSI. Behind her is her cousin, Levi, and a couple of his friends."

"Welcome to Delaney's," a blond waitress said. She winked at Quinn. "Great to see you again, Quinn. Been a long time since I've seen your cute face." When the buzz of conversation around the room picked up, she said to Quinn and the others, "This way, folks." As she led them to two side-by-side tables, she murmured to Quinn, "Call me. I've missed you."

His cheeks heated. Not going to happen. He'd made the mistake of giving in to Daisy McClintock's persistence and taken her out on two dates. A movie one night, a high school football game another. Twice was enough for Quinn to realize Daisy wasn't a good match for him. She needed more attention than he could give her. He'd had to postpone one of their dates because he'd been sent with his unit on a mission. She'd let him know how displeased she was to be pushed aside for work and then not been given a full explanation. That whole side of his life was shrouded in secrecy and would never change. Could Heidi handle the secrets? Considering the strength she'd already exhibited, the answer to that question was a resounding yes.

Quinn shook his head at the waitress smiling into his eyes with a hopeful expression. "Thanks for the offer, Daisy, but I'm off the market."

Her eyes widened. "Off the market? Since when?"

"It's recent." He pulled out Heidi's chair for her and sat beside her.

Daisy's smile became forced. She handed out the menus and took drink orders without looking at Quinn again, and hurried off to get the drinks.

"Should we ask for a different waitress?" Heidi asked. "I'm a little worried about the food she might deliver."

Quinn turned, relieved to see humor dancing in her eyes. "Daisy takes pride in her work. She won't let hurt feelings hamper the service." At least, he hoped she wouldn't.

"I don't know, man," Dane said. "She was unhappy. Former girlfriend?"

He shook his head. "Just a couple of dates. Daisy wanted more than I could offer."

"Shew. Hate to see how she'd react if you had been serious about her."

When the others were engaged in conversation, Heidi leaned closer. "Why did you tell Daisy you were off the market?"

"Because it's the truth."

Heidi frowned at him. "Then why did you kiss me?" she whispered, her eyes glittering.

Wow. Daisy wasn't the only one with a temper. "You're the reason I'm off the market, baby."

Daisy returned at that moment with her coffee pot in hand, then took breakfast orders. Once she left, Quinn said, "You want to ask me anything, Heidi?"

"You're serious? You took yourself out of the dating pool because of me."

"Problem?"

"No! I'm having a hard time processing it. We haven't even been on a date."

"Give me time. I'll remedy that. If you let me."

"What if we date and a relationship doesn't work out? We work together, Quinn. I don't want to sabotage my job at PSI and I don't want to make you uncomfortable."

"We're adults. We'll handle it. We need you in the S & R program. Besides, I'm not your direct boss. If this doesn't work, we'll figure out a working rhythm."

"Quinn, you said you wanted to talk about the past," Levi said. He glanced around the noisy restaurant, doubt on his face. "You want to do that in here? Might be hard to carry on a conversation in this place."

"I didn't realize the restaurant would be so busy this morning. We'll wait until we return to Heidi's place. We don't need an audience hearing our conversation." Sharing the information with future friends was up to Heidi. Quinn didn't want her past shared on the grapevine unless she disclosed the information herself.

Once breakfast was served, they demolished the food in short order. As always, the meal was perfect. Rio made them promise to stop at Darcy's deli the next morning. "You'll love the food. She's amazing in the kitchen, and out of it, too."

"Not biased are you, Rio?" Angel teased.

"No, ma'am. Just honest."

"And head-over-heels in love with that beautiful woman."

Quinn and the rest burst into laughter at Rio's flushed face. Seeing his friend so happy pleased Quinn. The medic deserved that classy pianist. She was a very special lady with a heart of gold and the courage of a warrior.

When they returned to Heidi's, a black SUV was parked in the driveway with a police cruiser idling behind it. As they unloaded from the vehicles, Josh climbed from his cruiser.

Their unit leader looked tired. Too many nights with little to no sleep. "Josh, why are you here?" Quinn asked.

"Babysitting your new ride. Bear and a buddy brought it to Otter Creek. We wanted to make sure no one had a chance to monkey with this one." A smile curved Josh's lips. "Bear said the next time you let one of his vehicles get blown up, he'll charge you double and give you the most trouble-prone vehicle he can find."

Quinn winced. "It wasn't my fault."

Dane snickered. "I don't think Bear agrees with you."

"You're moving better than I expected today, Heidi," Josh said. "How's the head?"

"Headache's gone."

A nod, then he shifted his attention to Quinn. "What's the plan for today?"

"Asking questions." He introduced Levi to Josh and explained about the tracker in Charlie's collar.

Josh whistled. "Maddox won't be happy about that. Somebody dropped the ball. Another reason I stopped is to tell you Remy and Lily Doucet will be here by noon. Ethan called in a favor with Maddox."

"Why are the Doucets coming?" Angel's voice was sharp. "I know we screwed up before, but we won't make the same mistake, and Levi promised to follow instructions."

Josh's eyebrows rose. "This is not about you, Martinez, although you should know if you mess up again, you'll be coming to PSI as trainees. I guarantee you won't make a mistake like that again by the time we're through with you. The Doucets will be protecting my niece or nephew. Ethan wants Durango ready to move on Muehller at a moment's notice without leaving Serena and the baby vulnerable."

"Sorry," she murmured. "Dane and I got an earful from Nate and Maddox. Guess I'm touchy."

"You're lucky nothing happened to your principal." A sharp look at Levi. "The next time he doesn't cooperate, tackle him."

"Hey!" Levi scowled.

"Better than being dead."

CHAPTER NINETEEN

Serena laughed, holding the sides of her stomach. "Nate, you're killing me. My bladder is the size of a thimble these days."

Durango's EOD man tossed her a wicked grin, his eyes sparkling with amusement. "Come on now, sugar. You know I can't help it. I have to get my revenge on Josh while he's not around. My unit leader knows too much about me for me to do this while he's around. He might spill embarrassing tales to my beautiful wife. I'd just as soon avoid that if I could."

"You think I'll be able to hide my secret knowledge from my brother? Ethan says my facial expressions give away every thought in my head. I couldn't lie to my parents, even by omission. They always knew something was wrong. Madison and Megan accused me many times of tattling on them as we were growing up. I never said a word, not that they believed me." She finished chopping the last of the celery and slid the cutting board across the counter to Nate, narrowing her eyes. "Did Josh really wear a burka or did you make that up?"

"Every word is true. Your brother doesn't make a pretty woman."

She grinned. "I'm not surprised. He wasn't a very cooperative model when we tried dressing him in Mom's wedding gown when we were four. He was an uncooperative nine-year-old who was mortified to wear a dress."

Nate burst into laughter. "I'd have given anything to see that."

"Did Josh's ruse work? He's tall for a man, much less a woman."

"Oh, it worked. He stayed seated so no one knew how tall he was and hid his face to disguise the beard shadow. Josh covered the kid with a blanket and he played possum for us."

Incredible. She didn't know many children who would have helped in an escape attempt. "I can't believe the boy cooperated."

"We told him we were playing a quiet game. Whoever stayed quiet the longest got a treat."

"Must have been a good treat. What was it?"

"Skittles. The kid was crazy about the candy. There was no way Josh could be quiet all the way back to the landing zone." Nate shrugged. "The kid was bound to win the game."

Thinking of all the things that could have gone wrong made Serena's stomach tighten into a hard ball. "And if the boy didn't cooperate long enough?"

"We had contingency plans."

She could imagine. Her brother and his unit would have done anything to protect that boy, even sacrifice themselves for his safety. Warmth spread in her chest. Her amazing husband would have done the same in his years as an Army Ranger. Serena thought about his shoulder scar and realized he'd already taken a bullet to protect a child when he was with the Las Vegas police.

Her gaze dropped to her stomach and she prayed Ethan wouldn't have to sacrifice himself to save her or their baby. "Thanks for keeping an eye on me, Nate."

"Any time, sugar. You know that. Working with you is never a hardship. Who else can I exchange recipes with?"

She couldn't imagine him wanting any of the home cooked meals she prepared for Home Runs. Nate was doing a favor for Josh and Ethan. Watching over her meant others scrambled to cover his responsibilities at PSI. "I still wish it wasn't necessary. I hate interfering with everybody's schedule."

"Only for a short time, Serena. In fact, we have a couple from Fortress arriving in a few hours to watch over your baby."

"Why? I thought Durango was switching off the babysitting duties."

"Maddox owes Ethan a few favors. Your husband is collecting one so we're free to help him corral Muehller."

Serena was relieved that her husband would have the whole team as backup this time. In the last confrontation with Muehller, Ethan had faced off with the assassin with Rod and a few green cops. Enough doom and gloom talk. Time for a change of subject. "Stella looks terrific."

Nate dumped the celery into the dutch oven along with the rest of the ingredients for beef stew and set it on the burner to simmer while he and Serena began preparing the next meal. "Makes two of us who think that. I'm crazy about that woman. She's the love of my life, Serena. I don't know what I would do without her."

Serena understood. She loved Ethan with every beat of her heart, with every breath she took. Two years of marriage and she was more in love with her husband than on the day she married him. Soon, they would add a baby to their family. She couldn't wait to hold her son or daughter.

She rubbed her aching lower back, then began chopping onions for the next dish.

"Back hurting?" Nate was watching her.

Serena shifted her weight. "Been aching for several hours. I'm fine, Nate. Stop worrying."

"That's not going to happen," he muttered. "Don't go into labor on me, all right? I'm inexperienced at impending fatherhood."

"I'll do my best," she said, her tone dry. If she had any control over labor, Baby Blackhawk would already be in her arms. "Do you and Stella want kids?"

"Eventually." He browned hamburger for chili. "We want a couple years to ourselves first. When she's ready, Stella's going to be a great mother."

"Is she happy working as a detective in a small town?"

"Otter Creek isn't small any more. Ten thousand people and growing each day." He smiled. "She loves small town policing. It's different from being a marshal. She protects friends and neighbors instead of setting up safe houses and alternate identities for witnesses or informants. Stella says this is the best job she's had and she loves her boss. Ethan is tough, fair, and one hundred percent behind his people."

Three hours later, she and Nate stored meals in the freezer except for the night's dinner which was in the refrigerator waiting for Nick to heat in the microwave. Serena's sister Madison was under strict instructions from her husband and the fire department not to touch the oven or microwave. Bad things happened when Maddie cooked. Serena didn't understand how a woman who created beautiful knitted masterpieces from intricate instructions consistently failed at reading recipe directions.

Nate carried Serena's equipment and food for Megan's meals to his SUV, then returned for her. When he opened the door, his expression was grim. "Ready?"

"What's wrong?" Had he heard from Ethan?

"Stay on my left side, sugar. Once we're outside, move as fast as you can."

"Nate, you're scaring me."

He cupped her cheek, holding her gaze. "I'll take care of you and your baby."

Serena straightened. No one was going to hurt her baby, including an international assassin with a thirst for vengeance. "Let's go."

Respect filled Nate's gaze. "Good girl," he murmured, turning toward the door. "Wait until I tell you it's clear." The operative stepped out on Madison's porch and scanned the neighborhood. His attention focused on the Endicott's home across the street. A moment later, Nate motioned for Serena to join him. "As fast as you can," he said, holding Serena's arm.

Good thing, too. Ten feet from the car, Serena stumbled and would have gone down had Nate not been holding her arm.

"Almost there," he said. "My SUV is reinforced. You'll be safe."

"Do you see anyone?"

"Not at the moment."

"But you did see someone suspicious earlier."

"Too far away for an ID."

She wrapped her coat and arms around the bulging belly. Not much protection against a sniper's bullet.

When they reached the SUV, Nate lifted Serena and placed her inside before rounding the hood and sliding behind the wheel. He cranked the engine. "Seatbelt."

Serena yanked the belt over her shoulder and belly as a wave of pain tightened her stomach muscles. Her gasp had him whipping his head her direction.

"Serena?"

"Contraction. I'm fine, Nate. Go."

"Contraction? You're in labor?" His voice rose.

She frowned. "I only had one contraction. I'll let you know if I have more."

"Yeah, you do that." He set the vehicle in motion. He drove onto the street. A crack sounded and the driver's side window became a spiderweb of cracks.

"Get down as far as possible, but don't undo the seatbelt," he snapped as he floored the gas pedal. The SUV raced down the street away from the threat. Nate activated his Bluetooth and called Ethan.

Seconds later, Ethan's voice came through the speakers. "Blackhawk."

"It's Nate. Serena's not hurt, but someone shot at my SUV."

Another pain hit Serena. A soft moan escaped.

"Baby, what's wrong?" Ethan asked.

"This is really bad timing, but I might be in labor."

"Nate, head for the hospital," Ethan ordered. "I'll meet you there."

"We're seven minutes out."

"Copy that. Serena, I'll have Dr. Anderson meet us at the hospital."

"I love you, Ethan."

His deep chuckle filled the interior of the vehicle. "I hope you say that in a few hours."

CHAPTER TWENTY

Heidi wrapped her hands around a mug of coffee, grateful for the warmth seeping into her cold hands. The coldness was due to the discussion which still lay ahead. She despised talking about her past. Sharing made her feel as though she were pulling the curtain back on her life and allowing anyone to see the movie of her life. A horror film instead of a sappy love story. So many lives touched by her father's selfishness.

She lifted her gaze to see Quinn watching her, understanding in his eyes. This discussion wouldn't be easy for him, either. Revisiting the worst time of your life? Not for the faint of heart. Yet more proof Quinn Gallagher was a hero in every sense of the word. He didn't shrink from the hard things. Quinn had experienced hardship and heartbreak in the years since she left Black River.

Heidi knew the basics of what Quinn had survived in their hometown. She'd searched for his name on the Internet over the years. The time when he'd been on active duty, there was no news in their hometown newspaper. Now that she knew about his work, Heidi wasn't surprised

Retribution

about the silence. Quinn kept a low profile even after he separated from the military.

"Whenever you're ready, babe," he murmured. "Take your time."

Might as well get this discussion behind her. Refusing to talk about the past hadn't made the memories easier to live with. Grabbing the tattered remnants of her courage, she said, "My sister and I were sleeping the night we were taken. We shared a room, much to my ten-year-old dismay. I didn't think I should be made to share a room with a baby of eight." She stopped as grief threatened to overwhelm her. Twenty years and the wound was jagged and fresh. Would she ever lose the pain over Moira's death?

Quinn covered her hand with his. The ugly story couldn't be told by anyone else. Drawing strength from the contact, she said, "Moira had a bad cold. We must have been sleeping for a few hours before we were taken from our beds."

"You don't remember being snatched and hauled outside?" Dane asked, skepticism evident.

"According to the police reports, Dad used chloroform on us so we wouldn't wake our sister or mother. The crime scene techs found two cloths reeking of chloroform on the floor of our bedroom. Dad and his partner carried us into the woods. A trail led to the subdivision with the house where we were held."

"Why didn't they drive to the hideout?" Angel asked. "Tough to carry dead weight."

"We lived in a small town," Quinn said. "Would have been easy for someone to recognize the car. Gossip was a local pastime. Secrets were impossible to keep, especially when someone was always awake." A small smile curved his lips. "I never got away with anything."

"When did you wake up, Heidi?" Dane asked.

"Moira and I were already inside the house when the chloroform wore off. We didn't know where we were."

"How did your father hide his identity?"

"He didn't. His partner stayed with us. Dad never returned to the house." Her lips curled. "He had a role to play, after all. The grieving father, desperate to save his children."

"Did his partner say anything to you?" Quinn asked. "Give any hints to his identity?"

"He whispered so we never heard his voice. If we had, we might have recognized him." She shivered. "It was creepy." Heidi swallowed hard. "Moira was so scared. I tried to comfort her, but I was as frightened as she was." Two terrified children shoring up each other. Impossible to do when neither understood what was happening or why.

"You're sure the other kidnapper was a man?"

"Positive. He had big, strong hands with dark hair on his arm."

"Caucasian?"

She nodded.

"Any distinguishing marks or scars?"

A hesitation, then, "A tattoo."

"What kind?"

Here came the disbelief. Why should they believe her when the police had been skeptical? "I don't know. I've blocked most of the details from my mind. I tried to picture the tattoo in my mind, but it's still a blur."

He squeezed her hand. "It's okay, baby. Did you see this man's face?"

Cold sweat formed on the back of her neck.

"That's enough, Quinn," Levi snapped. "Back off. Can't you see she's been traumatized enough?"

Quinn ignored her cousin. "Heidi?" His gaze held confidence that she'd handle the questions, no matter how tough. She prayed he was right.

"I don't know."

"Why do you say that?" Angel prompted.

"I still have nightmares about being held captive. In the dreams, I see a man's face, but it's shrouded in fog so I can't distinguish any features." She sighed. "Then again, I could be dreaming with no basis in reality, hoping to find closure for myself."

"Your father never identified his partner?" Quinn asked.

"I think Dad was afraid to identify him."

"Is it possible the partner is trying to kill you?" Dane asked.

"He's the only one I know of who might want me dead."

"What about your mother and sister?" Angel leaned her folded arms on the table. "Would they know who this man is? Can we ask them what they know?"

"They're dead, too."

Angel paled. "I'm so sorry. What happened?"

"House fire."

"Another arson?" This from Dane.

Rio freshened Heidi's coffee in silence. He squeezed her shoulder before starting a fresh pot of coffee.

"They died one week after my younger sister and I were abducted."

"Ironic," he muttered.

"Tragic," Quinn said with a pointed look at the younger Fortress operative. "Heidi, who investigated the kidnapping and fire?"

"Detective Ivan Bennett. Why?"

"Might be worth talking to him about what's been happening to you." He paused. "Unless you've touched base with him over the years."

"Not since I turned eighteen. Levi went with me to request a copy of the police report. My copy burned in one of the house fires. I never went back for another."

"Bennett might be willing to talk to us. Can't hurt to try."

Levi snorted. "If he's still alive. He was nearing retirement fifteen years ago."

"Won't take long to find out," Quinn said. "If he's dead, someone else will remember."

"We shouldn't leave town right now." Heidi sipped her coffee.

"Why not?" Her cousin scowled. "It's the safest thing for you to do. If the second kidnapper is trying to kill you, he won't expect you to return to Black River."

"She's right." Rio returned to the table and sat on the other side of Heidi. "The Otter Creek police might need her S & R skills in the next few days."

"Heidi's not putting her life in danger on the off chance that the cops might need her," Levi insisted.

"It's more than a chance," Heidi said. "I promised the police chief I would be available to track an escaped prisoner heading this direction. He might already be here for all I know. The bombing has kept me out of the loop."

"You can't track someone that dangerous."

If he only knew how dangerous Muehller was, Levi wouldn't allow her to leave the house. "Not your decision, Levi. This guy is targeting the chief's pregnant wife. Serena Blackhawk deserves to have her baby in peace and safety."

"If Heidi searches for Muehller, she won't be alone." Quinn laced his fingers through Heidi's. "My team and I will be with her. Nothing will happen to her on our watch."

"You can't guarantee that."

"He'd have to go through me to reach Heidi and that won't happen." Quinn turned to her. "Sweetheart, I don't want to make this harder than necessary. Finish the story. I know you were held two days before you escaped."

He was right. Time to finish the story and find out if someone else knew a fact that might help unravel the arsonist's identity. "Moira and I were kept in a room with the door locked."

"Windows?" Rio prompted.

"Boarded up. The only reason we knew it was daylight was the sunlight seeping through a crack in the wood. We had enough light to see each other."

"What about electricity? Were you able to turn on a light?"

She nodded. "Leaks in the roof left stains on one wall. It was damp and musty, smelled of mold and mildew. Moira was already sick. I think the conditions in that house made her worse. Her fever spiked and she cried constantly for Mom." Tears welled and spilled down Heidi's cheeks as the memory of her baby sister's misery swamped her. "The second kidnapper told her to shut up, that Moira was driving him insane." Her voice broke on that last word. "When she still cried, he used a pillow to muffle the sound. He suffocated her."

"How did you escape?" Quinn asked.

"The man panicked when he realized Moira was dead. He raced from the room to the phone and called someone to help him get rid of the body. In his panic, he forgot to lock me in. I slipped from the house. As soon as I was outside, I ran as fast as I could to find help for Moira. I hoped that the man was wrong and I could save her, but Moira was gone."

"How horrible," Angel murmured. "I'm sorry you went through that. How soon did the police realize your father was behind the kidnapping?"

"The day of my sister's funeral. I think they'd been piecing everything together." She wiped the tears from her face. "My father couldn't keep his story straight. Once he realized his partner killed Moira, everything fell apart. Dad confessed to everything."

"Why did he set this plan in motion?" Quinn pressed his jeans-clad thigh against hers. "What was his motive?"

"Money. Unknown to us, Dad was having an affair. He needed money to start a new life with this other woman in

Mexico. The lady wanted to live in Acapulco." Her lips curled.

"Were you aware of your father's activities?"

"He fooled all of us."

"Did you learn the woman's name?" Angel asked, a scowl on her face.

She shook her head.

"Your turn, Quinn," Rio said. "What happened from your side?"

"The night Heidi and Moira disappeared, my father received a phone call from his business partner, begging him for money to save his daughters. Dad urged Henderson to go to the police, told him kidnappings never ended well without the help of law enforcement, but he wouldn't hear of it. He had a note from the kidnappers threatening to kill the girls if he didn't come up with five million dollars in cash within 48 hours. The note said they were watching Henderson and would know if he contacted the police."

"Why didn't your father go to the cops?" Dane asked.

"You don't understand. Our parents were best friends. Dad never suspected Henderson was behind the ransom demand."

"Did your father get the money?"

"Oh, yeah."

"Where did he find that much cash?"

"The company coffers. Dad owned a majority stake in the company. He had to sign all financial transactions. G & H Industries was doing well at the time. That amount of money cleaned out the bank account and they still didn't have enough. So thinking about the sweet little girls who were in danger, Dad borrowed against our house. He also tapped his and Mom's personal account. To save Heidi and Moira, he drained every penny we had."

"Oh, Quinn." Heidi squeezed his hand. "You must have hated us. We ruined your life."

He gathered her into his arms despite her cousin's frown. "No, baby. Never you or the rest of your family. You were as much victims of the scheme as we were."

"Finish the story," Rio said.

"There isn't much more to tell. Dad believed Henderson was telling the truth until the police arrested him. Dad tried to keep the company afloat, but there wasn't enough cash to pay the bills and the bank refused to extend credit to G & H or to Dad personally. Within a few weeks, the company was bankrupt and so were we. My father took his own life. G & H employed half the people in Black River. When the company went under, most of them either went bankrupt or moved. It devastated the town. My father couldn't live with the guilt that he'd ruined so many people's lives with a desire to save children that weren't his own."

"But it was never his fault," Heidi protested. "Why didn't he lay the blame where it belonged, at my father's feet?"

Quinn hugged her a little tighter. "Dad had a lot of pride."

No wonder Quinn had been so angry when she first admitted her identity. What she found more amazing was that he saw past her name to the woman she had grown into.

"What about the five million dollars?" Dane asked. "Did the police recover the money?"

He shook his head. "They assumed the partner disappeared with the cash."

Angel looked at Heidi a moment, then shifted her attention to Quinn. "Why now?"

"What do you mean?" he asked.

"If the second kidnapper is behind Heidi's problems, why did he wait this long?"

"He didn't," Levi pointed out. "This creep has tried to burn us alive several times over the last fifteen years."

"Heidi has been attacked twice in as many days. There was a five year gap between when he killed her family and when he went after yours. From then on, the fires were about once a year. Why the sudden escalation now? He went from toying with you to real attempts to kill you. What changed?"

Heidi's eyes widened. Good question. What had changed?

CHAPTER TWENTY-ONE

Quinn glanced away from the road to Heidi for a few seconds. She'd been quiet since they climbed into his SUV to locate a map and explore Dunlap County. Too quiet. The discussion at her dining table had been difficult. No one wanted to visit the past, especially when that past was filled with so much heartache. Hadn't been a pleasant time of reminiscing for him, either.

No matter what it took, he'd unmask her arsonist. In the meantime, he would support and care for her. The truth was he did care. More than made logical sense and more than he wanted at this early stage of their dating relationship. So what did that mean? He didn't know, but he also couldn't wait to find out. "Talk to me, Heidi."

"We dug into the past and bared our souls, for all the good it did. No earth-shaking revelations, no spotlight on the killer. We dragged ourselves through the muck and mud for nothing."

"I'm not so sure about that. We can explore the connection to Detective Bennett now that we have his name."

"If he's willing to talk to us. Cops are a close-mouthed lot."

"With the exception of the kidnapping, you've been a suspect. I can't see why Bennett or his partner wouldn't share information. The money is still missing and the second kidnapper has yet to be identified. If Bennett or his partner would rather talk to another law enforcement officer, I'll have Nick contact him. If that fails, I'll turn the tech geeks at Fortress loose with their mad hacking skills, see if they get anywhere. If the information is in an electronic file, the techs will find it."

"What about the fires? A cop will suspect I'm behind the blazes. Bennett might wonder if I'm mentally stable. I'll be lucky if he doesn't take me in for a psych evaluation."

"There's no proof you started the fires. Besides, they can't be traced to you because you weren't using your birth name. The only fires Bennett knows about are the ones that killed the rest of your family. Whoever has this cold case will be interested in any information that could solve this case. Small town cop shops take murder personally, and when the victim is a child, everyone wants justice."

He drove to the Otter Creek town square and parked in front of Del's bookstore. Quinn opened the passenger door for Heidi, then escorted her inside the store.

Heidi gawked at the large stock of books Del kept on hand. "This is amazing!"

"Thank you." Del came around the counter, a broad smile on her face. "Welcome to Otter Creek Books, Heidi. I'm glad you stopped in." She gave Quinn a quick hug. "What can I help you find?"

Quinn turned to Heidi. "Do you want to look around while I talk to Del?"

She smiled. "I'd love to."

"Come to the coffee bar when you're finished."

Del glanced at her part-time sales assistant. "Annie, show Heidi around the store. I'll watch the front desk."

The red-haired grandmother of four rambunctious grandsons led Heidi to the second floor to start the tour, chattering as though Heidi were a long-lost friend. Typical Annie. She never met a stranger, which was a real boon for Del's business. Her assistant knew everybody in town. If you were a reader, she kept up with your reading habits, ready with a suggestion for the next book. Quinn smiled. That's how he'd ended up with so many books in his possession. Yeah, he loved to read before going to bed, but his towering TBR stack was due more to his reluctance to disappoint Annie than his desire for yet another book. By the time Annie brought Heidi back to the cash register, his girlfriend's arms would be full of books.

"How are you?" Del nudged Quinn toward the coffee bar. "Josh told me what happened yesterday."

"I'm fine."

One eyebrow went up.

He rolled his eyes. "I'm a little sore, but seriously, I'm okay."

"Heidi?"

"The same." The fact that she had recovered as well as she had spoke volumes about her fitness and the angle of impact with the wall and ground.

"She's lucky."

The sound of Heidi's laughter drifted down the stairs, drawing his attention to the second floor. "I know," he admitted, voice soft. He tried not to think about the "what-ifs." The worst hadn't happened. Heidi was still here and, by some miracle, had agreed to date him.

"Do you know who the mastermind was behind the bomb?"

"Not yet. My ride is in pieces and charred. Nate said the bomb was a simple design. I doubt Otter Creek's finest will find a signature left behind by a professional bomber. Fortress is looking into it as well."

Del slid him a mug of coffee across the counter. "Was the bomb aimed at you in retaliation for a mission?"

Quinn sipped the hot liquid, taking his time before replying. Wouldn't be fair to blow off her concern. She had a valid reason to worry. Del cared about each member of Durango. But her focus was on her husband's safety. "It's possible. Zane hasn't found anything to indicate that Durango is a target for revenge."

"If there had been rumors or threats against Josh or the rest of you, would you tell me?"

"I wouldn't have to, sweetheart." He squeezed her hand. "The minute a threat is suspected, our women will know. We don't take your safety lightly."

Her eyes closed a moment. When she opened them again, Del's gaze was filled with remorse. "I'm sorry. I know better. Josh has never held anything back from me. Wouldn't be like him to start now."

"The bomb shook you up, didn't it?"

Her eyes filled.

Oh, man. This was bad. Del never cried, at least not that he knew. Josh's wife was as tough as they came, a fitting companion for Durango's leader. To deal with Durango's missions, all the women had to be strong.

Every member of Durango would put their lives on the line to protect teammates or their spouses. Del had been around them long enough to know that. So where was this coming from?

"The target could have been Josh or the others." Del blotted her eyes with a napkin. "If you hadn't realized there was a bomb, we would have lost you and Heidi. I don't want to lose either of you. I like Heidi."

"Durango is well trained and experienced. We spent more than our fair share of time in war zones with targets on our backs. I recognized the sound."

"I wouldn't have known. Neither would the other women."

All these months, Del had been a rock. What changed? "Have you talked to Josh about this?"

She shook her head.

"You should. Might make you feel better." Quinn made a mental note to contact Josh and tell him about this conversation.

"I will. I promise. Now, tell me about you and Heidi."

He froze. "What about us?"

Del leaned across the counter until her face was inches from his. "Come on, Quinn. Spill."

"She's been here two days."

"And?"

Knowing how Otter Creek's grapevine worked, he rolled his eyes and capitulated. "We're dating."

Her mouth gaped. "After only two days? I never realized you were such a fast mover."

Irritation welled in Quinn. So he'd been a serial dater since arriving in Otter Creek. That didn't mean he moved through women like a shark went through a school of fish. Quinn wanted a permanent relationship. He was finished with dating for the sake of dating. His teammates were all either married or soon to be married. Though he acted like a happy guy who didn't worry about anything, he wanted a relationship like each of his friends had.

Maybe his handling of previous dates was wrong, but Quinn hadn't seen the point in continuing to date women who couldn't handle the demands of his life. Daisy was a case in point. He'd talked himself into giving her a chance when he'd suspected before the first date that a relationship wouldn't work between them. "I'm not a fast mover. Heidi and I are from the same hometown."

"Why didn't you mention that the other night?"

"I didn't recognize her. I hadn't seen her since she was ten. Besides, she was under orders from Maddox not to tell us her birth name unless it became necessary."

She dropped her voice to a low murmur. "Why couldn't she tell you the truth?"

"She's had trouble over the years. We think the trouble trailed her to Otter Creek."

Del's eyes widened. "The bombing?"

"And the fire."

"Do you know who it is?"

"Not yet. We will." He wouldn't rest until the culprit was caught.

She leaned closer, her expression fierce. "Make him sorry he tried to hurt Heidi."

Amusement made him smile. "Count on it."

"Why did you and Heidi stop by? To visit the store or something else?"

"We need a map of the area. Heidi and I are off today and she wants a feel for the area in case she's called out on an S & R mission."

"I have just what she needs. Stay here and enjoy your coffee." She hurried around the counter and down one of the aisles.

As she disappeared around a corner, the bell over the front door rang. Quinn turned in his seat and smiled. "Remy, Lily, welcome back to Otter Creek."

The Doucets crossed the floor. "We thought we'd say hello to Del before we reported to Blackhawk for baby duty," Remy said.

"She's finding a map for my girlfriend." He bussed Lily's forehead with a light kiss. "How are you? This big old Cajun treating you right?"

Lily's blue eyes twinkled. "He treats me like a princess. So does his family," she said, sounding bemused.

He understood her confusion. Lily was as tough and skilled as any Fortress operative he'd worked with and

Retribution

she'd practically raised herself in various foster homes and on the streets of Nashville. She was used to fending for herself. Being treated like royalty was foreign to her. "Good job, Remy."

Quick footsteps announced Del's return. She gasped. "Remy, Lily." She hugged each of them. "So good to see you again. Josh told me you might be coming."

"We're glad to help out," Lily said. "We wanted to stop in a minute before we reported to Blackhawk. How is Josh?"

Her face lit. "He's great. Sleeping right now. He was on duty last night. I know he'll want to see you."

"How about dinner tonight?" Quinn suggested. "If Remy and Lily are free."

Remy shrugged. "Depends on the baby."

"I'll have Josh call you," Del said. "You'd better go. Ethan is expecting you." After they left the store, she handed Quinn two maps. "One focuses on Dunlap County. The other is a broader view of Dunlap and the surrounding counties, including part of the Smokies. Many hikers visit the forest each year, some experienced, some not. Heidi will be called out on a search at some point. It's inevitable."

"Perfect. Thanks."

Minutes later, he and Heidi were on the street, maps in hand. "Where to first?" he asked.

"I'd love to walk around town. I need a sense of the layout. Walking will help me work out the soreness."

As they walked, Quinn introduced Heidi to people who stopped him to chat about the explosion. Most of them thought the loss of his SUV was from a mechanical malfunction. Suited him. He didn't want his friends and neighbors afraid to be around him or Heidi.

After a quick visit with Darcy in That's A Wrap, they returned to his SUV. "Mallory Road winds around the whole county. You'll get a good feel for the countryside."

"Perfect."

As they passed different landmarks, Quinn shared the history he'd picked up since moving to Otter Creek.

He had turned back toward town when his Bluetooth signaled an incoming call. He glanced at the readout. Ethan. "What do you need, Ethan?"

"Heidi."

Quinn's hands tightened around the steering wheel. "Muehller?"

"Maybe. Someone shot at Serena and Nate."

Not what he wanted to hear. "They okay?"

The police chief was silent a moment.

"Ethan?" His gut tightened into a knot at the thought of the chief's sweet wife injured from a sniper's bullet. He'd seen up close the damage Alex's bullets could do.

"Neither of them were injured by the bullet. Serena might be in labor, though."

Ah. That explained the odd sound in the voice of the father-to-be. "Where was the attack?"

"Outside Madison's house."

Quinn whistled. Nick would be livid. The three sisters were identical. The only distinction between them was Madison's limp and facial scar. If Madison faced the right direction and stood still, the shooter could have mistaken her for Serena. His lips curved. As long as they didn't see Madison's flat stomach. "I assume Madison and Megan know to be cautious."

"They do. I need Heidi and Charlie at the scene to see if they can track the shooter."

Heidi straightened. "Chief Blackhawk, Charlie needs a scent. Has the prison sent Muehller's clothes yet?"

"I received them this morning. Nick will meet you at his house with one of the plastic bags."

"What about Deke and Ace?"

"Deke is out of town until tonight. He flew to Charlotte to testify in a trial. It's a leftover from his job as a marshal.

Look, Heidi, I know you were injured yesterday. If you're not up to this, say so. I'd rather have you rested and ready when we're positive Muehller is involved. This might be someone after Nick. The shooter could have mistaken Serena for Madison."

Heidi frowned. "How?"

"My wife and her sisters are identical triplets. I expect the truth from my people so be straight with me. Are you up to the task today?"

"We need to pick up Charlie. Tell Detective Santana to expect us in thirty minutes."

"I'll pass along your message when I give him the clothes. Thanks, Heidi."

"Don't thank me yet. We may not find what you hope."

"I want confirmation that Muehller is behind this attempt on Serena. We'll go from there. Quinn?"

"Sir?"

"Keep a close eye on your girlfriend. Muehller won't think twice about sacrificing an innocent to achieve his goal. I don't want Heidi to pay the price for helping me."

Quinn planned to watch over his girlfriend. He'd protect Heidi from Muehller and her own personal enemy.

CHAPTER TWENTY-TWO

As soon as Quinn stopped the vehicle, Heidi exited the SUV and opened the back door for Charlie. She clipped his lead to the red harness. "Let's go to work, Charlie." The Lab yipped and wagged his tail.

The three of them crossed the street and approached one of the patrolmen steering onlookers away from the actual crime scene. The young policeman held up his hand and said, "You can't bring your dog through here, ma'am."

"It's okay, Martin," Nick Santana called. "The chief sent them."

Officer Martin's face reddened. "Sorry, ma'am."

"No problem, Officer Martin. I'm Heidi Thompson." She laid her hand on her black Lab's head. "Would you like to meet Charlie?" She suspected this wouldn't be the only time she and Charlie encountered resistance. Might as well make friends when they could.

Martin brightened. "Sure." He crouched down and extended his fist for Charlie to sniff. "We always had dogs when I was a kid. Loads of fun."

"They keep life interesting. Charlie, greet."

The Lab sat and raised his paw for Martin to shake, much to the policeman's delight.

"Charlie is part of PSI's S & R program," Heidi explained. "We'll be training other dogs and their partners to be part of search teams."

"Wow. That's great." He shook Charlie's paw. "Good boy, Charlie." Martin raised the crime scene tape. "Go on through, ma'am. See you later, Charlie."

She and Quinn ducked under the yellow tape and crossed the yard. They dodged crime scene techs searching the area with flashlights.

"Thanks for coming." Nick dug into his crime scene kit and pulled out a sealed plastic bag containing a white shirt. He handed the bag to Heidi. "This arrived special delivery this morning. We haven't opened it. There's a second bag in Ethan's office for Deke and Ace."

Quinn frowned. "Ethan said the shot was fired at your place."

"I talked to Nate. The shot was fired from the corner of this house, aimed across the street to mine."

"No one was hurt?"

He shook his head. "I found the bullet in the street. Nate was driving away from the house when the shot was fired. Bullet hit the driver's side window."

"I don't understand how Nate or Serena weren't injured or killed." Heidi signaled Charlie to sit. "The shooter must have been a bad shot."

Nick grimaced. "If the shooter is Muehller, he's an expert marksman. The bullet hit where this guy was aiming."

"The glass in Nate's SUV is bullet resistant," Quinn said. "All our vehicles use that kind of glass as well as armor plating." He lifted one shoulder. "Pays to be cautious in our line of work."

"I'm glad they are safe." She turned to Nick. "What is Muehller's first name again?"

"Hans."

"Is it all right if we search the area now?" When he agreed, she turned to Charlie and gave him a hand signal, telling the Lab it was time to work. Heidi opened the bag and let Charlie sniff the contents. She pushed enthusiasm and excitement into her voice. "This is Hans. We have to find Hans. Find Hans." After sealing the bag again, she straightened, watching her dog.

Charlie stood, raised his nose into the air and sniffed the currents. He walked one way, then another. The Lab zeroed in on the side of the house. With a bark, he trotted to the corner of the house and followed a scent trail to the fence encircling the backyard. He whined, turned his head toward Heidi. She glanced at Nick for permission to touch the gate. When he motioned for her to proceed, she opened the gate and followed Charlie into the yard. He led her to the back fence. No gate this time. Guess the shooter hopped the fence. "We need to go around."

They retraced their steps and circled to the alley which separated two rows of houses. When Charlie acted as though he couldn't find the scent, she opened the bag and refreshed his memory. The Lab searched around the back of the fence, but came up with nothing. He sat and stared at Heidi with a whine.

Disappointment spiraled through her. He'd lost the scent. The shooter must have climbed into a vehicle.

Perhaps Quinn wouldn't mind playing a game with Charlie. Otherwise, she would have to be the "lost" one. Her furry buddy needed a successful search.

"What's wrong?" Nick asked, gaze on the Lab.

"He lost the scent. My guess is the shooter got into a vehicle. That's why the scent disappeared so abruptly."

"Do you know if Muehller was the shooter?" Quinn asked.

"Charlie was following Muehller's scent."

"So when he failed to kill Nate or Serena, he took off to regroup." Nick sighed. "Fantastic. He's in the wind again."

"Look at it this way," Quinn said. "Now you know Muehller is behind the shooting, and you aren't a target nor is Madison."

"Yeah?" The detective's expression grew grim. "I wish someone was after me rather than Ethan or Serena. The only criminals I've come up against are run of the mill bad guys, not anyone like Muehller. All Ethan's ever done was protect the innocents and the people he loves. He shouldn't be punished for doing his job."

"Doesn't work that way. You knew the risk when you signed up to be a cop, Nick." Quinn dropped his hand on his friend's shoulder. "Ethan knew the risks going in. We all did. The important thing is Muehller failed. Again."

"He might not next time. We can't stay on high alert forever. Muehller will wait until our guard is down, then strike. I've got a crime scene to process. Thanks for your help, Heidi." He stalked away.

"Wow. Is Detective Santana always that intense?"

"When his wife's family is at risk."

Heidi frowned. "He's not that intense about his own?"

"Nick doesn't have family except for the Cahills. His parents and brother were murdered while he was in college. There is no one else."

She sucked in a breath, sympathy flooding her. Yeah, she knew that kind of devastating loss. She felt for the detective. His fierce protectiveness of Ethan and Serena Blackhawk made sense. "You up for a game, Quinn?"

His eyebrows winged upward. "Sure. What kind?"

"Search for Quinn." She inclined her head toward Charlie who was now laying on the ground, head on his paws, the picture of dejection. "Give me your jacket and go hide."

"Right." He shrugged out of his jacket and jogged down the alleyway and around a corner of a house away from the crime scene.

Heidi gave him another minute before she signaled Charlie it was time to work. She let him sniff the jacket and said, "This is Quinn. We need to find Quinn. Find Quinn."

Charlie smelled the air currents and immediately began the search for Quinn. Tail wagging, the Lab trotted down the alley and around the corner of the house where Quinn had disappeared from sight.

Charlie led her past another row of houses and beyond the tree line. Behind a large fir tree, they found Quinn seated on the ground, one arm resting on his upraised knees, a grin on his face. "Good boy, Charlie. You did it. You found Quinn." After a full body rub and hug, she fed her buddy a treat.

"May I have my jacket back now?" A wink from her boyfriend. "It's cold out here."

"Oh, sure. Sorry." Although the truth was she wanted to keep the jacket. It was warm and carried Quinn's unique scent. Yep, she was a card-carrying sap. "Thanks for playing victim for Charlie."

"No problem. What if I hadn't been a cooperative victim?"

"Can't imagine you disappointing him. However, if you didn't want to play along, I would have hidden and let you search with him. A successful search keeps him happy."

"Huh." He turned his speculative vision toward the dog. "Might be a good exercise. Would he respond to my commands?"

"If you gave him the right commands. Why?"

"In a few days, we'll be actively engaged in training S & R teams. We should know what you and Deke do. Who knows if we'll be called on to be part of an S & R mission?"

"You will," she pointed out. "If Deke or I have to find Muehller for Chief Blackhawk, you or one of your teammates will be along for the journey."

"I'll be with you," he insisted. "I'm not handing over your safety to someone else. You're mine to protect, baby. Ready to leave?"

"Definitely. Charlie's ready for some playtime."

They drove to Heidi's house. No other vehicle was in the drive and the house was empty. Guess Levi and his bodyguards were out. Their presence in town wasn't a secret. The arsonist knew she and Levi were in town.

Once she gave Charlie water, she and Quinn led the Lab into the backyard and took turns tossing a ball for her furry buddy to chase. Near the end of their play session, Quinn's cell phone rang.

When Heidi paused, Charlie flopped down on the ground, panting. She rubbed his ears as Quinn answered his phone.

"What do you have for me, Zane?"

"Nothing good. We have a problem."

CHAPTER TWENTY-THREE

A ball of ice formed in Quinn's stomach. "Talk to me, Z."

"The bots I set up to search the Net are getting multiple hits."

That was the last thing he wanted to hear. Were his teammates and their ladies safe? "On who?"

"You and Heidi."

Ah, man. Definitely not good. His head whipped her direction. "Hold on," he muttered and pressed the speaker button. "Heidi is with me. You're on speaker. Repeat what you just said."

A pause, then, "Hello, Heidi. Zane Murphy here."

"Hi, Zane. You must be the tech guru that Quinn mentions with such admiration over your skills."

"Ah, okay." He drew out the last word.

Made Quinn's lips curve to hear such discomfort coming from the Navy SEAL. Zane was used to working in the shadows where no one noticed him. Durango counted him as a vital part of their team, even if he was a frog boy instead of an Army grunt. They wouldn't let him hide in the darkness. They also had a soft spot for his lady. Claire

Walker was a world-class photographer and a spitfire to boot. His gaze shifted to the woman by his side. Claire reminded Quinn of Heidi. Determination, grit, courage. Words which described the woman who owned Zane's heart and Heidi, too.

"Heidi, I've been scouring the Internet for any mention of the members of Durango."

She stiffened, worry clouding her gaze. "Oh, dear. You wouldn't call about the search unless there was a problem. What did you find?"

"Quinn's teammates are safe. You and Quinn, on the other hand, are not."

"I don't understand. If you were looking for compromises to Durango's safety, why were you finding references to me? Wait. Which one of my identities has hits?"

"Very good, Heidi. You have a smart girlfriend, Quinn."

"I have excellent taste." He cupped the back of her neck and gently drew her against him, offering silent support against the blow he suspected was coming. "Tell us something we don't know."

"Heidi, when Fortress is protecting identities of clients, we watch for signs their information has been compromised. That means we have bots constantly scouring the Internet for any mention of the old identity or the new one. The good news is the protocol worked and the bots caught references to you."

"And the bad news?"

"All of your identities have been compromised, including the latest one as Heidi Thompson."

At those words, Quinn scowled. "How is that possible? No one should know all her identities. I don't even know them." He stopped. "Only three people besides Heidi have that information. Levi, Maddox, and the arsonist-kidnapper dogging her every step for the last twenty years."

177

"No!" Heidi protested. "Levi wouldn't do this. Could the leak be originating with Fortress?"

"Unlikely." Quinn sympathized. Levi and Heidi had been watching each other's backs for years. While he understood, Quinn wouldn't allow her silent pleading to stop him from doing everything he could to protect her, even if that meant disillusioning Heidi about her only remaining relative, a man she'd depended on to survive. "Have you been able to trace the source of the leak, Z?"

A grunt from his friend. "Of course."

"Who?"

"Levi Thompson."

Heidi pressed her face against Quinn's neck. He tightened his hold, wishing he could spare her any more pain and heartache. This turn of events puzzled him, though. He usually had a good feel for people. This latest news had blindsided him. He just didn't see her cousin doing this. Was it possible Quinn had been wrong and Levi was the one trying to kill his cousin? He had plenty of motive, but unless he had slipped away from his bodyguards to set the fire in the garage, then raced back to Knoxville before his bodyguards realized he was gone, Levi would have been forced to hire a partner. The more people involved in a conspiracy, the greater chance of a leak. Quinn had learned long ago most people couldn't keep secrets. Aside from money, the partner would have no reason to maintain secrecy.

If he had hired a partner, how would Levi set up the fire at this house? Maddox was obsessive about security, especially after recently finding two traitors in the Fortress ranks. The boss would have gone to extra lengths to protect Heidi and Levi's locations from each other as well as anyone else who might have nefarious plans for them.

Quinn needed to check Levi's cell phone, see who he called. If he'd wiped his call history, Zane could find the numbers.

Quinn frowned. He still wasn't convinced. Was it possible the real arsonist had enough computer skills to frame Levi? But why bother? He'd tried to kill both Heidi and Levi in the past. Wouldn't he want Levi dead instead of discredited? If revenge was the motive, it shouldn't matter whether Heidi and Levi were together or not. The arsonist would stay after them until he completed his goal or until Quinn stopped him. "Keep digging."

"You believe I made a mistake?"

He snorted. "Nope. You don't make those kinds of mistakes. I think it sounds like a perfect solution handed to us on a silver platter and wrapped in bright paper with a satin ribbon. The solution is too perfect. Nothing is that easy. I think Levi is a scapegoat."

Heidi lifted her head. Her eyes were wide, hoping shining in their depths. "Zane?"

"Yes, Heidi?"

"Levi would never betray me. He put his life on the line over and over for me. If he hadn't rescued me two months ago, I would be dead." Her face turned toward Charlie. "Charlie, too. Levi was on duty at the fire station when the fire was reported. He has a fire hall of witnesses who will vouch for his whereabouts."

Quinn didn't bother pointing out that Levi could have had an accomplice. Zane was a sharp guy. Nothing much slipped past his friend. In fact, he figured the SEAL had suspected the validity of his search results and wanted their take on the matter.

"I'll keep looking," he promised. "You may not like my findings."

"I want the truth, no matter where it leads. I don't want to live my life in fear any more. If the results of your search hurt, I'll mend. I need a name, Zane."

"Copy that. Quinn?"

"Yep."

"This one's a keeper. Hang on to her."

His gaze locked with hers. Heart hammering in his chest, Quinn uttered the words he thought would never come from his mouth, especially not this soon. "I plan on it."

Heidi jerked in reaction to his statement.

Yeah, it shocked him, too. He'd loved her when she was a kid, viewed himself as her big brother. As an adult, he was head-over-heels in love with the woman she'd become. He wanted to spend the rest of his life protecting her and loving her with every breath he took. He didn't know if she felt the same way. If she didn't, he'd convince her to take a chance on him, on a life with him. She had the strength to deal with his work and a spine of steel to keep him in line when he went overboard to protect her from life. Not possible to protect her to that extent. Wouldn't prevent him from trying. He gave a mental shrug. Protecting those he loved was in his DNA. Heidi had dealt with enough crap in her lifetime. He'd love to spare her more hardship.

He wanted to bring joy to her life, be the answer to her dreams of a lifetime of love. Heidi Thompson, whatever name she used, was the woman who brought color to his barren world, the one who brought light to his soul. Her emerald eyes, red hair, and creamy skin drew him, no question. But the woman he fell in love with? She was even more beautiful inside than her gorgeous exterior. In short, she was perfect for him. Now he had to convince her he was worth taking the risk, their love worth the gamble.

"I'll keep you posted, Quinn. I have to report to the boss."

"Understood." Maddox wasn't going to like what he heard. Quinn didn't, either. Another problem would develop if Maddox believed Levi was the culprit who sabotaged his and Heidi's covers. The promised protection for Levi was shaky at best after the problems he'd given Angel and Dane. If Maddox became convinced of Levi's guilt, the Fortress CEO would cut him loose and let Heidi's cousin fend for himself.

"Need anything else from me?" Zane asked.

"Find me contact information for an Ivan Bennett. He was a detective with the Black River Police Department twenty years ago. He investigated the kidnapping of Katie Henderson and her younger sister Moira."

"Twenty years ago, huh? Hope this guy was young twenty years ago. Otherwise, I'm likely to fail. You think Bennett might know something?"

"The only way to stop the attacks on Heidi is figure out the identity of the second kidnapper."

"Makes sense unless Heidi's been breaking men's hearts and casting them aside. I'll send you the information as soon as I find it, whatever the result. Shouldn't take long."

"Copy that. If it's not possible to talk to Bennett, find his partner."

"I'll get back to you." And with that, Zane was gone.

Quinn slid the phone into his pocket, wrapped his free arm around Heidi, and waited.

For a moment she said nothing, simply searched his face. Perhaps looking for a measure of his sincerity? He meant every word.

"You told Zane you planned to keep me. Did you mean it?"

"I did." He wasn't backing down from his statement. Did she understand what he was telling her?

"What does that mean?"

Guess not. "What I said was literal, baby. I'm keeping you."

"For how long? A month? Longer?"

He leaned down and kissed her, long and deep, before answering. Her kisses were fast becoming as necessary to him as breathing. The heat and silky texture of her mouth drew him as nothing else ever had. He'd kissed other women. Their names, faces, and taste had disappeared the moment his mouth took Heidi's for the first time. "Is forever too long?"

Heidi's breath caught. "Forever?"

"You don't have to say anything. I know we've only been back together for a few days. But the truth is we laid the foundation twenty years ago, Heidi. I adored the child born as Katie Henderson. I'm in love with the woman now known as Heidi Thompson. If you give me the chance, I'll spend the rest of my life making you happy. I'll protect you until my last breath. I'd love raising a family when we're ready. Say yes, baby. Say you'll throw caution to the wind and take a chance on the love of a lifetime. Choose a lifetime with me."

Tears welled in her eyes and slid down her cheeks.

Oh, man. Was that a bad sign? Quinn squelched the panic bubbling inside. He cupped her face between his palms and brushed the tears away with his thumbs. "I didn't mean to make you cry, honey. Am I scaring you?"

He could wait while she grew used to the idea. Maybe. Man, he was crazy about her. The thought of slowing down or backing off almost took him to his knees. But to have forever with her? Yeah, he'd make himself wait. Didn't mean abandoning his campaign to win her heart. He'd just be more subtle.

Romance. That was the key to a woman's heart according to his mother and sisters. So he would romance Heidi Thompson. Flowers, dinners, movie dates, hiking the trails in the area. The Churchill trail was a great place to walk. Picnics when the weather grew warmer. His brain filled with ideas to win Heidi for his own.

"These are happy tears. I never thought I'd hear you say those words to me. I thought my father had destroyed any good feeling you might have left in your soul for Katie Henderson."

"Never. I don't care what name you go by, I will always love you."

A wide, beautiful smile curved her lips. "I loved you as Katie Henderson. You were my hero, the boy I measured all others against. As I grew older, I believed I would never see you again and I mourned the loss of my hero. As Heidi Thompson, I'm so in love with you, Quinn Gallagher. Spending a lifetime loving you would be a dream come true."

He stilled, hardly daring to believe what he was hearing from Heidi's lips. "So you'll marry me, Heidi?" He wanted absolute clarification so they both understood where their relationship was heading. Love, marriage, kids, grandkids, sitting in side-by-side rocking chairs on the porch, watching their family grow up and make the world a better place. That's what he longed for. But only with Heidi.

"Marriage?" she whispered. "You want to marry me?"

"The sooner the better. I don't want you to slip away. Will you marry me, baby?"

"Just try and stop me."

He laughed, tugging her tight against him. Joy and relief surged through his body. Thank God. She had just agreed to be his partner for a lifetime. His gaze dropped to the bare ring finger of her left hand. Quinn needed to stop by the jewelry store. He wanted a ring on her finger as soon as possible. "Not a chance. You made the promise. I'm holding you to it, even if you wise up later and rescind the agreement."

Eyes sparkling, Heidi laughed.

The back door opened. "Hey, what's going on?" Angel asked, her expression one of curiosity.

Not telling yet, he decided. He wanted to savor the shift in their relationship and to place that ring on her finger before they made the announcement. Rather than divulge what they had been talking about, Quinn glanced over her shoulder. "Where's Levi?"

"Right here." The man stepped around Angel, a frown on his face as he glanced first at Heidi, then at Quinn. "Everything okay?"

"You tell me. Got something you need to tell us, Levi?"

"Dane and Angel went with me to the bookstore. I was going crazy with nothing to do here. Heidi hasn't hooked up the cable in the house yet."

"We invited you to explore the area with us. You opted to stay here." He was worried about the cable? "Been surfing the Internet lately, Levi?"

"Sure, until we came here. Maddox said it was okay as long as I didn't access any accounts from a former name. Why?"

"Hand over your cell phone."

"What is the problem, Gallagher?" he asked, voice sharp. "I think I have the right to know what's going on."

Dane flanked Angel. "What's up?"

"I need to check Levi's phone," Quinn said.

With a raised eyebrow, Dane glanced at Heidi's cousin. "Hand it over. Now."

"I want to know why."

"This is you cooperating, Levi?" Angel asked, scowling. "I'd hate to see what happened if you were any more cooperative."

"Okay, fine." Levi pulled the phone from his pocket and handed it to Dane who tossed it to Quinn.

He tapped the screen and pulled up the call history. Nothing but calls to Heidi. Quinn would have Zane check from his end to make sure nothing had been deleted. If there was an electronic trail, the SEAL would find it. Nothing escaped his notice. "Get your computer."

"Wait a minute." Levi scowled. "I don't have to let you invade my privacy like this. That wasn't part of the protection deal."

Quinn looked at Dane who left immediately. He returned his attention to Levi. "Someone is leaking information on the Internet."

"What kind of information?"

Was he that good an actor or was he innocent as Quinn and Heidi thought? "Heidi's names. All of them. My name is also getting hits in connection to Heidi."

Shocked, Levi stared at Heidi. "And you suspect me?"

"No, I don't. But someone knows about me. If they know about me, they also know about you. We have to find out who's leaking the information and stop it, Levi. It's bad enough that my name is out there. Quinn can't have publicity and stay safe. People more dangerous than an arsonist are interested in hurting him."

"Three people know all of Heidi's identities aside from her," Quinn said, hoping to get the conversation back on track. "Maddox, the kidnapper, and you."

"It's not me. I would never do that to Heidi."

"The good news is I don't think you're to blame."

"And the bad?"

"We have to eliminate you as a suspect so we can hunt the real culprit."

"How about you take a look at your rejected girlfriend. That Daisy woman. She looked pretty angry this morning when you announced you were off the dating market. Maybe she's the guilty one."

"She doesn't know about Heidi's other identities. You, on the other hand, have means, motive, and opportunity to take revenge against Heidi."

"Why would I wait fifteen years to pay her back for something she didn't do? Heidi was just a kid. The fault belonged to her old man."

"If she hadn't moved into your home, your family would still be alive." When Heidi made a small sound of distress, Quinn tucked her closer to his chest. "She cost you everything so maybe you decided to make her suffer before you killed her."

"You're insane, Gallagher," Levi snapped. "I would never hurt Heidi." He turned to her. "You believe me, don't you, sweetheart? You know I love you."

Dane returned with a laptop. "Where do you want me to set up?"

"Table."

"I don't have the Internet hooked up yet," Heidi said. "There hasn't been enough time."

"No problem," Angel said. "We all have hotspots."

Quinn glanced around the area, the back of his neck itching. "Let's move this inside." He wanted Heidi and Levi out of sight.

Heidi signaled for Charlie to come with her. Once in the kitchen, all of them sat around the table while Dane checked Levi's online activities. Levi sat back in his chair, arms crossed, a mulish expression on his face.

Quinn didn't blame him for being upset. However, the sooner they completed the search, the faster they could move on to find the true betrayer. "Levi, while Dane is searching through your computer, tell me what you know about Ivan Bennett."

A snort from the other man. "That old war horse? What do you want to know?"

"What was your impression of him?"

"Thorough, old."

"How old?"

Levi stopped, thought a moment. His cheeks flushed. "Not so old. He was nearing retirement age. The officers were eligible to retire at fifty-five."

Quinn's lips curved into a slight smile. "That age is looking younger all the time."

"Tell me about it," Dane muttered.

"Anything else you remember about Bennett?" Quinn asked Levi.

Heidi's cousin started to shake his head, stopped. "He had a son. I think he was a cop, too."

CHAPTER TWENTY-FOUR

Ethan cradled his son, tears trickling down his cheeks as he stared at face of his sleeping child. He was tiny and made him feel as though he would break the boy if he held on too tight. Ethan had to smile at the head full of black hair and dark eyes along with the skin tone that so closely mirrored his own, evidence of the dominance of his Native American DNA. Such a long wait to see the fulfillment of a dream. Pride, blinding love, and pure terror mixed in a bubbling brew inside Ethan. Who knew someone so small could generate such bone-deep fear? What if he couldn't do this?

For a moment, melancholy stole into Ethan's contemplation of the changes ahead. If he could alter one thing it would be to lay his son into the arms of Ethan's mother. She would have loved holding her grandson. She'd been a great mother despite her hard life. More than once, she placed herself in danger to protect him. That practice continued until Ethan had been old enough and big enough to realize what she was doing. From that moment until his mother had been killed in a car accident, Ethan had refused to stand behind her. Losing her had devastated him and his father.

"He's beautiful, isn't he?" Serena gave Ethan a tired smile. "He's going to be a mini Ethan."

He shook his head. "Lucas Blackhawk will be his own man, not a copy of me. Unlike what my father did to me, I'll protect and support him, encourage him to do what he's called to do. We may not always see eye to eye, but Lucas will never question if I love him." With his free hand, he wiped the tears from his face. "Thank you, my love."

"For what, sweetheart?"

"Giving me the greatest gift of my life aside from your love."

A soft knock sounded on the hospital room door. Ethan tensed, his free hand dropping to his sidearm. He relaxed when Lily Doucet peered into the room. "What is it, Lily?"

"Serena's parents are here, sir. They're anxious to see the baby."

He glanced at his wife. "You ready for the Cahill mob?"

"Let the party begin."

A minute later, Aaron and Liz Cahill came through the doorway. As soon as Liz saw Lucas, her eyes filled with tears of joy. Yeah, Ethan understood that sentiment. His son had Ethan's heart in his two tiny fists. How was it possible to love someone this much so fast? "Come meet your grandson." He stood and laid Lucas in her outstretched arms. "This is Lucas Aaron."

Serena's father cleared his throat. "Oh, Ethan. You don't know how much that means to me."

"You're the father figure I always wanted and needed in my life growing up. I can't think of a more fitting name to give him."

Aaron wrapped him in a tight hug. "We love you, son. Thank you for that honor." When he stepped back, Aaron crossed to Serena's bedside and pressed a kiss to her forehead. "How do you feel, baby?"

She grinned. "Like I just had a baby. Other than tired, I'm fine, Dad."

"You did good, kid. He's beautiful. Looks like his father, though. You'll have to do better with the next one."

She rolled her eyes. "I'll do my best, but I can't control genetics. Is Ruth here yet? She'll be anxious to hold Lucas, too."

Ethan turned, his eyes narrowing. He'd tried calling his aunt several times over the past few hours but as usual Ruth either hadn't charged her cell phone or bothered to turn it on. That Ruth was out of touch for this long concerned him. Word would have gotten around town within minutes of Serena being admitted to the maternity ward. His aunt must know by now even if she hadn't checked her land line or cell. Otter Creek's grapevine was almost as effective at spreading the word as the Internet.

Uneasiness swelled in his gut. He'd been growing more worried in the last couple hours. But with Serena laboring to bring Lucas into the world, his focus has been on his wife and child, not his aunt. Ruth was a smart, tough woman. She'd encountered Muehller and his cohort when Ethan first arrived in Otter Creek and had come out of the skirmish victorious. There was no indication the international assassin had targeted Ethan's aunt. But Ruth should have been at the hospital by now.

Ethan pulled out his cell phone and walked to the doorway. "I'll be back in a few minutes, love." He stepped into the hall. Remy and Lily were standing on either side of the door, weapons evident. Under the circumstances, he'd cleared the Fortress operatives' armed presence with the head of hospital security. No one would question the extreme measures when there was a threat to the safety of his wife and child.

"I need to make a few calls," he murmured to the Fortress operatives.

Lily grinned and rubbed her hands together. "I get first dibs on baby duty."

Remy chuckled. "Fine. I'll stay on the door. Don't worry, Ethan. We'll look after them."

"I'm counting on it. Anything happens, put it down hard." As he walked down the hall, he passed Madison and Megan, Serena's sisters. Both of them were carrying gift bags and almost running in their excitement.

"How are Serena and the baby?" Madison asked.

"Great. Your mom and dad are with them." He smiled. "Liz needs to decide what name she wants the baby to call her when he starts to talk."

Megan laughed. "It's a little early for that, but I have a list of suggestions for her. She asked me to research popular nicknames for grandmothers last week."

Bet that list was an interesting one. As editor of the *Otter Creek Gazette*, his sister-in-law was quite a wordsmith. "Can't wait to hear the results. I need to track down Ruth. Have you seen her?"

She frowned. "She left the newspaper office four hours ago. One of her murder book club cronies was meeting her at Ruth's place to brainstorm a sticky plot point in her latest manuscript. After that, Ruth planned to come here."

Ethan's gut tightened. Maybe his aunt and her friend had lost track of time. He doubted it, though. Ruth had been looking forward to holding Lucas as much as the rest of Serena's family. No, something wasn't right. "Thanks, Meg. I'll try her at home."

"Do you want one of us to find her?" Madison laid her small hand on his arm. "You shouldn't have to worry about that right now. You have a new baby to enjoy."

"I appreciate the offer, Madison, but I know you're anxious to get your hands on your nephew. I'll have the rest of my life to enjoy my son."

"If you're sure."

"Go on." He smiled. "Serena's expecting you." Ethan waited until both women had been admitted to the room before heading further down the hall. Once he was away from foot traffic, he called his aunt's home. Nothing. He tried her cell phone. The call went straight to voice mail where he left another terse message for her to call him. His next call went to Rod Kelter.

"Yeah, Kelter."

"I need a favor."

"Name it."

"Go by Ruth's house. She's not answering her land line or cell phone. According to Meg, Ruth was to meet one of her book club buddies at the house, then come here."

"I'll call you as soon as I know anything."

"Rod." Command rang in his tone.

"Yes, sir?"

"Watch your back. If Nick's available, take him with you. If he's not, grab someone else."

Silence for a couple heartbeats. "Muehller?"

"I don't have anything to go on but my gut and it's not happy."

Rod gave a low whistle. "I'll be careful."

Ethan returned the phone to his pocket, debating whether or not to leave the hospital and meet his brother-in-law. Gaze shifting to the room where his wife and son were waiting for him, he knew for the moment his priority was them. He prayed Ruth had just gotten sidetracked and would be here soon, embarrassed by all the concern. Rod was smart and experienced. His chief of detectives knew how to handle himself. He trusted Meg's husband or he wouldn't have Rod working for him, related by marriage or not. The police chief retraced his steps, pausing in front of Remy.

"Problem?" the other man murmured, his gaze scanning the corridor, assessing each person as they walked past the room.

"My aunt has been out of touch for several hours. A couple of my people are headed to Ruth's place to check on her. Stay alert."

"Yes, sir." A small smile from Remy. "Go enjoy your family, Ethan."

He clapped the operative on the shoulder and walked past him into the room. His heart skipped a beat to see Madison sitting in a chair, holding Lucas. A huge smile was on her face even as slow tears slid down her cheeks. Man, this had to be so hard for her. Due to injuries sustained in a car accident, Madison wasn't able to have children. When Serena had found out she was pregnant with Lucas, Nick had taken Madison out of town for a couple of days to romance the love of his life and remind her how much he loved her. Watching her now made Ethan wonder if Nick had another outing in mind for Madison. Maybe not, though. While she appeared delicate, Madison Santana had faced the loss of her first husband, her own son, and nearly been killed herself. No, this amazing woman wasn't weak. If anyone could handle the emotional storm, it was his gentle sister-in-law.

While the others laughed and talked, Ethan crossed the room and crouched beside Madison. "Aaron says Serena will have to do better next time."

Her jaw dropped. "What? He's perfect! Why would Dad say that?"

"Because he looks like a small replica of me."

A soft laugh from Madison. "That dark hair and brown eyes do seem to be dominant in the gene pool for this one. At least Serena only had one baby."

"Tell me about it," he murmured. "I was afraid the multiple births prediction might become reality. Don't think my heart could take more than one at a time."

"There's always next time." She gave him a wicked grin. "Sorry, but there's not enough of Lucas to go around. I'm putting in a request for at least twins."

He winced. "Thanks a lot." Might revise his opinion about Madison's sweetness.

"Would you like to hold your son?"

Yeah, he did, but Madison looked content now that the tears had stopped. "Lucas looks pretty relaxed. I'd say you're well on your way to favorite aunt status."

Meg tossed a grin over her shoulder. "Ha! He hasn't been bribed by his Aunt Megan yet. Just wait until I hold him."

When she turned her attention to answer a question from Liz, Ethan leaned over and pressed a soft kiss to the top of the baby's head.

"You're going to be a great father, Ethan."

Startled, he glanced at Madison. "I didn't have the best example, Maddie." His father had been an abusive alcoholic. Ethan still had the scars to prove it. "I don't know what I'm doing."

"No one knows what to do. Babies don't come with instruction manuals. You'll figure it out along the way. I know a couple of important things already."

His eyebrows rose.

"You are nothing like your father, Ethan Blackhawk. You are a good, honorable man who adores his wife and son. They are blessed to have you in their lives." She smiled. "We all are."

His phone signaled an incoming call. Ethan rose. "Thanks for the vote of confidence." With the volume of conversations rising in the room, he returned to the hallway. "Blackhawk."

"It's Rod."

His detective's grim voice sent Ethan's heart rate soaring. "Talk to me."

"You need to come to Ruth's house. She's missing and her friend has been murdered."

CHAPTER TWENTY-FIVE

Ethan raced across the lawn to his aunt's home. A rookie with green-tinged skin stepped aside to let him enter. He should have his sergeant talk to him. After he found Ruth. Everything else would wait until she returned, safe and sound.

His chief of detectives turned, fury burning in his gaze. Rod inclined his head toward Ruth's maroon recliner.

Ethan shifted his attention to the body slumped in the chair. Regret and anger mixed in a toxic brew at the sight of one of his own citizens. The elderly woman was named Alice Prescott and was Ruth's best friend. His aunt would be heartbroken by her loss as would the town. Alice was quite a character, always sharing a smile, known for a spunky attitude no matter what life threw at her. She happily volunteered for committees, especially ones involving planning parties or festivals with the infamous events committee. To the puzzlement of many, Alice actually liked the work. As a former high school English teacher, the sweet lady knew many of the town's citizens and she had the ability to sweet talk folks into volunteering.

She not only talked them into helping, she pitched in herself and made the work fun.

Her death was senseless. No reason to kill the English teacher except she'd seen the killer's face. He tugged on the rubber gloves Rod handed him and moved closer to the recliner. "One shot to the forehead," he murmured. "Close range."

"Muehller?" Rod asked.

"That's his signature. Looks like a .40 caliber, a favorite of his. Have you called the coroner?"

"He'll be here in two hours. Caught him out of town eating dinner with his in-laws."

With a nod, he turned away from Alice for the moment. The living took precedence over the dead. If Alice were alive, she would tell him as much. "Ruth?"

"Her car is in the garage. Alice's vehicle is parked on the street in front of the house. Ruth made a pot of tea. They never had a chance to drink it." He stopped, glanced at Ethan.

"Talk to me, Rod."

He sighed. "There's blood in the kitchen. Not a lot, but enough. Ruth didn't go voluntarily with whoever took her."

Ethan's jaw flexed. Go down easy? Fat chance, not with the indomitable Ruth Rollins. One thing he knew for sure. Whoever took her would pay, a payment Ethan looked forward to exacting. "Show me."

Rod led him to the kitchen. Ethan pulled up short at the sight of the serving tray in the middle of the floor, red ceramic tea pot shattered. Light-colored tea had spread in thin streams from the remains of the pot. Probably green tea, a favorite of his aunt. Two china cups lay broken along with two saucers, a plate upside down on the linoleum, cookies scattered. On the other side of the tea tray was a trail of blood. His gut clenched. Ruth had to be all right. Muehller had no reason to hurt her. She was bait for Ethan.

Then again, there'd been no reason to kill Alice. She was harmless and Muehller knew Otter Creek PD would identify him sooner or later as Ruth's abductor. Ethan prayed Muehller viewed Ruth's good health as necessary to obtain revenge on him. He was the target, not his family. The problem was criminals didn't focus only on law enforcement instead of innocents.

Ethan followed the blood trail to the back door. Once outside, he tracked the intruder through the backyard, spotting footprints in the muddy terrain leading to the fence, then followed the trail out the gate. The signs of passage disappeared. "He put her in a vehicle here." He scanned the area, noted a few security cameras and the addresses of the homes where they were located. Maybe one of them actually worked. If not, there was the chance a traffic camera had caught the vehicle driving away from the scene. All he needed was a top-notch tech who worked fast. Time was not on their side. Muehller had at least a two hour head start. Good thing he knew of a couple outstanding cyber techs who might do him a favor.

"That's my take on it," Rod agreed. "This scene is similar to the one near Madison's house."

"How?"

"While Muehller didn't go inside Maddie's home, Heidi and Charlie confirmed he was at the scene and stood exactly where the shooter took the shot at Nate. Muehller scaled a fence and climbed into a vehicle parked in the alley."

So when he couldn't grab Serena, Muehller went after the only other family Ethan had left. Ruth. His fist clenched. "I'll get in touch with Quinn and have Charlie brought here to confirm Muehller took Ruth. What else do you need from me?"

"Stella and Nick if they're free. The sooner I process this place, the better. We need to find Ruth fast, Ethan."

"I know. I'll call in Nick and Stella. Rod, we do need to find Ruth quickly, but, we can't move so fast we miss something. We'll waste more time if we have to backtrack because we weren't careful. Once I've made the calls, I'll get my crime scene kit and give you a hand."

"You should be with Serena and your son."

He quelled Rod's protest with a look. "Serena and Lucas are safe. Ruth isn't." Ethan stepped around the tea tray mess. "Have you notified Alice's next of kin?"

"She doesn't have any."

A sad thing to hear about a wonderful woman. The town would mourn her passing. He'd get justice for Alice. Wouldn't change Alice's death, but the next time Muehller was behind bars, he wouldn't slip out again. Hans Muehller wouldn't be seeing daylight for a long time.

After sending Rod into the house, Ethan called Nick. "How close are you to finishing that scene?"

"Wrapping up now. Why?"

"I need you to help Rod process Ruth's house. She's missing and her friend Alice Prescott has been murdered."

"Muehller?"

"Looks like it. Call Stella. Have her come as well. Clock's ticking."

"Copy that. I'll be there as soon as I can."

That done, Ethan made another call.

"Murphy."

"Zane, it's Ethan Blackhawk. I need a favor."

"On the books or off?"

"Off." He didn't have time for a warrant. Ruth's life was on the line. He didn't care what obstacles he had to circumvent. Ethan owed his aunt his life.

"What do you need?"

He surveyed the area to be sure he was alone. "For you to hack into traffic cams and security cams in Otter Creek." He rattled off Ruth's address. "I need footage from the past four hours. A woman's life is at stake."

The sound of a computer keyboard clicking reached Ethan's ears. "Working on it now. What's going on, Ethan? I haven't heard of a problem from Remy or Lily."

"Serena and my son are safe. Ruth Rollins, my aunt, is missing and her best friend has been murdered."

"The assassin took Ms. Rollins?" Zane's voice was grim.

"Appears so."

"I'm sorry. Congratulations on the birth of your son, by the way. Lily says he'll be a heartbreaker when he grows up."

Despite the worry weighing on his thoughts, Ethan smiled. "Thanks. When is your wedding day?"

"Two weeks. We wanted to marry sooner, but Claire wanted Adam to attend the wedding."

Ethan remembered Josh mentioning the Fortress operative's injuries which were sustained during a mission. Adam had been captured and tortured by a drug lord in Belize a few weeks earlier. "How is he?"

"Recovering well. He'll need plastic surgery, but he's lucky to be alive." A pause, more finger tapping on Zane's keyboard, then, "Ah. Got something for you. Two security cameras are online. I hacked into their systems, trusting that you'll put in a good word for me with a judge if I'm found out."

Doubt he'd need to do that. From what he'd heard over the last couple years, Zane Murphy was a world-class hacker who never left a trail behind. "Send me the file." Ethan gave Zane an email address that couldn't be traced back to him directly. One of those alternate identities Quinn suspected he had. "What about the traffic cameras?"

"Working on that now."

"I want the feeds on roads heading out of town. I need to know if he left town, and if he did, which direction he took."

"Got it. Your town's system is antiquated, by the way."

"Yeah?" Amusement swirled through him. "In this case, that's a good thing. Should make it easier for you to hack the system."

"Ethan, do you have a laptop handy?"

"I don't, but I can access my aunt's computer."

"I'm going to send the traffic cam footage, but the time frame you gave me is wide. I can narrow it down for you if I know which vehicle to scan for. Otherwise, you'll be spending several hours looking through the footage. You don't have that luxury."

"I'm going inside to the computer. I'll call you in two minutes." Ethan jogged through the yard and over the threshold of Ruth's back door. He skirted Rod who glanced up at his entrance.

"Anything?"

"Zane Murphy is lending a hand with a search. Don't ask details. I'll let you know if he comes up with anything. Nick and Stella should arrive soon."

With a nod, the detective returned to his task.

Ethan walked to Ruth's office. He turned on her laptop and typed in Ruth's password when the dialog box popped up, grateful his aunt had made a point of giving him full access to her computer in case something happened to her. At the time, she'd mentioned something about him making sure her latest manuscript went to her publisher if something should happen to her. This was one time he was glad for her precaution, but determined not to contact that publisher. His aunt would send her electronic file of her manuscript herself.

Before he logged into his account, he called Quinn. "It's Ethan. I need Heidi and Charlie."

"Where?"

"My aunt's house. She's missing, Quinn. I think Muehller took her and I need Charlie to confirm."

"We'll leave as soon as we load up Charlie. Be there in ten minutes."

He logged into his account and clicked on the file Murphy sent. He fast forwarded through the footage of one security cam until he spotted a dark SUV with tinted windows speeding down the alley about the right time. Ethan called Murphy and put the phone on speaker. "I'm looking at the footage from the first security cam. The dark SUV?"

"Yep. The second security cam showed the same thing. There was another vehicle that came through the alley during the four-hour time frame you gave me. The windows were clear and the driver was a teenage boy."

"Track the first SUV. I want to know where that vehicle went when it left here." Ethan manipulated the video clip until he caught the image of the driver. Too blurry to make out the facial features. Maybe Murphy could clean it up and get him an image. Hopefully, Charlie would confirm Muehller was their culprit. Shouldn't take much for the Fortress tech to provide an image. "After you've done that, see if you can isolate the driver's face and clean it up enough for a positive identification."

"Jon Smith is in the building. He can help with the ID. I'll get back to you when I have the route nailed down and a face to go with the SUV."

"Hurry, Zane." His throat tightened at the thought of his aunt, somewhere around Otter Creek, hurt and at the mercy of a killer with a thirst for vengeance.

CHAPTER TWENTY-SIX

Quinn pushed back from the table. "Ethan needs you and Charlie," he said to Heidi.

She rose, grabbing Charlie's work harness and leash. "What's going on?"

"Someone kidnapped Ethan's aunt. He suspects Muehller and needs you and Charlie to tell him if he's right."

Poor Ethan, dealing with one thing after another at a time when he should be with his wife and child. She turned to the Labrador. "Sit, Charlie."

The dog sat and remained still while she strapped on his harness. Not sure what to expect, she said, "Might be wise to take our tracking gear, just in case. We can leave it in your SUV until we need it."

Quinn smiled. "I always carry my Go bag in the vehicle. The rest of my unit also carries their gear wherever they go. Fortress has been known to send a jet to pick us up if they need us bad enough."

Good to know they were always ready for a mission. Didn't surprise Heidi. Preparation was the mark of a Special Forces soldier. What had surprised her was Quinn's declaration of love so soon after reconnecting. She thought about that as she hurried to change into her boots, grab her gear bag, and her weather-proof coat. Heidi never thought she would hear those three precious words from Quinn Gallagher.

Why choose her? In Heidi's eyes, she was nothing special. In fact, she came with a truckload of trouble. She didn't want Quinn to regret falling in love with her. She wanted a marriage filled with love, laughter, and loyalty. Heidi thought she might be able to achieve that with Quinn and she would work hard to make that happen. She didn't want her home to be a war zone with constant bickering and fighting. She'd had enough of that as a kid.

Heidi double-checked the contents of her bag. Food for herself and Charlie, first-aid supplies, mylar blanket, lightweight tent if they should be caught in the elements and be unable to return to base camp. To the bag, she added the maps. She'd love to use one of those maps to find Ethan's aunt.

Would Quinn have a supply of food in his bag? If they were sent on a search, Heidi didn't have enough stores for him. She returned to the kitchen where Quinn, Charlie, and the others waited. "Quinn, do you have food in your bag? If not, we should pick up some. What I have won't be enough."

"I have MREs. I'll be fine."

She wrinkled her nose. Didn't sound tasty. Better than going hungry, though.

Levi closed the gap between them and pulled her into a hug. "Be careful, Heidi."

She tightened her arms around his waist. Levi felt like home and safety to her. Now that she thought about it, she felt the same way with Quinn. Maybe that's why she'd been comfortable with him from the moment she saw him at PSI. He'd been her hero as a kid. Now he was everything to her. She prayed she would be the same for him. "We may not have anything to go on, Levi. This could be a false alarm or the trail might disappear like it did at Madison's house a few hours ago."

Her cousin's troubled gaze met hers. "Don't take any chances. Please."

"I have a great bodyguard. We'll be fine."

Levi turned to Quinn. "Take care of her. I want her back in one piece."

Instead of taking offense and spouting off, the Fortress operative acknowledged the order with a snappy salute. He glanced at Dane and Angel. "Stay alert. While we're chasing international assassins, the arsonist is still gunning for your principal. If you think something isn't right, call PSI and get backup."

Dane frowned. "Why not call one of your teammates?"

"If we go after Muehller, the rest of Durango will be with us."

"Yes, sir."

Heidi snapped her fingers. "Charlie, come."

Minutes later, Quinn parked a few houses away from the police activity at one house. Heidi's attention shifted to an ambulance parked nearby. No lights, no hurried activity. Dread coiled in her stomach. Were they too late to help Ruth? She prayed that wasn't the case. Ethan needed a break.

"Heidi, we won't be allowed to take Charlie inside the house so we don't contaminate the crime scene." He hesitated, then said, "A friend of Ruth's was murdered in the house, baby."

She gasped. "That's terrible. Ethan thinks Muehller is behind this?"

"That's what he needs you and Charlie to confirm."

"I gave Nick the shirt from Muehller. Charlie will need access to it to refresh the scent in his mind."

"No problem." Quinn nodded at the SUV ahead of theirs. "That's Nick's vehicle. He'll have the bag for

Charlie." He circled the hood and helped Heidi to the pavement, turning her insides to mush. Quinn treated her with honor and respect without acting as if she were helpless and unable to care for herself. A fine balance for men to walk and he made it look easy. He must have learned well while caring for his mother and sisters after his father died.

She opened the door for Charlie and clipped his leash to the harness. "Find Ethan and tell him we're ready to work. Charlie and I will wait here." Might make her a coward, but she didn't want to catch a glimpse of a dead body, even from a distance. She'd had enough of death, thank you very much.

Quinn skirted law enforcement personnel as he crossed the lawn. Heidi was fascinated with all the activity as was Charlie. He seemed particularly interested in the two policemen who were about eighteen inches apart, walking the lawn with flashlights in their hands. Looking for signs of the killer? Perhaps they would find a clue indicating an identity, adding weight to the evidence the police needed.

Within two minutes, Quinn returned with the police chief following close behind. Ethan's purposeful strides ate up the distance quickly. Heidi swallowed hard. She would hate to have him come after her. Ethan Blackhawk looked strong and capable, confidence oozing with every step. At well over six feet, he was a powerful man without an ounce of flab on him.

"Thanks for coming," Ethan said as he unlocked the detective's SUV.

"We're happy to help. How's Serena?"

The somber look on his face lifted for a brief moment as his mouth curved into a smile. "Fantastic. She and Lucas are doing great."

Aww. Her heart melted. "Lucas is your new son?"

"He was born two hours ago. He's perfect, like his gorgeous mother. I almost can't believe he's mine." Ethan opened the hatchback and unlocked a secured box in the back. Inside was the plastic bag containing Muehller's shirt. He handed Heidi the bag. "Should I show you where we think the killer came into the house?"

Grateful he hadn't offered to take her inside the place, she nodded. She and Quinn followed the police chief to the back of the house, Charlie close to Heidi's side. The white house looked like a nice place to live. So did the neighborhood from what she'd seen as they drove here. The murder was sure to be a shock to the neighbors. She and Charlie had to find Ethan's aunt in time.

The policeman stopped at the edge of the yard and pointed to the back door where Nick Santana worked. "Evidence indicates he came through there and surprised Ruth in the kitchen." Ethan glanced at her. "How will we know if the Lab detects Muehller's scent?"

She lifted the bag. "This is the only scent Charlie is hunting for. If the intruder isn't Muehller, Charlie won't find his scent." Heidi knelt in front of Charlie and again forced enthusiasm into her voice. "Charlie, this is Hans. Find Hans."

Her partner sniffed the contents of the bag and wagged his tail. Sniffed again.

"Find Hans. Find him."

Charlie lifted his nose into the air, sniffed, paced. Watching his body language, Heidi knew he had caught the scent. Charlie headed for the back door where Nick paused in his task to observe the dog at work. "Find Hans, Charlie," Heidi said. "Where's Hans?"

The Lab moved toward the back of the yard and stopped at the gate. A whine and a glance at her. "Can we go through the gate?" she asked Ethan.

"Absolutely." With a gloved hand, he unlatched and opened the gate. Charlie darted to an alley where he paced, nose lifted, searching for a scent. Her Lab sat. "He's lost the scent. The killer must have gotten into a vehicle right here."

"It was Muehller?" Ethan pressed.

She nodded, holding up the bag. "This scent is what he searched for and found."

"Excellent. Now, if Zane will get back to me on the traffic cams, we'll have an idea where to start the search for my aunt." He gave a wry smile which didn't reach his eyes. "Provided Muehller didn't avoid the cameras."

"Doubt Muehller had time to locate all the cameras in the area," Quinn said. "He has to know the Otter Creek PD is hunting for him. If there's anything to see, Z will find it."

At that moment, Ethan's phone signaled an incoming call. "Blackhawk." The policeman listened a moment, a look of satisfaction growing on his face. "Send me everything you have. Thanks, Murphy. I owe you one."

"What did he find?" Quinn asked as he rubbed Charlie's head.

"He tracked the SUV down Main Street and out to Highway 18. From there, he lost the vehicle between two traffic cameras."

"Narrows down the search grid. At least we have a direction to start. Did he get a license plate or a face?"

"Oh, yeah. Zane Murphy is worth his weight in gold. If I wasn't worried about Maddox putting a bounty on my head, I'd do my best to convince him and Claire to move here. I can use someone with his talent in the police department."

Quinn barked out a laugh. "Sorry, Ethan. You can't pay him enough. I guarantee, the boss will exceed any offer you make to keep him. Besides, Z and the boss go way back. Those frog boys stick together."

Ethan grunted. "Figured as much." He turned to Heidi. "You up for a field trip if I can narrow down the search area?"

"We're ready. My gear is in Quinn's vehicle."

"I don't have to ask if you're ready, Quinn."

"Want me to contact the others?"

"Not yet. You and Heidi come with me. I want to see the video feed Zane sent to my email."

Quinn sent Ethan a pointed look. "I don't want Heidi inside the house."

That tight knot of dread in Heidi's stomach eased. Thank goodness. Quinn must have guessed her reluctance to enter the house. Heidi also wasn't sure how Charlie would react.

"Understood. That won't be necessary. Nick has a laptop inside his vehicle. I can access my inbox from his computer." He led them to Nick's SUV and grabbed the laptop. Once logged in, he clicked on the video Zane sent. He paused the forward movement on one frame and zoomed in. The face of the driver was grainy, but recognizable.

"Well?" Quinn demanded. "Is it Muehller?"

CHAPTER TWENTY-SEVEN

"Muehller took Ruth." Ethan tapped a couple keys and the video progressed again.

Quinn moved closer to the computer. His eyebrows rose as he noted the familiar stores and cross streets in the passing frames. Muehller drove right down Main Street. No turning his head as he passed places with obvious traffic cameras, almost as if he wanted Ethan to know who had Ruth. Probably did. Nothing like taunting the object of your vengeance, the ploy sure to add pressure to the lawman. However, if the assassin hoped to rattle Ethan Blackhawk, he was out of luck. Ethan didn't rattle. He planned every move and adjusted when something didn't work. Ethan was like a bulldog. Once he got his teeth into something, he didn't let go. Muehller wouldn't get away with this and Quinn couldn't wait to see his face when Ethan took him down. "Did you see Ruth in the frames?"

Ethan shook his head. He tapped another key and sent the video into fast forward. "There was blood in the kitchen. That's where we think Muehller grabbed my aunt."

The police chief stopped talking abruptly, his hand bunching into a powerful fist.

"If she's injured, then Ruth is either unconscious or Muehller tied her up and forced her to lay flat." Man, this had to be tearing Ethan apart. He adored his aunt.

"That's my guess as well." His voice sounded gruffer than normal. "Ruth wouldn't have gone down without a fight."

"No, she wouldn't." Quinn squeezed Ethan's shoulder a moment. "She's tough and smart. Ruth knows you're coming for her. That knowledge will comfort her and give her the grit to survive no matter what Muehller does."

"She's in her seventies, Quinn." His voice cracked. "Although she thinks she's invincible, Ruth can't handle the shocks she did when she was younger and had to raise a punk teenager on her own."

He snorted, thinking of the police chief as a trouble-making teen. Hard to picture that as Ethan was the face of law and order in Otter Creek. "I don't believe for a minute Ruth is that fragile."

"Why do you say that?"

"Because your aunt took a teenage punk to task last week in the town square. This boy topped Ruth by a good six inches. Didn't bother her. Never seen anything like that from her. Fragile, Ethan? Not in this lifetime."

"How do you know about this incident?"

"I witnessed it firsthand. The teen had been harassing his younger brother, calling him stupid and making him cry. I was about to stop to him, but Ruth got there first." He moved closer and dropped his voice to a murmur. "You know what I do for a living, Ethan. I wouldn't want to tangle with your aunt under any circumstances. Muehller won't get the best of her. Besides, didn't Ruth take on this guy two years ago and come out the victor?"

"She wasn't the focus of his interest. Serena was."

"She's not the focus now, either. You are. The point of the grab-and-go with Ruth is that Muehller wants you to pay for putting him in prison and your aunt is the bait. This guy is smart. He won't kill Ruth until he has you where he wants you."

"Which is where?"

"On your knees, watching him pull the trigger when he kills her. And if he is stupid enough to be inclined to do that before you arrive, Ruth will persuade him otherwise. She writes best-selling murder mysteries, Ethan. She knows how criminals think. Plus, Serena just gave your aunt a great reason to stay alive. Ruth Rollins will fight for the chance to hold your son."

Ethan cleared his throat. "Thanks." He returned his attention to the computer screen. His eyes narrowed. "That's Highway 18, the Rosedale exit."

Quinn leaned closer to the frozen frame on the screen. "That's all the footage?"

"The SUV disappeared before Rolling Meadows."

Which was the next exit. At least it was a start. Quinn rubbed a hand over his jaw, his fingers rasping over the beard growth. Now they knew a general direction However, Muehller could have taken many different back roads from that point. They needed a more focused starting point for Heidi and Charlie to work from. Even with Deke and Ace, they wouldn't have enough search teams to cover the area. The closest trained S & R team was several hours away. Until Muehller left the vehicle, Charlie wouldn't have a scent trail to follow. If they could find the vehicle Muehller drove, they would have a better idea where to look. "There's a lot of open countryside out there, Ethan. A few subdivisions scattered around, too." Plenty of places to hide, more hostages to take if Muehller thought he needed them. A stupid move, though. The more people you must control, the greater likelihood you'd fail. Under stressful circumstances, people weren't predictable.

Retribution

"I know. While this helps, it isn't enough. We need more for Charlie to go on."

Ethan's phone signaled an incoming call. He glanced at the screen, then put the call on speaker. "Blackhawk."

"Chief, received a call from old man Lawrence. He wants you to call him immediately."

The police dispatcher sounded frazzled. Amusement zoomed through Quinn at her words. Mr. Lawrence was infamous around town, surly most of the time. The town folks loved his wife and enjoyed the farmer's two camels, Bonnie and Clyde. Elementary school kids looked forward to field trips to the Lawrence farm each fall and spring to see the animals, including the camels the old man bought for his now-grown granddaughter.

"If this is about his escape-artist camel, Bonnie, tell him I can't help him right now, Suzie. He'll have to look for her himself. We're shorthanded at the moment."

"He said you'd say that. He also informed me the call wasn't about Bonnie, but he refused to talk to anyone but you. Look, Ethan, I know you're slammed with the investigations right now. Talking to Lawrence will only take a couple minutes and will save the rest of us aggravation. You know he won't stop calling until you talk to him."

Ethan scowled. "I'll take care of it." He tapped his screen and pulled up his contact list. He placed the call and put this one on speaker as well while he restarted the video feed. A moment later, a deep, raspy voice answered the phone. "Mr. Lawrence, it's Ethan Blackhawk. Suzie said you called. I've only got a minute. What do you need?"

"Why didn't you let the town know that Mitch Harrington fella was out of prison?"

The police chief paused the video feed, stared at the phone. "Hans Muehller is the guy's real name, Mr. Lawrence. Are you telling me you've seen him recently?"

"I sure did. Not more than two hours ago. That boy was nothing but trouble when he was here before. Why would he think he's welcome back in this town after serving his time? And let me tell you, spending a little over a year in prison for all the ugly crimes he committed is not justice in my book. You ought to do something about that, Blackhawk."

Quinn wanted to laugh at the old man's belief that Ethan could do anything to right injustice in the correctional system. Ethan was good, all right, but not that good. No one was. All you could do was your best to see justice served. Thankfully, more often than not, the justice system worked.

"Where did you see Muehller?" Ethan asked.

"Driving down Forest Road. Can't figure out why he's going back in there. This ain't tourist season."

Quinn thought about that. Isolated location, far enough away from town to prevent any undue attention. Forest Road led to cabins tourists rented during the spring, summer, and fall seasons. Muehller had to stay somewhere while stalking Ethan, Serena, and Ruth. If Ethan was right about Muehller having money and alternate IDs stashed around the country, there was no telling how he'd registered, if he'd even bothered to do so. Quinn wouldn't. Not that many people around camping or staying in the cabins. With no one registered for a cabin, Muehller wouldn't worry about housekeeping walking in on him and his hostage.

Then again, Quinn wouldn't be caught in a building at all if the layout wasn't good for security. Too many walls and too few windows limited the line of sight, not something with which he and his teammates were comfortable. Would Muehller think the same way? Maybe not. He wasn't trained as a Special Forces soldier. Also, based on what Josh had told him, the assassin had an ego problem. He might not believe the Otter Creek police would track him down.

In a way, Quinn hoped that was the case. He hated to think of Ruth out in the elements. No snow on the ground, but it was cold and damp, the ground wet. Not good for anyone to be exposed to the weather long, especially someone older.

"No, it's not tourist season," Ethan agreed. "He's not a tourist. Muehller escaped from prison a few days ago. I need to find him, fast. What was he driving, Mr. Lawrence?"

"Dark blue SUV. Nevada plates. Couldn't catch any letters or numbers. Boy was going too fast and my eyes ain't as good as they used to be when I was your age. Heard about Ruth so I know you're busy. Want me to see if I can locate him for you?"

Quinn's blood ran cold. If the farmer actually managed to locate the assassin, Lawrence would try to apprehend Muehller himself instead of calling the cops.

"No, but I appreciate the offer of assistance. Muehller is as dangerous as they come. He wouldn't think twice about killing you. I don't want to explain to your sweet wife that you were helping me with an investigation. She'd have my hide."

A bark of laughter from the grizzled old farmer. "Guess you got a point there. She's not so sweet when she's riled. I ought to know. Done more than my fair share of riling over the years. To be honest, I'm surprised she stayed with me."

A quick grin from the police chief at that last comment. "Thanks, Mr. Lawrence. Appreciate the information."

"Yep." And Lawrence ended the call.

Ethan logged off the laptop. "Need to check the campground and cabins."

"We'll follow you," Quinn said.

He paused, glancing over his shoulder. "Might be a wild goose chase."

"Could be right on target as well. Ethan, let us help. You don't have to do this alone." In fact, he shouldn't. Quinn had complete faith in his friend's skills, but even a Special Forces soldier needed a battle buddy to watch his back.

Ethan studied Heidi's face a moment. "I know Quinn is up for this. But after the injuries you sustained in the blast yesterday, are you ready for work?"

Heidi nodded. "I'm fine. Maddox made sure I had some training. I'm not in Quinn's league or yours, but I can hold my own. I'm armed and comfortable with my Glock. I trained in self-defense. I won't take chances, Ethan. I promise." Her gaze slid to Quinn's. "I have too much to live for."

"Have you tracked at night?" Quinn asked. "It's almost dark now. By the time we get to Forest Road, there won't be any sunlight left."

"A couple times, but it's dangerous. The shadows mask the depth of depressions and hide tree roots. The risk of injury to me and Charlie is high. Why? What are you thinking?"

"NVGs. Night vision goggles."

Heidi smiled. "That's not part of my gear bag."

"I have a pair in mine. Standard equipment. Ethan, what about you?"

"I do have a pair. Risky, though, Quinn. If we stumble on Muehller, he could blind us for critical seconds with a flashlight."

True enough. Ruth's life was at stake, though. They couldn't sit on the sidelines if there was a chance to find her and bring her home. "We'll have to take the risk. Might also be a theoretical discussion. If we don't find Muehller at the cabins or campground, we may have to wait until morning."

"If Ethan's aunt is injured, we don't have a choice but to start a search if we know where to begin," Heidi said. "Charlie and I will depend on you and your NVGs to keep us safe as we chase the scent trail."

"Are you sure you are ready to do a full on search?" Ethan asked, his expression troubled. "You were just released from the hospital last night with a concussion."

"Ruth's safety is on the line. I'm sure my new bosses will allow me another day to recuperate if I ask."

"No problem." No one was going to give her grief over a second day off, especially if she helped them locate and rescue Ruth. All the members of Durango had a crush on Ethan's aunt.

"All right." Ethan returned the laptop to Nick's SUV and locked the doors. "Let me tell my detectives what's going on and where we're headed." He pointed a finger at Quinn. "Don't leave before I return, Gallagher."

Quinn grinned. Yeah, the police chief knew him well. That's exactly what he'd wanted to do. "Yes, sir."

Ethan strode away.

"Are you sure you want to do this, Heidi?" Quinn pulled her against him and wrapped his arms around her. "Ethan's right, you know. What we're doing is against the doctor's orders."

"I'm well enough." She shrugged. "I'll rest better knowing Ruth is safe and well."

Yet another reason why he loved this beautiful woman. "All right. Here are the rules. While I will defer to you and Charlie on the search, if we find Muehller, do exactly what I tell you to do. No questions or hesitation. The arsonist is nothing compared Hans Muehller."

"We have to try, Quinn. I couldn't live with myself if we lost Ethan's aunt because I wimped out."

Ethan returned. "Let's go."

Quinn followed Ethan through town and to the highway which skirted Otter Creek. Thirty minutes later, Ethan turned off his headlights.

"What's he doing?" Heidi leaned closer to the windshield. "I don't see anything wrong with his vehicle."

He followed Ethan's lead and turned off his own headlights. "There shouldn't be many people out here. If Muehller is holed up in one of the cabins, we don't want to alert him to our presence before we assess the situation. If we go in blind, Ruth could be injured further."

Quarter of a mile down the road was the entrance to the hunting lodge and cabins. They parked a few hundred yards from the parking lot and got out of the vehicles. Heidi attached Charlie's leash to his harness and slipped her gear bag onto her back while Quinn shrugged into his own.

When Ethan glanced back at them, Quinn nodded. He and Heidi were ready. The police chief tossed Quinn the bag with Muehller's shirt, which he shoved into his pack.

They walked the remaining distance, pausing at the tree line to scan the area. Quinn's heart sank. No sign of occupancy at the lodge or cabins. A few more cabins were in the trees behind the lodge. Ethan signaled them to wait, then walked across the parking lot to the lodge office.

He returned a couple minutes later. "Nothing," he whispered. "Mr. Phillips says there's no one staying here right now. I told him I would look around to make sure Muehller hadn't broken into a cabin." Ethan turned, pointed to the dirt trail leading through the forest. "This path will lead us to the other cabins without exposing us to view until we're ready to be seen."

Ethan and Quinn pulled out their NVGs and slipped them on. Quinn threaded his fingers through Heidi's and led her down the trail after Ethan. Though he was the one with the visual help, Heidi moved quietly with confidence.

At the edge of a clearing, Ethan again signaled them to stop. Quinn moved Heidi behind him. "Stay here," he whispered. He moved into position beside Ethan.

A hundred yards in front of them sat a cabin with a dark SUV parked at the back. "I'll check the vehicle's plates," Quinn murmured as he shrugged off his pack. He handed Ethan a thermal imager. "Check the cabin for occupants. I'll be back in a minute."

Weapon in hand, he slipped into the trees and worked his way to the far side of the cabin near the vehicle. Couldn't make out the color in the darkness. Might be blue, black, or a dark green. However, the plates were issued in Nevada. They'd found Muehller's ride.

Quinn scanned the windows. Didn't see any lights, not even a candle flickering or a fire in the fireplace. Of course, either of those would be a dead giveaway of cabin occupancy.

He circled back around to Ethan and Heidi.

"Is it the right vehicle?" Heidi asked.

"Nevada plates. Can't tell about the color in the darkness." He glanced at Ethan. "You'll need to get prints to confirm, but I'd say this is Muehller's ride. Anything on the imager?"

Ethan shook his head. "No heat signatures. There's no one inside that cabin."

Quinn stared, puzzled. If the cabin was empty, where were Muehller and Ruth?

CHAPTER TWENTY-EIGHT

Heidi's heart sank. Where was Ruth? She turned her gaze to the cabin shrouded in darkness. While she prayed nothing bad had happened to Ruth, how long would it take for a dead body to cool off enough the thermal imaging device Ethan used wouldn't pick up that person? From the grimness of Ethan's expression he'd already thought of that terrible possibility. Oh, man. She didn't want that heartbreak for Ethan and Serena on the day their son was born. They shouldn't have ugly memories of this day. Little Lucas's birthday should be a happy occasion, not one where sadness crept in to mar the celebration.

"We need to check the cabin," Ethan murmured. He turned to Heidi. "I want you and Charlie stay here in the safety of the trees."

"Yes, sir."

Quinn cupped Heidi's cheek with his palm, leaned in, and kissed her. "Stay out of sight no matter what you hear, baby. Ethan and I can take care of ourselves much better if we don't have to worry about you charging into the line of fire. We will put your safety first, but Muehller won't be so kind. He'll see you as another target to eliminate."

"I promise to stay hidden." She didn't want to be a distraction that might cause him or Ethan harm. Heidi didn't mind admitting she was no match for an international assassin despite the training from Fortress. The operatives had done their best, but the training time was too short. The training was to be used if she was separated from her bodyguards and had to defend herself to survive. In a one-on-one confrontation with the assassin, she would come out on the losing end.

Her boyfriend inclined his head toward a thick stand of trees to the left. "That's your best bet for cover. Muehller would have to stumble over you to know you're there as long as you're quiet." He glanced at Charlie. "What about him? Will he stay quiet if something happens?"

Heidi gave a quick nod. "Don't worry about him. He's well trained. Be careful, Quinn. I have plans for you." She leaned in close. "A lot of them."

With a soft chuckle, he gave her a quick, hard kiss before nudging her toward the stand of trees. Heidi signaled Charlie to follow her and together they moved into the shadowed landscape. Once satisfied that she was as safe as possible under the circumstances, Quinn followed Ethan into the clearing. Both of them had guns in their hands.

Better have her own weapon ready in case she needed it. She reached behind her back. Wrapping her fingers around the grip of her Glock, she held the gun by her thigh as she knelt beside a silent Charlie. Her search partner knew something dangerous was happening because he stood stock still, alert and watchful.

She turned her attention to the clearing on the other side of the trees, checking on the progress of the men. Heidi watched in fascination as Ethan and Quinn worked their way from shadow to shadow in absolute silence. No footfalls, no cracking branches or twigs, and only a series of hand signals used for communication. Made her wonder if they had worked missions together before. As they neared the cabin, Quinn broke off and moved around the back of the structure while Ethan continued to move toward the front.

He checked around the front window, then angled toward the door. Standing to the side, Ethan reached out and turned the knob. Gun hand raised and ready, he pushed open the door and slipped inside the dark cabin.

The wait seemed an eternity now that Ethan and Quinn were out of sight. She worried the next sound she heard might be gunfire shattering the night's quiet. However, before much time passed, Quinn came to the front door and trotted across the clearing to Heidi and Charlie. "What did you find?" she asked.

"Basic medical supplies, bloody bandages, and discarded boxes of takeout food, most likely from a nearby town. There's no way Muehller could show his face in town and someone not recognize him. Ruth and Muehller are gone."

"Where could he have taken Ethan's aunt?" Heidi frowned. "He doesn't have his vehicle."

"Could have stolen another one, babe. This clown is pretty resourceful from what I understand. That's why we need you and Charlie. You can give us an idea of whether or not Muehller put Ruth in another vehicle, walked her out of here, or carried her away. Josh said this guy carried Serena a half mile when he abducted her. With his line of work, he had to stay in shape. Muehller's had nothing but time on his hands since he went to prison. To kill time, many prisoners lift weights and jog. If this guy followed the norm, he shouldn't have any trouble carrying Ruth a short distance."

He clasped her hand and led her and Charlie across the clearing, steering her around rocks and tree roots, and helping her over the uneven terrain. Ethan met them at the front of the cabin, phone pressed to his ear.

"I need another team out here at the lodge, Rod. Cabin eight. Quinn and I found Muehller's SUV and the cabin where he took Ruth. They're gone, though. We'll see whether Charlie can tell us if Muehller drove off in another vehicle with Ruth or if they're somewhere out in the forest." A minute later, Ethan slid his phone into his pocket. "Stella will be here to process the scene in a few minutes. Quinn, you have the bag with Muehller's shirt?"

"Right here. Stella should have someone with her when she processes the scene. Muehller might return."

Ethan palmed his phone and fired off a text. "Done."

Quinn slid off his pack, pulled out the plastic bag, and handed it to Heidi. "Let's see if Charlie has a successful search this time. If not, I vote we let Ethan play the lost victim."

His friend's eyebrows rose. "What's this?"

"Charlie becomes depressed if he can't locate his target. This afternoon, I had to play hide-and-seek with Charlie."

"I take it he found you."

"Yep. Took him all of ten minutes."

Heidi opened the bag for a third time and held it out to Charlie. He sniffed, looked up at her, sniffed again, then wagged his tail. "This is Hans, Charlie. Find Hans."

Charlie raised his nose and paced, searching for the scent. He trotted around the side of the house to the back near the SUV and lunged toward the forest.

Heidi held tight to the leash. "He's picked up the trail. Looks like Muehller when into the forest recently."

Ethan scanned the area. "Quinn, call in the rest of your team. Let's run this guy down."

"Copy that." He walked away a few steps and placed a call. In less than a minute, Quinn was back. "Twenty minutes. Josh said to wait for Durango to arrive before you make a move on Muehller."

"If I can," Ethan said. "No promises. Ruth's safety comes before mine."

"Fair enough. Heidi, you ready?"

"Let's do this. I'm ready for a mug of hot coffee. This damp has chilled me down to my bones." Charlie yipped, impatient to find Muehller. "Find Hans, Charlie." Heidi allowed the Lab to take the lead.

Quinn held Heidi's hand as they hurried after Charlie with Ethan close behind. The Lab led them through the trees, around bushes and boulders. When Heidi stumbled over a couple exposed tree roots she couldn't see in the darkness, Quinn kept her upright and on the move. Might be wise to add a pair of NVGs to her gear bag. She would ask Quinn later about helping her choose a good pair.

"I hope you know where we are," she murmured to Quinn. "Every tree looks alike to me and I haven't been able to learn the terrain yet."

"Of course I do."

She glanced at him before returning her attention to the unfamiliar ground in front of her. "Are you being serious?"

"What do you think?"

Heidi analyzed what she heard in his voice. "I'm not positive. I hear a couple of things in your voice. Humor and confidence. Knowing you, though, I suspect you do know where we are."

"I have GPS. I can get us back to the lodge."

Good thing. It was pitch black out here. It would take her forever to find her way back if it weren't for Charlie or Quinn. Charlie was excellent at retracing his steps. Without Quinn and his handy NVGs, she and her search partner would be forced to wait until morning to head back to the lodge, not something she wanted on this cold winter night. Holing up for a night of undesired camping was better than trying to return to the lodge without light and ending up with a sprained ankle or worse.

When she noticed Charlie panting, she stopped him and slid her pack off her shoulders. "Rest break for Charlie," she whispered. "Can't afford for him to become exhausted."

"Understood," Ethan said. "How long?"

"Fifteen minutes if we can spare it."

With a quick nod, he said, "I'll return soon, then we can head out again." Within a few steps, he disappeared from sight through the trees.

Heidi frowned as she filled the collapsible bowl with water for her partner. Once Charlie drank his fill, Heidi emptied out the remaining water and returned the bowl to her pack along with the half-filled water bottle. "Where did Ethan go?"

"Scouting the area to see if he can find traces of Muehller's passage."

"By himself? In the dark?" She didn't understand how he could see anything out here.

"First, he's an Army Ranger and a very experienced cop. He can take care of himself. Second, Ethan's the best tracker around. Even a bent grass blade can tell him volumes. If you're lost, he's the man you want looking for you."

Maybe. She would rather have Quinn and his teammates hunting for her. There was something about them that told her they would never give up the chase no matter what obstacles they had to overcome or how long the search for her lasted. She trusted them with her life.

Heidi stared at the place where Ethan had disappeared. Perhaps the police chief was the same. Despite not knowing him for long, she believed he would never stop looking for his aunt. Anyone with eyes could see Ethan Blackhawk adored Ruth. She was a lucky woman to be so loved.

At the fifteen minute mark on the dot, Ethan returned. "Ready?"

"Find anything?" Quinn asked as he helped Heidi to her feet.

"Signs of recent passage up ahead. Let's see if Charlie agrees with me on the direction Muehller took."

Heidi refreshed the scent for Charlie and they set off again, heading the direction Ethan had taken into the trees. Guess Ethan was right about the recent passage. Muehller must have come this way. How did he carry Ruth this far? Prison workout fit or not, they must have walked at least a mile from the lodge.

She thought about the distance and the strength necessary to carry a person that far. Scary thought if the assassin had done just that. Perhaps he hadn't had to carry Ethan's aunt the whole distance. If Ruth wasn't too badly hurt, she could have walked some of the distance on her own.

Ethan came up beside them. "There's a forest ranger's cabin up ahead," he said softly. "Charlie's been heading straight for that structure."

"Is the ranger in residence at this time of year?" Quinn asked, skepticism in his voice.

The police chief shook his head. "There shouldn't be anyone there. The ranger came through here three days ago to scout the area for trouble. He's not due to return until next week."

Amazed that he knew this particular bit of information, Heidi asked, "How did you find that out?"

"Called the forest ranger while I was tracking. He's a friend. As far as he knows, this is the only permanent structure in the area besides the lodge and cabins. Muehller doesn't like roughing it. The man likes his luxuries which is why I'm happy he's been in prison for the last two years. No luxuries to be had." Ethan stepped in front of Heidi and Quinn and held up his closed fist.

When Quinn pulled her to a stop, Heidi recalled Charlie with a soft whistle. He trotted back to her side, tail wagging, tongue hanging out. Her buddy would need to eat soon. He was burning calories in this search.

The police chief turned with a finger to his lips and motioned for them to remain in place. Between one breath and the next, he had moved off to the left without even a branch quivering to show his passage.

Goodness, Heidi would love to learn how to do that. Might be a great skill to have in her arsenal one day. Quinn nudged her deeper into the shadow of a large tree and tugged her against his side.

"Okay?" he whispered.

She nodded, snuggling closer, careful not to obstruct his view or impede his gun hand. Charlie laid down at her feet. With his dark fur, he blended into the darkness. "Why are we waiting?"

"Ethan must have seen or heard something. He's checking it out."

Grateful for people so much more experienced in this stealth business, Heidi subsided into silence so Quinn would hear if someone approached their position.

A couple minutes later, Ethan returned as silently as he'd left. "I heard a door shut in the distance. The ranger's cabin is about six hundred yards ahead. While it's supposed to be empty, there's a flickering light in there. Someone lit a fire in the fireplace. Curtains are closed so I can't see inside the structure. I hear someone walking around because the floor's creaking."

At that moment, Ethan's phone must have vibrated because he removed it from his pocket and glanced at the screen. "Dispatch," he murmured. He pressed the phone to his ear. "Blackhawk."

The night was so quiet and, with Ethan close, Heidi and Quinn heard the other side of the conversation.

"Chief, there's an urgent call for you. The man won't identify himself, but he says he has your aunt."

His face hardened. "Patch him through." A second later, Ethan said, "Blackhawk."

"It's been a long time, Blackhawk," growled a male voice.

"Not long enough, Muehller."

"Now, now, that's not very civil of you."

"You want civil? Turn yourself in. I'll be happy to escort you to my jail cell until the feds haul you off to prison."

Soft laughter sent chill bumps surging over Heidi. Hans Muehller sounded evil to her and he meant to hurt Ethan if he could. They couldn't let Muehller have his way. Lucas needed his father. Like she and Quinn had needed their fathers. If they'd been men like Otter Creek's police chief, would her life and Quinn's have been different? She'd like to believe so. At the very least, their fathers would have made different choices. Maybe she and Quinn would have gotten together sooner. They could already have a son or daughter.

"I don't think so, Blackhawk. I have something you want. If you want to see your aunt alive again, you will do exactly what I tell you. Otherwise, you'll find her dead with a bullet to the forehead."

CHAPTER TWENTY-NINE

Quinn shifted Heidi closer to his side as anger settled on Ethan's expression. He already knew where this conversation was going before Muehller said anything else.

"Where and when?" Ethan asked.

Yep, that's what he had thought the police chief would say. The question was, how soon would the assassin try to push Ethan's buttons and rattle him?

"That easy?" The assassin sounded suspicious.

"You have my aunt. I love her," he said simply.

"Aren't you going to thank me?"

"For what?"

"Leaving your precious wife alone. Your pregnant wife. She glows, doesn't she?"

"Left her alone, huh? What do you call shooting at the SUV she was riding in? No, I don't think so, Muehller. You blame both of us for spending the last two years of your miserable life in prison. I can't see you letting that go out of the goodness of your heart."

Soft laughter drifted through the speaker. "Very good, Blackhawk. You're right, of course. Both of you will pay for subjecting me to dull prison life. Serena is more beautiful than I remembered. After you're dead, I might reacquaint myself with her. Have to get rid of the brat, though. Squalling babies aren't my thing."

Rage filled Ethan's face.

Quinn squeezed Ethan's shoulder to get the other man's attention. "Don't let him get to you," he mouthed.

His friend visibly relaxed, gave a quick nod of thanks for the reminder. "I want to talk to Ruth. Otherwise, no matter what you ask, the answer will be no."

A little fumbling sounded over the phone's speaker, then a female voice said, "Ethan." Aggravation and weakness came through in the woman's tone.

"How badly are you hurt, Ruth?" he asked.

"This bozo hit the back of my head when he broke into my house. I imagine I need stitches. The bleeding has continued since he dragged me into his vehicle, then carried me off through the woods to some rustic cabin."

Quinn had to admire the fact Ruth was trying to give Ethan as much information as she could without angering her captor.

"Head wounds tend to bleed a lot," Ethan said.

"I think I know that from my research and now from personal experience," she said tartly. "Tell me something I don't know."

Her spunky attitude made Quinn grin. If she was fifty years younger, he might have been tempted to make a play for her himself. No wonder she'd been able to handle Ethan as a teenager. She was indeed a force to be reckoned with.

"Help is coming."

Silence, then, "I see. Good."

More fumbling, then Muehller returned. "For shame. You shouldn't give your aunt false hope. If I'm feeling generous, the old bat might survive. You and your wife will not. Too bad about the baby. Enough chitchat, Blackhawk. You satisfied your aunt is in reasonably good health?"

"Tell me where and when. I'll be there."

"No one else, just you."

"Where and when?" Ethan repeated without addressing Muehller's demand that he come alone to surrender himself.

Quinn's eyes narrowed. If Ethan thought for one minute Quinn would let him walk into danger alone, he was doomed to disappointment. Not happening, not on his watch.

"There's a cabin back in the woods about a mile from the lodge."

Satisfaction gleamed in Ethan's gaze. "I know it."

"Be here in an hour. Alone, Blackhawk. If you don't follow my instructions, the first bullet goes into your aunt, the second into you. You know I don't miss."

"One condition."

A sigh. "What now?"

"You leave my wife and child alone as well as Ruth. You don't go after them now or at any time in the future. Serena was an innocent bystander who happened to be in the wrong place at the wrong time. I'm the one you want, not Serena. I know from your history you don't hurt children. I'm asking you to honor that as well. And Ruth? She's just a pawn for you to get to me. Don't waste your bullet."

Laughter from Muehller. "I could promise each of those things and renege after you're dead. Why would you trust anything I said?"

"Because you're a man of your word. While I don't condone your career choice, I appreciate a man who keeps his promises and that's you, Muehller. If you promise me you'll leave my wife, child and aunt alone, I'll surrender to you."

A moment of silence, then, "Very well. Serena, the brat, and the old bat are off limits. Come alone to this godforsaken cabin in an hour. Say your goodbyes to your pretty wife because she is soon to be a pretty widow."

"One hour." Ethan ended the call. "How far out is the rest of Durango, Quinn?"

Quinn pulled out his phone and fired off a text. He got a response seconds later. "Five minutes."

"How do they know where we are?" Heidi asked.

"Fortress operatives have GPS trackers embedded under the skin. Josh is tracking me using his phone." He turned his attention back to Ethan. "You're not going to sacrifice yourself for Ruth. You know we love her, but Lucas needs his father and Serena needs her husband."

"I have no intention of dying."

"Good to hear. Do you have a plan?"

"I'm working on it."

"Yeah? Work faster. We need to catch this clown by surprise. That means we need to beat the one hour deadline."

"My thought exactly." He stared at Quinn a moment, expression thoughtful. "You have a plan."

He did. Didn't like it, but when Durango arrived, they'd hash out the fine details. "Yep, a bad one."

"We'll make the plan better. Let's hear this flawed masterpiece."

Quinn turned his head to look at Heidi. "My girlfriend and I got lost in the woods while we were walking our dog. We've been wandering around for hours and happened upon this cabin with a fire going in the fireplace. We stopped to ask for directions."

"No," Ethan snapped. "It's too dangerous for Heidi. If you use this scenario, do it without her."

Quinn shook his head, worry knotting his gut. The idea of putting Heidi directly in the line of fire and in the crosshairs of a killer made him feel ill. "Can't. Doesn't work for a guy alone to ask for directions. Any man would be more likely to try and figure a way back on his own."

"And get more hopelessly lost," Heidi muttered. "I've rescued a couple of them. Ethan, Quinn is right. This could work. Will your aunt give us away?"

A snort from the police chief. "Are you kidding? Ruth has a poker face. I never knew what she was thinking and I lived with her for years. No way will Muehller learn that she knows Quinn. Easy in your case since she's never met you. Fair warning, though. Ruth will be fascinated with Charlie. He'll more than likely appear in her next mystery novel."

Heidi grinned. "Hear that, Charlie? You're going to be famous."

A soft whistle was the only warning before the rest of Durango walked through the trees to them. All of them, like Quinn, were dressed in the black uniform they used on missions.

Rio frowned at Heidi and Quinn. "So much for following the doctor's orders," he said.

Quinn scowled at his teammate. "Couldn't be helped. Muehller has Ruth and she's hurt."

Durango's medic stilled. "How bad?"

"She says Muehller hit the back of her head. She's been bleeding for about five hours," Ethan said. "Might need stitches."

"Do you know if she lost consciousness for any length of time?"

"Didn't get a chance to ask her. Muehller called, demanding I surrender so he can kill me. He let me talk to her for a minute. Based on what I saw on the way here, Ruth was unconscious for a time. Muehller carried her for a quarter mile or so, then forced her to walk." His jaw flexed.

"You tracked them through the woods at night?" Josh asked, eyebrows raised.

"Charlie did most of the work."

"Good job, buddy," Alex murmured, rubbing the Lab's head.

Charlie wagged his tail.

"So what's the plan, Ethan?" Josh asked. "You aren't going to walk in and let this guy kill you."

"I don't have plans to die tonight. However, any plan we come up with will involve me surrendering to Muehller. Anything else will endanger Ruth further. Plus, she needs medical attention sooner than later. I'm not letting Muehller kill her."

"Of course not," Nate said. "We love her, too, Ethan. Where did Muehller take her?"

"Forest ranger's cabin about six hundred yards north of here."

"Do you know the layout or are we working blind?"

Ethan grabbed a nearby stick and drew the cabin in the dirt, pointing out the windows and front and back entrances. "Here's the problem. If we go in guns blazing, Ruth could well be caught in the crossfire. I can't take that chance."

Josh frowned as he studied the crude drawing. "Suggestions?"

"Quinn came up with a lame plan."

"Hey, the plan might be lame, but it will get me inside the cabin where I can help you."

"It also puts Heidi and Charlie in the line of fire," Ethan insisted.

"Let's hear it," Josh said.

Quinn laid out his idea and waited for his teammates' reaction.

"Lame," Alex agreed. "But it'll work to get you some help inside that cabin, Ethan." He gave a quick grin. "Not that you'll need it."

"Let's plan this out," Josh said. "Ethan, what's your deadline?"

"Less than an hour."

"Then let's figure out what we need to do to help Heidi and Charlie stay safe, as well as Ruth."

CHAPTER THIRTY

Heidi's hands grew clammy the closer she and Quinn walked to the darkened log cabin where Ruth was being held captive. Just the thought of having to face down a professional killer made her wish she hadn't eaten anything recently. She planned to treat herself to some decadent dessert after they rescued Ethan's aunt. Something laced with chocolate.

"You okay, baby?" Quinn murmured.

"Not really."

"We worked through every possible scenario. This option seemed the best."

"I know. I agreed with your logic. This plan makes the most sense and is the most plausible explanation for our sudden appearance at Muehller's front door." Heidi squeezed his hand, feeling bad for causing him more distress. During the discussion with Durango and Ethan, Quinn's reluctance to use his own plan was obvious. No one else had a better suggestion. "I want to help. I trust you and your teammates to keep me and Charlie safe."

"Stick to the plan, Heidi. You can do this. I have confidence in you."

Despite the fear, those words warmed a corner of her heart. No one else but Levi had ever believed in her. To have the man she hoped to marry soon express that kind of confidence in her was more than she hoped for at this stage in their relationship.

Through the ear piece Alex placed in her ear, Durango's sniper said, "We've got your back, sugar. We won't let anything happen to you."

Josh chimed in. "Drop the second we tell you to hit the floor. Your job is to protect Charlie. We'll take care of you."

"No problem my knees are knocking already. Don't worry. I'll do what I'm supposed to do. Sorry to sound like a wuss. I won't let you down."

Nate snorted. "You're not a wuss, Heidi. Any smart person would be afraid in this situation."

That should have made her feel better. It didn't. She was terrified. Heidi decided to cut herself a break. Hans Muehller was an evil man. She was right to be afraid of him. But she'd told Quinn the truth. She did trust him and his teammates. If anyone could pull this off with minimal injuries, it was the Durango team.

Even though Heidi wouldn't admit it out loud, she was more terrified for Quinn than for herself. When the bullets flew, and they would, he'd put himself between her and Muehller's gun. The man she loved with all her heart wasn't wearing a bulletproof vest and, based on the discussion between Ethan and Durango, Muehller didn't miss his targets. When Charlie pressed against her leg, she caressed the Lab's head as much to comfort him as to comfort herself. She didn't want to lose Quinn now that she'd found him again. They had so much life left to live together, to create the family neither of them had growing up.

"On task. Report," Josh murmured through the Fortress comm system.

"In position," Alex said. The sniper was in the fork of a nearby tree, scoped rifle in hand. Another man who didn't miss his targets.

Nate, Rio, and Ethan checked in.

"Copy," Durango's leader said. "Hold positions. Quinn, you and Heidi are up. Watch yourselves."

"Roger that," Quinn murmured.

Show time. Hand in hand, Heidi and Quinn crossed the remaining distance to the front of the cabin with only a couple of stumbles. Quinn kept her upright, though he tried to look as though he were injured in case the assassin watched their progress. To prevent further suspicions than Muehller already would have when two strangers appeared on his doorstep, Quinn ditched the NVGs and his gear bag at the stand of trees where Heidi hid. She left her equipment bag with his along with their cell phones. Couldn't claim they were unprepared for the great outdoors if they were well equipped with a mapping system in their phones. Wonder how Quinn would explain the lack of modern communication technology?

"Let's do this." Quinn draped his arm across Heidi's shoulders, limped the remaining distance to the cabin door and knocked.

"Hello?" Heidi called out. "Is anyone home? We need help."

No answer.

"Again," Josh murmured. "Heat signature shows Muehller stopped pacing. He's approaching the door."

Quinn knocked again, harder.

"Please," Heidi said. "We need help. My boyfriend is injured."

The knob turned and the wooden door opened. A blond-haired man about six feet tall with icy blue eyes stood in the doorway, scowling, glancing over their shoulders before settling on their faces again. "What do you want?" he snapped. "You're trespassing."

Charlie let out three barks, tail wagging furiously. He'd found Hans, all right. A grumpy Hans. The assassin was a fine one to talk about trespassing since he was holed up in the ranger's cabin.

She used a hand signal to tell Charlie not to bark any more, then fed him a treat as a reward for a successful search. "That's enough, Charlie." To Muehller, she said, "My boyfriend sprained his ankle. We've been walking for hours, trying to get back to the lodge, and now we're hopelessly lost. Every tree looks alike. I swear we passed the same rock formation three times. Can you help us?"

"I could have figured out where we are," Quinn growled. "You wouldn't give me a chance."

She frowned at him. "Right. That's why we've been walking in circles. No more chances or trying to spare your male pride, baby. I'm tired, cold, and have blisters on top of blisters on my feet. We're getting directions."

"Can you have this lover's quarrel somewhere else? I'm busy." Muehller scanned the area again. Would he see Durango or Ethan? No, of course not. They were professionals. The assassin wouldn't see them until it was much too late.

"Move this inside," Josh murmured in the comm system. "Old Hans is pretty twitchy."

"I can't go another step," Heidi whined. "I need to use the bathroom and my boyfriend needs ice for his ankle. I promise we won't stay long. Just point us in the right direction after we rest a couple minutes, and we'll get out of your way."

Muehller let his gaze drift slowly over Heidi. Instant revulsion made her shudder. Good grief. How could she have forgotten that Muehller had been in prison for two years? That was a long time to be in solitary confinement and away from women. Quinn tightened his hold on her shoulder. He wouldn't let Muehller touch her and his teammates were less than two minutes away from the cabin. One word and they would storm the place. A look might make her want to barf but it wouldn't kill her to endure the lechery for a short time.

"Maybe you should come in," the assassin almost purred. "I'm always willing to help a damsel in distress." He stepped back and opened the door wider.

He distressed and disgusted her. Heidi swallowed the bile surging into her throat. She couldn't vomit all over Muehller's shoes. He'd kick them out for sure and Quinn wouldn't be able to assist Ethan. "Thank you," she murmured as she pretended to help Quinn limp into the cabin. As they moved deeper into the room, Heidi's gaze collided with the alarmed one of Ethan's aunt. The police chief had told her to be proactive, that she would catch the cues fast. "Hello, I'm Heidi. This is my boyfriend, Quinn. Thank you for letting us impose on you for a few minutes."

That fast, Ruth Rollins put on her game face, relief in her eyes when she recognized Quinn. "Of course, my dear. I'm Ruth."

"Enough," Muehller snapped. "You two, get over by the old bat and shut up."

She turned her head to look at Muehller. He had a gun pointed their direction. Heidi gasped, feeling the blood drain from her face.

"Steady, sugar," Rio whispered through the comm system.

"Hey, buddy, what's going on? There's no need to use a gun." Quinn shifted to stand between the women and Muehller. "We're not here to hurt you."

Laughter from the blond man. "That's rich."

Heidi had to admit that was funny considering Muehller's occupation. The assassin had no way of knowing about Quinn and his teammates. Otherwise, he would have already killed the most dangerous person in the room. Quinn. The assassin might be the star of nightmares, but Quinn was better trained and more disciplined.

"I'm not worried about you hurting me. Both of you, empty your pockets." Muehller waggled the gun. "Don't make me wait long." A grin. "My trigger finger is itchy."

Quinn didn't budge. "We don't have any money on us, mister. If you're looking for a quick score, you're out of luck."

A snort. "I'm looking for cell phones or a gun, wise guy. Empty the pockets or I'll simply shoot you and check them myself. Of course, your pretty girlfriend might be hurt in the process. Want to take that chance?"

Despite the roaring fire in the fireplace, Heidi trembled. The adrenaline rush Quinn had warned her about. He must have felt her shivering because he dropped back a step so she was pressed up against his back. Grateful for the warmth and reminder that he would watch out for her, Heidi leaned her head against his shoulder and absorbed the comfort.

Charlie growled, his body vibrating with tension. Afraid he would attract Muehller's attention, she signaled him to remain quiet. The growling stopped, but Charlie remained tense and alert.

"Pockets," Muehller snapped. "Or I pull the trigger and be done with both of you."

"Do it," Josh murmured. "Nate, go."

"Copy," Nate whispered.

"Okay, buddy. Chill." Quinn slowly moved his hands to the sides of his black pants and turned the pockets inside out. Empty, of course. He'd taken the precaution of emptying everything before approaching the cabin. "See? Nothing."

"Turn around."

He cocked his head. "Why?"

Muchller raised the gun and aimed at Quinn's chest.

"All right, fine. Just don't hurt us." He turned and placed his hands on Heidi's waist. With his back to the assassin, he winked at Ruth. "Satisfied?" he asked Muehller.

"No. Now your woman. Get over here, sweet cheeks. I'll search you myself. I don't want to miss anything important." A broad smile. "You might be an assassin, after all." He broke out into laughter at that statement.

Heidi narrowed her eyes. Jerk.

Quinn's hands tightened. "No way, man. No one touches my girlfriend but me. I'm the possessive sort."

"Ethan, go," Josh whispered.

"Moving in now," Ethan murmured.

"The possessive sort, huh? You're going to be dead if your woman doesn't do exactly as I say in the next five seconds."

"That's enough," Ruth snapped. "You have no cause to hurt either of these young people."

"Shut up, Ruth. You've been more than enough trouble for me already. Heidi, if you don't want your boyfriend to die right where he stands, move away from him."

"Move enough for Muehller to see you," Josh said softly through the ear piece. "Don't get near him, Heidi. He'll use you as a human shield."

Quinn growled.

"Look, I don't want to make my boyfriend angry. You don't know what he's like. You want to see my pockets? Here." Heidi moved to the side of Quinn who stubbornly retained his hold on her, not allowing her to move far. She turned her pockets inside out. "Nothing, just like Quinn."

"Why would you let him talk you into going anywhere without your cell phone? Are you so spineless you won't speak up for yourself?" Muehller looked disgusted.

Quinn glared over his shoulder. "I wanted to be alone without our nosy families interfering. Since they won't give us a moment's peace, we left the phones at the lodge. If we can't hear the phones, we can't answer them."

A knock sounded on the door.

"Sit down beside the old bat, both of you. If you move from there, you die." Muehller waited until they complied before going to the door.

Quinn's muscles bunched.

"No shot," Alex murmured.

"Wait, Quinn," Josh said.

On the pretense of rubbing his injured ankle, he kept his hand near the gun strapped to his leg.

Heidi glanced at Ruth and noticed her skin was pale. She reached over and clasped the other woman's hand. "You'll be fine," she whispered. "Wait and see." Heidi prayed she was right. So much rode on the next few minutes, not the least of which was Ruth's safety. If something went wrong, Ruth could die. Not acceptable.

With a quick glance to make sure she and Quinn remained seated, Muehller opened the door. He sneered. "Long time, Blackhawk. Come join our little party."

"Where's my aunt?"

"Come inside and see. Oh, but first, drop all of your weapons on the floor."

Ruth's hand trembled. Heidi patted the older woman's hand, mentally readying herself to move on the prearranged cue.

Still standing in the doorway, Ethan removed his sidearm and placed it on the floor, waited.

"Come now, Chief. Don't take me for a fool. Backup piece, too. And don't bother trying to tell me you didn't bring it. You don't leave things to chance."

A slow move to his right ankle and a second gun joined the first.

"That's all?" Muehller frowned.

"No other guns," Ethan said.

"Don't consider me much of a threat, do you?"

Ethan said nothing in response.

Heidi kept her face blank. Ethan might not have other guns, but he had two wicked looking knives, one strapped to his calf, the other strapped to the inside of his forearm. One way or the other, the police chief intended to take Muehller down before he hurt anyone else.

Muehller inclined his head toward the guns on the floor. "Kick them out of reach."

Ethan complied, kicking one close to Heidi.

The assassin motioned for Ethan to turn around with the barrel of his gun. Once he was satisfied there wasn't another gun on the lawman, he gave Ethan a wide berth as he shifted to the side of the room. He stopped near the front windows.

"Heidi," Alex murmured. "Be ready."

"Say your goodbyes to your aunt." Muehller grinned. "If I were you, I wouldn't waste time. You don't have long before my patience runs out. I have a bullet with your name on it and I've been waiting a long time to see you bleed out in front of me."

"Ethan," Ruth said, voice breaking.

"It's okay, Ruth." Ethan glanced at Muehller. "I'm giving her one last hug."

Suspicion glittered in those ice blue eyes. "You touch the gun by sweet Heidi, and I will kill her first, then the old woman. You aren't fast enough to prevent me from killing them."

Quinn moved a scant inch closer to Heidi.

"Ah, ah, Quinn. Don't make me kill you any sooner than I have to."

"Hey, man, we're just asking for directions. We don't have anything to do with what's going down here."

"On my mark," Josh said.

"You don't have to do this," Quinn said. "Let us go and we won't tell the cops. You can disappear."

Another burst of laughter from Muehller. "You're an idiot, you know that, Quinn? You should have chosen a better man, sweet cheeks. For your information, Quinn, Blackhawk is a cop. He's still going to die. Jury's out on you and your woman. But I've got to be honest, it's not looking good for either of you. Can't abide stupid or weak people."

Ethan crossed the room to kneel in front of his aunt and pulled her into his arms for a hug. "How bad?" he murmured.

"Not bad enough that I can't box that hoodlum's ears if he gets close enough," she muttered. "I have a massive headache, extreme nausea, and I just want to lay down and take a nap. If I stood up, I'd fall flat I'm so dizzy. The idiot caught me by surprise."

"Concussion, blood loss at least," Rio said. "We need to get her to the hospital."

"You're wasting time, Chief," Muehller said.

Ethan glared over his shoulder, then returned his attention to his aunt. "I love you, Ruth. You literally saved my life. I'll never be able to thank you enough for sacrificing so much for me."

Tears glittered in her eyes. "You're a good man, Ethan. I'm proud of the man you've become."

Muehller sighed, shifted. "Enough. It's time for you to die, Ethan Blackhawk."

"Nate," Josh snapped.

A second later, the back door blew open and Josh and Nate barreled through the doorway with a crouching run and Rio kicked down the front door. At the same time, Ethan wrapped his arms around his aunt, tugged her to the couch cushions and covered her with his body. Heidi dived on top of Charlie and Quinn wrapped himself around her and the dog, his gun aimed at the assassin.

Rage filled Muehller's face as he raised his gun and aimed at Ethan's head. A split second later, glass shattered and blood blossomed on the assassin's shoulder. Ethan reared up, snatched his weapon from the floor and, when Muehller squeezed the trigger, shot the fugitive in the forehead at the same time multiple shots were fired by Josh, Nate and Quinn.

Muehller would never get up under his own power again. Heidi buried her face in Quinn's neck as the stink of cordite stung her nostrils.

"You okay, baby?" Quinn shoved his gun into his waistband and, wrapping his arms tight around her, drew Heidi close. "Are you hurt?"

"I'm fine," she whispered. "Is everybody else safe?" Heidi glanced around, careful to avoid looking at the blood and gore from Muehller. She gasped as her gaze scanned Ethan. "Ethan's hurt."

CHAPTER THIRTY-ONE

Quinn's head whipped toward Ethan. Oh, man. The sleeve of Ethan's shirt was soaked with blood. "Ethan?" He crawled off Heidi and rushed to the police chief's side. Rio shoved his weapon into his thigh holster and raced out the front door to return a minute later with his Mike bag.

Ethan shrugged off Quinn's hold. "It's nothing," he said, weapon still aimed at Muehller. "Make sure he's dead, Rio."

Josh nodded for Rio to do as Ethan directed.

The medic knelt, checked for a pulse. He glanced at Ethan. "Gone."

"Check Ruth next."

Rio's eyes flared. "She's kept for six hours. She'll keep for five more minutes while I see if you'll bleed to death in front of her eyes if I treat her first. Sit down, Ethan."

Quinn thought the lawman would argue, but he swayed on his feet. Stubborn man. To take the decision out of his hands, Quinn steered him to a seat beside Ruth. "What do you need, Rio?"

"Light. Firelight isn't good for anything except romance. If I wasn't marrying the most incredible woman on the planet, I'd make a play for you, Ruth."

The injured author smiled.

Alex strode into the cabin at that moment and turned on the light switch. Glaring light filled the cabin and made apparent Ethan's pallor. That was saying something considering his copper complexion.

"Ethan, please," Ruth said. "Let Rio see how bad the injury is. If you won't do it for me, do it for Serena and the baby."

The chief grimaced as he nodded.

Rio ripped Ethan's shirt and eased the material away from his body. After a cursory examination, he said, "Straight through the biceps, my friend. You're lucky. Muehller could have hit your brachial artery or shattered the bone. This is messy but recoverable."

"Doesn't make it feel any better," he griped.

"Shoot faster next time." Rio tugged on rubber gloves, tore open pressure bandages, and placed them on both sides of the wound. "That will hold you until the EMTs take you to the hospital."

"Why is Rio being snarky?" Heidi whispered. "Shouldn't he be a little bit sympathetic?"

"Keeps Ethan's mind off his pain and helps Rio evaluate his responses." Didn't want to tell Heidi the medic watched for signs the police chief was losing too much blood.

"Ambulance should be here within ten minutes," Josh said as he slid his phone into his pocket. "Nick and Rod just finished processing Ruth's place. Stella will meet them here. They'll arrive soon."

"Tell the Doucets to stay at their post until we determine whether or not Muehller had someone working with him."

"I'll take care of it."

Rio ripped off his soiled gloves and grabbed a fresh pair. "Your turn, Ruth. You're holding up better than your nephew."

"Who do you think taught him to be tough?"

The medic grinned. "Somehow, that doesn't surprise me in the least. Let me check your pupil reaction, beautiful." Everyone was quiet while Rio assessed Ruth's condition. "Good news and bad news, sweetheart. The good news is you're going to survive this ordeal in a lot better shape than old Hans here."

"And the bad?"

"You're going to have a monster headache for a while and quite a few stitches at the back of your head. Makes laying on your back to sleep a literal pain."

"Can you do the stitches? I have a book deadline to meet."

"If we were on the battlefield, I'd be honored to stitch your wound. As for the book deadline, email your publisher and tell them you'll be a few days late."

Ruth snorted. "Watch me, young man. I've never missed a deadline in forty years. I don't intend to start now."

Rio chuckled while bandaging her head. "I hope you're right. I'm looking forward to the next Tutweiler mystery. One thing I know for certain. We aren't letting Ethan live this down."

"I have a hole in my arm," Ethan pointed out. "Ruth has a tiny cut."

"Not so tiny. I'm sorry, buddy. She wins the grit award today."

"She cheated. Played the old age card." Ethan sank against the sofa back. "You're not fooling me, Rio. If Darcy wises up and dumps you before Saturday, you'll try sweet talking Ruth into marrying you out of pity."

"Just proves he has good taste," Ruth said.

The ambulance arrived followed by Nick and Rod. The detectives walked into the living area first and surveyed the scene. Rod crouched beside Muehller. "Can't say I'm sorry he won't be coming back to threaten our families again, but I looked forward to seeing him rot behind bars for the rest of his life."

Nick knelt in front of Ruth. "How are you, Ruth?"

"According to Rio, I'll live."

He grinned. "Good to know. Ethan?"

"I'll live, too. Don't tell Serena about the gunshot yet. I don't want to worry her."

"Better not wait too long. Word will spread like wildfire. Your sweet wife will make you pay if she learns about your injury from another source."

By the time they arrived at the hospital, Serena had already heard and insisted on seeing Ethan.

"I'll talk to her," Quinn volunteered. "I want to introduce Heidi to her anyway. I also want to hold my new nephew."

Josh waved him on as he spoke softly into his phone. Sounded like he was reporting to Maddox.

"Come on." He urged Heidi down the hall with a hand resting at the small of her back. Before coming to the hospital, they dropped Charlie off at the house with a bowl of dog food, some water, and a chew bone as a reward for tracking down Hans Muehller. According to Heidi, her search partner should sleep for several hours.

Quinn wanted to leave Heidi with Levi and his bodyguards since she was exhausted as well, but she insisted on going to the hospital to check on Ruth and Ethan. Unlike Heidi, Quinn trusted the word of his medic teammate. He was confident his two friends would recover.

As they neared Serena's room, Quinn saw Remy and Lily Doucet standing watch at her door. Lily grinned at him and Heidi. "Congratulations on your mission, Quinn. Any word on Ethan?"

"Doc's in with him now. Rio says he'll be fine, though."

"Good. Serena can use a distraction. She's concerned, afraid we're keeping information from her."

As he brushed past the two operatives, Remy clapped him on the shoulder and murmured, "Good job, man."

After a light knock on the door, he and Heidi walked inside the dimly lit room. Quinn smiled at the beautiful new mother. "How are you, sugar?" He leaned down and pressed a light kiss to her forehead.

"Quinn, how is Ethan? Please, tell me the truth."

"The truth is he's going to be fine. Rio says the bullet went through the muscle in his arm. Missed the bone and a major artery."

She sank back against her pillow with a sigh of relief. "Thank God. Muehller's really dead?"

"He'll never be a danger to anyone again. Serena, this is my girlfriend, Heidi Thompson. Sweetheart, this is Serena Blackhawk, Ethan's wife."

While Serena and Heidi got acquainted, Quinn wandered over to the bassinet. Man, the kid had a head full of black hair. When Lucas scrunched up his face like he was getting ready to cry, Quinn glanced at Serena, eyebrow raised to see if she wanted him to pick up her son.

"Go ahead." She smiled. "Looks like you want to hold him."

Fantastic. He'd waited for months to hold this little boy. For the next hour, he and Heidi took turns rocking Lucas. Finally, Ethan walked into the room, headed straight to his wife and kissed her, long and deep.

"I'm okay, love. Doc Anderson says I'm not to lift anything heavier than Lucas for a while, but I'll recover with no repercussions."

"I was so afraid for you," Serena choked out.

"It's over, baby. Muehller's gone for good." Ethan turned to Quinn and Heidi. "Thanks to both of you for the help tonight. Heidi, you and Charlie are an amazing team. We're very lucky to have you in Otter Creek. Charlie's nose gave us the advantage we needed. I owe you and Quinn a favor. Any time, any place."

She placed Lucas into Serena's arms. "No favors owed between friends. I'm glad we could help."

"I'm taking Heidi home now. Let us know if you need anything else." Quinn threaded his fingers through Heidi's and they left the small family to celebrate and bond.

Back in the hall, Lily asked, "How is Ethan's aunt?"

"Grousing about being on enforced bed rest for two days until she realized reading books and working on her laptop counted as quiet activities. She told the doctor she couldn't promise to stay in bed, but she would stay home and rest." He shrugged. "With the irrepressible Ruth, that's as good as you can get."

"I'm glad. Serena and her family were worried about the lady."

"They had reason to be concerned. Muehller would have killed her once he'd taken care of Ethan."

"Glad he didn't have that chance," Remy said. "Where are you headed now?"

"Home with Heidi. You need someone to spell you?"

"Rio is taking over while we go sleep at Liz and Aaron's house."

He and Heidi left the hospital and were soon parked in her driveway. The house was dark except for a lamp burning in the living room.

"Looks like everyone's gone to bed," Heidi said.

"Either Dane or Angel will be keeping watch." Quinn noted Heidi's stiff movements as she exited the SUV. "Soreness kicking in?"

"Pain reliever wore off. What now, Quinn?"

"Sleep for both of us, then we'll tackle our remaining problem."

She sighed. "The arsonist. I wish he would leave us alone."

"We'll talk about everything tomorrow, baby. Are you hungry?"

"Too tired to eat. I just want to go to bed."

He ushered Heidi to the front door and unlocked it with the key she'd given him. He wondered if her appetite was diminished because of the events in the cabin. "Come on. Let me walk you to your door."

She grinned. "Like a real date?"

"A gentleman always sees a lady to her door."

Once inside the house, Quinn nodded to Dane who had drawn this duty shift and walked with Heidi to her bedroom. He nudged her inside and followed her, closing the door behind himself.

"Quinn?"

"Shh. I need to hold you for a minute." He wrapped his arms around her. "You were incredible tonight, baby. You faced down a monster and didn't flinch."

"Charlie did all the work."

"He was amazing," Quinn agreed. "But you made the difference. You're the only reason Muehller let us in the cabin. If I'd been me alone, he would have shot me where I stood on the porch."

Heidi shuddered and held him tighter. "Then I'm doubly glad I went with you."

He lifted her chin and took his time kissing her. Quinn could spend the rest of his life kissing Heidi and never get enough. No question in his mind. He was crazy about Heidi Thompson.

When he felt his control slip, Quinn eased back, breaking the kiss while still keeping her in his arms for a moment longer. "I love you, Heidi. Sleep well." A last kiss, this one to her neck, and he forced himself to release her and walk from the room.

"I love you, too," Heidi whispered as she shut her door.

With a smile on his face, Quinn went into his room. The adrenaline crash was hitting him hard. Dane and Angel could keep an eye on things for the night. Minutes later, he climbed into bed and fell into a deep sleep.

He walked into the kitchen early the next morning to see Angel pouring a mug of coffee. "Morning."

The operative turned, handed him the mug without comment. Quinn's lips curved. He must look wrung out. Felt like it, too. "Anything happen while I was asleep?"

"Murphy called. He said to get in touch when you woke up."

He blinked. "Why didn't he call me?"

"Josh kept him updated along with Maddox. Murphy didn't want to disturb you, said his information could wait a few hours."

Huh. Sounded like Z might have something. He hoped the information might lead him to an answer for Heidi. "Thanks." He finished most of the mug of coffee before refilling it and stepping outside on the deck to call Zane.

"About time you woke up," Zane groused as his greeting. "Figured you would have already called by now."

"Yeah, yeah. What have you got, Z?"

"Information on Bennett. He's dead."

CHAPTER THIRTY-TWO

Disappointment spiraled through Quinn. Untangling this mystery would be much easier if they could have talked to the original investigating detective. He and Heidi would have to go about finding the answers a different way. "When did Bennett die?"

"Two years ago in January. Get this, though. Before he died, Bennett had been in a mental institution for years. In fact, he was admitted about five years after Heidi's kidnapping."

Quinn stilled. "Diagnosis?"

"Had a mental breakdown and never recovered. He retreated into his own mind and stayed there."

He sat on the deck steps, took a sip of coffee while he thought about that. "Any idea why he had the breakdown to begin with?"

"Not that I could find. Your best source of information is going to be his son, Ivan Bennett, Junior."

"Where can I find him?"

"Same place you would have found his old man before the breakdown."

Huh. Hadn't seen that coming. "He's on the job in Black River?"

"He's a detective, just like his father."

Interesting. Also annoying. Chances were good Detective Bennett wouldn't be willing to talk about his father. "Any other children?" Perhaps he might learn information from another relative.

"A daughter. She won't be any help, though. Aurora Bennett is also in a mental institution, the same one to which her father had been admitted."

Quinn frowned. A tragedy, but were the two connected? "Dig into Aurora's background. Junior's background, too. I want to know everything you can find."

"I sent Junior's contact information to your email. I'll get back to you about anything else I dig up." He ended the conversation by simply ending the call.

Quinn sipped the rest of his coffee, letting the caffeine and cold morning breeze clear the cobwebs from his mind. Bennett being admitted to a mental institution not long after Heidi's kidnapping raised a red flag. There may not be a connection, but his gut told him otherwise. Was Detective Bennett involved in the kidnapping? Was he the one who accidentally killed Moira Henderson?

His hands clenched around his now empty coffee mug. Maybe that's why his father never got the sense that the police were looking into the kidnapping and missing money. Bennett might not have been interested in pushing the case forward because to do so would have implicated him. Was the detective partially responsible for the death of Quinn's father?

The back door opened and Heidi stepped out of the house accompanied by Charlie. The Lab trotted to Quinn and, after a few head rubs, went to visit the grass.

Heidi sat down beside him on the step and scooted close. "Hey."

"Morning, sweetheart." He leaned over and kissed her thoroughly, something he looked forward to doing for years to come. "How do you feel?"

"Good. No headache. A few muscle twinges. You?"

"Same."

"Why are you up so early?"

He grinned. "Military training, babe. Can't sleep more than about four hours at a time. What about you? Why are you awake at this time of morning?"

She wrinkled her nose. "Charlie needed to go outside. I tried to roll over for a little more sleep. He wasn't having it. Nothing like a wet dog nose pressed to your ear before the sun has risen."

Heidi studied his face for a couple of beats. "You found out something." A statement, not a question. Smart lady.

"Zane called. Detective Bennett is dead."

"So much for getting information from the original detective. Now what will we do?"

"Explore other options. We see if his partner is still alive and willing to talk to us. Second, Z also found out Bennett has a son currently on the Black River police force. He's also a detective. He might be a source of information."

"Might?"

"Cops aren't known for being forthcoming with information on anything, especially their families. What's interesting is the senior Bennett was admitted to a mental institution a few years after your kidnapping." He paused for effect, then said, "And so was his daughter."

Heidi's eyes widened. "His daughter?"

"That's right. And get this. According to Z, father and daughter were in the same institution until he died two years ago."

"What are the odds of that?" she muttered.

Probably astronomical. "Now that the danger to Ethan is over, what do you say to a trip to the past?"

Heidi's body jerked. "Are you talking about hypnosis or an actual trip to Black River?"

"Both."

"I've already tried the hypnosis route. I didn't see anything different than I do in my dreams."

"You couldn't remember any more details about the second man?"

She shook her head. "Do you really think a trip back home will help us figure out who's trying to kill me and Levi?"

"Everything seems to stem back to your kidnapping, honey." He wrapped his arm around Heidi's waist and drew her up against his side. Though he enjoyed the feel of her body against his, Quinn had noticed Heidi shivering, a combination of the cold morning breeze and nerves. "I hate putting you through this, but I think we must if we want to learn the truth." The thought of taking her back to a place filled with such ugly memories made him feel ill. The last thing he wanted was to cause her more pain. If he didn't think it might help, he wouldn't subject her to Black River's ire. Facing them down would take courage, a trait she had in spades.

"The townspeople hate me," she said, staring off into the distance.

"I know," he murmured. "It was unfair. You were just a kid and had nothing to do with your father's scheme except as an innocent victim."

"Doesn't seem to matter. The last time Levi took me to Black River, I still generated a lot of hostility. They blame me and my family for the loss of G & H Industries. Many of their lives were ruined because of my father."

He gently turned her face toward him. "You're not going home alone, babe. I'll be by your side."

She didn't comment, just leaned her head against his shoulder.

"Unless you're not up to the trip, I'd like to leave this morning."

"I want to wait until Levi is awake so we can tell him where we're going."

When Charlie returned, they went into the house and found Levi and Angel in the kitchen, not speaking to each other, mugs of coffee in hand and bleary eyed.

"Good morning, Levi." Heidi brushed his cheek with a kiss.

A grunt in response.

"I'm fine, thank you," she said, a smile curving her mouth.

Levi rolled his eyes. "When did you get in?" he muttered.

"A little after midnight."

"Did you find Ethan's aunt?" Angel asked.

Quinn nodded. "She was admitted to the hospital with a scalp laceration and concussion. Ethan suffered a gunshot wound to the arm. Both of them will recover."

"I was afraid Durango wouldn't find her in time."

Quinn had feared the same thing. Muehller had had minimal incentive to keep Ruth alive. Losing his aunt would have devastated the lawman.

"So what's next?" Levi asked. "When are you going to do something about this maniac trying to kill me and Heidi?"

His temper spiked, but he answered with a mild tone. "Glad you asked. I'm taking Heidi back to Black River."

"Those people hate her. The residents of the town think Heidi should have died with her sister."

"G & H Industries still would have closed down because of the money loss. The outcome would have been the same whether she was alive or not."

"Don't you think I know that? But these people have long memories. The name Henderson is synonymous with thief in that town. No one will tell her anything. They wouldn't help us the last time we asked. Why would that change today?"

"I wasn't with you. Black River sees me and my family as victims. Where they might not talk to you, they will talk to me."

Levi scowled. "I don't like it. Heidi, please don't do this. If lover boy thinks these attempts to kill us stem from the fiasco with your father, it would be crazy to head right into the heart of the enemy camp."

Heidi held up her hand to halt the flow of words from her cousin. "No more running. The only way to stop this guy is to unmask him. I want a normal life, Levi." She paused, threaded her fingers through Quinn's. "We want a normal life together."

"You and Gallagher?" His voice rose. "You've only been together for a few days. You can't be serious."

"It's my life, Levi. You want me to be happy. Quinn makes me happy."

Levi turned to Quinn, a warning in his eyes. "Hurt her and I will take you down hard. I don't care if you are a crack soldier. I love her."

"That makes two of us, buddy. I'll make it my life mission to keep her happy, whatever it takes."

"So how are we going to do this?" her cousin asked.

"Not we, Levi. Heidi and I will go to Black River alone. We'll attract less attention as a couple than as a pack of five."

"You might need help protecting her."

Quinn's lips curved. "I won't need help. You have my word that I'll keep her safe. No one means more to me than Heidi."

"How long will we be gone?" Heidi asked.

"Until we find answers. Pack for a few days."

"Where will we stay? I doubt any rooming place in town will rent to me."

"Let me worry about that. I'll find us a place to stay." He had a place in mind, one she would object to if she knew ahead of time. He'd beg for forgiveness later. At least he'd know Heidi was safe.

An hour later, he and Heidi drove out of town. Knowing he might be pushing to get back to Otter Creek in time for Rio's wedding rehearsal, Quinn placed a call to his friend.

"Do you know what time it is?" Rio groused. "I've only been asleep a couple hours."

Quinn chuckled. "You'll survive. Listen, I'm taking Heidi to Black River."

"Wait." Rio yawned. "Give me a second to splash water on my face." When he returned to the phone, the medic said, "Why are you going back to Black River? You hate that town."

True enough. He hadn't been home for years, always managing to meet his family in other cities. "It's where all of Heidi's troubles began, Rio." He went on to explain what Zane had learned about the Bennett family.

His friend gave a soft whistle. "Timing is interesting."

"That's what Z and I thought."

"Sometimes mental illnesses are from genetics. Other times they aren't. I've known some psychiatric patients who couldn't deal with a traumatic event in their lives. A few slipped into a catatonic state. Need help with your hunt?"

Quinn's throat tightened. Rio should be concentrating on his upcoming wedding, not worrying about catching some determined arsonist. "No thanks, buddy. Spend your time romancing your almost wife. Don't want her to change her mind. I just wanted to let you know I might be late for the rehearsal, but I'll be there."

"You better be, Gallagher. You're the best man. Heidi?"

"I'm here."

"How do you feel today?"

"A little sick to my stomach at the thought of returning home, but good other than that. No more headache and only a few muscle twinges."

"Excellent. Provided there aren't any unpleasant happenings in Black River, you should be clear to work Monday. Deke said he'll get in touch with you Sunday night about the class schedule for Monday. Your first session isn't until ten o'clock."

"Great. Thanks for letting me know."

"Yep. Quinn?"

"Yeah?"

"Watch your back."

"Copy that."

Three hours later, Quinn took the Black River exit off Interstate 40. He glanced at Heidi. She was still slumped against the passenger-side door, sound asleep. Might as well go to his mother's place and drop off their luggage before tracking down Detective Bennett or his father's former partner.

As he drove through town, Quinn noted the changes. The old movie theater in the center of town was now a restaurant. Several stores he remembered frequenting while he grew up were gone, replaced by boutique stores he'd never step foot in unless Heidi wanted to visit them. The ice cream shop was still in business. That place had the best ice cream. Don't know if the store changed policy, but the original owners had made ice cream themselves every day.

When he turned into his mother's driveway and shut off the engine, Heidi stirred and opened her eyes. She glanced around, froze. "Oh, Quinn, no," she said. "Your mother won't want me to stay here. Seeing me will hurt her."

"Do you trust me, babe?"

She nodded without hesitation which had warmth blooming inside his chest. Man, he loved this woman.

"Mom wants you to stay in her home. She told me so when I called to tell her we were coming." He leaned close and kissed her. "It will be fine, Heidi."

His girlfriend wrapped her arms around his neck and shared another kiss. "I hope we don't regret coming here," she whispered against his lips.

Unsure whether she meant coming to his mother's, Black River, or both, he pressed another kiss to her soft lips, then exited the SUV. With their bags in hand, he escorted Heidi to the front door and knocked. He still felt weird about walking into his mother's house without knocking even though he had a key. This wasn't his home anymore.

A moment later, locks disengaged and there stood his mother. Her blond hair was a little lighter than the last time he'd seen her and she'd cut it a different way. Hmm. Noreen Gallagher was trying out a new look.

She grinned. "Quinn!" Noreen launched herself at her son and wrapped him in a tight hug. "Great to see you, baby. And look at this beautiful young lady." She released Quinn and enveloped Heidi in a gentle hug. "Welcome home, sweetheart. It's been a long time."

"Thank you," Heidi choked out. Tears swam in her eyes.

"Oh now, none of that." Noreen released her and stepped out of their way. "Come in. Quinn, take Heidi's gear to the girls' room. Your old room is ready for you. You'll have to work around the toys."

Quinn chuckled. "How are my nieces and nephews?"

"Very excited that Uncle Quinn is in town for a couple days. The whole clan will be here for dinner tonight."

At Heidi's deer-in-the-headlights look, Quinn said, "You have nothing to worry about, honey. We all know you weren't responsible for anything that happened years ago. You're safe here."

"Sweetheart, why don't you deliver those bags while I take Heidi to the kitchen." Noreen sent Heidi a knowing look. "I imagine she could use a good cup of coffee about now."

"Sounds great," she agreed, though she looked a little uneasy at the thought of being alone with Quinn's mother.

He leaned down and brushed Heidi's mouth with a soft kiss. "I won't be long," he murmured.

With a nod, she followed his mother. Once he'd deposited the bags in the rooms, he retraced his steps downstairs to the kitchen and found Heidi looking comfortable as she relaxed on the barstool at the counter.

"So, Quinn Gallagher, do you have something to tell me?" Noreen slid a mug of coffee across the counter to him.

"Like what?"

His mother waggled her finger at him. "Spill. What's going on with you and Heidi?"

"I'm going to marry Heidi Thompson as soon as she'll have me."

The silence grew thick in the kitchen. "Marriage?" A broad smile curved Noreen's lips. "Oh, Quinn." Tears gathered in her eyes.

"Mom?"

"These are happy tears. Congratulations to both of you."

"You don't mind?" Heidi asked. "Even after everything that happened?"

"If you make my son happy, then you have my blessing." She turned to Quinn. "What's first on your agenda?"

"Tracking down Ivan Bennett, Junior and Bennett Senior's partner. Do you have the key I asked about?"

A troubled expression settled on Noreen's face. "I wish you would reconsider."

"If it's not necessary, I won't use the key, Mom."

She pulled the key from her pocket and slid it across the counter. "After this is resolved, I'm bulldozing the place."

Once all their questions were answered, Quinn planned to drive the dozer himself to flatten that house of horrors. But first, he had a murderer to catch.

CHAPTER THIRTY-THREE

Heidi's cheeks burned as she and Quinn walked to the police station. She should have worn a bulletproof vest. Many people greeted Quinn pleasantly enough. Those same folks lost the smile when they recognized her. Most didn't bother to acknowledge her at all. Nothing like being treated as if you were a pariah or invisible. Either one was equally bad in her book. She wished they'd say their piece and be done with it. At least she could defend herself. This way she had no recourse except to duck and run. She just hoped PSI's insurance coverage was excellent because if the glares were anything to go by, she wouldn't return to Otter Creek unscathed.

"Wonder if they'll change their minds about you when we discover the identity of the second kidnapper?" Quinn murmured.

"I doubt it. I'll still be the person they all love to hate. I'm glad they're talking to you. Maybe you can find answers."

"I'm counting on the guilt factor."

She slid him a sideways glance. "Guilt factor?"

"Yep. By the time I'm finished with them, they'll feel guilty for blaming an innocent kid and rush to spill their guts to make up for the injustice."

"Right. Good luck with that." Heidi would believe that when it actually happened. If it actually happened. She wasn't holding her breath. The people of Black River never forgot their history, and unfortunately the name Henderson brought back feelings of anger, grief, and betrayal.

Inside the police station lobby, she and Quinn approached the desk sergeant and waited for him to finish his phone conversation. When the lawman ended his call, Quinn said, "We need to see Ivan Bennett."

"He's at a crime scene. You can leave him a message." He slid a notepad and pen to Quinn.

Another message. A fifth message in the past three hours. Heidi resisted the urge to scowl at the policeman. She'd learned on the drive into town that Quinn had left voice mail messages for Bennett to get in touch with him and had yet to hear back from the detective. She suspected this message would end up in the garbage can without Quinn receiving a call back. Didn't seem as though the detective was interested in talking to them, which puzzled her.

He was a law enforcement officer. Shouldn't he be interested in seeing justice done, in closing a case that his father couldn't close? Heidi thought every cop hated unsolved cases. She sighed. Maybe he didn't want to solve the case if his father was the culprit behind Moira's death. Although she wouldn't know from personal experience, perhaps Bennett, Junior believed loyalty trumped truth when it came to protecting his father's good name.

Once Quinn finished scrawling another message for Bennett to call him, he asked, "Do you know who Bennett, Senior's partner was at the time of the Henderson kidnapping?"

The desk sergeant scowled, suspicion growing in his gaze. "What do you want to know that for? It's ancient history."

"I don't care how old the case is, I want to know the truth," Heidi said. "I'm the surviving child in that kidnapping case. I want to talk to a detective connected to my case and I know Detective Bennett passed away. If you won't give me the information, I will go over your head, Sergeant."

His eyes grew cold. "You're Katie Henderson?"

"I go by the name Heidi Thompson now. Katie Henderson has painful baggage in her past weighing her down. Heidi Thompson doesn't." She couldn't say the same for the rest of her assumed identities.

A snort. "Changing your name doesn't get rid of the baggage. Follows you wherever you go and however far you run."

"A new name changes how I feel about myself and my past, and also provides separation. Will you help me find answers? I can't go back and save my sister, but I can bring resolution and close that part of my past for good. Please, Sergeant Banks. Moira was only eight. She didn't deserve to die."

He was silent so long Heidi thought he wouldn't help her and that she and Quinn would be forced to ask Zane for more computer hacking. She hated to ask him to break the law, especially since she didn't know if the case file was accessible. Durango believed their fellow Fortress operative could get any information they needed. Those hacking skills wouldn't be useful if this backward police department didn't have the files in a computer hard drive Zane might access. Heidi wouldn't put it past the Black River Police Department to keep everything in paper files. They weren't known to be cutting edge on anything, at least not that she'd learned in visiting their website over the years. She had zero skill in creating websites, but even she recognized amateur workmanship when she saw it.

"I have a granddaughter that age," Banks muttered. "If Kelsey had been murdered like that, I wouldn't rest until I'd run the perp down like a dog. Hang on." He turned to the side, glanced around to see if anyone was watching, and tapped on the computer keyboard. Banks scanned the screen, scrolled down, then said in a soft voice, "Albert Graham. Need an address?"

Quinn shook his head. "Thank you. No need to compromise yourself any further, Sergeant Banks. We'll take it from here."

"You find out anything, you let us handle it, you hear? This is police business, not a job for civilians. You might get hurt."

Heidi bit back a laugh. If Sergeant Banks only knew what Quinn did for a living, he wouldn't have worried about her boyfriend being hurt. The policeman should be more concerned about the kidnapper's safety. Quinn's family had been hurt by the scheme her father and the kidnapper cooked up.

Banks frowned at Quinn. "You look familiar. Do I know you?"

A smile from her boyfriend. "Probably. I used to live here." He shook the desk sergeant's hand. "Quinn Gallagher. Caleb Gallagher was my father."

"Bad business all around. Sorry about what happened to your dad. He was a good man."

"Thanks." He inclined his head toward the note. "See that Bennett gets the message."

"Can't guarantee he'll call." Banks' mouth curled. "Junior doesn't bother himself with a lot of things these days. He ain't nothing like his old man used to be. I wouldn't depend on him to spit on me if I was on fire."

What did that mean? Bennett, Junior wasn't good at his job? Heidi turned away after thanking the sergeant for his help and walked from the building hand-in-hand with Quinn. "Will you call Zane for help in locating Graham?"

"I know exactly where to find Al. He's a good friend of my family, but I wasn't aware that he investigated this case. Too consumed with my own anger and grief." He threaded his fingers through hers. "I think I need to introduce my future wife to Al. He'll be thrilled to meet you."

Heidi hoped Quinn knew what he was doing. If Mr. Graham was like the rest of the town, he wouldn't be pleased to witness her return to Black River. Ten minutes later, he parked in front of a red brick ranch-style house with gray shutters. As they walked to the porch, the living room curtains fluttered. Someone was home, all right. Question was, would the person let them inside the house?

She got the answer to her question before they rang the doorbell. The white door opened wide and a gray-haired man stood in the doorway, brown eyes curious.

He squinted at Quinn's face. Recognition lit the man's gaze. "Quinn! How are you, son?" He shook Quinn's hand. "Your mother's been keeping me updated on your career over the years. Special Forces in the Army and now working for an exclusive private outfit. Can't tell you how proud I am of your accomplishments. Your dad would have been pleased, too."

"Thank you, sir. May we come in for a few minutes?"

"Of course." He waved them inside to the sofa and sat across from them in a recliner. "Who is this beautiful young lady?"

"This is Heidi Thompson, the woman who has agreed to marry me, soon I hope." He grinned. "If I have anything to do with it, she'll be marrying me within a couple weeks."

Startled, she stared into his twinkling eyes. Was he serious? Heidi had a feeling he told Mr. Graham the truth. Butterflies took flight in her stomach at the thought of marrying Quinn Gallagher so soon. She couldn't wait to be his wife, a permanent part of his life and work. None of the other Durango wives were able to work with their husbands.

Al Graham studied her face. "Heidi Thompson. Why do you look familiar? I feel I should know you as well, my dear."

Heidi watched him carefully. "I used to go by the name Katie Henderson."

Sorrow settled on his face. "I see. I'm sorry we weren't able to figure out who the second kidnapper was, Heidi. Ivan and I wore down a lot of shoe leather over the years trying to find a new lead. Our efforts were unsuccessful. Your case was the only one we never solved. That sticks in my craw. Felt like a failure when I couldn't give you closure."

He sighed. "And to lose the rest of your family the next week in a house fire was devastating for all of us. Never had an arsonist in Black River that I remember. Where did you go after leaving town?"

"To live with my cousins."

"Why did you change your name?" Graham's piercing gaze held hers.

The detective hadn't forgotten how to interrogate another person. Heidi ought to know. She'd been interrogated by the best over the past twenty years. Graham had skill. "I didn't for the first five years. My aunt and uncle raised me until I turned 15. My aunt and uncle and all my cousins but one were killed in a house fire."

The old detective cocked his head. "Arson?"

"The police accused me of setting the fire."

"Did you?"

She shook her head. "I loved them. I would never hurt them."

"Cops ever find the arsonist?"

"No, sir."

He was silent a moment. "We don't believe in coincidence in this business, Heidi. The chances of you being the victim of two different arsonists are slim."

"I know. The fire that killed my cousin's family wasn't the last one. My cousin, Levi, and I were dogged with fires wherever we settled. About once a year, our house or apartment went up in flames. We changed names, changed cities, changed jobs, everything we could think of. All of the fires were deliberately set."

Laurens turned his gaze to Quinn, his expression grim. "What do you need from me, son?"

"Your knowledge of Heidi's case and your experience. She had a copy of her case file, but it was lost in the last house fire. Would you have a copy of the file?"

Satisfaction gleamed in his eyes. "I do, indeed. Still break out the file once in a while to reread it, see if something catches my attention or spurs a new avenue to explore. I might be retired, but I'm not dead yet. I want this case closed before I die. You could ask one of the cold case detectives for a copy, you know."

"We could," Quinn agreed. "Not sure how willing he or she would be to cooperate. Heidi is generating animosity in Black River by simply being in town."

"Hmm. I could make some inquiries for you, perhaps get a copy of the file from the station. All I have is my case notes. Could be the current detective has a tidbit of new information I don't."

"Don't put yourself in any danger, Mr. Graham." Just the thought of this man being in danger made her want to forbid him from helping.

"Not to worry, young lady. I haven't forgotten my training. I'll be careful. Besides, who would think a doddering old man is a threat?"

"Al, we understand that your partner was admitted to a psychiatric facility. Do you remember when that happened?"

Graham stared out the window for a time. When he turned back, he said, "Not long after Heidi and her cousin came to Black River to talk to Ivan. I was out of town at the time, or I would have been involved in the interview as well."

"Did he say anything to you about our visit?" Heidi asked. "Was he disturbed by our presence?"

"I don't know how he felt about it, Heidi. I never saw him again. By the time I returned from vacation, Ivan had already gone into the facility for evaluation. He never came out and refused all visitors. Within a couple months, he had retreated into his own mind to such an extent, he didn't communicate at all, not even with his physicians. Shook all of us up. My colleagues and I didn't see any warning signs. Made us wonder which one would be next."

Heidi exchanged a glance with Quinn. The timing of admittance to the psychiatric facility bothered her. Was it a coincidence or a way to avoid being prosecuted for arson and murder?

Even if he was guilty, he certainly couldn't have been involved in the incidents over the past two years. Was it possible there was a third partner involved in the kidnapping and arsons?

CHAPTER THIRTY-FOUR

"If you can obtain a copy of the file from the police station without endangering yourself, we'd appreciate it." Quinn stopped, tilted his head to better hear the radio he'd noticed in the background. At first, he thought Al was listening to talk radio. Now he realized the speech sounded like the radio chatter in Josh's patrol car. "You have a police radio?"

His friend's cheeks blazed. "Old habit. Like to know what's happening around town."

"Did you happen to hear where Bennett, Junior might be working a crime scene?"

His friend smirked. "I might have heard he's on Winston Drive working a possible homicide. Why?"

"He's been avoiding my calls. We want to talk to him about his family, see if his father spoke about the kidnapping case with Junior since he's also a cop. Any insight will be helpful in our search for the second kidnapper."

"You won't have much help there. Junior's nothing like Ivan, which is a shame. His father was a fine police officer."

"We've heard some things about Junior around town. I'd like your take. Tell us about him."

"He's lazy, arrogant, and self-important. He does enough work to get by and shoves the rest of his responsibilities onto his partner, a long-suffering detective named Anne Marie Salinger. She's a real go-getter. Any cases they solve is because of her work, not Junior's. He couldn't care less about the victims or their families. As far as he's concerned, all the vics get what they deserve. He believes they're the scum of the earth and Black River is better off without them."

"Sounds like he's a real peach," Quinn muttered.

"More like the pit," Heidi said.

Al burst into laughter. "You're a keeper, Heidi Thompson."

"I'll remind Quinn of that when I make him angry."

"Who has been assigned to the case?" Quinn asked. "I assume in a small department, everybody has a cold case or two sitting on the back burner. Who has the Henderson case?"

The old man grew thoughtful. "Now that you mention it, Junior demanded the case. Claimed he wanted to help his father achieve a perfect record."

"But you don't believe that."

"Not a chance. Junior didn't care about his father or Ivan's record."

So why did he demand the case? Maybe if Salinger stumbled across the identity of the second kidnapper, Junior would reap the notoriety of solving the one case his father couldn't. "Do you think Detective Salinger will talk to us?"

A shrug. "Probably. You need to catch her without Junior. He'll stonewall you and dominate the conversation.

You won't learn squat from her with him around. He doesn't want anyone talking about his family, and that includes Salinger. The boy's touchy about it, embarrassed that his sister and Ivan were in a psych hospital."

He paused. "Salinger's not fond of her partner, but don't spread that around. She still has to work with this clown and live here after you return home. You already know the people in this place have long memories. Salinger is taking care of aging parents who don't want to move. She can't relocate no matter how unpleasant life here becomes. They need her. Don't make it impossible for her to remain."

Quinn rubbed his jaw, his beard rasping against his fingers. Would Al tell him where Salinger lived? Cops, retired ones included, were very protective of their own. He decided to approach the question from another angle even though he and Heidi had no intention of hurting the detective. Al knew the truth. Quinn didn't want to make Al the target of cruelty and disloyalty if he could avoid it.

If Salinger wasn't comfortable sharing information about her partner and his family, Quinn and Heidi would look elsewhere. Someone, somewhere in this town, knew enough information to blow this case wide open. They just had to find that person and convince him to tell what he knew. "Where does she hang out?"

"Diner on Sixth."

He hazarded a guess. "Jake's Place?"

"That's the one. Salinger's not married and she doesn't cook. When she's off shift, that's the first place she heads. Can't give you an exact time although her shift is officially over at five. Detectives don't punch a time clock. The work takes as long as it takes."

Quinn understood that. He and his teammates weren't tied to the clock either. Wasn't uncommon for them to work around the clock on an op. "I understand. We'll wait for her arrival."

"I'll see what I can do to get a copy of your file, Heidi. Quinn, I'll call when I have the information and we'll set up a time to meet."

Quinn and Heidi stood. "Be careful, Al. Word will get around that we're looking into Moira's death. Someone has been trying to kill Heidi for twenty years. A retired police detective will be just as much of a target, maybe more so because you're a real threat and know the right questions to ask. I don't want to lose you."

Looking into Al Graham's eyes, he saw a world of weariness in their depths. His family friend had witnessed ugly things in his career. That darkness shadowed Al's gaze. Probably the same shadows that darkened his own and haunted Quinn's dreams. The nightmares and flashbacks were the reason he had stacks of books stashed around the house to read. Bless Del's heart, she recognized the PTSD symptoms and kept him supplied. The books distracted him from the skin-crawling memories when the nights were too long and dark.

"Evil wins if we do nothing," Al said. "You know all about that, don't you, son?"

Got him there. He'd stared at much evil over the years and been scarred by it. Evidence of knife and bullet wounds riddled his body courtesy of terrorists the world over. His lips curved. "Yes, sir."

"You stand in the face of evil no matter when it comes at you. You've fought the battle for years. I can't do any less. It's the creed I live by."

Sounded familiar. He and his teammates stepped up when the need arose. "Sir, you put in your time. I have other sources I can tap for this information. I want you safe."

Al waved that aside. "The call to duty doesn't stop because I turned in my badge. You want a life with this beautiful young lady, son? She'll never be safe if the veil of deceit and murder isn't ripped away. I want you and Heidi to have freedom, for you to be free from fear for your wife's safety while you're away on assignments."

Cold chills raced over his body. He glanced at the woman he loved with every fiber of his being. Quinn had to end the danger to Heidi or he might receive a call one day telling him his wife had been murdered in a house fire. No, a thousand times no. He couldn't lose her.

Al continued. "One moment of distraction could end your life and leave Heidi to live a half life at best. Let me do this for you, Quinn. Copying a file is a small enough favor to ask."

Logically, he knew Al was right. The file was a small favor and Al could get it faster than a request from Heidi to the police department. Somehow Quinn believed the request would either be denied or delayed through a mountain of red tape. Though he longed to forbid the former detective from involving himself in Heidi's case any further, he couldn't wrap his friend in bubble wrap. Al Graham was a seasoned professional. Quinn would have to trust the man to watch his own back. Hopefully, his long-term service and retired status would provide some protection. If Al died, people would talk and ask questions, not something a murderer wanted.

But small-town secrets were hard to keep, a fact Quinn was counting on. People in Black River loved nothing more than to gossip. "We won't bother requesting the file unless you fail to secure a copy."

"Probably best," Al agreed. "For you to ask for it now would call too much attention to you and Heidi early on. Word will spread fast enough why you're here."

The gossip wire was likely already buzzing though he didn't remind Al of that fact. Quinn hugged his family friend. "Talk to you soon." As he walked with Heidi to his SUV, he felt the hairs prickle at the back of his neck.

With a casual glance, he scanned the area for the watcher. No obvious signs and he couldn't dissect each sector the way he would on a mission without tipping off the watcher that Quinn was aware of his presence. Several good places to keep them under surveillance without being seen. Quinn's fingers itched to grab his rifle and check their surroundings through the scope.

He unlocked the vehicle, lifted Heidi inside, and bent to kiss her. "We've attracted attention," he murmured.

"How do you know?"

"I feel the stare." He'd learned over the years not to stare at his targets. Some instinct clued the targets in to the surveillance.

"What about Mr. Graham? He's not safe if the killer knows we've spent time with him." She clamped a hand over his forearm. "We have to warn him, Quinn."

His heart warmed at her concern for a man she'd spent mere minutes with. "I'll call Al, then we'll head to Winston Drive to see if Bennett is still working the crime scene. If not, maybe we can track him down for a quick interview."

He hustled around the back of the SUV and climbed behind the wheel. Once he cranked the engine, Quinn punched in a call to Al. "It's Quinn. Got eyes on your place, my friend."

A sigh sounded over the speakers. "So it's begun. I was hoping for more time before word spread. Very well, then. I'd best get Heidi's file soon. I think I need to pay my friends down at the police station a visit. Be safe, Quinn."

"Same to you, Al."

His stomach knotted with worry. Much as Al protested that he knew what he was doing, Quinn's gut said the killer would fight back quickly. He didn't want his family friend caught in the crossfire. Short of hogtying the man, there was nothing he could do to prevent him from aiding their investigation. He had a vested interest in solving the cold case as much as Heidi did.

On Winston Drive, he and Heidi surveyed the bustling activity around a small gray house. More like a bungalow, compact and with a neat, well-landscaped yard. An ambulance sat waiting on the street, the rear doors wide open, EMTs nowhere in sight. Patrolmen worked crowd control as neighbors pressed close to the perimeter to catch of glimpse of the people inside the house.

No one seemed in too much of a hurry to render medical aid and transport a patient to the hospital which told Quinn there was no need for haste. The relaxed attitude of the cops milling around the area led him to conclude this might not be a homicide. Otherwise, the pace of activity would be more frenetic.

"Doesn't look as if Bennett will be free any time soon." Heidi glanced at Quinn. "What do you want to do?"

"Wait and observe for a bit." He watched the proceedings for a while. No sign of Junior. Had he left already? "I'm not sure if Bennett is here. I don't see an unmarked car, only prowl cars. Based on what we've heard about Junior's personality and attitude, I doubt he'd drive a black-and-white. This might be a simple unattended death."

"Great. So how do we find this guy?" She frowned. "It's a sure bet he won't return your calls."

"We could drive around Black River since it's not that large, or return to Al's place and check the police scanner." The police station was another option. Perhaps the desk sergeant might offer another tip. Last resort, though. He didn't want the sergeant to face a reprimand.

Quinn searched the faces of the responding officers, recognizing a few from his high school years. One of them might be willing to confirm Bennett's absence from the scene. "I'll ask some questions of officers I know. Wait here."

"No way. I want to go with you."

He turned. "Baby, it's cold outside and you're a target. I'm trying to keep you comfortable and alive which is easier to do if you're not out in the open."

"I'll warm up soon enough, especially if we stop and purchase coffee when we're finished here," she pointed out. "The killer hasn't tried to shoot me, Quinn. His weapon of choice is fire. Unless he's acquired a flame thrower, I should be safe. I doubt the killer would be foolish enough to try something with me surrounded by law enforcement officers."

He blew out a breath in frustration and reminded himself he couldn't put her in bubble wrap, either. This wasn't a life or death situation where he had cause to overrule her wishes. Heidi wanted to be part of solving her sister's murder and he couldn't blame her for that decision. Quinn wanted a chance to bring down the person who caused his father to take his own life.

After a quick nod, he climbed from the vehicle and met her on the sidewalk. "Let's see if my old friends recognize you."

Holding hands, they made their way through the crowd and walked to the closest cop on the perimeter of the scene.

"Help you?" the cop muttered.

"You haven't changed a bit since high school, Sully." Quinn smiled at the startled officer. "How's your family, buddy?"

"Quinn! Haven't seen you since graduation, man. You look great. Where have you been all these years?"

"Deployed around the globe. I enlisted in the Army as soon as the ink dried on my high school diploma. Spent twelve years in, then transitioned to a private security firm."

"Wow. No wonder we haven't seen you around town. What kind of work do you do for that firm? Is it like a rent-a-cop business?"

Amusement had his lips twitching. "Not quite. We specialize in high value target security and hostage rescue." A very low key description of a high octane job. "What have you been up to since high school?"

"Couple years of community college, then started working for the police department when I couldn't find anything else that suited me."

"You like the job?"

Sully rolled his eyes. "Some days. Most of the time, though, I'm stuck on traffic detail or crowd control. We get our share of looky-loos at wrecks and crime scenes. People are a bunch of busybodies."

Quinn tilted his head, considering his friend's words and the tone with which he'd said them. "So you're a twelve-year vet of the police force and still doing grunt work?"

"Got to know somebody to get your detective shield. More politics than skill and knowledge." A wry smile curved his friend's mouth." Guess I don't know the right people."

"Does Detective Bennett know the right people?"

A scowl marred Sully's face. "Oh, yeah. His old man had a lot of clout in this town and on the force. Can't do nothing wrong."

"What kind of detective is he?"

He leaned close. "Lousy, but don't repeat that. Why are you asking about Bennett?"

"He might have information that could help us solve a cold case."

Sully blinked, then shifted his gaze to Heidi. "Who are you?"

She held out her hand. "I'm Heidi Thompson, Quinn's girlfriend."

"Soon to be wife," he corrected with a smile. "Heidi used to live here, Sully. Been twenty years ago. She went by the name Katie Henderson then."

The policeman froze. "Your old man caused my family to end up in bankruptcy court."

"Lot of that going around in those days. I'm sorry, Sully. What my father did was wrong on so many levels and hurt most of the town. He also hurt my family as well. His selfishness led to my sister's death."

"How old were you when all that went down?"

"Ten."

"Just a kid," he muttered, glancing around. "So what do you want to know? Maybe I can help."

Quinn doubted that was the case. Sully had been in high school with Quinn at the time of the kidnapping. They'd been more interested in football and girls than a kidnapping, at least until the fallout washed through the town's families. "We heard Bennett was here working a crime scene. Any chance we can talk to him for a minute?"

"Nope. Sorry, man. The detective left here thirty or forty minutes ago to head to another call."

Huh. Interesting timing. That was about the time Quinn and Heidi arrived at Al's place. "Did you happen to hear where he was going?"

A head shake. "Just somewhere on the east side of town. I can ask one of my buddies if you want, see if they overhead a specific location."

"The call didn't go through dispatch?"

"Not that I heard. Figured he was notified by cell."

"Is that normal?"

"Nope. Might be meeting an informant. Those calls don't go over the radio."

"What about his partner, Salinger?" Heidi asked. "Is she here or did she leave, too?"

"They work in pairs, like the big city detectives, though if you ask me, Anne Marie is the one carrying the lion's share of the load in that pair. She left when he did."

"Thanks for talking to us, Sully," Quinn said. "We won't keep you any longer."

"Sure. Great seeing you again. Don't be such a stranger."

"You bet."

Back in the SUV, Quinn cranked the engine and turned the heat on high to alleviate Heidi's shivering. His cell phone rang. He glanced at the readout. Al. Had he copied the file so soon? "Hey, Al."

"Anne Marie is here at the station alone. Don't know where Junior got off to."

"Do you think she'd talk to us at work?"

"I think so. I'm in the copy room right now. Should be safe enough if I commandeer an interview room and ask questions about the case. I don't want to alert anyone that she's helping you. No one would be surprised that I'm still poking a stick at this case. We've all got cases we couldn't close that haunt us. The Henderson kidnapping is mine."

"We'll be there soon, Al." Quinn ended the call, praying they caught a break from Anne Marie Salinger. He had a feeling time was running out.

CHAPTER THIRTY-FIVE

Quinn opened the front door of the police station and escorted Heidi inside. Sergeant Banks glanced up, eyes widening when he recognized them.

"Can I help you?" His eyes shifted slightly to the left toward a group of cops gathered nearby, talking quietly.

"We're here to see Al Graham. He's a family friend, told me to look him up when I was in town. He said he'd be here for a while, shooting the breeze with his friends. Will you tell him we're here?"

Banks relaxed a fraction. "Sure. Wait over there," he said, indicating a row of benches for visitors. The group of cops glanced at Quinn and Heidi with varying expressions, ranging from curiosity to suspicion to outright hostility.

Tough crowd. He and Heidi sat, waited. Five minutes later, Banks waved them over. "Through the double doors, down the hall to your left. Second door."

"Thanks, Sergeant."

He pressed his hand to the small of Heidi's back and urged her past the knot of cops who stopped talking as they drew near. Locating the right room, Quinn opened the heavy wooden door.

"Quinn!" Al grinned, rose, and wrapped him in a tight hug. "Good to see you, my boy. And who is this beautiful young woman?"

Quinn went along with the ruse, seeing the subterfuge as a way to protect Al as much as possible. He introduced Heidi again to his friend, then turned to the curious woman seated at the interrogation table, papers strewn across the flat surface in front of her. He held out his hand. "Quinn Gallagher. This is my girlfriend, Heidi."

"Nice to meet a friend of Al's. I'm Anne Marie Salinger." The detective stood. "I'll get out of your way so you three can talk."

Al closed the door to the interrogation room and leaned back against it. "Actually, we'd like for you to stay if you have time. We need your help, Anne Marie."

She resumed her seat and waved them to seats across from her. "What's going on?"

Quinn glanced at the camera in the corner of the ceiling. No red light. No way to be sure someone wouldn't slip into the observation room next door, but he didn't have the luxury of waiting. Bennett could return to the station any time and when he did he would find his partner. "Heidi and I used to live in Black River twenty years ago. My family still lives here."

"Noreen Gallagher." Anne Marie's face brightened. "She's a sweet lady."

"Yes, she is." She was also tough as nails. His mother would still get in his face if she thought his behavior was foolish. Nothing like being taken to task by a woman thirty years your senior and almost a foot shorter. Noreen Gallagher didn't put up with any garbage from her children even if they were all adults. "Heidi used to go by the name Katie Henderson."

Her startled gaze shifted to Heidi. "You've been gone a long time. Why did you return?"

"Justice. I want to find my sister's killer."

The detective's face hardened. "That's our job, Ms. Henderson. Civilians messing around in law enforcement investigations run a high risk of being hurt."

"Thompson. Heidi Thompson. Katie Henderson is my past. This is who I am now, a woman seeking answers to a mystery that still haunts me to this day."

"Look, the kidnapping was a tragedy for you and your family. No one's arguing that. We've never stopped looking into your case, but we haven't found new leads. Nothing but dead ends."

"I know you want to close this case," Quinn said.

"No cop wants an unsolved case on the record. I'm working with the son of the original investigator, as I'm sure Al told you since it's obvious now you came to talk to me. Bennett and I chased every investigative avenue and got nowhere." She turned to Heidi. "What prompted you to return to Black River now?" Suspicion lit her gaze.

Anne Marie Salinger was pure cop, suspicious of everyone's motives. One thing he'd learned over the years in dealing with terrorists. Everybody lied. Some with good intentions, some with bad.

"Quinn and I are getting married soon."

Anne Marie blinked. "Congratulations. What does that have to do with me?"

"We'll be constantly looking over our shoulders, wondering when the next fire will be set." Heidi leaned forward, arms folded on the table. "Our future children will be in danger until the second kidnapper is caught and put behind bars. I don't want to lose my sons and daughters the way I lost my mother and older sister."

"Next fire?" The detective's eyes narrowed. "What do you mean by that? You aren't talking about the fire that killed your family, are you?"

"That was the first of many incidents over the years." She explained the sequence of events, touching on each of the fires, ending with the latest one at her rental house. "I can't take the chance that something will happen to Quinn or our family. I won't hide from this coward any more. It's time to end this thing once and for all before someone else dies."

The detective remained silent a moment, then said, "How can I help?"

A simple statement that had Quinn's fists loosening. "What can you tell us about Bennett?"

Like a door slamming shut, her expression closed off.

Yep, that's what he expected to happen. Quinn admitted to himself that he would close ranks if someone went after a member of his Delta unit. That's what happened when the feds had looked at Alex for the murder of his father, a U.S. senator. "Look, I know it seems disloyal to talk about your partner behind his back. I appreciate your reluctance, but Bennett won't be willing to talk to us about his family. That's the information we need. Will you help us?"

"You're right about Ivan." Her fingers drummed on the table top. "He doesn't like to talk about his family. Can you blame him? His sister's in a psych hospital and so was his father until he died. My partner is worried the higher ups in the department will begin questioning his judgment."

"What about you?" Heidi asked. "Do you question his judgment?"

Anne Marie's expression became guarded again. "I've never had reason to."

Something there, but what? Quinn would circle back around to that.

"You said you and Bennett continue to investigate," Al reminded her. "Learn anything new recently?"

"You know I can't talk about an open investigation," she muttered.

"Come now, Anne Marie." Al sat in the one free chair. "We both know it's not uncommon to interview witnesses and victims again in an attempt to unearth another avenue to explore." He inclined his head toward Heidi. "Here's your witness and victim. To ignore a golden opportunity to move this investigation forward would be remiss of you."

Humor sparked in her eyes. "I guess it would. So, Heidi, would you be willing to answer questions?"

"Try me." Under cover of the table, Heidi clasped Quinn's hand. "I'll answer what I can. I still have gaps in my memory from the kidnapping."

"Traumatic amnesia?"

"That's what the therapists said."

"More than one?"

"A string of them when I was living with my aunt and uncle. They worried I wasn't coping well with the loss of my family."

"What prompted that?"

"I wouldn't talk for months after my home burned and my father went to prison. My aunt and uncle thought talking to a professional might help me move through the grief and shock faster."

"Were they right?"

"I started talking again not long after beginning therapy so I suppose it worked. So, Detective Salinger, what do you want to ask me?"

Quinn listened without comment as the detective took Heidi back through the painful events of her kidnapping. In spite of a growing pressure to punch the closest wall, he kept his feet firmly planted on the tile floor of the interrogation room and his body glued to the chair as the woman he loved described the last moments of her sister's life and her own desperate flight into the darkness to find help for Moira.

He couldn't go back in time and prevent the heartbreak and trauma of those days. He could, however, support her the only way at his disposal. Holding her hand was nothing considering he wanted the second kidnapper centered in his rifle scope. But he'd hold her hand forever if it reminded her of his love and support.

"Do you remember what the second kidnapper looked like?" Al asked. Quinn's friend had fallen into an easy rhythm of asking questions along with Anne Marie. The younger detective didn't seem to mind.

"His face is a blur," Heidi whispered, her gaze focused on the scarred wooden table.

"The second kidnapper is a man?" Anne Marie asked. "You're positive?"

Quinn watched Bennett's partner. Had there been some doubt as to the sex of the second kidnapper? This was the second time he had listened to Heidi recount her experience and she hadn't changed her statement. She believed her father's partner was a man. No reason to ask this particular question unless the cops believed Henderson involved the woman he'd been having an affair with in his kidnapping scheme. Did the suspicion surface during Al's time?

He glanced at his friend who gave him a slight head shake. Ah. So the information was new.

"It was a man," Heidi insisted. "A woman's hands wouldn't look like the kidnapper's."

"You remember the hands but not the face?"

"That's right."

"How did the hands look?"

"Big, strong, wiry black hair on the backs. I told Al and his partner the second kidnapper was a man right after I escaped."

"How old do you think this guy was at the time of the kidnapping?"

Heidi raised her head, her gaze locking with Quinn's.

He straightened at the pure terror in the depths of her eyes. Decades old terror. "Baby, what is it?" he asked, his voice soft and low.

Perspiration beaded on her forehead. "I...." Her voice trailed off.

Quinn reached cupped her face with his palm. "No one will get through me to you. I'll protect you with my life." He brushed his lips over hers in a light kiss, a reminder that he would stand between her and the danger stalking her. "You know what I'm capable of, sweetheart. Trust me."

She gave a short nod and eased back from Quinn. Her hand clenched on his as she turned to Anne Marie and Al. "The second kidnapper was young, maybe late teens or early twenties. He didn't move with the same assurance of an older man. I can't tell you exactly why I think that except to say he felt young and inexperienced to me. Of course, as a kid, I wouldn't have been able to voice that distinction." A wry smile curved her lips. "After I lost my mother and older sister in that house fire, I didn't speak at all for almost a year."

"Not a bad assessment of the perp for a traumatized ten-year-old." Al nodded his approval. "Did he have any distinguishing marks or mannerisms?"

She shuddered. "A tattoo on his hand. I keep seeing it in my dreams. I can't wait until we find this guy so I can stop having the same nightmares over and over again."

"What kind of tattoo?" Anne Marie's pen hovered over her notepad.

"I can't remember. The image never takes shape."

"The knowledge is buried in your mind, babe. The mist you told me about is your mind's way of protecting you from remembering the trauma." Quinn lifted their joined hands and kissed the back of hers. "You've been dreaming about this for years, obsessively watching for tattoos in case you spotted one like the kidnapper's ink job, haven't you? I had buddies in the military who were into tattoos before the top brass started regulating how much and what type of ink we could get."

She eyed him curiously. "You have a tattoo?"

He grinned at her. "Pay attention to my left shoulder blade when I have my shirt off." Quinn sobered. "What one category of tattoos made you react negatively every time you saw it, Heidi?"

She stared at the table again, frowning in concentration. "I don't like snake tattoos, but I don't like snakes in general."

"Don't blame you," Anne Marie said. "Creepy things. Aside from the snakes, which tattoos made you break out into a sweat?"

Heidi's head jerked up. "Naval symbols."

"Naval symbols," Al repeated slowly, his expression controlled. "Like a sail?"

"Maybe, although that doesn't sound right to me."

"A sailboat?" This from Anne Marie.

Her eyes widened. Quinn could almost see the mist parting in a wave of insight. "An anchor, as in the military symbol for the Navy."

The door to the interrogation room burst open and a middle-aged man with black hair barged in. His brown eyes narrowed at the sight of Al sitting at the table. "Got to roll, Salinger. You, too, Al."

This must be the elusive Ivan Bennett, Junior.

"Me?" Al's eyebrows rose. "I'm retired, son. I don't have to roll anywhere, at least not yet."

"You'll want to roll for this call, old man. A neighbor reported a fire at your house."

CHAPTER THIRTY-SIX

Heidi leaned forward in the SUV to see Al's house better. Two firefighters wielded axes on the roof while the others from the Black River Volunteer Fire Department maneuvered hoses for better angles to attack the raging fire. Smoke billowed from windows, tongues of red, orange, and blue licking at the late afternoon air.

Oh, man. Al's house was engulfed in flames. She was not an expert, but his house appeared a total loss. Heidi glanced over her shoulder at the old man watching the flames in silence, sympathy and horror fighting for dominance. How could this have happened? Quinn's friend had done nothing wrong. "I'm so sorry, Al. This is all my fault."

Ancient blue eyes turned her direction. "Nonsense, young lady. This could have been an accident."

"You don't believe that," Quinn said, his fingers tightening around the steering wheel, glaring at the ongoing destruction.

Al was silent a moment. "With the fires in Heidi's past, I don't believe this is a coincidence. My concern is how quickly Bennett will point a finger at her."

Her stomach clenched. Not again. At least this time she had multiple witnesses to her location when the fire started. "Can't blame me this time. I wasn't near your house when the fire started and I have several policemen who saw me somewhere else."

"Doesn't mean he won't try, Heidi."

They watched in silence for more than two hours until the fire crews climbed aboard the trucks and left the scene. Nearer to the smoldering remains of Al's house, Anne Marie and Ivan stood, arguing. They couldn't hear the conversation, but the evidence was clear. Red faces, finger pointing, scowls, all with Ivan towering over his more petite partner. Anne Marie finally stalked away toward the other side of what remained of the house. Ivan strode toward Quinn's SUV.

"I'll head him off," Quinn murmured, opening his door.

"We'll all get out," Al said. "I need to see what's left anyway."

Heidi surveyed the charred structure. Al must want closure. Although the fire crew had fought hard, nothing but ash and leaning towers of blackened building material were left.

Outside the SUV, Heidi and the others started toward Graham's house. The acrid scent of smoke and burned plastic stung their noses as they neared the structure.

Ivan stopped five feet from them, arms crossed, body blocking the sidewalk. "Sorry, old man," he said to Al, a smirk on his face. "Fire marshal says it's a total loss."

"I see. Good thing I have insurance."

"Yeah, about that. It's going to be a while before your claim will be processed."

"Why?"

Heidi could guess. She'd heard this song and dance before. Many times before.

"The fire was deliberately set."

"How do you know it wasn't an electrical short? The house was old."

"Unless you routinely set old fashioned gas cans against the side of your house, I'd say this is going to be a slam dunk for the arson investigator." He turned his cold gaze to Heidi. "It will be my job to find evidence against the little firebug and toss her behind bars."

Quinn edged in front of Heidi. "Her? You insinuating that Heidi set this fire, Bennett?"

"Katie Henderson has a history of setting fires, Gallagher."

"I was never charged with arson, Detective." Heidi wondered at his words. He knew her birth name already? When had the detective had time to run a background check on her? Or had he learned the truth from his partner? She wasn't keeping her birth name a secret. The one thing she was careful not to reveal to Anne Marie was all the identity changes. She and Levi hadn't gone through official channels to change their identities. What good would it have done to do so? The arsonist/kidnapper would have known where she was and blown the reason for hiding her identity in the first place. "I was just a kid. Why would I burn my own house down?"

"Two houses, Henderson. Killed two families in the process."

"That's enough, Ivan," Al snapped. "You have no proof. You know better than to accuse Heidi Thompson of something with no proof."

"You should be backing me, old man. I'm doing the job you and Dad never finished."

"No proof, Ivan. You seem to think Heidi is behind this fire. Why?"

"She's a firebug, Graham, with a long history of suspicious fires associated with her. Neighbors saw her at your house not long ago."

"Heidi and I both were here," Quinn said. "We were together the whole time when we visited with Al."

"He's right," Al said flatly. "She never left the living room and neither did Quinn. Where does the fire marshal think the fire started?"

"Office," Bennett muttered.

"She didn't set the fire, Ivan."

"So maybe Henderson didn't leave your sight." The detective tossed a glance full of suspicion at Heidi. "An accelerant was used to spur the fire along. Who's to say she didn't pour gasoline around the outside of your house and strike a match. Wouldn't take long and lover boy here would cover for her."

Quinn got up into Bennett's face. "You better get your facts lined up before you start throwing accusations around, Bennett. As soon as we left Al's place, Heidi and I drove to Winston Drive to look for you. We talked to Sully. He can verify our story. Then we went to the station to talk to your partner. Since Heidi was in town, she figured you and Anne Marie might like to talk to the only kidnapping witness. After all, you've been assigned the cold case. I'm assuming you want to solve it."

"What's this about gasoline?" Heidi asked. "The fire marshal says gas was the accelerant?"

"Hard to miss an old-fashioned red gas can near the point of origin, Henderson."

An invisible band tightened around Heidi's chest so she felt as though she couldn't draw a breath. How was this possible? She'd only been in town a few hours. Who hated her that much?

"You're nothing but trouble, Henderson. Why are you in town?"

Quinn reached behind himself and grasped her hand. "We came for two reason. First, we came to tell my family that Heidi and I are getting married. Second, we need to find out who kidnapped Heidi when she was a child."

"That's my job."

"Yeah? You're doing a lousy job of it, Bennett. When you have proof Heidi's behind this fire, you come find us. Al, you ready to go?"

"This is a crime scene," Bennett snapped. "You can't trespass."

"It's his house and he used to be a cop. He knows how this works. Al wants to see what's left. That's what we're going to do. You don't trust us? Tag along and make sure we don't make off with any evidence of our guilt." He turned, circled Heidi's waist with his arm and urged her past the glowering detective.

The stench grew stronger the closer they came to the blackened structure. Al circled what remained of his house, sadness in his eyes. His attention paused on the gas can near the corner of the house. He turned toward Quinn. "Someone is trying to set up your girlfriend, son," he murmured. "The arsonist hasn't been able to kill her. Could be he or she wants to put her in prison to get her out of the way."

"Or shut her up." Quinn pressed a gentle kiss to Heidi's forehead. "Al, let's get out of here. There's nothing for you to salvage. I'm sorry, sir."

The former detective waved that aside. "It's only a house, which can be replaced. I'm glad no one was hurt. Well, I suppose I should find somewhere to stay for a while."

"Come with us." Quinn dropped a hand on his shoulder. "Mom has extra room and you know she'll be glad to have the company. You can stay with her until you decide what to do next."

A short nod. "Thank you. I think I might do that." His expression hardened. "I assume you have an extra weapon handy."

Quinn smiled. "Along with the ammunition."

"Good. Someone destroyed mine. I'd like to borrow yours until I arrange to purchase a new one. Staying in your mother's home will allow me to keep an eye on her. I'm afraid none of us will be safe until the arsonist is behind bars."

CHAPTER THIRTY-SEVEN

Quinn leaned close to Heidi and whispered in her ear. "I'll be back in a few minutes."

"Everything okay?"

"Need to report to Josh and Maddox." After dropping a light kiss on her perfect lips, he rose from the sofa and left Heidi in the company of his family and Al. Quinn walked into the kitchen, snagged his jacket off the barstool, and stepped outside on the deck, closing the door behind himself.

A crisp, cool breeze blew against his face, a welcome respite from the warmth of the house, teeming with family. Though he loved them all fiercely, that many people in such close proximity got to him after a while. He zipped his jacket, settled in the deck chair, and propped his feet on the railing. Quinn called Josh first, knowing his friend would be on duty soon.

"Quinn, how's it going?"

He didn't bother with niceties. "There's been another fire."

"Sit rep."

"This time a family friend lost his home. He was one of the original detectives who investigated Heidi's kidnapping. Some of the local cops think Heidi's to blame for the latest fire."

Silence a moment. "Is she?"

"No. She had no motive or opportunity. It was the arsonist, Josh. He left behind a gas can similar to the one he left at her place and all the other fires."

"Guess that confirms your theory that Heidi's problems stem from her kidnapping. Sounds like this guy is desperate."

Quinn frowned, thinking back through the conversations he'd had with Anne Marie and Ivan. "There must be a woman involved in this somewhere."

"A woman? Why do you say that?"

"Anne Marie Salinger, one of the detectives investigating the case, kept asking Heidi if she was sure the second kidnapper was a man. Something must have led them to believe a woman might have been Henderson's partner."

"Wouldn't the detectives assigned the original case have interviewed Heidi at the time?"

"They did. She said she told them it was a man, but right after her interview, the rest of her family was murdered and she just quit talking for a few months." He explained about the new information his girlfriend had given Anne Marie. "Bennett is convinced Heidi is guilty, Josh. According to those who know him, he won't bother digging deep into the case. Anne Marie does the work which solves most of their cases."

"You have to see it from their perspective, Quinn. On the surface, Heidi looks guilty. When a suspect's name pops up that many times in the course of investigations, there's usually a reason and it won't be a good one."

"She's a victim, not a criminal."

"I believe that, too. Doesn't change the appearance."

"Then why did you ask me if she set the fire?"

"You need to be sure of her before you get in any deeper with Heidi emotionally."

Quinn huffed out a laugh. "Too late, my friend."

"You're in love with her, aren't you?"

"Head over heels. I'm going to marry that woman as soon as possible."

"There's no chance she's pulling a fast one?"

"None," he said, voice firm. "Heidi was with me in a station full of cops when Al's house was torched."

A chuckle from Durango's leader. "A fact which probably frosts the real arsonist. Hard to pin this fire on her with so many credible witnesses. Do you need Durango in Black River?"

"Rio is marrying Darcy in two days. He shouldn't be concerned about anything but his bride to be."

"The rest of us can make the drive easily."

"I appreciate the offer, but I can handle this on my own."

"If you need us, call. We'll be there. What does Maddox say?"

"He's the next call." After that, he'd touch base with Zane. Hopefully, he'd completed the background checks on the Bennetts. Now, Quinn had a new name. Anne Marie Salinger. He thought she was clean. With Heidi's safety on the line, he wasn't leaving anything to chance.

"Call him. Get his take on this. Let me know if you need us."

"Copy that, Major." He ended the call, then reported to Maddox.

His boss sighed. "Not what I wanted to hear. Your friend has insurance?"

"Yes, sir."

"I'll have Zane look into it. Maybe we can move things faster for him. Levi cooperating?"

Quinn debated telling Maddox how much trouble Heidi's cousin had been causing. Since threatened with losing his protection detail, Levi had at least made an effort to cooperate. "He's fine."

"Angel and Dane?"

"Green." No other way to say it. They needed more training, but at least they were teachable.

"Agreed. You can expect them to join your training classes after you wrap up the arsonist."

Wonderful. Did that mean Levi would be sticking around Otter Creek? "Yes, sir."

"What do you need from me?"

"Zane. He's doing research for me."

"Anything else?"

"Check on the whereabouts of the trainees we cut loose from PSI. I want to make sure they aren't in the mix."

"I'll get back to you as soon as I confirm their locations." He ended the call.

Zane answered on the first ring. "I was getting ready to call. How is it going?"

Quinn brought his friend up to speed.

"No injuries?"

"No one was home."

"Lucky."

"Not so much for the arsonist."

"Oh?"

"The Black River cops think Heidi set the fire." His lips curved. "She's amazing, but even she can't be in two places at once. We were at the police station in the interrogation room when the fire started."

Zane burst into laughter. "Nice. Listen, I dug into the background of Ivan Bennett and his children."

Quinn gripped his cell phone tighter. "And?"

"Bennett Senior had a solid record, several commendations in his file. Close rate was pretty good. Not as good as Ethan Blackhawk's, but noteworthy. From all accounts, he adored his wife and kids."

"Wife still alive?"

"Died in a car wreck ten years ago."

"Finances?"

"Well, that's the interesting thing. He lived off his salary and a small inheritance left to him by his grandmother. The psychiatric facility Aurora is in is a private one. Very exclusive."

"In others words, very expensive."

"No way could he pay for that with his monthly cash flow."

"Is it possible someone high up in the facility owed Bennett a favor or he knew someone who cut him a break on the price?"

"Not that I can find. Looks like he paid full price in cash every month."

Quinn sat up, feet dropping to the wooden deck. "Cash?"

"That's right. I can't find a source for that cash, Quinn. I'll keep digging, but $5,000 a month isn't chump change."

"Insurance didn't cover the expense?"

"The insurance kicks in a thousand every month."

So where did Bennett get the money? He could guess. Five million dollars would last a long time if you only spent $5,000 a month. The question he needed to answer was which male Bennett was involved, the father or the son? "Who covered the expenses after Bennett Senior was admitted to the facility?"

"Junior. Same deal. Cash payments. And before you ask, I can't find a source for his cash flow either."

"Keep digging. What did you find on Aurora?"

"She's been in the Hermitage Hills facility for twenty years."

"How long after Heidi's kidnapping was she institutionalized?"

"A few weeks. She had been seeing a psychiatrist for years, though."

"Any idea why?"

"Not for the treatment as she was growing up. However, when I dug into the Hermitage Hills records, I learned Aurora was institutionalized after her boyfriend was arrested and convicted of kidnapping Heidi and her sister. She was Caleb Henderson's lover."

CHAPTER THIRTY-EIGHT

Heidi glanced at her watch again. Where was Quinn? He'd been gone for almost an hour. He must have learned something more. Otherwise he would have returned by now. His friends and co-workers rocked at research so coming up with no information didn't seem possible. Since she couldn't concentrate on the conversations around her, Heidi excused herself and went in search of her boyfriend.

She found him standing in the darkened kitchen, staring out into the night through the French doors. Though the light was dim, the lines of his body revealed Quinn's inner tension. Heidi pressed a hand to her stomach. Something was wrong, but what? "Quinn."

He extended his arm, inviting her into his embrace, without saying a word. Quinn gathered her close and, for several minutes, simply held her.

Gradually, he relaxed against Heidi as though her nearness brought him comfort. She hoped that was true. "What's wrong?"

"What do you know about Aurora Bennett?"

Heidi frowned as she looped her arms tighter around his trim waist. "Nothing. Should I? Wait. Bennett? She's a relative of Bennett Junior?"

"Sister. She worked at G & H Industries." He glanced down at her. "Aurora was your father's lover, sweetheart."

Stunned, she stared at him. She'd heard rumors that her father was having an affair. This was the first time she had a name. Why would he hurt Heidi's mother that way? She'd thought her parents were blissfully in love, but the only bliss in her childhood home was in Heidi's imagination. "She was the woman he was running away with."

"Zane said the affair had been ongoing for almost a year, that he was obsessed with this woman."

"Did he tell you where she is? Maybe she has an idea who Dad's partner was."

"I wish it was that simple. Aurora Bennett was institutionalized not long after your kidnapping. She's been in the private facility ever since. According to Zane, she's not allowed to have any visitors other than her brother."

"Couldn't we try? We have to talk to her, Quinn. She might be able to help us stop these fires. The next time one is set, we might not be so lucky."

"If I thought it would do any good, I'd find a way to get us in there. Aurora is missing. She escaped from the facility last week."

She could be anywhere by now. "Do they have any idea where she might go?"

He shook his head. "Junior hasn't filed a missing person report on her so no one's looking."

"Why not?" Why would Junior endanger his sister that way? No food, no warm place to stay, no medicine if she took any.

"Don't know." He gave her a wolfish grin. "We'll ask the next time we see him." Quinn cupped the back of her neck and kissed her.

Good grief, Quinn Gallagher had skills. When he broke the kiss, they both were short of breath. "What do we do now?" she asked, her voice raspy. Yep, definite skills.

"Since we can't get to Aurora, we need to resurrect your memories of the kidnapping."

A wave of nausea swept over her. "How?"

"I have an idea." He tightened his hold on her as though buffering her against his next words. "The experience won't be pleasant, baby, but I don't know what else to do."

"Let's hear this lousy idea."

"Let's go for a drive. Will you trust me?"

"Always."

"Good. Wait here while I tell Mom we'll be gone for a while." When Quinn returned, they left the house through the back door. Once inside the SUV, he reached into his pocket and pulled out black material.

"What's that?"

He captured her gaze with his, one hand covering hers. "A blindfold."

"You want to blindfold me," she whispered. Adrenaline raced through her bloodstream. She didn't know about this. Intellectually, she understood what he was doing. Recreating the night of the kidnapping. Understanding his reasons didn't make the prospect less daunting. She hated the dark. Now that she thought about it, her fear probably stemmed from the kidnapping. Heidi couldn't remember being afraid of the dark before that incident.

"It's the only way I can think of to jar your memory. Your choice, Heidi. If you don't want to do this, we'll think of something else."

Though she didn't want to comply, Heidi knew they didn't have many other options. She'd already been hypnotized with and without drugs to stop the nightmares, and put the remaining kidnapper behind bars, all to no avail. "Will you take me back to that house?" The house where her baby sister died. The house of her nightmares.

Quinn didn't say a word. He didn't have to.

Heidi steeled herself. "Do it." She wanted answers and this appeared the only way to get them.

He leaned forward and raised his hands. Breath stalled in her lungs as he moved closer. But instead of wrapping that fabric around her head, he kissed her until she thought about him, not the blindfold.

Quinn eased away, whispering, "Keep your eyes closed. Trust me, Heidi. I won't let anything happen to you." A moment later, he covered her eyes with the soft, silky black material. His thumbs brushed her cheeks with a gentle touch. "You look beautiful in black."

The comment surprised her into a brief smile. "Thanks."

"I'm going to buckle your seatbelt for you." His breath tickled her face as he leaned close. "I love you, baby. Thank you for trusting me."

"Hurry, Quinn." She didn't know how long she could hold herself together. Already the darkness was closing in, making it difficult to breathe.

"No longer than ten minutes, I promise."

The whole drive, he asked questions about the night of the kidnapping, most of which she couldn't answer. The chloroform had knocked her and her sister out for a couple hours by the estimation of the police and the physician who examined her at the hospital. All Heidi remembered was waking in the dark with her sister, locked in that horrible room.

When Heidi thought she might have to yank that stupid blindfold off, Quinn slowed the SUV to a stop. Now she didn't know which was worse. Still wearing that blindfold or knowing Quinn was taking her into the house of death. She couldn't think of that place without remembering Moira's last moments on this earth.

Quinn turned off the ignition. "Are you ready?" he asked, his voice soft.

"Never. Let's get this over with. Maybe then, we'll have the answers we need. I want you, our future children, and your family to be safe."

"Stay still. I'll come around to help you."

Cold air filled the SUV when Quinn opened his door. Seconds later, he opened Heidi's door and unlatched her seatbelt. His hand cupped her cheek. "I know this is hard, but you're doing great, babe. Hang in there a little longer."

"Do you really think this is going to work?"

"We won't know until we try. I'm going to help you to the ground, then lift you into my arms. I don't want you stumbling out here. There isn't much light aside from the moon and a streetlight down the road. Mom told me the people in this neighborhood slowly began to sell or abandon their homes after your kidnapping. Some of them were affected by G & H's shutdown. Others didn't want to live in this neighborhood anymore. As a result, not many people live near this house."

"Is that why your mother hasn't been able to sell it?"

"She didn't see the point of trying to sell when people around town knew the history of the house."

"She mentioned something about knocking it down."

"That's right. I think she's planning to sell the property to the city for a park for children. The mayor approached her about the possibility a couple months ago." He brushed the side of her neck with a light kiss. "Ready, Heidi?"

Heidi's chest tightened. "I need to take off this blindfold," she said, voice shaky.

"Five more minutes, baby."

"How will we get into the house?"

"Mom gave me the key."

"And if she hadn't?"

He swung her legs to the side of the seat, then eased her to the ground. "I would have picked the lock. Special

Forces taught me all kinds of interesting skills." The door closed with a soft snick.

If she hadn't been so focused on not ripping off the black material hiding the world from her eyes, Heidi would have laughed at the stealth Quinn was using. He probably didn't even realize he wasn't making much noise. The military trained him well.

"Put your arms around my neck." When she complied, he murmured, "Hold on." Quinn placed one arm across Heidi's back, the other behind her knees, and then she was airborne.

Heidi buried her face in his neck, breathing in the familiar scent of the man she loved, that mixture of forest and Quinn. Wood creaked and Quinn stopped.

"I need to unlock the door." He set her feet on the ground, keeping one arm around her waist. A moment later, the screech of rusty hinges being forced to work echoed in the night. "I'll carry you inside."

She nodded despite the building fear. Heidi hadn't thought this experiment of Quinn's would work. Maybe the sensory deprivation was having an effect on her memory because the whole kidnapping experience was right at the edge of her consciousness. For Quinn and their future children, for herself, she wanted to remember, perhaps for the first time since that fateful event. Until now, Heidi had just wanted to forget.

Quinn picked her up again and maneuvered her inside the house. Heidi's nose wrinkled. The scent of dampness, mustiness, and mildew assaulted her sense of smell. "I hope no one lives here."

"Not since your kidnapping. People say the place is haunted."

Heidi jerked. "By Moira's spirit? That's ridiculous."

"I agree. There's a logical explanation. Probably kids or teens meeting here at night, maybe to party, maybe to scare themselves with stories about the kidnapping."

"Does the house still look the same?"

"Mom didn't change anything inside or outside. Once the police finished their investigation, she locked up the place and walked away." Quinn twisted and a few seconds later, she was in another room.

"I'm going to set you down, baby. I'll remove the blindfold, but I want you to keep your eyes closed. Listen to the sounds of the house. Breathe in the scents. Remember," he whispered.

She gave a short nod, hands trembling. Quinn set her feet on the floor once again and held her while she found her balance. His scent intensified, then the blindfold was gone. Heidi wanted to open her eyes, but refused to give in to the fear. The house was dark. She doubted Noreen had kept the electricity on. Somehow, though, having the material away from her face helped her breath easier.

"What do you want me to do?" she asked.

"Let me hold you." The warmth of his chest pressed against her back and his arms wrapped around her. "Think back to the day of your kidnapping. Tell me what you remember leading up to the kidnapping."

Some of the knots in Heidi's muscles loosened as memories of the day surfaced. She relayed her efforts to keep Moira entertained until her mother returned from work.

"Where was your older sister?"

She laughed, surprised that she could in this house in the darkness. "On the phone with her boyfriend. She was in love with this long-haired wannabe rock star. Anyway, when our parents came home, they fed us dinner, watched a Disney movie with us, then sent us to bed. Andrea, our older sister, was allowed to stay up later. I remember waking a couple hours later and hearing my parents fighting."

"The fighting woke you."

She snuggled deeper into his embrace. "We hated the fights."

"Did you talk to them?"

Heidi shook her head. "Doing that would make them mad at me. They had turned on us before when we tried to stop them."

Quinn stilled the soothing motion of his hand. "They hurt you and your sisters?"

She didn't answer. Ancient history now. Her father would never slap her or her sisters again. Her mother would never scream at them in frustration and rage, ugly, hateful words spewing from her lips.

"Know that I will never lay a hand on you or our children in anger. I will never hurt you, baby."

Heidi turned then, opening her eyes to see his beloved face. "I know, Quinn. You use your strength and training to protect the innocent, not hurt." She framed his face with her palms. "I'm not worried that you'll be like my father."

"If we'd known, my father would have confronted Caleb. He might have been able to stop the abuse."

"It's over, sweetheart. I survived."

"Your father shouldn't have gotten away with it."

The corners of her lips curved. "Slaps on the face didn't raise eyebrows in those days. Neither did my mother's verbal abuse."

"Didn't make how they treated you and your sisters right. I promise you, our home will be different than the one you were raised in. I will always treat you with love and respect, even when we disagree."

She rested her head against his shoulder. "I love you, Quinn."

From the doorway, a woman screamed, "Liar!"

CHAPTER THIRTY-NINE

Between one heartbeat and the next, Quinn spun to face the threat in the doorway, his body blocking the woman's view of Heidi. "What am I lying about?" he asked, silently chastising himself for becoming distracted enough to miss her approach.

"Not you. Her. Caleb's daughter. She lies about her father. My Caleb was a good man."

"You must be Aurora Bennett." He reached back and pulled Heidi closer to his back, then moved both of them a couple steps to the right. The meager moonlight shined on the face of the woman standing in the threshold. He recognized her from the photo Zane had emailed him earlier in the evening.

She tilted her head. "You know me?"

"I know about you."

"How?"

"I used to live in Black River. My name is Quinn."

"You are Gallagher's son. He was a nice man." Aurora frowned. "Why did you come back here? You should have stayed away."

"I came to see my family. People are looking for you, Aurora."

Disbelief shone on her face. "They never look for me. I go back to the doctors when I want. I don't need them right now."

Based on what he observed, she did need to be back in the institution. The Bennett woman had an almost childlike demeanor. Didn't make her any less dangerous. He'd been in plenty of places where children killed as easily as adults.

Heidi peered around his shoulder. "What do you need, Aurora?"

Hatred gleamed in her eyes. "Retribution. You must die. Then I will be free to start a new life, one filled with laughter and love. Someone else will fall in love with me and take me away from this place."

Cold chills zipped up his spine. "Killing Heidi isn't on the table," Quinn said, drawing Aurora's attention back to him. "I love her and I'm not letting you hurt her."

"Katie. She's Katie Henderson, not Heidi Thompson. She lies to everybody, even you."

"I know who she is and who she's been. Heidi told me everything. You've been setting those fires and trying to kill her, aren't you?"

"I tried everything, but she won't die!"

Quinn mentally connected the dots in a flash. "You went to Otter Creek, keyed my vehicle, and destroyed it with a bomb. Did you plant the tracking device on Charlie?"

"It was easy. I pretended to be the new dog washer at the groomers. Charlie's a sweet boy. But Katie has to die. If not for her, I would be happy."

"I don't understand. How is she to blame for your unhappiness?"

"My Caleb is dead. If Katie and Moira had cooperated, he wouldn't have gone to jail. We would have started a new life in a new country. I would have my own children by now. Instead, I'm alone. It's Caleb's bratty kids' fault that he's dead. My Caleb is gone so Katie doesn't deserve to live."

While she talked, Quinn scanned the room and the woman blocking their exit. Heidi's description of this room was spot on. This was a box and Aurora was holding a lighter. He breathed deep and caught the scent of gasoline. Crap. He'd bet anything she spread gasoline around the house before confronting them. This place was old and filled with rotting wood. One flick of that lighter and this place would burn to the ground in a matter of minutes.

"Heidi was only a kid, ten years old when she was kidnapped. How is this her fault?"

"She told on Caleb," Aurora said. "If she had kept her mouth shut, he wouldn't have been arrested and died in prison."

"I didn't know Dad was the mastermind behind the kidnapping," Heidi said. "I never saw him or heard his voice in this house. But the police suspected him before I escaped and found help. Did you kill my sister Moira?"

"What? No! I like children. I would never hurt them."

"But you set the fire at my home that killed my mother and older sister."

"They weren't children. A better mother would have woken up and saved her daughter. I would have been a good mother. Now, I'll never have that chance. Your fault."

"You know who the second kidnapper is." Quinn's gaze dropped to the lighter which Aurora had flicked to life. The flame burned bright in the gloomy room. "What is his name?"

She gave a harsh laugh. "You think I would tell you?"

"What can it hurt? You're going to kill us."

"Not you. Katie. You can leave."

Did she believe he would walk away? Quinn shook his head. "I won't leave her."

"You have to leave," Aurora insisted. "Your father gave me the money to have a new life. I don't want to hurt you."

"Tell me the other kidnapper's name."

She shook her head. "No, I have to protect him. It's only right."

"Why is it the right thing to do?"

"Because he protects me."

Protects. Present tense. Was she talking about her brother, Ivan? A dark shadow moved behind her shoulder.

"Shut up, Aurora. I told you to get out of town and leave them to me. You never listen to anything I tell you."

Ivan Bennett, Junior shoved past his sister, weapon pointed at Quinn. "My sister is right. You should have stayed away from Black River. Now I don't have a choice but to take care of both of you."

"We can't hurt Quinn, Ivan." Aurora frowned at her brother.

"No choice, Sis. He'll tell on us. Do you want me to die in prison like Caleb?"

Face crumpling, she shook her head.

"What are you going to do, Bennett?" Heidi asked. "Shoot us in cold blood? That would spark a lot of questions."

"I won't shoot you if I don't have to. No, I'll let you die in a tragic fire of your own making. Too bad you killed your boyfriend by accident." He aimed his weapon at Quinn's heart.

Quinn shifted his weight subtly. He had to get Heidi out of this house before they burned alive. "The cops won't believe this set up."

Ivan chuckled. "Of course they will. I'm their star detective and since your deaths will be linked to the Henderson case, I'll be assigned this one, too. The evidence will support my story. I'll make sure it does."

"Manufactured evidence."

A shrug. "No one will question me."

Quinn thought Junior overestimated his skill and reputation. "So you killed Moira."

The detective scowled. "Her death was an accident. I wanted a couple minutes of peace. She wouldn't quit crying."

"What did Dad promise you?" Heidi asked. "Money?"

"I helped for Aurora's sake. Caleb promised he would keep her safe and happy." He used his free hand to shove his sister out the door. "Get out now, Aurora. Start the fire as soon as I'm clear."

"Was your father part of the kidnapping?" Quinn asked.

Ivan scoffed. "Are you kidding? Dear old Dad was horrified when he realized I was the second kidnapper. Somehow he put all the pieces together and figured out Aurora and I were both involved in what had been happening to Katie."

"So he admitted himself to the private mental hospital to protect you both instead of turning you in."

"Where's the money?" Heidi pressed against Quinn's back. Though he kept his face impassive, he wondered what she was doing.

He grinned. "I keep it close. Can't trust banks, you know." Ivan stepped back. "I'll be sure to give my condolences to your mother, Quinn." With a laugh, he slammed the door shut and Quinn heard a bolt slide home. Seconds later, a loud whoosh told him that Aurora had dropped the lighter.

He crossed the room and tried kicking open the door. While the house was a ramshackle affair, the bolt must be attached deep to a stud. Quinn could eventually break down the door, but he suspected they didn't have much time. The door was already growing hot.

"What do we do now?" Heidi gripped his arm.

He glanced around the room again, yanked out his phone.

"I already texted Anne Marie what was happening."

"Good. We don't have time to wait for her to arrive. This place is going to be a pile of rubble in minutes." He used his flashlight app to see what he had to work with.

Bed, nightstand, old lamp, plywood covered window. Even as he scanned the room, smoke drifted under the door. "Shove that bedspread against the door."

Heidi nodded and hurried to do as he asked.

Quinn rushed to the window and ran his fingers along the wood, searching for a gap to slide his fingers in and tug the sheet of plywood away from the wall. He found one, inched his fingers in as far as he could and yanked. A cracking sound filled the room. Not enough leverage. Whoever put up the plywood did a good job.

He crossed to the bed in three strides and tossed the mattress and box springs. Quinn used the flashlight app again to examine the bed frame. Oh, yeah. This would work.

Within a couple minutes, he had the frame separated and returned to the window. He slipped the metal under the edge of the wood and pulled. Half the wood tore away from the wall and window. Dropping the metal, Quinn grabbed the ragged edge with both hands and yanked off the rest of the covering.

He threw the wood aside and tried unlocking the window. The mechanism was rusted shut. He used the metal bed frame to break out the glass. Quinn grabbed his weapon. "Sweetheart, stay near the window on the floor. I don't know if Junior and his sister stayed to watch the show or if they took off. If he's still here, Junior will try to shoot us."

"What about you?" After a sustained bout of coughing, she said, "He'll kill you."

"He'll try. He won't succeed. I have a great incentive for staying alive. I plan to marry you soon, baby."

Another round of coughing. "I'm holding you to it. Be careful."

Without waiting any further, Quinn dived through the gaping hole where the window used to be, and rolled to a crouch, gun tracking. He quartered the area. No gunfire, no sounds of anything except sirens approaching in the distance. He heard Heidi's racking cough and knew he had to take a chance. He must get her out of that house.

Backing up to the wall beside the opening, he said, "Heidi, come through the window as fast as you can."

A rustling sound warned him she was on the move. Seconds later, she climbed through the opening.

Quinn hurried her to the stand of trees off to the right. They couldn't stay near the house where they were backlit by the flames eating the old structure.

Gunshots echoed in the night. A bullet slammed into Quinn's side, spinning him away from Heidi.

CHAPTER FORTY

"Get down!"

Quinn scrambled to where Heidi had dropped and dove on top of her. The shots had come from behind the car parked in the drive. Had to belong to Junior. From his current position, Quinn couldn't get a bead on the shooter.

"How bad are you hurt, Quinn?" Heidi's voice shook.

"I'm fine, I promise. Bullet grazed my side." At least, he hoped that was the extent of the damage. Burned something fierce. "Cops should be here in minutes." Quinn longed to go after this guy, but his priority was protecting Heidi. If he left her alone, Junior or his sister could slip past Quinn and hurt Heidi. He couldn't take that chance.

More shots were fired. Dirt flew up. Leaves jerked. Nowhere close to their position. Quinn frowned. For a cop, Junior's aim was lousy.

The hairs at the back of his neck prickled. The lousy shot was probably Aurora which meant Junior was on the move, zeroing in on their position.

"Get up nice and slow, Gallagher."

Quinn considered refusing, discarded the plan. A bullet might pass through him and strike Heidi. "Stay down no matter what happens," he whispered in Heidi's ear, then slowly climbed to his feet. Blood ran down his side. He could use Rio's medical skills about now. Quinn faced Ivan Bennett, pistol still in his hand.

"Drop the weapon."

"Planning to shoot an unarmed man?" he asked, doing as he was told. He shifted slightly, nudging the pistol into the shadows close to Heidi's hand. Quinn had a backup piece, but he couldn't reach it before Bennett took him down. Even if he were a terrible shot, Bennett couldn't miss at this range. With Quinn dead, Heidi didn't have a chance. "Won't work. Your cop buddies will be here any minute. You and Aurora won't get away with this."

"Want to bet? This is perfect, much better than my crazy sister's plan. I caught you both leaving the scene of an arson. You drew your weapon and fired at me to protect your woman. I had no choice but to return fire." Bennett grinned. "I'm a better shot than you."

Not on Quinn's worst day would that be the case. Law enforcement training didn't hold a candle to his training in Delta. "Last chance, Junior. You can walk away alive."

Bennett aimed his weapon. "After all the trouble you caused, I'm looking forward to this."

A gunshot rang out.

The detective looked down at his chest where a blood stain spread rapidly. His eyes rolled back in his head and he dropped to the ground.

"No!" Aurora screamed as she rushed toward them, firing the gun repeatedly in their direction.

Quinn dived to the side, grabbing his backup weapon as he fell. One shot and Aurora Bennett crumpled beside her brother. He kept his weapon trained on the two as he approached them. "Are you hurt, baby?"

"I'm okay."

Excellent. "Stay still while I secure their weapons." And see if they were still alive. With the placement of the shots, he doubted it. Quinn approached Junior first, as he was the bigger threat if he was still alive. He kicked aside the Glock and checked for a pulse. Nothing. At least he wouldn't have to worry about Bennett coming after them.

"Is he...?" Heidi's voice choked off.

"Yeah, he is. Nice shot."

"I didn't mean to kill him," she said.

"If you hadn't, he would have killed us. You did what was necessary." He knelt beside Aurora, nudged aside the weapon and checked for a pulse. Zip.

Anne Marie Salinger shouted their names.

"Over here," he called back. Now came the long explanations.

He sat down beside Heidi. Quinn held out his hand. "Give me the weapon, babe." When she placed the pistol in his hand, he placed it along with his backup weapon on the ground for Anne Marie, then tugged her into his arms. "You were amazing. You saved both our lives, Heidi."

She pressed her face into his neck and cried in silence. Not knowing what else to do, he simply held her while the cops swarmed the area.

After checking both bodies for a pulse, Anne Marie turned. "What happened?"

Quinn explained the sequence of events. "So what now, Detective Salinger?"

"Looks like we need to transport you and Heidi to the hospital. Once you're patched up, we'll talk again." With that, she waved the EMTs closer. "Those two are dead. Take these two to the hospital for treatment. Jordan."

"Yes, ma'am."

"You go with them. Don't let them out of your sight."

Quinn huffed out a laugh. "You afraid we're going to bolt, Detective?"

"I'm making sure you don't leave before I have every question answered."

He gave her a snappy salute. "Yes, ma'am."

The night seemed to pass in slow motion. The physician at the hospital stitched his side and gave Heidi a clean bill of health. Officer Jordan then transported them to the police station where Quinn and Heidi were separated and questioned for hours.

When they left the building, the sun was peeking over the horizon. The dawn of a brand new day, the first day of true freedom for Heidi. Quinn wrapped his arms around her and kissed her. "I love you, Heidi."

"I love you, too, Quinn. What do we do now?"

"We go home. We have a wedding to attend."

CHAPTER FORTY-ONE

Heidi slipped away from Rio and Darcy's wedding reception to stand in the vestibule doorway. The rain continued to fall, the gray and gloomy evening matching her own mood.

A gust of cool wind ruffled her hair as she listened to the soft rhythm and thought about her family and the Bennetts. Two days since she'd been forced to kill a man to save herself and Quinn from certain death and the sky wept at the senselessness of the deaths of so many people in a doomed bid for retribution. No wonder Bennett Senior never expended much effort to solve Moira's murder. When Al Graham understood the truth, he'd been equal parts furious with his partner and guilt ridden for not having pushed harder himself.

Because Bennett had been determined to save his own family, he'd chosen to sacrifice Heidi's. So much loss and heartbreak as a result.

"Heidi?"

She turned. "You should be with your friends."

Quinn slid his arms around her waist. "Are you all right?"

"I will be." Heidi laid her head on his shoulder, taking comfort in his nearness and warmth. "When will the dreams stop?" Each night since they had returned to Otter Creek, her dreams had been filled with replays of the night the Bennetts died.

He shifted closer. "It takes time. Longer for some than others."

"Do you have them? The nightmares?"

"Not of the Bennetts. Missions with Delta and Fortress. The more time passes, the greater the gap in recurrence."

"I keep dreaming of other ways to handle the situation."

"It's normal, Heidi. No matter what your mind tells you, we didn't have another option. If there had been, I would have chosen a different alternative." Quinn cupped the nape of Heidi's neck and kissed her, his touch gentle. When he lifted his head, he said, "Come with me." Lacing their fingers, he led her into the sanctuary where candles still burned in the dimly lit auditorium of Cornerstone Church. They stopped under the flowered arch on the stage.

Quinn gathered her hands in his. "Heidi, you closed a chapter of your life this week. A chapter filled with pain and loss. I can't wipe away the hurt or bring your family back. I can promise to fill your future with love and laughter. I adore you, Heidi Thompson. You've brought light and joy into my life." His lips curved. "You also brought an awesome dog."

Heidi laughed. Quinn was right. Charlie was a great dog.

Quinn reached into his pocket and dropped to one knee. "I love you, baby. Will you marry me and make my life complete?"

"I'm so blessed to have you in my life, Quinn. I never dreamed something good could come of my broken past.

You are a dream come true. I love you, Quinn Gallagher, and I would be honored to be your wife."

Quinn slipped a ring on her finger, then jumped to his feet and dragged her into his arms for a long, hot kiss. By the time he let her come up for air, Heidi realized the back of the auditorium was filled with Quinn's cheering and clapping friends and co-workers, and Levi. Her cousin grinned.

Time to write a new chapter in her life. One filled with fun, family, and friends. And the best thing? She got to share it all with the man of her dreams.

Retribution

ABOUT THE AUTHOR

Rebecca Deel is a preacher's kid with a black belt in karate. She teaches business classes at a private four-year college in Nashville, Tennessee. She plays the piano at church, writes freelance articles, and runs interference for the family dogs. She's been married to her amazing husband for more than 20 years and is the proud mom of two grown sons. She delivers monthly devotions to the women's group at her church and conducts seminars in personal safety, money management, and writing. Her articles have been published in *ONE Magazine*, *Contact*, and *Co-Laborer*, and she was profiled in the June 2010 Williamson edition of *Nashville Christian Family* magazine. Rebecca completed her Doctor of Arts degree in Economics and wears her favorite Dallas Cowboys sweatshirt when life turns ugly.

For more information on Rebecca . . .
Sign up for Rebecca's newsletter: http://eepurl.com/_B6w9
Visit Rebecca's website: www.rebeccadeelbooks.com

Printed in Great Britain
by Amazon